What's the secret ingredient for a lively romance?

Just Add Children

Two complete novels by your favourite authors!

Catherine George was born in Wales, and early developed a passion for reading which eventually fuelled her compulsion to write. Marriage to an engineer led to nine years in Brazil, but during his later travels the education of her son and daughter kept her in the UK. Instead of reading to pass her lonely evenings she began to write the first of her romantic novels. When not writing and reading she loves to cook, listen to opera, browse in antique shops and walk the labrador.

Emma Goldrick was born and raised in Puerto Rico, where she met and married her husband Bob, a career military man. Thirty years and four children later they retired and took up nursing and teaching. In 1980 they turned to collaborative writing. After sixty years of living over half the world, and a full year of studying the Mills & Boon style, their first submission was accepted. They have never looked back. Goldrick's hobbies include grandchildren, flower gardens, reading and travel.

Just Add Children

THE PERFECT SOLUTION
by
Catherine George

DOUBLY DELICIOUS
by
Emma Goldrick

MILLS & BOON

Harlequin Mills & Boon Limited,
Eton House, 18-24 Paradise Road, Richmond, Surrey, TW9 1SR

The Perfect Solution and *Doubly Delicious*
were first published in separate, single volumes by
Mills & Boon Limited. *The Perfect Solution* in 1992 and
Doubly Delicious in 1991.

ISBN 0 263 79539 X

Set in Times Roman 11 on 12 pt
05-9512-102194 C

Printed in Great Britain by
BPC Paperbacks Ltd

THE PERFECT SOLUTION

CHAPTER ONE

BY THREE in the afternoon the ordeal seemed endless. But at long last the subdued buffet lunch was over and the mourners began to depart. Reiterating condolences to the pale young widow, some shook her hand, others kissed her cold cheek, closer friends gave swift, sympathetic hugs. Eventually Joanna Clifford closed the door on the final compassionate face, the shell of her composure at cracking point now it was all over.

Except that it wasn't over, quite. There was still some unfinished business to attend to before she came to grips with the everyday reality of widowhood. First on her list of priorities came a vote of heartfelt thanks to Doris Mills. Doris, who normally came in twice a week from the village to help with the housework, had been a tower of strength since early morning, her eagle eye everywhere as the hired caterers served the funeral feast. She brushed aside Joanna's thanks in her usual no-nonsense manner.

'No trouble at all, Mrs Clifford. I've seen the caterers off and everything's in order. I'll be off now. See you in the morning. There's a nice fresh pot of coffee waiting for you in the drawing-room.'

This last unlooked-for solicitude was almost too much for Joanna. She blinked hard, squeezing Doris's hand by way of thanks, then went back to the drawing-room, where Jim Fowler, financial adviser to her dead husband, waited in front of the fireplace. Joanna poured coffee for them both, then sat back in silence, waiting for him to begin. Jim Fowler was a thin man in his late forties. Through thick-lensed spectacles his eyes peered at her, red-rimmed, their normal shrewd gleam replaced by a blend of grief and misgiving as he confronted his friend's weary young widow. He'd been hit hard, Joanna knew. Jim Fowler and Paul Clifford had been born and brought up in the same part of London's East End, thick as thieves all their lives, each one the only man the other ever trusted.

'How do you feel, Jo?' he asked. 'Really feel, I mean. You look terrible.'

'So do you.' Joanna leaned back in the corner of the sofa, allowing herself to relax now only Jim was there to see. Her eyes met his with a trace of defiance. 'If you want the truth, the only emotion I seem capable of is guilt.'

'*Guilt?* What the devil have you got to be guilty about? It's Paul——' He stopped, biting his lip.

'I feel guilty, Jim,' went on Joanna, eyeing him curiously, 'because after five years of marriage surely I should feel some grief for Paul! But at the moment I don't. There's a great deal I need explained before I can bury my dead. So start talking, Jim.'

He gazed at her hopelessly. 'I feel like one of those old-time messengers who got their heads chopped off when they brought bad news.'

Joanna smiled sadly. 'Don't worry, Jim. I'm handier with a garden trowel than a hatchet.' She looked towards the window, her eyes heavy. 'In fact I was planting wallflowers when the police arrived to tell me Paul was killed. They were so kind. They even made tea for me in my own kitchen. For shock.' She turned her head to look Jim in the eye. 'More shock than they knew. I thought Paul was in America. Instead he was smashing himself up in his Ferrari right here in the UK. And he wasn't alone in the car when he did it, either.'

Jim rotated his head wearily to ease his tense neck muscles. He sighed. 'All right, love. I wish it weren't me who had to tell you. But I will.'

Joanna sat up, bracing herself, her eyes like blue flames in her pale face. 'Thank you, Jim. Perhaps afterwards I can get on with the rest of my life.'

He nodded, opening the briefcase he was never without. He looked across at her with a wry smile. 'In those old films it was always the family lawyer who got this job, not a run-of-the-mill accountant.'

Joanna, who knew that Jim Fowler was a great deal more than that, paid close attention as the shrewd financial adviser took over from the family friend. Jim began by explaining that Paul's factories had taken a recent hammering due to high interest rates and fierce competition.

'To put it in a nutshell, PC Plastics is in a bad way, Jo.'

'How bad?'

'On the verge of bankruptcy——'

'Bankruptcy!'

'Paul's trip to the States was a last bid to save it from the chop.' He rubbed a hand over his face wearily. 'It was no use. He came back early. Even if he'd lived it would still be curtains for PCP.'

Joanna stared at him in shock. 'Dear heaven, Jim, I had no idea. Paul never said——' She stopped short, shrugging. 'But then, Paul rarely said anything at all to me lately.' She frowned in concern. 'But what will happen to you, Jim—and all the others?'

He shrugged. 'Don't worry about me. I've got plenty of irons in the fire. And the rest are young enough to find jobs. You need to look out for yourself, love.'

There was a brief, tense silence. Joanna's mouth took on a bitter curve as she looked about her at the familiar, comfortable room. 'Rather a joke if I'm forced to sell the house in the end, after all.'

Jim mopped his forehead with a handkerchief. 'It needn't come to that. This house is your personal property. The mews cottage in Chelsea will have to go, of course.'

'But Paul sold that years ago!'

'No, he didn't. He—well, he just told you he did.'

Her eyes widened. 'What are you saying?'

Jim looked miserable. 'I wish there was some way I could put this that wouldn't sound like a slap in the face. But there isn't.'

'Oh, for crying out loud!' snapped Joanna, suddenly at the end of her tether. 'Get on with it, Jim.'

'He kept the Chelsea place because——' Jim swallowed. 'Because that's where he spent a lot of his time when he wasn't down here with you.'

She stared at him blankly. 'What are you talking about? He always stayed at his club.'

'Did you ever speak to him there?'

She thought for a moment. 'No—now I come to think of it, I suppose not. I left messages when necessary, which was once in a blue moon.'

Jim nodded. 'He stayed there part of the week, the rest of the time he went off to Chelsea—and Rosa.'

Joanna felt the colour leave her face. Jim sprang to his feet, but she waved him away, managing a smile. 'I'm all right.' She leaned forward to pour herself more coffee, her hand shaking only slightly as she filled the cup. She sipped in silence, then raised blank blue eyes to Jim Fowler. 'Who is Rosa? No need to ask, I suppose. There was bound to be another woman. For years all I've been to Paul is a presentable doll to produce for special occasions.'

'Not in the beginning.'

'No,' she repeated in a dead voice. 'Not in the beginning.' There was an awkward silence. 'This Rosa,' went on Joanna after a while. 'I suppose she was the passenger with him in the crash?'

Jim nodded.

'And did she survive?'

'Only for a few hours.' Jim came to sit beside her, taking her cold hand in his. 'Jo, I'd give anything in the world to avoid hurting you like this——'

'But you knew,' she said dully. 'You knew all the time.'

'Yes, love. So did my Maisie. But we couldn't tell you.'

'No. I can see that.' Joanna shrugged. 'Right. So Paul had a mistress. I don't know why I'm making such a fuss. Besides, as Marlowe says, "the wench is dead". And so is Paul.' Suddenly her self-control disintegrated. Snatching her hand away from Jim, she turned her face into the sofa cushion and gave way to the tears she'd kept at bay for days.

Jim watched in anguish for a moment, then bent over her, patting her shoulder awkwardly. It was a long time before Joanna could pull herself together. She accepted the starched handkerchief he offered, mopping herself up vigorously.

'Sorry,' she croaked when she could speak.

'Nothing to be sorry for, girl. You needed to let go.'

'I suppose so.' Joanna sat straight. 'But don't misunderstand. I'm crying for myself, Jim. Don't pretend you don't know what it was like between Paul and me lately. Because of his religion there was no possibility of divorce. But he wouldn't hear of a separation. To him it was a public admission of failure, and Paul hated failure.' Joanna looked up sharply. 'Jim—he didn't—I mean the accident wasn't some kind of suicide attempt, was it, because Paul failed to get American backing?'

Jim looked shocked. 'Not with Rosa in the car, Jo!' He shifted in his seat uncomfortably. 'Besides, Paul was brought up a strict Catholic, remember. He'd never have killed himself.'

'But he did, in the end, didn't he?' Joanna sighed heavily. 'It's getting late. You should be getting back to Maisie. How's her arthritis, Jim?'

'Bad. That's why she isn't here today. She wanted to come. I wouldn't let her.'

'Give her my love. Tell her I'll come and see her.'

'She told me to bring you back with me tonight, wants you to stay with us for a bit.'

Joanna shook her head. 'Tell your lovely wife I'm grateful, but for the moment I'm better on my own—heaven knows I'm used to it.'

Jim reached across for his papers. 'If that's what you want, Jo. If you change your mind, any time, you know where to come. Now. Sorry to keep at you, but I'd like to get the financial position straight before I go.'

'I won't touch a penny of Paul's money,' said Joanna vehemently.

'Now then, love. I can understand how you feel. You've had a bloody awful shock.' Jim smiled tiredly. 'But you'll feel different tomorrow. You love this house. And if you refuse any money at all you might have to sell it.'

'Perhaps I should! If it weren't for this place things might have been a lot different. On the other hand,' she added bleakly, 'you know where you are with a house.'

Jim gave her an unhappy look, then plunged into a morass of facts and figures. The factory itself, although no longer viable as a going concern in its present form, was situated on land wanted urgently by a property developer. Once the sale had gone through the widow of Paul Clifford could not only keep her home, but live there in reasonable comfort.

'So if I could just have Paul's will, Joanna,' said Jim, standing up.

She frowned. 'Haven't you got it?'

'No. It wasn't with the rest of the papers. I assumed it must be down here.'

'Paul never mentioned it. Perhaps it's in his desk in the study. You look for it, Jim. I'll make more coffee.'

But when Jim rejoined her in the drawing-room he looked grim. 'Not a sign of it. I suppose it could be in the Chelsea house.'

Joanna shrugged. 'Perhaps he altered it in favour of his mysterious Rosa. Cut me off with the proverbial shilling.'

'Don't talk like that! Have a look upstairs, please,' said Jim rather sharply. 'The damn thing must be somewhere.'

Paul Clifford had been obsessive about tidiness. The search through his belongings, though undertaken with reluctance, took Joanna no time at all.

'Sorry,' she said, as she rejoined Jim. 'Nothing. Not even a scented billet-doux in one of his pockets. Paul covered his tracks very efficiently—the same way he did everything else.'

'Try not to be bitter, Jo. Paul was proud of you in his own way. Rosa was—was something separate.'

Joanna bit back a cutting retort. 'Was she, indeed! Just who the blazes was she, anyway? Rosa what?'

'Rosa Anstey. She was Paul's secretary for years. You used to know her quite well.'

Joanna's eyes widened incredulously. 'Miss Anstey! Are you serious?' She shook her head, trying to take it in. 'But I was very fond of Paul's invaluable Miss Anstey. She was such a friendly person, warm dark eyes and rather plump—not even very young!' She stared at him blankly. 'I assumed Paul's mistress would be some brainless young bimbo.'

Jim took in a deep breath. 'Jo. There's something else——' He broke off as the telephone interrupted them.

Joanna answered it then handed it over to Jim in consternation. 'Jim, it's for you. Maisie's had a fall!'

Jim barked a few staccato sentences into the receiver, then crashed it back on the handset, looking distraught. 'She's in hospital. Tried to reach something on a high shelf and fell. Broken her leg.' Feverishly he stuffed papers in his briefcase, then raced outside to his car, with Joanna hard on his heels. He opened the car window, and waved a peremptory finger at her. 'Look for that will again, Jo.'

'Stuff the wretched will!' snapped Joanna. 'Just get yourself off to Maisie, and you mind you ring me tonight and tell me how she is!'

Joanna watched the car out of sight then went back into the house, utterly shattered by Jim's various revelations. Then, as she looked about her at the square familiar hall, she became conscious, for the first time in years, of feeling totally alone. The house felt eerily empty. She shook off the feeling impatiently. She was used to solitude here. Paul had never been in the house for more than two or three days at a time during their entire marriage. Their holidays together, such as they were, had been spent abroad.

And the rest of his life had belonged to Rosa Anstey.

I wonder, thought Joanna bitterly, what Rosa did on weekends? Did she have a weekend lover, in the way that I had a weekend husband? What did I lack that plain, unassuming Rosa Anstey was able to supply?

She paced through the familiar rooms of her home like a tigress in a cage, humiliation and resentment burning inside her. If Paul's mistress had been younger and sexier than herself it would have been easier to bear. But Rosa Anstey had been ten years older and so thoroughly *nice*.

Joanna made a sudden dash for the stairs, wrenching down the zip of her dress as she went, unable to bear her mourning black a moment longer. She ran into her bedroom, peeling off the dress as she went. She pulled on a bright yellow sweatshirt and faded Levis, thrusting her feet into ancient old sneakers, the type of clothes Paul had detested. She tugged the pins from her hair, releasing the heavy, straight weight of it to brush it until it shone like expensive butterscotch against the creamy pallor of her face. Red patches of colour burned along her cheekbones as she wielded the brush, accentuating the kingfisher-blue of eyes which gazed back at her in defiance. Portrait of Joanna Clifford, widow, she thought scathingly.

She turned away, her attention caught by the king-sized bed. It was hard to believe now that Paul had ever shared it with her. Now he never would again. In the beginning it had been so different. In the early days of their marriage he would rush her upstairs to bed the minute he arrived for the weekend, eloquent in his delight with the bride who made him feel like a young stud again. But all that had ended, abruptly, long before their first anniversary. Nothing was ever the same again. She sighed. What a gullible fool she'd been never to suspect that Paul had a mistress.

The struggle to come to terms with her husband's long-term infidelity bleached the transient colour from Joanna's face. She slumped down on the bed in deep depression, huddling there for a long, black interval, until the telephone shrilled, intruding on her misery. Who, she thought in despair, could possibly want to talk to her tonight, of all nights? Only the possibility that it might be Jim Fowler moved her to pick up the receiver at last.

'Mrs Clifford?' asked an unfamiliar male voice.

'Yes.'

There was a pause. 'My name is Marc Anstey——'

Joanna dropped the telephone. She grabbed at it, her hand shaking as she put the receiver to her ear.

'Hello?' said the caller. 'Mrs Clifford? Are you still there?'

'Yes,' she said tonelessly. 'I'm still here. Would you repeat your name, please?'

'Anstey. Marc Anstey. And it's very important that I see you as soon as possible. Tonight, if you will.'

'No!' she said vehemently. 'I mean—this isn't a good time. There's been a funeral here today.'

'I know.' The voice was distinctive, with a gravel-based timbre which hinted of origins other than Anglo-Saxon. 'I've just been to one myself, Mrs Clifford—Rosa's funeral. She was my sister.'

Joanna was silenced. 'I'm sorry,' she said after a moment. 'But why should you want to see me, Mr Anstey?'

'I promised to deliver something to you. From Rosa.'

Joanna felt suddenly cold. 'From Rosa? I don't understand.'

'It's not something one can discuss over the phone,' he said curtly. 'If you'd be kind enough to spare me a few minutes I'd be grateful, Mrs Clifford. I won't keep you long. I quite understand your reluctance to talk to me under the circumstances, but I promised Rosa I'd get in touch with you personally to carry out her wishes.'

What about my wishes? thought Joanna with resentment. 'Oh, very well, Mr Anstey. Where are you?'

'About a mile away in the village. I can be with you in ten minutes.'

'Make it half an hour, please,' she said firmly.

'Very well. Half an hour, then. And thank you,' he added.

Joanna replaced the phone in a daze, wondering if her nervous system could stand much more in the way of shocks. What could Rosa's brother want with her?

She wondered whether to change back into the black dress, but decided against it. This Anstey man could take her as she was. In her particular circumstance mourning black was sheer hypocrisy anyway.

By the time the doorbell rang Joanna had herself firmly under control, all her defences shored up and ready as she opened the door to face a man who was enough like Rosa Anstey to confirm his identity. But where Rosa had been round and plump this man was tall and lean, a curious look on his face as he took in her appearance.

'Mr Anstey, I presume,' she said coolly. 'I'm Joanna Clifford.'

He nodded, taking something from a pocket to hold out to her. 'Would you like some identification?'

Surprised, Joanna took the yellow card from him. The photograph and signature confirmed not only that he was Marc Anstey, as he said, but also that he was a member of the National Union of Journalists, and worked for the *Sentinel*, one of the major national newspapers.

Her eyes flew to his face. 'You're a journalist?' She almost threw the card back at him. 'If you're here in a professional capacity, Mr Anstey——'

'Of course I'm not,' he said wearily. 'I'm on leave. And I don't deal in gossip, Mrs Clifford. I'm a foreign correspondent for the *Sentinel*. My business with you here tonight is strictly personal.'

Joanna looked at him in silence for a moment, then held the door open. 'I suppose you'd better come in.'

'Thank you.' Her unwelcome visitor stood very still in the hall, watching her as she bolted the door. He looked like she felt, thought Joanna. His close-curling black hair gave a spurious impression of youthfulness contradicted by his olive-skinned face, which was haggard with grief. His black eyes narrowed a little as he registered her appearance.

'I've just changed,' Joanna said without thinking, then could have bitten her tongue. What she chose to wear was nothing to do with her unwelcome visitor.

'Did your heart sing a gay *Te Deum* as you discarded your widow's weeds?' he asked, his voice accentless, but with a gravelly huskiness even more pronounced now they were talking face to face.

Joanna stared in affront. 'I beg your pardon!'

He rubbed a hand over his face wearily. 'I apologise. To you and to Noel Coward. The last thing I want is to antagonise you, Mrs Clifford.'

She opened the drawing-room door and motioned him through. 'Perhaps you'd better sit down and tell me what it is, precisely, that you do want. And what it can possibly have to do with me.'

Marc Anstey took the chair she indicated, looking bleak and self-contained, and nothing at all like Joanna's idea of a journalist in a dark, well-cut suit, his black tie reminding her all too forcibly of his connection with Rosa Anstey, aka Paul Clifford's mistress.

'I'm sorry to intrude at what must be the worst possible time for you.' He looked at her levelly. 'At the moment I'm based in Washington, but as luck would have it I'd just arrived on leave in the UK when the accident happened. I managed to get to the hospital in time to be with Rosa before she died.' His jaw tightened as he reached a hand into an inside pocket and drew out a long, legal-looking envelope. 'Before she died Rosa gave me this and told me to bring it to you.'

Joanna took the envelope from him, trembling inside at the thought of what it might contain.

'Would you read it, please?' he said tersely. 'I can't stay long. I've got someone with me in the car.'

Joanna sat down on the edge of the sofa, her face set. 'It must be very important, Mr Anstey, to bring you here the very day of my husband's funeral.'

His mouth took on a sardonic twist. 'It was not an errand I relished, believe me.'

Joanna drew a document from the envelope, unsurprised to find she was looking at the last will and testament of Paul Clifford, dated only weeks before his death. It was brief enough to read very rapidly. To his wife, Joanna Clifford, he bequeathed the painting by Stubbs from the Chelsea house. To James Frederick Fowler, lifelong and devoted friend, he left his gold watch and cufflinks. To Rosa Maria Anstey he bequeathed the company known as PC Plastics, or whatever sum was received for the sale of said company, this sum to be used for the education of Paola Anstey. In the event of Rosa Anstey's death the legacy would pass to said Paola Anstey, daughter of Rosa Anstey and Paul Clifford.

Joanna read through the document a second time in disbelief. Paola, she thought in anguish, daughter of Paul Clifford. Marc Anstey, watching her closely, leaned forward abruptly.

'Are you all right?'

Joanna nodded, ashen-faced. Marc Anstey gave a quick glance round the room, then went over to the silver salver on a side-table, poured brandy into a glass and brought it back to her. 'Drink some of that. You'll feel better.'

'I loathe brandy,' she protested.

'It'll do you good.'

Joanna took a reluctant sip of Paul's best cognac, vaguely resentful when her visitor was proved right.

'You've had a hard day,' said Marc Anstey stiffly.

'It gets worse as it goes on.'

'Mine hasn't been too wonderful either.' He rubbed a hand over his face.

'No,' agreed Joanna, surprised by an unexpected pang of remorse. 'I imagine not. You were obviously very close to your sister.'

He nodded grimly. 'I loved Rosa very much. Otherwise, Mrs Clifford, I wouldn't be here right now. Rosa begged me to come, made me promise as she—as she was dying. I've always dismissed deathbed promises as so much melodramatic poppycock. When they happen to one personally it's a different kettle of fish, believe me.'

Joanna nodded. 'I know.'

He frowned. 'But I thought your husband was killed instantly.'

'He was. My particular promise was made to my father.'

'Were you able to keep it?'

'At some personal cost, yes.' Joanna regarded the haggard, attractive man with curiosity. 'Is your promise anything to do with me, then, Mr Anstey?'

'Yes, very much so.' He looked her in the eye. 'There's no point in beating about the bush, Mrs Clifford. I've come here to make a suggestion you're going to find totally unacceptable. Insane, in fact. By way of explanation, you have to understand that my sister couldn't bear to think of her child in the hands of strangers. She knew that owing to the nature of my work I can't care for my niece myself for the time being. So Rosa made me swear I'd come to see you in person and ask *you* to take Paola, your husband's child, until I'm in a position to do so myself.'

Joanna stared at him incredulously, her face so pale again he moved towards her swiftly, but she held up her hand. 'I'm not ill—just appalled that you should use such emotional blackmail. Whatever vow you made to your sister is nothing to do with me, Mr Anstey. It's—it's outrageous. You can't possibly expect me to do such a thing!'

He lifted one shoulder in a gesture which contrived to convey derision, hostility and scorn all at once. 'I don't. I never thought for a moment you'd agree. It was my sister, not I, who was convinced you were the right one to have her child.'

'I can't think why!'

He looked her over assessingly. 'Having met you, neither can I, Mrs Clifford.' He met her outraged eyes levelly. 'But there's something you've overlooked. By the terms of Paul Clifford's will Paola now owns PC Plastics. However, Rosa left a will, appointing me trustee to look after my niece's interests. And if I block the sale of PCP to the developer all its present resources will be swallowed up to meet its debts, including your house, Mrs Clifford.'

CHAPTER TWO

JOANNA stared at him, her blue eyes icy with outrage. 'May I ask you a question?' she said after a taut silence.

'By all means.'

'If, Mr Anstey, *you* are the trustee in the case, why did your sister want me to take care of the child?'

He shrugged. 'Make no mistake, Mrs Clifford, I couldn't love my niece more if she were my own child. But I'm single, and I lead a peripatetic sort of existence. After spells in Moscow and Tokyo I'm presently based in Washington.' His mouth tightened. 'When Rosa moved into your husband's Chelsea house I took over her studio flat as a London base, but neither the flat nor my lifestyle is suitable for looking after a child.'

'In the circumstances your sister must have been very fond of you to consider you a suitable guardian for her daughter!'

'She was. As I was of her. Rosa knew perfectly well I wasn't in an ideal position to bring up Paola myself—not yet, anyway. But I swore to her I'd see that her daughter received the best of care—and love.'

Joanna nodded, eyeing him. 'I see. So let me just get this straight. I am to have the responsibility of bringing up the child, but you are the—er—treasurer, shall we say?'

The black eyes narrowed to a hard gleam. 'Precisely. Not that *I* gain anything, Mrs Clifford. Whatever comes to the child will be held in trust for her. If you had agreed to give her a home an ample allowance would have been yours for your trouble.' He shrugged indifferently. 'I knew it was a mistake to come here. I apologise for my intrusion—believe me, it was the last thing I felt like tonight. Nevertheless, I've now carried out my sister's wishes as I promised, so my part in all this is over. Goodnight.'

'Wait,' said Joanna, springing to her feet. 'What are you going to do?'

He turned, one eyebrow raised. 'Do? About the sale?'

'No, I don't care a damn about the sale!' she snapped. 'I meant what about—about the child?'

He rubbed a hand along his shadowed chin wearily. 'I don't know yet. But I'll think of something. My problem is the time factor. I've only got a week's leave to sort things out.'

Joanna bit her lip, eyeing him. 'Where is—is your niece now?'

'Outside in the car.'

'What?'

He shrugged. 'Since Rosa died she tends to cling to me like grim death. A friend of mine came to the funeral with us, and stayed in the car with her until it was over.'

'Is your friend outside in the car too?'

His face hardened. 'No. An hour spent with a crying child put paid to the lady's maternal instincts. The moment the funeral was over she took off in a taxi. I came here alone. Paola was so worn out I just wrapped her up in a rug on the back seat of the car and she went off to sleep—which reminds me, I'd better see if she's all right.'

'Could I see her?' said Joanna impulsively.

'Why?' His eyes narrowed in suspicion.

She looked at him in appeal. 'Look, until tonight I didn't even know she existed. I just want to see her for a moment, that's all.'

Marc Anstey shrugged, then made for the door. 'As you like.'

Joanna followed him outside towards the car parked at the far edge of the gravel circle in front of the house. He put a finger to his lips as he leaned forward to peer into the back seat.

'She's still fast asleep,' he said under his breath. 'I won't open the door. Satisfy your curiosity, Mrs Clifford, then I'll be off.'

Joanna's throat tightened as she gazed through the car window at a tangle of black curls and sleeping, tear-stained face.

'Well?' he demanded in an undertone. 'Have you seen enough?'

Joanna shook her head slowly. 'As she's asleep will you come back into the house for a moment? You can leave the door open to watch out for her.'

'If I must.'

They went back into the hall and stood in the open doorway, both of them looking fixedly at the car rather than at each other.

'Mr Anstey,' began Joanna, choosing her words with care, 'this has all come as a great shock. It's only a couple of hours since I learned about my husband's association with your sister. To discover there's a child as well is hard to take in. I can't think straight. But I'm not heartless. I see your difficulty, and——' she breathed in shakily '—I feel for the child. Deeply. On the other hand you can't expect me to decide something so important as this off the top of my head.'

'I don't *expect* anything,' he said curtly. 'In fact, a moment ago I seem to recall you dismissed my sister's request as melodramatic nonsense.'

Joanna's chin lifted. 'Look, Mr Anstey, if you mean to be unpleasant there's no point in going on with this.'

He controlled himself with visible effort. 'I'm sorry. This isn't easy for either of us. Believe me, the last thing I wanted was to come barging in on you tonight, of all nights. But I've got so little time to get things settled.' One black eyebrow lifted. 'And I assumed you'd need the will. It seemed best to get it over with. Not best for you, nor for me, but for Polly.' He smiled wryly at her questioning look. 'Her favourite song, "Polly Wolly Doodle". The name stuck.'

'I see.' Joanna looked at her watch, then over at the car. 'Are you driving back to London now?'

'No. I haven't slept much lately. I couldn't face the drive back to town tonight. On the way here I booked a room at the Lamb and Flag in the village. The landlady's organising some supper, after which my plan is to tuck Polly up in one bed and crash out in the other myself.'

'I see.' Joanna braced herself. 'In that case, Mr Anstey, would you consider bringing your—bringing Polly to see me in the morning?'

'On approval, you mean?' he queried scathingly.

'No!' Joanna's nails bit into her palms. 'I'd just like to make Polly's acquaintance. I knew your sister quite well at one time, and I liked her very much. But I find it very hard to visualise her as Paul's mistress.' She paused as Marc Anstey winced. 'I'm sorry. What I'm trying to say is that her relationship with Paul won't prejudice me on the subject of her child's welfare. But right now would be a bad time for Polly and me to meet. In the morning she should feel better, and I—well, shall we say I shall have had time to get used to certain aspects of my husband's life unknown to me until today?' She met his black, assessing eyes candidly. 'I'm not saying I'll do what your sister wanted. For one thing, Polly might hate the sight of me. But what I am saying is that I won't dismiss the idea out of hand.'

'No.' He showed strong white teeth in a mirthless smile. 'Because if you do you lose your money and your house.'

Joanna gave him a patronising little smile. 'As it happens, I don't, Mr Anstey. The house is mine. I was born here. And with care I can continue to live here. I don't need money. Your blackmail wouldn't have worked.'

For a moment Marc Anstey was silent, then he gave her a mocking little bow. 'I apologise, Mrs Clifford. I got the facts wrong.'

'And you a journalist—how *very* strange!'

He threw up a hand, smiling faintly. 'All right, Mrs Clifford. I'll bring Polly here after breakfast in the morning. Just for a few minutes. But she's a little human being, remember, not a puppy. If you do take her you can't send her off to the dogs' home if it doesn't work out.'

Only the memory of a small, tear-stained face prevented Joanna from slamming the door in his face. 'I won't bother to answer that, Mr Anstey. I'll see you at ten in the morning.'

A disquieting gleam flashed in the dark eyes for an instant before Marc Anstey turned away. He paused under the portico light to look at her. 'By the way, I should have said this before. Please accept my condolences. Belated, I'm afraid. If you find it hard to think of Rosa as Paul Clifford's mistress, I find it damned impossible to think of you as his wife.'

'But I'm not his wife, Mr Anstey. I'm his widow. Goodnight.'

Which, thought Joanna, as she bolted the door yet again, was about right. After the revelations of the day it was difficult to remember she'd ever been Paul Clifford's wife. Rosa Anstey and Polly had probably seen far more of Paul than she had during the entire duration of her marriage.

Jim rang later to say his wife's leg was in plaster, and other than feeling mad with herself for doing something so stupid Maisie was in good heart. 'How are you, love?' he asked.

'Like Maisie, as well as can be expected. Give her my love and tell her I'll visit her.' Joanna paused, then told him about the unexpected visitor who'd brought the missing will. 'So I know about the child now, Jim. Paul's left everything to the daughter I never knew he possessed.' She gave a mirthless little laugh. 'He left me the Stubbs painting. You know the one, a grey rather like my poor Saladin. Liked his joke, did Paul.'

Jim groaned. 'I kept trying to tell you about the little girl, love,' he said, 'then the shock about Maisie sent everything out of my head. How do you feel about it?'

'I'll let you know when I've had time to get used to the idea.' She explained about the terms of the will and Rosa Anstey's dying wish regarding her child.

'You've got to be joking!' said Jim, flabbergasted. 'She couldn't have known what she was saying.' He paused. 'I've never met this brother of hers. Heard of him, mind. A bit of a high-flyer, tipped for the top, so I hear. A kid could cramp his style. He might be trying to pull a fast one, Jo, dumping the kid on you to evade his own responsibility.'

'No,' said Joanna, thinking it over. 'I don't think so. In fact, Jim, I rather got the impression that the high-flying Mr Anstey isn't in the least keen to hand his niece over to me. Which is natural enough. He knows nothing about me, after all.'

Jim cleared his throat noisily, sounding embarrassed. 'But Rosa did, love. She admired you no end. I know for a fact she felt pretty bad about what happened with you and Paul. It might seem crazy, but she must have really believed you were the best one to look after her child.'

'She may have,' said Joanna sharply. 'It doesn't mean I'm going to, though, Jim.'

'No, no, of course not.' Jim paused. 'But if this Anstey chap kicks up rough about the will it's going to make things a bit difficult for us all at PCP.'

* * *

Joanna went early to bed, but not to sleep. She lay tossing and turning all night, certain she must be insane even to contemplate taking Rosa's child. But the small, tear-stained face of Polly Anstey kept rising to haunt her, along with harrowing thoughts of a dying woman's plea. If she refused to take the child, Joanna had a sinking feeling she'd regret it for the rest of her life.

She smiled bitterly as she realised that Paul had achieved his family in the end, after all, though not in the precise way he'd wanted it. Paola Anstey's great drawback in his eyes would have been her sex. Paul had been so desperate for a son. Joanna shook her head in the darkness, marvelling at her husband's talent for deception. Paul Clifford had lived a lie for years, juggling two separate lives with the skill of a magician. If he hadn't been killed she might never have known. Suddenly Joanna felt a searing pang of inadequacy, depressed at the lack in herself which had sent her husband into the arms of another woman. She wept a few bitter tears into her pillow, then pulled herself together, sniffing, knowing full well she was weeping from wounded pride, rather than grief.

The tears disappeared altogether when Joanna finally acknowledged the inescapable fact that Polly Anstey's pathetic little face was not the only one keeping her awake. As the night wore on she found it harder and harder to dismiss Marc Anstey's dark, haggard features from her mind. Joanna heaved over on to her back restlessly, assuring herself it was only natural to feel *some* sympathy for Marc Anstey. And not for *him* exactly, but for his dilemma. His sister had left him in a pretty pickle one way and another. Joanna's lip trembled. It wasn't fair of Rosa to make her feel guilty like this. Why should she be expected to take charge of another woman's child? Why had Rosa thought she could solve her problem by passing it on to Joanna Clifford? Only the problem wasn't an 'it'. It was a desolate little girl, crying for her mother. And probably for her father, too.

Joanna stared miserably at the ceiling, watching the changes of light as clouds played tag with the moon outside. Why me? she thought for the hundredth time. Were there no suitable relatives? And, even if there weren't, surely there was enough money from the sale of PCP to provide the child with suitable care? But Rosa had evidently wanted more than that. She'd wanted Paul's wife to take over responsibility for his child. Which was madness. How did she know Joanna Clifford wouldn't make Polly's life a misery? Unless she'd instructed her brother to make regular inspections, satisfy himself that Polly was being treated properly. It all seemed very unlikely—Joanna lay suddenly still. Unless, of course, Paul had told Rosa about the accident.

Joanna got up very early next morning, had a hot bath, dithered for a while, then pulled on a scarlet sweater with the same faded Levis of the night before. Feeling on edge and irritable, she passed the time until ten by making muffins, wondering if they were the sort of thing little girls liked. She fidgeted about, tidying up, arranging and rearranging sprays of leaves in a copper jar, until by the time her visitors were due Joanna's nerves were as taut as piano-wire.

Pulling herself together impatiently, she ran upstairs to brush her hair. She eyed her reddened eyelids and pale face, then shrugged and went downstairs. Marc Anstey could take her as she was.

She was at the window when the car turned into the drive. Prey to a sharp attack of nerves, she opened the door and stood under the portico as Marc Anstey, still in his formal suit, helped a small girl from the car and led her towards the house.

Sleeping, Polly had looked like a sad little angel. Awake and unwilling, she was a sturdy little creature with bright black eyes in a round face still blotchy from weeping, her dark curls untidy. She wore navy shorts and a white T-shirt and clung to her uncle's hand, shrinking against him as he tried to pull her forward. Something eased inside Joanna as she realised that together Marc and Paola Anstey could have been taken for father and daughter. The child bore no resemblance at all to Paul Clifford.

'Hello,' she called casually.

'Good morning,' said Marc Anstey, picking up his niece bodily. 'This is very kind of you, Mrs Clifford. You must excuse Polly. She's in a very unsociable mood.'

'Never mind. Come in and have some coffee. I'm dying for some.' Joanna led them to the bright, cheerful kitchen, waving Marc to a chair at the table. He set Polly on his knee, where she snuggled against him, thumb in mouth, her eyes fixed on Joanna.

All fingers and thumbs under the black, unblinking scrutiny, Joanna made coffee and carried a tray to the table, then sat down in a chair opposite her visitors, smiling brightly.

'How was breakfast at the Lamb and Flag?'

'Difficult.' Marc sighed wearily as he shifted the child more comfortably on his lap. 'Polly wasn't in an eating mood. And after twenty minutes of intensive coaxing neither was I.'

Joanna poured hot, strong coffee into two tall mugs, then looked enquiringly at the child. 'How about you, Polly? Do you like coffee?'

No response.

'Milk? Orange juice?'

A flicker of interest lit the dark eyes. Taking it for assent, Joanna poured juice from a carton into a beaker and set it within the child's reach.

'I don't suppose you'd fancy a muffin, Mr Anstey?' she asked casually.

Marc Anstey's eyes brightened. 'English muffins? Wonderful! I haven't tasted one in years.'

Battening down the hatches on her emotions, Joanna applied herself to toasting and buttering. She kept up a light, superficial conversation with Marc Anstey, making no attempt to talk to the little girl as she handed out plates and napkins. Marc Anstey polished off two muffins at flattering speed, while Polly, finding no one was taking any notice of her, warily tasted the fragment of muffin her uncle tossed on her plate for her to try.

'I like it,' she said in a hoarse, weary little voice.

Joanna smiled. 'Good. Shall I toast a fresh one for you?'

Polly nodded mutely, then as Marc sent her a meaning look she muttered, 'Yes, please.'

While the adults drank more coffee the child ate her muffin to the last crumb, then drank a second beaker of orange juice.

'The catering seems more popular here than the Lamb and Flag,' said Marc lightly, then gave Joanna a significant look. 'We must be going soon.'

'Not yet!' Joanna looked up with a smile of relief as Doris arrived. 'Morning, Doris. This is Mr Marc Anstey, and the lady on his knee is Polly.'

'Pleased to meet you,' said Doris, beaming at the little girl.

Polly favoured Doris with one of her unwinking scrutinies, then her orange-rimmed mouth curved in a faint suggestion of a smile. She slid down from her uncle's knee. 'Loo, please,' she said imperiously.

Doris held out her hand. 'Right you are, young miss. Will you come with me?'

Polly nodded serenely, surrendered her hand to the firm, rough grasp, and trotted off without a backward glance.

Joanna looked at Marc in astonishment. 'Well!'

'Three cheers for Doris.' He leaned forward, his face suddenly urgent. 'Look, since we're out of Polly's earshot so unexpectedly, can you tell me how you feel now you've met her? Or is it too soon?'

She looked at him, defeated. 'I lay awake all night wrestling with my conscience.'

He tensed, his face colourless with strain. 'And?'

'I decided the best thing was to have Polly to stay for a day or two before we come to any hasty decisions.'

Marc's eyes narrowed. 'It could mean quite a hold-up for the sale of PCP.'

Joanna's eyes smouldered. 'Mr Anstey, you can do whatever you like with Polly's inheritance. As I told you last night, I don't need——' She bit her lip, as it suddenly occurred to her that if she had a child to bring up and educate this was not exactly true.

'If you do take Polly,' he said swiftly, 'provision—generous provision—would be made for her, and for you.'

They looked at each other in silence for a moment, then Joanna nodded reluctantly. 'I'd have to accept it, for Polly's sake—*if* she stays with me.' She eyed him curiously. 'Mr Anstey, what I find so extraordinary is that you don't have anyone else who could take Polly.'

'If I had, do you think I'd have come to you, Mrs Clifford?' He turned away, grimacing. 'I'm sorry. I could have put that more gracefully. What I mean is that our parents are dead, Rosa and I the only children. My father's family washed their hands of him when he married the orphaned Sicilian girl he found wandering the streets of Naples towards the end of the war. I do have relatives, yes. But I've never met any of them, nor do I wish to.' He swung round suddenly. 'And you know Paul had no one, either. Or no one he'd admit to.'

Joanna's eyes narrowed. Something in his tone suggested Marc Anstey and Paul Clifford had never been soul-mates.

'Nevertheless, Mr Anstey, I'm still surprised that your sister thought *I'd* take Polly.'

Marc Anstey's black eyes shuttered. 'If you want the truth, Mrs Clifford, I'll give you her reasons verbatim—even at the risk of alienating you completely. Rosa said you lost a child, and couldn't have any more. She seemed to think that by handing Paul's daughter over to you she was making up for that. I thought it was a lousy idea. But I couldn't say so—not when it was damn near the last thing I was ever going to say to her.' He swallowed convulsively and turned away, his fists clenched at his side.

Joanna's hand went out to him, then dropped hastily as Doris ushered in a washed and tidied Polly. Joanna's heart contracted at the tenderness in Marc Anstey's smile as he greeted the little girl.

'Polly would like a walk in the garden,' announced Doris. 'Is it all right if I take her round the stables, Mrs Clifford?'

'You'd like that, Polly?' asked Joanna.

The child nodded vigorously. She went off with Doris, chattering in a hoarse little voice, leaving Joanna with a wistful feeling she identified with some surprise. She wanted Polly's approval, too.

'Are the stables in use?' asked Marc.

Joanna began clearing away, her back to him. 'No. Not any more.'

'It was you who used to ride, I take it. I can't see Paul on a horse.'

She shot him a glance over her shoulder. 'You obviously disliked Paul.'

One shoulder lifted in a very Latin shrug. 'Not exactly. I disapproved.'

'Because of Rosa?'

'Exactly.' He smiled without mirth. 'Most of the time I behave like your average Brit, but the Sicilian in me rose up in revolt when Paul Clifford set my sister up as his mistress.'

'An old-fashioned word.'

'Rosa *was* old-fashioned. She never looked at another man from the first day she went to work for Paul Clifford. He was the one great love of her life.' One black eyebrow rose sardonically. 'I don't think he felt the same about her, by any means.'

Joanna turned to face him. 'Since she gave him a child I imagine he cared for her a lot. Paul wanted a family very much.'

Marc examined his fingernails intently. 'Polly owes her existence to the fact that it was Rosa whom Paul turned to when you lost *your* child. She offered comfort, and because she'd been in love with him for years the inevitable happened. They became lovers. She became pregnant.'

'Whereupon Paul moved her into the Chelsea house and engaged a new secretary.' Joanna tried to smile and failed. 'From then on my marriage was virtually over. When Paul learned I couldn't have any more children, I think——' She thought for a moment. 'I think Paul felt cheated. As though he'd made a bad bargain.'

'Bargain?'

Joanna nodded. 'He made it possible for me to keep this house. In return I married him and promised to provide him with children.'

Marc frowned. 'Did you love him?'

'I thought I did. I wouldn't have married him otherwise. I'd just lost my father, and Paul—well, I suppose I looked on Paul as the ideal person to take his place. But I was never *in* love with Paul. He was twenty years older than me. In the beginning the gap didn't seem to matter. He——' she stopped, flushing.

'Enjoyed having a young, beautiful bride,' said Marc drily.

Her eyes frosted over. 'Quite so. Perhaps we should go outside. No doubt you'll want to satisfy yourself that my house and garden are suitable as a home for Polly.'

He nodded distantly. 'Thank you—Mrs Clifford.'

They went out into the damp, misty morning to find Polly helping Doris pick blackberries from the thornless bushes in the orchard beyond the stables. She ran to Marc, flushed and very different from the woebegone child of earlier on.

'Marco! Look—they've got apples on trees here!'

He laughed and picked her up, kissing her cheek. 'Of course they do, you little townie.'

'Can we stay to lunch?' demanded the child.

Marc shook his head. 'We ought to be going.'

'Would you like to stay, Polly?' asked Joanna.

Polly nodded, smiling at Joanna for the first time. 'Yes.'

'Please!' prompted Marc.

The child repeated it obediently, wriggling to get down.

'I'm helping Doris,' she said importantly. She ran off without a backward glance, leaving a strained silence behind her.

'She seems to like it here,' said Marc, as he strolled with Joanna towards the stables.

'I hope so.'

'When shall I leave her with you?'

Joanna opened the top half of one of the doors, gazing into the empty manger. 'Whenever suits you, Mr Anstey.'

He was silent for a moment, leaning beside her. 'I'm due back in Washington next week. If I brought Polly here the day after tomorrow, I could put up in the Lamb and Flag for a couple of days, stay within reach in case——'

'I'm beating her regularly?'

'No,' he said wearily. 'In case I'm needed. If the arrangement doesn't work I'll just have to engage a full-time nanny and find a bigger flat.'

Joanna thought about it in silence. If Marc Anstey was on hand for a time at the beginning it might ease the initial stages of her relationship with Polly. As yet the little girl was far more taken with Doris than her dead father's wife. Joanna squared her shoulders.

'All right. Let's do that.'

Marc turned to her. 'Are you sure?'

'Yes.'

He held out his hand formally. 'Let's shake on it, then.'

Joanna smiled coolly and put her hand in his for an instant, then detached her fingers hastily, horrified to find her pulse racing at his touch. She turned back to the empty stable, saying the first thing that came into her head. 'I had a horse called Saladin who used to live in here.'

'Did you sell him?'

'No. Paul had him destroyed.'

Marc shot a startled glance at her. 'Why?'

'I had a fall when I was riding him. It was my fault, not Saladin's. But I lost the baby. Paul went berserk, took his anger and disappointment out on the horse. I was told I'd have miscarried anyway, fall or no fall, but by the time I was discharged from the hospital Saladin was dead.'

They stared into the dark stable for some time in silence.

'Couldn't you have bought another horse?' Marc asked at last.

'No.' Joanna cleared her throat. 'Paul held the purse-strings. I had no money of my own.'

Marc Anstey turned to watch his niece running about on the grass in the distance. 'Couldn't you have got a job—earned some money of your own?'

The open disapproval in his tone stung Joanna. 'That's a very personal remark! As it happens I did find a way to earn money. Eventually. But not enough for luxuries like horses.' She paused, shaken to find herself so angry. 'Mr Anstey, I think we should get certain things straight. The only thing you and I have in common is Polly. You have my assurance that if she stays with me I'll do my utmost to give her a good home and make her happy. But I want everything legally sorted out beforehand, including your rights where she's concerned—reasonable access and so on. Beyond that, you and I need have nothing to do with each other.'

Marc Anstey said something under his breath, a leap of dislike in his eyes as they clashed with hers. 'Rosa was wrong. This just isn't going to work.'

Joanna shrugged disdainfully. 'I don't see why not. The equation's obvious. Polly lost a mother. I lost a child. I lay awake most of last night thinking it over, and came to the conclusion that Rosa was right. It's the perfect solution.'

He looked at her moodily for a long, tense moment. 'I'll reserve judgement until this trial period's over—but, whichever way things turn out, keep one thing very much in mind,' he added, with sinister emphasis. 'Polly might lack a mother, but she's not alone in the world. Anyone who harms a single hair of her head will have me to contend with. And I can fight dirty, Mrs Clifford. Believe me.'

CHAPTER THREE

JOANNA'S home was late Georgian, quite small, and classically simple in design. A single pillar supported the porch. Above it a half-moon window formed a pleasing note of contrast among the oblong sash windows flanking the main door of Swan House, which stood in three acres of land mainly given over to woodland and orchard. As a child Joanna had run free there with her friends, and was convinced that in time Polly could be just as happy in the same surroundings.

But much as she loved her home, the day Joanna was expecting Marc Anstey with Polly it felt like a cage. After her sudden tirade at the stable door Marc had called his niece to him and taken her away at once, deaf to the child's pleas to stay for lunch, and Joanna's last view of Polly had been a forlorn little hand waving from the back window of the car. Marc Anstey had made it plain that diplomatic relations between himself and Paul Clifford's widow were at an end. Not, Joanna assured herself, that she minded. Her view of the entire male sex was somewhat jaundiced after her experience with Paul.

As the time grew closer to Polly's arrival Joanna began to get cold feet, more convinced by the minute that she'd been mad even to think of trying to bring up someone else's child. It wasn't as if she had experience of motherhood in any form herself.

Her own mother had taken off with a lover before her daughter could walk, leaving Joanna to the loving but eccentric care of a father who looked on dogs, horses, music and literature as the only necessities in life other than food. Urged by relatives to send his child away to school, Richard Swan had refused point-blank. In his view the local schools and his own efforts could provide his child with all the education necessary right up to university entrance, and his pleasure was enormous when Joanna proved him right by gaining a first-class degree in art history.

Joanna smiled wryly. Instead of art history and her subsequent secretarial course she'd have done better to train as a nanny for her present undertaking.

She tensed as she heard a car crunch to a halt on the gravel outside. When the bell rang she made herself wait for a moment or two, then opened the door, her smile of welcome fading when she found Marc Anstey alone, looking even more haggard than before.

'Good morning, Mr Anstey,' she said formally. 'Where's Polly?'

'Good morning, Mrs Clifford.' He shrugged, nodding in the direction of the car. 'She fell asleep on the way down. I thought we might have a word out here before I wake her up.'

'By all means.'

He thrust his hands into his pockets, eyeing her warily. 'I suppose I should have rung. To ask if you'd changed your mind.'

Joanna looked past him towards the row of wallflowers she'd planted on the day Paul died. 'I never change my mind once it's made up.'

'I admire your certainty.'

'Obstinacy, my father called it.'

His eyes, black-ringed with weariness, studied her coolly. 'You were pretty frank last time I was here—regarding any personal dealings between you and me. So I've a suggestion to make.'

'I'm listening,' said Joanna, who had regretted her outburst almost the moment it was made.

'Do you have a solicitor?' he asked.

'I generally leave money matters to Jim Fowler, Paul's financial adviser. He's an old friend.'

Marc nodded. 'I've already been in contact with him over the will. Would he agree to a meeting between the three of us? In the role of Polly's trustee I'd like some kind of contract drawn up and ratified, with your role—and mine—clearly defined where my niece is concerned.'

'I'll arrange it,' said Joanna promptly. 'If he can get down here this evening perhaps the three of us can thrash it out over dinner.'

'Are you asking me to break bread with you, Mrs Clifford?' he asked drily. 'I thought personal contact was to be minimal.'

Joanna's chin lifted. 'Mr Anstey, I'm sorry I was so outspoken the other day. My—my emotions were still pretty raw right then. I've had time to think since, and I realise that it would be very bad for Polly if you and I remain hostile to each other.'

'*You* were hostile, Mrs Clifford, not me.'

Joanna fought down her resentment. 'And I'm trying hard not to be now,' she said tightly. 'What

I'm saying is, shall we start again? If not as friends, at least as two people prepared to make the best of a difficult situation.'

'I'll go for that.' Marc Anstey gave her a faint smile which metamorphosed almost at once into a mammoth yawn.

'You look tired,' commented Joanna.

'Polly wakes up in the night crying for her mother.' He shot a sombre look at her. 'Will you be able to cope with that?'

Joanna ignored a sudden rush of panic. 'I'll do my utmost to cope, I promise. I know none of it will be easy, Mr Anstey——'

'It might be just a bit easier if you call me Marc.'

'All right. You know I'm Joanna.'

'Yes. I know.'

There was a pause while each took stock of the other. Then Marc gave her a twisted smile. 'A shame we had to meet under such bloody awful circumstances.'

'Amen to that,' agreed Joanna bleakly. 'Shall we get Polly out of the car?'

After her nap Polly was sleepy and irritable until she realised she was back in the house with the orchard. The discovery smoothed over the initial stages as the child ran through the house and out into the garden to play there for a while before lunch.

'Does this mean I'm bidden to two meals today?' enquired Marc suavely, eyeing the three places laid at the kitchen table.

Joanna turned away to take hot rolls from the oven. 'I haven't contacted Jim yet. Dinner tonight depends on him.'

Lunch was a difficult meal. Polly, deeply disappointed because Doris was missing, refused to eat more than a spoonful or two of the vegetable soup, which she pronounced different from the soup Mamma made.

'Will Mamma make soup in heaven?' she asked Marc, who looked as though he'd been kicked in the stomach.

'Of course she will, *cara*,' he said gruffly. A pulse throbbed at the corner of his mouth as he fed her a morsel of hot buttered roll. 'The angels will love Mamma's soup. Not,' he added hastily, 'that Joanna's soup isn't delicious.'

Joanna smiled brightly. 'Just different,' she agreed. 'You wouldn't have any recipes, I suppose?'

'Don't worry. It might be best to do your own thing right from the start.'

After lunch the moment Joanna had been dreading came all too soon. Marc, obviously ready to drop, said goodbye to Polly before departing for a rest in his room at the Lamb and Flag. The little girl stared at him incredulously, tears welling up in her dark eyes.

'Want to come too!' she clamoured hoarsely, clinging to his hand like grim death. *'Marco——'*

'No, Polly,' he said coaxingly. 'You stay here with Joanna. I'll see you later. I promise.'

The ensuing scene was every bit as bad as Joanna had feared. Worse, she thought in desperation, as she hung on to a hysterical little girl once Marc

Anstey had torn himself away, his face pale and drawn as he gunned his car down the drive.

Joanna managed to get the screaming, kicking child indoors, then struggled upstairs with her to a small bedroom at the back of the house. She sat down on the bed with the distraught child in her arms, rocking Polly back and forth, murmuring soothing, wordless noises of comfort for a very long time before the exhausted child lapsed into normal tears. Her head burrowed against Joanna's shoulder at last as she wept, the small body shaken by the occasional hiccup as the storm of weeping gradually died away. Joanna, utterly shattered, smoothed a trembling hand over the tangled black curls, her other arm holding Polly close. At last she turned the swollen, forlorn face up to hers and smiled tenderly.

'Polly. I want you to listen to me.'

She felt the little body tense.

'I used to know your Mamma quite well,' Joanna began with care. 'So before Mamma had to go to heaven, she asked your Uncle Marc——'

'Marco,' corrected Polly hoarsely.

Joanna bit her lip. 'Right. Marco. She asked him to give you to me to look after.'

A quiver ran through the small body. 'Why?' demanded Polly.

'Because I don't have a little girl, you see. Your Mamma knew I wanted one. So she gave you to me. Won't you stay with me so I won't be lonely any more?'

'Marco too?' asked Polly hopefully.

Joanna blinked. 'Your uncle's job means he has to be in America a lot, so he can't *live* here. But he can come and see you whenever he wants, I promise. Look. Cross my heart!'

Polly's forehead creased in a frown while her dazed little mind grappled with the new idea. Joanna waited, tense, then at long last the curly black head nodded slowly, one small shoulder lifting in exact imitation of her uncle.

'Suppose so,' said Polly listlessly, then brightened. 'Doris? Will I see Doris if I live with you?'

'Most days,' Joanna promised. 'She helps me with the house.'

Polly sat up, beginning to take in her surroundings. Her eyes went from the pictures of Winnie-the-Pooh on the wall, to the row of battered teddy bears sitting on a shelf, then opened saucer-wide as they saw the doll's house in the corner. 'Does a little girl live here?'

Joanna let Polly get down to explore. 'Not now. This used to be my room when I was a little girl like you.'

Polly looked surprised. 'Yours?'

'Yes. If you open that chest over there you'll find more toys. They used to be mine, but you can have them now. If you like,' added Joanna casually.

But Polly wasn't listening. Her attention was riveted on the large Victorian doll's house filled from kitchen to attic with miniature nineteenth-century furniture. She turned to Joanna in wonder. 'Yours, too?'

'Yes. My daddy made it for me.'

Polly looked wistful. 'I haven't got a daddy.'

Joanna's heart stood still. 'Haven't you, darling?'

'No. Only Marco—and Uncle Paul.'

Joanna swallowed. 'Uncle Paul?'

Polly nodded absently, her attention on the wonders of the doll's house. 'He came to our house a lot. But he's gone to heaven now too.'

Deciding it was dangerous to continue the conversation without advice from Marc Anstey, Joanna showed Polly how to unfasten the wall of the doll's house to reveal the rooms inside. 'Would you like to play up here for a minute while I make a telephone call?'

'Can I take out the dollies?' entreated Polly.

'Yes, of course. Only they like to go back in their places afterwards. When I come back I'll tell you their names, if you like.'

The child nodded fervently, then turned back to the house, her small hands reverent as she lifted the baby doll out of the cradle.

Joanna flew to her bedroom and whisked her wedding photograph into a drawer. Then she went systematically through the entire house, removing what few traces of Paul she could find. Her relationship with Polly was likely to be so fragile and difficult for a while that she had no intention of allowing Paul to make life any more difficult than he had already, for Polly's sake as well as her own.

Afterwards Joanna rang Jim Fowler to ask him to dinner. He promised to be with her by eight after he'd been to visit his wife in the hospital.

'What's up, Jo?' he asked uneasily. 'Anstey kicking up rough?'

'No. He just wants everything on a legal footing. I think it's a good idea,' she added firmly. 'See you tonight, Jim.'

She rang the Lamb and Flag, left a message to the effect that the appointment Mr Anstey required had been made, then went back to Polly to suggest they unpack Polly's belongings and put them away.

'Tell you what,' said Joanna. 'Once we've done that I'll take the doll's house down to the kitchen and put it on the table there if you like. I've got a friend coming to dinner, your uncle too, so I've got to get busy.'

Polly assented rapturously, trotting back and forth industriously as they put her clothes away. Joanna's heart contracted as she hung up little dresses exquisitely smocked and embroidered by a loving hand that could only have belonged to Rosa. When everything was put away and a long-maned lion lay on the bed guarding Polly's pyjamas, Joanna took the little girl on a tour of the upper floor, ending with one of the bathrooms, where Polly needed only a little assistance before they went back to collect the doll's house.

Later, as rain lashed against the kitchen windows, Joanna was conscious of an unexpected feeling of peace as she glanced across at the absorbed child from time to time. As she made her preparations for dinner it occurred to her that fate had given her a child of Paul's after all. But in the last way she would have wished.

Once the vegetables were done and the pork tenderloin stood absorbing its flavours of garlic and mustard, ready to cook later, Joanna sat down at the kitchen table to tell Polly the names the youthful Joanna had given her dolls. To a child of the nineties some of the names were very funny. When Polly laughed Joanna rejoiced. If Polly could laugh now and then things wouldn't be too bad. Not, she thought, that she had any delusions about being a substitute for Rosa Anstey. Nor had she any intention of trying to take Rosa's place, even if such a thing were possible. It was essential that she create a role of her own where Polly was concerned.

The first argument arose over the subject of supper. None of Joanna's suggestions appealed to Polly in the slightest.

'You must eat,' said Joanna briskly. 'You hardly had any lunch.'

'Not hungry,' Polly said.

Joanna shrugged. 'OK.'

Polly, plainly expecting to be coaxed, looked taken aback. Her eyes were baffled as Joanna dropped the subject and helped her put all the dolls back in their places in their house.

'Bathtime now,' announced Joanna.

'Don't want a bath,' said Polly, eyeing her.

Joanna returned the bright black stare serenely. 'You can go without supper if you like, Polly, but in my house you can't go without a bath. Only clean little girls sleep in my beds. OK?'

Something in Joanna's manner decided Polly not to argue. She sighed gustily. 'OK.'

Matters improved slightly at bathtime, where a flotilla of battered rubber ducks were produced to liven the proceedings. Afterwards, when the little figure was clean and cosy in pyjamas and dressing-gown, her black curls gleaming, Polly unbent towards Joanna sufficiently to confide that her teddy's name was Benno and her pyjama-case was Leone.

'Uncle Paul gave him to me,' she announced as they went downstairs, hand in hand.

Joanna's stomach lurched. 'That's nice. Now, if you don't fancy supper, how about a glass of milk instead?'

Polly, however, had changed her mind. If she could have scrambled eggs on toast she would have some supper.

'Done!' said Joanna.

With delicious smells coming from the oven, the radio playing music softly in the background, the kitchen was a bright, welcoming place as Polly ate her supper with a speed which showed a hunger she'd been determined to hide. She was halfway through a large bowl of ice-cream when her uncle arrived.

'Good evening.' Marc Anstey's smile was a little crooked as Joanna opened the door, his eyes on the smear of flour on her cheek.

'You're early,' she said shortly, wishing she'd thought to remove her striped butcher's apron before letting him in.

'I thought you might need a hand with Polly.' He stopped in the kitchen doorway as a small projectile hurtled across the room and into his arms.

'Marco, Marco, she's got a doll's house—over there—look! She did scrambled egg for me and she made me have a bath but there were ducks——'

'Steady!' laughed Marc, looking vastly relieved. 'What a time you've had, *tesoro*. But it's not good manners to say "she" all the time.' He raised an eyebrow in Joanna's direction. 'How would you like Polly to address you?'

'Joanna?' She smiled a little. 'Or Jo, perhaps. My friends call me that.'

Marc held Polly away from him a little. 'How about it, Polly Wolly Doodle? Are you Joanna's friend? Will you call her Jo?'

Polly cast a thoughtful glance in Joanna's direction, then nodded. 'Jo.' She smiled graciously.

Marc cuddled the curly head against his shoulder, his eyes questioning as he looked at Joanna. 'All right?' he asked softly.

She nodded. 'I think so. Drink?'

The scene in the kitchen could have been any one of thousands like it all over the country at that time of night. The child finishing her supper, the lady of the house preparing dinner, the man of the house just returned from his day in the outside world.

Joanna smiled in secret amusement as she handed Marc a glass of wine.

His eyebrows rose as he thanked her. 'Our acquaintance is short, I know, but I think that's the first smile you've managed other than the lady-of-the-manor social variety.'

Joanna turned away to check on the apples simmering on the hob set into the pine counter. 'It just struck me how strange this is. A few days ago the three of us had never laid eyes on each other. Now——'

'Now here we are, the perfect picture of domesticity!'

'To the casual observer only,' said Joanna tartly.

Marc took a suddenly sleepy Polly on his knee and held her close, his eyes on Joanna over the dark curls. 'Funny, really, you're not in the least what I expected.'

'You can't have known much about what *to* expect, surely!'

'My sister talked about you a great deal.' He looked away. 'Rosa suffered agonies of guilt where you're concerned.'

Joanna winced. 'I'd rather not talk about—about that, please.'

His head swivelled, his eyes holding hers. 'You mean we just shut the past away and pretend she—and your husband—never existed?'

'Not exactly.' Joanna looked at the now sleeping child closely. 'If the little one wants to talk about her mother we'll talk. As much as she wants. But what do I do about Paul? I'm terrified of putting my foot in it with Polly,' she whispered urgently.

Marc nodded, comprehending. 'Show me where to put Polly to bed, then we'll sort a few things out before Fowler gets here.'

The wear and tear on Polly's emotions over the previous few days had finally taken their toll. When Joanna conducted Marc to the small bedroom overlooking the orchard the child was too deeply asleep to stir when he slid her beneath the covers. He tucked Polly's teddy in beside her then stood looking down at the flushed, sleeping face for a moment before following Joanna from the room.

'If we leave the door ajar we'll hear if she cries,' said Joanna, then paused at the head of the stairs. 'Dinner's well in hand. Would you go down to the drawing-room, help yourself to a drink while I tidy myself up? I shan't be long.'

While Marc went downstairs Joanna turned back into Polly's room to move the lamp so that its faint glow was away from the child's face. Her throat tightened as she looked down at the sleeping child, and she turned away blindly, hurrying to take a swift shower and change her clothes. Resisting a surprising urge to dress in something eye-catching, she put on the black dress worn for the funeral, knowing Jim would expect a show of mourning. With sudden distaste she pushed aside the jewellery Paul had bought her. Instead she found a silver filigree butterfly her father had given her years before and pinned it to the severe dress, then made up her face with care and brushed back her heavy hair, securing it at the nape of her neck with a black velvet ribbon.

Marc laid down the daily paper and stood up as she entered the softly lit drawing-room, the appreciation in his eyes very gratifying. 'You look very elegant.'

'Thank you.' Joanna smiled politely. 'I must put my chef's hat on again for a while. Would you care to listen to some music while I put the finishing touches to the meal?'

'No,' he said flatly. 'I prefer to watch you. Even help, if you like.'

Joanna had never been offered help in the kitchen, other than Doris's. Not sure she cared for the idea, nor for Marc Anstey's company while she worked, she found herself flustered by the intent dark eyes which followed every move she made as she set to work.

'Are you sure I can't peel something, or wash dishes?' he asked.

'All done, thanks,' she said, her back to him. 'I did most of it earlier while Polly played with the doll's house.'

There was silence for a while.

'Joanna,' said Marc at last.

She turned. 'Yes?'

'Before we get bogged down in facts and figures with Fowler, I want you to know how much I appreciate what you're doing for Polly.' His eyes held hers. 'I know how hard it must be for you—in the circumstances.'

'It's hard for all of us.' She detached her gaze with effort. 'I just hope it works out well. For Polly, I mean.'

'Children adapt, even to loss.'

'I know.'

'Did *you* lose someone?'

'In a way. My mother left my father before I could walk. She drowned in a sailing accident shortly afterwards with her lover. So I suppose you could say I lost her—or she lost me.'

Marc's eyes softened. 'I see. No wonder you feel sympathy for Polly's situation.'

Joanna shook her head as she began to roll out some suet crust. 'It's much worse for Polly. Rosa was always there for her. I never really knew my mother. My father was the centre of *my* little universe.'

'You still miss him?'

'Yes, all the time. He'd have been a great help with Polly.' Joanna spooned apple slices carefully on to the crust, wrapped it in a cloth and put it in a steamer on the hob.

Marc watched, fascinated. 'What on earth is that?'

'Apple dumpling.' She smiled a little. 'Jim's favourite. If you're chicken you eat cheese instead.'

He grinned back, then sobered. 'Strange. I forget now and then.'

She nodded. 'I know. But life has to go on. Tell me, why does Polly believe Paul was her uncle?'

Rosa Anstey had been surprisingly obstinate on the subject of her child's paternity. Because divorce was out of the question she'd insisted Polly never knew Paul Clifford was her father.

'Would you have wanted to divorce him if you'd known?' added Marc, eyeing her.

'You bet I would! Not that I could have done. Paul was a Catholic.'

'Don't I know it!' he said bitterly. 'It was his alibi for not marrying Rosa. While she, devout Catholic though she was, loved him enough to live in sin. Because believe me, Joanna, it *was* sin to her. Thank God she lived long enough to receive the last rites.' His mouth tightened. 'I'd have hated Rosa to die unshriven.'

Joanna looked sick for a moment. 'Paul did.'

Marc stood up abruptly, his dark face brooding under the bright overhead light. 'I can't pretend to be sorry. I didn't care much for your husband.'

'I could hardly fail to realise that!'

'Would you prefer me to go? I could leave the notes I've made. About the agreement for Polly. I could meet Fowler separately another time.'

Joanna considered him thoughtfully. 'You may as well stay now you're here. I've catered for three.'

He raised an eyebrow. 'Do you *want* me to stay?'

She looked away, conscious suddenly that they were discussing more than a mere invitation to dinner. 'Of course,' she said, deliberately casual. 'I'd like to get everything sorted out tonight if possible.'

Marc resumed his seat, refusing a second glass of wine. 'I'd better keep a clear head. I'm still too tired to risk much alcohol.'

'Have some coffee, then.'

'Good Italian coffee?'

She smiled. 'No. Good Brazilian coffee.'

The tension in the air eased. Joanna filled the cafetière, then left Marc to help himself while she put potatoes to roast.

'I hadn't pictured you as so domesticated,' he said, watching her.

'I'm still surprised you know anything about me at all!'

He smiled wryly. 'Rosa couldn't seem to help talking about you. You impressed her no end. She said you were friendly and warm, but at the same time very British and poised, the end product of an expensive education.'

Joanna chuckled. 'I'm British, certainly. But contrary to Rosa's belief I went to the village school and the local comprehensive, then on to a polytechnic, Mr Anstey. Though I must own up to a quite wonderful private tutor as well. My father did Greats at Oxford and bombarded my youthful brain with as much literature and philosophy as it could absorb, with a fair bit of Greek and Roman history thrown in.'

Marc shook his head sorrowfully. 'While I'm just a humble hack, making a living by my pen.'

'Not the way I heard it,' she said sceptically.

He grinned, changing the subject to comment on the way the kitchen was fitted out. 'It's very state-of-the-art in here. Unlike the rest of the house.'

Paul Clifford had wanted to do over the entire house when they had married, meeting with firm resistance from Joanna, who liked it exactly the way it was. To appease him she had given in over the kitchen. 'I admit it was a bit primitive in here. The cupboards and cooker were ancient so I finally gave in and let Paul loose in here with his idea of the country-house kitchen.' She made a face. 'Rather a contrast to the rest of Swan House.'

'Why the name? I haven't seen any swans about, unless you're hiding a moat somewhere.'

She looked at him levelly. 'Before I was married I was Joanna Swan. We Swans have lived here for two hundred years, good yeomen all.'

Marc Anstey smiled wryly. 'Whereas I spring from exotic but unknown Sicilian stock mixed with British die-hard respectability.'

'And Jim Fowler, who's due here any minute, is a product of London's Docklands—long before it was fashionable to live there!' Joanna removed her apron. 'I think we're what we are, not who we are. Paul could never reconcile himself to that point of view. He married me in his urge for upward mobility, to become part of a world he felt was different from his own. He was disappointed. All he achieved was an invitation or two to charity functions and an occasional dinner party with the rector and his wife—who's my closest friend.' She stopped suddenly, embarrassed. 'I'm sorry. I don't know why I'm telling you all this. You can't possibly be interested in my bizarre marriage.'

Marc moved towards her, holding her eyes with his. 'On the contrary. The subject interests me very much indeed——' He broke off as the doorbell put an end to the oddly intimate little moment. 'Ah. Your visitor. Time to get down to business.'

CHAPTER FOUR

DINNER with Jim Fowler was more of a strain than lunch with Polly. Long before it was over Joanna wished she'd arranged a meeting over morning coffee instead of a three-course meal. While they ate it was impossible to get down to business, yet the very reason for the meeting made polite dinner conversation uphill work. Joanna was glad when the time came to take coffee into the drawing-room, though even then both men leapt simultaneously to take the tray, like dogs with a bone. When they finally got down to business the atmosphere was thick with constraint as they began to discuss the proposals Marc had ready regarding the small person of Paola Anstey.

'I am Paola's guardian, of course,' began Marc.

'Legally?' pounced Jim.

Marc looked down his nose at the accountant. 'A year ago my sister called in a solicitor and made the necessary arrangements.' He reached in an inside pocket and took out a legal document. 'I think you'll find it in order.'

Jim studied it swiftly, then handed it to Joanna, who barely glanced at it before handing it back.

'What prompted your sister to do that?' asked Jim.

Marc eyed him militantly. 'Why shouldn't she?'

'All I'm saying is that she was relatively young. At her age women don't generally think of wills and guardians and so on,' said Jim, making an obvious effort to sound reasonable.

'My sister was Paul Clifford's mistress. To Rosa this was flying in the face of her upbringing and religious beliefs.' Marc's face darkened. 'She made provision for her daughter's future because she was convinced God would punish her sooner or later.'

'But that's ridiculous——' began Jim, then subsided at a searing blue look from Joanna.

'Some people might think Rosa's been proved right,' she reminded him.

'*I* don't,' said Marc bitingly. 'Paul drove like a maniac. *He* killed Rosa, not God.'

The silence following this statement was so unbearable that Joanna rushed to break it. 'Where was Polly when it happened?'

'At home with the woman who came in to help Rosa.' Marc smiled faintly at Joanna. 'Mrs Tucker is a lot like your Doris Mills, by the way. When Rosa failed to appear she contacted me. You know the rest.' Marc breathed in deeply, then laid out a typed list in front of Jim Fowler, who scanned it through his thick-lensed glasses in silence for a while before giving it to Joanna.

'Anyone would think you were doing Joanna a favour by handing the kid over to her,' said Jim, eyeing Marc challengingly. 'It seems to me you get the penny and the bun. You've got the say-so about the child's education and so on, while Jo here gets all the work and responsibility.'

Marc looked dangerous for a moment. 'I know damn well it looks that way, but this wasn't my idea, remember. I'm merely carrying out my sister's dying wishes. I thought it was a crazy idea to ask Mrs Clifford to take my niece. Frankly I expected her to slam the door in my face.'

'What would you have done if she had?' asked Jim promptly.

'Bought a bigger flat and engaged a nanny I could trust Polly to while I'm away. Which I can still do,' Marc added bluntly, 'if the trial period agreed on between Mrs Clifford and myself proves that the arrangement won't work.'

'It will work,' said Joanna. 'After what Polly's been through it must work, for her sake.' She picked up the sheet of regulations. 'Now. You don't say much about education, other than the money available for it, which, incidentally, is more than enough to send her to a very expensive boarding-school.'

Marc nodded. 'But not yet, surely!'

'Of course not yet! But I think I should be allowed an opinion on the choice of school,' said Joanna.

'I should bloody well hope so!' exploded Jim. 'You're the one left holding the baby, my girl.'

'Yes, I know, Jim,' said Joanna patiently. 'This is all very difficult as it is. Let's not make it worse.'

'Sorry, love.' Jim subsided, glaring at Marc.

'The village school here is very good,' said Joanna in a businesslike way aimed at lightening the tension. 'If you're agreeable I'd prefer that Polly start her education there after Christmas. We can leave decisions about other schools until she's older. Much older.'

Relief smoothed some of the lines etched at Marc's mouth and eyes. 'Thank you,' he said quietly. 'I'm grateful.'

'I can do a little extra-curricular coaching myself,' she said, warming to the idea. 'Drawing and reading and so on.'

'What about your own work?' demanded Jim. 'Won't that suffer?'

'I can fit that in around Polly,' said Joanna, unconcerned.

Marc frowned. 'I'd forgotten your job. What exactly do you do?'

'Don't worry. I do it at home.'

'She writes children's books. *And* illustrates them,' said Jim proudly.

Marc eyed Joanna with a hint of accusation in his dark eyes. 'In that case surely Polly will be a hindrance?'

'Probably. But only at first. I'll just organise my day differently, that's all.' She smiled sweetly. 'They're not three-volume novels.'

'Perhaps you'll show me some time.'

'If you like.' Joanna turned back to the agreement. 'Shall we get the rest of this settled, please?'

The other items were routine matters which Jim vetted quickly, agreeing to all the financial arrangements with such readiness that Joanna knew they were generous rather than merely fair. When Marc agreed that the sale of the factory should go through at once the atmosphere between the two men thawed slightly. Then Joanna came across a final item over the page. She read it through twice, her eyes narrowing. She looked up at Marc with sudden hostility.

'I don't care for the tone of this last bit.'

Jim snatched the paper from her, frowning as he read the final clause. 'In the event of Mrs Clifford's remarriage, all the foregoing would be subject to review.' He eyed Marc Anstey belligerently. 'What the hell does that mean?'

'If Mrs Clifford remarries I shall want Polly back in my sole care immediately.'

'Why?' snapped Joanna, her eyes like chips of blue ice.

Marc shrugged. 'Part of the reason Rosa was so desperate for you to have her child was that I'm not married, and the very nature of my job makes it difficult to provide a permanent base for Polly for the time being. Rosa was adamant that a child needs stability as well as love. But I'm damn sure she wouldn't want Polly at the mercy of some step-father figure if you marry again.'

'Did she say so?' demanded Jim.

'She didn't have to!'

'But you've got nothing in writing.'

Marc jumped to his feet. 'Writing or not, those are my conditions, take it or leave it.'

Joanna got up more slowly. 'I need time to think it over. Before I do, may I ask a personal question?'

'Of course.'

'What happens if *you* marry? Will I be expected to hand Polly back?'

He shrugged, a grim little smile playing at the corners of his mouth. 'Marriage is a snare I've done my best to avoid. The situation's unlikely to arise.' He paused, one eyebrow raised in the way Joanna was beginning to know. 'How about you, Mrs Clifford? Have you anyone in mind to replace Paul?'

Joanna waved a furious Jim out of the way. 'No, Mr Anstey, not yet. It's only a few days since he died—not much to cast around for a suitable candidate. I'll let you know the moment I sort one out.' She paused, two spots of colour burning along her cheekbones. 'How about lovers? Am I allowed those?'

His nostrils flared. 'I'm glad you find this all so amusing——'

'On the contrary,' she snapped. 'I don't find it amusing at all!'

'Look here, Anstey——' began Jim heatedly.

'Leave it, Jim,' ordered Joanna. 'I'm determined the trial period will continue as agreed. Discussion over for tonight, if you don't mind, gentlemen.'

Joanna knew perfectly well that Marc Anstey was reluctant to leave at the same time as Jim Fowler, but she made it crystal-clear she was bidding goodnight to both men. Marc was forced to return to the Lamb and Flag without the private word he so clearly wanted.

Joanna, suddenly wakeful after an energetic burst of clearing up after the meal, went upstairs to check that all was well with Polly, then took a bath to calm her anger over the proviso at the end of Marc Anstey's set of rules. It seemed that as long as she remained a widow she was allowed to function as a surrogate mother to Paola Anstey, for which service she would receive an allowance generous enough to render the sale of Swan House unnecessary. Which, of course, was a relief. She hated the thought of losing her home, and as yet her earnings from the series of Snowbird books were not quite enough to banish the spectre altogether. At the same time she had no intention of letting anyone try to run her private life for her, Marc Anstey in particular.

Joanna felt irritated and depressed as she got ready for bed. A few days ago she'd never heard of Marc Anstey, nor of Polly. Yet now both uncle and niece loomed large in her life, an advantage in one way, since it left her precious little time for bitterness and recrimination where Paul was concerned.

She took her wedding photograph from the drawer and stared at it, trying to remember how she'd felt that day five years before. The wedding had been a quiet, private affair, soon after her father's death. Paul, as short of relatives as his bride, had requested as few people as possible. The only guests at the brief ceremony, and at the lunch at the Ritz afterwards, had been Jim and Maisie Fowler. Joanna had felt very much alone without even Mary Lavenham to lend her support. But her staunchest friend, who would otherwise have seen her through thick and thin, had been too close to presenting her husband with twins to act as bridesmaid.

Joanna gazed at the fair, laughing girl in the simple silk suit and tilted hat, and marvelled at her youth. She felt at least a hundred years older now than the Joanna of her wedding day. Paul, maturely handsome in his morning suit, looked triumphant as he grinned at the camera. How pleased he'd been with himself. And with his bride. Yet once his hope of a family had been snatched from him all that had died a very sudden death.

The telephone startled Joanna out of her reverie. She snatched off the receiver, her voice sharp as she snapped her name.

'Marc Anstey here.'

Joanna frowned. 'Yes? Is something wrong? It's very late.'

'I know. I'm sorry.' He paused, then said stiffly, 'I offended you this evening. I was rude. I apologise.'

'I was surprised rather than offended,' she assured him, calm again.

'And very unapproachable. Too much so for me to ask when I could visit Polly tomorrow.'

'Come whenever you like. But if you want her full attention I'd make it after lunch. Doris will be here in the morning.'

'Which brings me to one of the things I meant to mention tonight. The news about your writing came as a surprise. If I allot you a larger allowance, would Doris come in every day from now on to leave you more time for your work?'

'I'd already thought of that. But I don't need extra money for her wages.'

'You mean you'd rather not accept anything else from me.'

'But it isn't from you, Mr Anstey, is it? The money will come from the sale of PCP in Polly's name.'

'I used the word "allot", not "give",' he pointed out coldly. 'Thank you. I'll be round about two tomorrow. If that's convenient.'

'Perfectly. Goodnight.'

Joanna took some time to get to sleep, then woke in the middle of the night, heart pounding and disorientated, to the sound of crying. She slid out of bed to run to Polly's room, where the child lay in a crumpled heap, sobbing, heartbroken, for her mother.

Joanna took the little girl into her arms and held her tightly, waiting patiently for the storm to pass. It was a long time before Polly quietened. At last she yawned widely, then snuggled her head against Joanna with a shuddering sigh.

'Thirsty,' she said hoarsely.

Joanna mopped the sodden little face with a handkerchief, then poured orange juice from the insulated flask she'd filled earlier. Polly drank deeply, consented to a trip to the bathroom, then allowed herself to be tucked back into bed, wide black eyes fixed imploringly on Joanna's.

'Story. Please?'

'All right. Just a little one. I'll tell you about a pony called Snowbird.'

With the hot, damp little hand held tightly in hers Joanna began on the story she'd been working on before Polly's advent. Snowbird was a white pony whose adventures were gratifyingly popular with under-tens both nationwide and overseas. Joanna did full dramatic justice to the latest episode in Snowbird's career, making a mental note of a new twist in the plot as she went along. Polly was fascinated. At first her reddened eyes never left Joanna's face, but as the minutes ticked by her lids began to droop. Joanna's voice grew quieter and quieter until she was sure the child was asleep, then she tiptoed from the room and slid into her own bed with a sigh. Looking after a grieving, motherless little girl promised to be no sinecure. But if Polly wanted to stay at Swan House she was determined to make a success of it. And not for Rosa, either, nor even Marc, but for Polly. And, Joanna realised with sudden insight, for herself, too. Even with all the problems which came as part of the package she knew with sudden conviction that the child was exactly what she needed to fill the aching, empty void in her life.

Joanna woke next morning to see Polly perched on the end of her bed, watching her.

'Good morning, Polly,' she said, yawning, and looked at the clock. 'You're early.'

'Can I come in your bed?'

Joanna smiled drowsily. 'Yes, of course.'

Polly wriggled down under the covers, then turned her face on the pillows towards Joanna. 'What a lovely big bed! Bigger than Mamma's.'

'Is it?'

'Uncle Paul sleeped in Mamma's bed sometimes.'

Joanna swallowed, suddenly wide awake. 'Really?'

Polly nodded vigorously. 'I didn't go in Mamma's bed when he was there.'

'No room, I expect.'

'Mamma said I mustn't.'

'I see,' said Joanna faintly, and changed the subject. 'What would you like for breakfast?'

The morning went by on wings, due principally to Polly's delight at seeing Doris Mills, who in her usual unfussy style handed the child a duster and enlisted her help. Polly trotted round after her all morning, proudly helping while the day's chores were dispatched with Doris's usual efficiency and speed.

When Marc Anstey arrived, dead on the stroke of two, Polly leapt up into his outstretched arms, burying her head on his shoulder without a word. Joanna looked on in dismay. The morning had gone so smoothly with Doris around she'd expected Polly to greet her uncle with a torrent of excited chatter. Instead the little girl clung to her uncle like a limpet as he carried her in the house.

'Hey,' said Marc teasingly, as he detached Polly's clinging arms to give her a big kiss. 'Aren't you going to say hello?'

'Tell Uncle Marc——' began Joanna.

'Marco!' interrupted Polly peremptorily. 'I *told* you.'

Joanna flushed. 'Tell—tell Marco what you've been doing all morning.'

Polly brightened, her face suddenly animated as she told Marc how she'd helped Doris with the housework. Then Jo had taken her out to explore the stables and she'd helped tidy the little house where Jo's horse used to live.

'*And* I swept the floor, but I got dirty and she—Jo,' added Polly hastily at the look in Marc's eye, 'Jo made me have *another* bath because I got muddy. And I had pancakes for lunch,' she finished triumphantly.

'Lucky old you,' said Marc, smiling. 'I didn't. Now then, the sun's come out, so perhaps the lady of the house will take two townies like us for a walk and show us some of the local countryside.'

Joanna smiled. 'Good idea. Come on, Polly, let's change our shoes.'

'How's she been?' asked Marc later, as Polly ran on ahead through the orchard towards the woods beyond the boundary wall, looking as carefree as though the moment of melancholy had never happened.

'She cried for Rosa in the night. But I expected that.'

'What did you do?'

Joanna eyed him caustically. 'What do you think? I cuddled her and mopped her up and gave her a drink. Then I told her a story. Before it was finished she was asleep.'

Marc lifted a shoulder. 'I wasn't criticising, believe it or not. I just wondered how you felt about coping with a situation that's likely to crop up pretty often for a while. The doctor says she'll adjust in time——'

'Doctor?' Joanna asked swiftly.

Marc nodded as they resumed their progress towards an impatient Polly. 'Before I brought her down I took her to Rosa's GP. He's known Polly from birth. It seemed a good idea to know what shots she's been given and so on, what illnesses she's had. Unfortunately for you, she hasn't had anything much so far except the odd sore throat and a cold or two.'

'Unfortunately for me,' repeated Joanna. 'Does that mean you've made up your mind about leaving her with me then?'

He stopped dead, his hand on her arm. 'Do you still want her?'

'Of course I want her——' Joanna broke off as Polly ran towards her, demanding to know where they were going.

The afternoon was warm, more like summer than the beginning of autumn. Joanna put all her worries firmly from her mind as she took pride in showing off the beauty of her home surroundings to her guests. They crunched their way through woods carpeted with the first multicoloured fall of leaves. Polly paddled happily through them in her green rubber boots, reluctant to leave until Joanna suggested they climb the hill which gave them a view of the village of Swancote below.

When they reached the top, breathless and a little dishevelled after the climb, Marc rested a foot on an outcrop of rock at the summit and leaned forward to look down at the village. 'Is it called Swancote after your family?'

'Locals say so, but I doubt it. More likely to be a corruption of Swinecote, according to George Lavenham, the rector.' Joanna retied the scarf holding her hair in place at the nape of her neck, one eye on Polly, who was clambering happily over a rocky mound behind them, the other on Marc, who looked far more at home in his surroundings than Joanna had expected. The high-flyer in the expensive suit was missing today, replaced by a relaxed man in a suede bomber-jacket and rubbed corduroys, a red handkerchief knotted at the open neck of his shirt. Even his gypsyish black hair and swarthy skin seemed very much in harmony with the patchwork backdrop of woods and fields in the soft, hazy sunshine.

'I feel like a specimen on a slide,' he said in an undertone, so that Polly wouldn't hear. 'Why the analytical look? Am I dressed incorrectly for a stroll in the country?'

'On the contrary,' said Joanna. 'It was Paul——' She stopped, biting her lip.

'Go on,' he prompted. 'Paul what?'

'It seems disloyal to say so, but Paul insisted on wearing a waxed jacket and flat cap if he so much as went outside the door down here.' Joanna shrugged. 'It looked all wrong on him, somehow. Paul was at his best on city pavements—but I shouldn't be saying so.'

'Because he's dead?'

Joanna nodded. 'Yes, because he's dead. And can't defend himself.'

Marc jumped to his feet and held out a hand to Polly. 'Come on, *cara*. Time to go back.'

Polly protested for a while, but, at the promise of more toasted muffins when they reached the house, trotted off happily enough, the other two following a little way behind.

'I leave tomorrow,' said Marc abruptly. 'We need to talk.' He glanced sideways at Joanna. 'I'd like to ask you out to dinner——'

'Not possible, I'm afraid. I'd need a baby-sitter, even if——'

'Even if you wanted to dine with me, which you don't!'

'I didn't say that. And I agree we need to talk.' She hesitated. 'You're welcome to share my supper, if you like. But it won't be anything elaborate tonight.'

He kicked his way through the leaves, his face sombre. 'I could eat at the pub and come back afterwards.'

'As you like,' she said indifferently.

'I don't like,' he said with sudden violence, then checked himself, breathing deeply. 'Look, I don't care a damn what we eat. But I'd like to talk to you without Jim Fowler glowering as if I intended nicking the silver. And I'd like to pay for the meal, organise it. As it is I feel like some bloody gigolo on the make for a rich widow.'

At Joanna's spontaneous giggle Polly turned to come running towards them, attracted by the sound.

'I'm hungry,' she announced.

'Good.' Joanna took her hand, motioning to Marc to take the other. 'Let's see how fast we can run home, then.'

Marc went back to the Lamb and Flag once Polly was in bed and asleep. His male pride appeased by Joanna's offer of bacon and eggs eaten at the kitchen table, he returned to Swan House so quickly that she had barely enough time to get ready before he was back, showered and shaved, and wearing a fresh shirt, but otherwise looking much as he'd done earlier on.

He eyed her well-worn Levis and outsize scarlet sweater with approval. 'Much better. You look approachable like that.'

'It seemed the right outfit for bacon and eggs,' she said lightly, 'but why should it make me more approachable?'

'Last night, in your mourning black, you were very much Paul Clifford's widow.' He strolled after her into the kitchen. 'Tonight it's easier to see the woman behind all that, the one Rosa trusted to take care of Polly.'

'I hope she was right.' Joanna handed him some cutlery and napkins and told him to lay the table. 'Would you like a drink?'

'No, thanks. I must get back to London tonight, ready to tie up a few loose ends in the morning before I go back to Washington. Shall I cut some of this bread?'

'Yes, please. I shan't be long.'

Marc sat in one of the kitchen chairs, watching Joanna as she moved deftly about her lavishly equipped kitchen. 'You like cooking,' he stated.

'Yes. There's something satisfactory about producing an appetising meal.' She slid sausages and several rashers of bacon under the grill then smiled across at him as she sliced mushrooms and tomatoes. 'In my father's opinion, my real preference, degree or no degree, was marriage, a home—preferably this one—plus a couple of children, a dog or two, a horse if I was lucky, and a room to myself to write my great novel. How do you like your eggs?'

'Any way you care to cook them.' He studied her with narrowed eyes. 'But isn't that, more or less, what Paul offered you?'

'I certainly thought so when he proposed.' Joanna turned her back to supervise the food under the grill, then took out a frying-pan for the eggs. 'What I actually got was quite a bit different. Paul made it possible for me to keep the house, of course. But I found he hated dogs. He wouldn't let me look for a job, yet he regarded my Snowbird stories as a waste of time. Until the first one was accepted. He changed his mind then; stopped being so patronising. But I could have coped with all that. The real damage was done because he was so wrapped up in his rage and anguish over the miscarriage that he never gave a thought to the fact that I was suffering too. He left me alone, took off to London, and you know what happened after that.'

Marc looked grim. 'Yes. None better.'

Joanna took warm plates from under the grill and began to serve out their meal, making a face as she eyed the finished results. 'Very definitely not in the health-food bracket, but rather nice now and again, just the same.'

Marc received his plate with relish. 'Absolutely. Besides, better a dinner of herbs——' He stopped abruptly.

Joanna smiled brightly. 'Not quite in context, but I know what you mean. Now then, it's your turn. You've heard all about me. Talk about yourself for a change.'

Marc Anstey, plainly aware that she needed a change of subject, began to talk about the work he did in Washington for the *Sentinel*. Joanna listened, fascinated, as he opened a window for her into a world which sounded frenetic and glamorous to someone based in a quiet Oxfordshire village. Marc Anstey was in constant contact with people in the world of diplomacy, politics, business, with a sprinkling of the arts and entertainment industry as icing on the cake. Joanna was reluctantly impressed to hear that he spent a lot of time making use of a substantial expense account to wine and dine contacts, and travelled all over the United States to cover stories, as well as writing a weekly feature column for his newspaper.

'It all sounds a far cry from Swancote,' said Joanna wryly, as they sat over coffee at the kitchen table. 'Do you have a house or a flat of your own there?'

Marc shook his head. 'The perks of the job mean my own office, a car and a company apartment in return for my services.'

'You must be very well up in your profession!'

'Not as high as I intend to be, I assure you.' He smiled. 'I've been in the business a long time. In a couple of years I'll be forty. Sometimes I feel I've missed out on certain things in life.'

Joanna laughed. 'Not many, by what you've been saying.'

'I've never had a wife and family,' he said very quietly. 'Regular visits to see Rosa and Polly are the nearest thing I've ever managed in that direction.'

'No girlfriends?' Joanna couldn't help asking.

'Lady, I'm perfectly normal!' he retorted. 'Of course I've had girlfriends. I even considered a permanent relationship with one or two—but not for long.'

'Very wise,' said Joanna lightly. 'Saves a lot of wear and tear on the emotions, I assure you.'

'Some people have very successful, happy marriages,' he said, his eyes on the coffee he was stirring.

'I know. My best friend has one of those. Luck of the draw, I suppose—I got the short straw in mine.' Joanna jumped up to stack the tray, in sudden need of occupation.

'Since I couldn't pay for the meal, at least let me wash up,' said Marc.

'No need. The dishwasher Paul insisted on does that,' said Joanna cheerfully. 'I'll just load it up and we can go into the drawing-room—unless you mean to rush off straight away.'

'I don't,' said Marc emphatically, watching her as she moved about the kitchen. 'We haven't really touched on the points which need discussion.' He got up as she came towards him, looking at her in a way which flustered her a little. 'You know, don't you, that I find it hard to remember we met such a short time ago?'

Joanna's heart gave an errant thump as she led the way to the drawing-room, and she was thankful her face was hidden from him for a moment. By the time she'd curled up on the sofa and waved Marc to a chair she had herself well in hand again.

'It's only natural that you would feel like that,' she said reasonably. 'The circumstances which brought the meeting about were so traumatic it would be useless to pretend we're normal, polite acquaintances. Especially as Polly provides a constant reminder of—of the link between us.'

'You admit to a link, then?' he asked swiftly.

Joanna looked at him. 'I could hardly fail to, with Rosa and Paul to haunt us.'

He grimaced. 'Do you think one day you might bring yourself to think of me as just an ordinary guy? Not Rosa's brother or even Polly's uncle? Hell, Joanna, I possess an identity of my own, in case you hadn't noticed.'

Joanna smiled a little. 'Oh, I'd noticed.'

His eyes lit with an unsettling gleam. 'Good. Because although you bracket me with Rosa, there's no way I can think of you as Paul's wife.'

'Probably because for the past four years Paul couldn't, either——' Joanna stopped dead, turning her head away, furious to find herself close to tears. She sniffed hard, blinked violently, but it was no use. Suddenly the tears won, and she put her hands over her face in shame at her lack of self-control.

Marc crossed the room swiftly and took her in his arms, encouraging her as she sobbed without inhibition into his shirt front. She heard his voice, deep and husky as he murmured comfort, felt his hand on her hair, smoothing the heavy strands away from her forehead, and shut her eyes tightly as he put a fingertip under her chin to raise her face. She felt his lips brush her forehead, felt his arms tighten, then his mouth was hard and warm against hers and her quivering lips parted in surprise to the kiss which began as a caress meant to comfort, but metamorphosed into something different with alarming speed. In seconds Marc's arms were threatening to crack her ribs, and she was kissing him back, her tears drying on her burning cheeks.

Joanna pulled away, staring with drenched blue eyes into Marc's taut, astonished face as he reluctantly dropped his arms.

'I suppose I should say I'm sorry,' he muttered. 'Could I have a drink?'

'Yes.' Joanna cleared her throat. 'Yes, of course.'

'It won't affect my driving—just one finger of Scotch. I need it.' He got up without looking at her and went over to the tray of decanters Paul had insisted Joanna keep in readiness for visitors who rarely came to Swan House when he was there. 'Would you care for something?'

Joanna smoothed back her tumbled hair with an unsteady hand. 'Yes. Sherry, please. Dry.'

Marc handed her a glass, then went back to his chair, looking shaken. 'It was never my intention——'

'No, I realise that.' She downed half the sherry like medicine. 'I didn't mean to cry, either. I haven't much since—since Paul died.'

'It's no sin to cry.' He shrugged, staring down into his glass.

'Unless it's for the wrong reasons.'

He looked up sharply. 'What do you mean?'

Joanna looked bleak. 'What tears I've shed have been for myself, not Paul. At the funeral everyone thought I was grieving like a good widow should, and I felt sick inside at my own hypocrisy.'

'Stop it,' he said sharply. 'Paul was hardly the epitome of the normal, loving husband, was he? Why the hell should you grieve? Because it's the done thing in your particular social circles?'

'Don't talk rot,' she snapped, then glared at his sudden grin.

'That's better. Your eyes look beautiful when they smoulder. Much better than drowned in tears.'

Her eyes went on smouldering for a moment, then Joanna smiled reluctantly. 'I admit it's a relief to be able to explain to someone who knew—knew the truth. Of course I'm deeply sorry that Paul died in such a horrible way, but I just don't feel any great sense of personal loss. The real tragedy is that in the process of killing himself Paul had to kill Rosa too, and leave Polly motherless.'

'Is that why you agreed to take her?'

'No, not entirely.' Joanna hesitated. 'My reasons are less altruistic. I was shattered when I found I'd never have more babies after my accident. It may sound melodramatic, but taking on Polly fills a void nothing else can.' She jumped up restlessly. 'Enough soul-searching. Like some more coffee?'

Marc was tactful enough to go upstairs to check on Polly while she made it. By the time he rejoined Joanna in the drawing-room she was in full command of herself again and was able to greet Marc with a composed little smile, as though the kiss had never occurred.

'Polly all right?'

'Fine.' Marc looked at her searchingly. 'Are *you* all right, too?'

She nodded. 'Though why some people enjoy a good cry beats me. I feel like a wreck.'

He smiled. 'A very beautiful wreck.'

Joanna's lips twitched. 'Such tact!'

'Not at all. It's the truth.' He took a cup from her, his eyes meeting hers. 'Believe me, Joanna, I'm sorry I annoyed you last night. About the remarriage bit.'

She shrugged. 'When I'd calmed down a bit I could see your point.'

'How do you feel about marrying again?' he asked very quietly.

Joanna finished her coffee and replaced the cup on the tray with precision. 'To be honest, my experience of marriage, both my parents' and my own, has left me with a profound reluctance to repeat the experiment. Ever.'

'It could be different with another man.'

'Possibly. If I meet anyone likely to change my mind I'll let you know.'

Marc jumped up, unsmiling. 'Time I was off, I think.'

Joanna rose to her feet, dismayed to find that she quite badly wanted him to stay for a while. 'But there were things you needed to discuss.'

'I think we've covered everything.' He pulled on his jacket then paused in the hall. 'Give my love to Polly. May I come to see her when I get back? I don't know quite when it'll be.'

'Of course.' Joanna hesitated. 'Please believe that where access to Polly is concerned...' She halted, losing the thread of what she was saying as she met the look in his eyes. 'I—I mean you're welcome to come here as often as you want.'

'Am I?' He smiled sardonically. 'I know that's true where Polly's concerned. How about the lady of the house? Will I get a welcome from her, too?'

Joanna tore her eyes away from the hypnotic black gaze. 'Of course. Not quite as demonstrative, perhaps.'

'Why, Joanna?' Marc moved closer. 'Are you afraid of demonstrations of affection? Are you too much a coward to want to touch, to follow your natural, human instincts?'

Joanna backed away. 'No, of course not. I find it very easy to kiss and cuddle Polly.'

He followed her, backing her up against the newel post of the stairs, cutting off her retreat. 'For once I'm not concerned with Polly,' he said softly, his voice so caressing that her knees began to knock together. 'Won't you wish me *bon voyage* and speed me on my way with a goodbye kiss, Joanna? Something I can remember when I'm far away?'

She swallowed. 'What happened just now was an accident; you just meant to comfort me——'

'Right. Now I want a little comfort from you, Joanna.'

'Oh, very well,' she said impatiently, and held up her face. Marc laughed softly against her mouth as his arms closed around her. Joanna, aghast at her body's response to his nearness, clutched at his jacket and he picked her up by the elbows and stood her on the bottom stair so that her face was level with his. The fire in his dark, explicit eyes took her breath away, her lips parting in a gasp his mouth stifled with a hard, demanding kiss which had little to do with comfort. For a long, dizzying interval Joanna gave herself up to an embrace so intimate that she was left in no doubt that the man holding her so close badly wanted a great deal more from her than mere kisses. She burned with the knowledge that given the least encouragement he would have carried her up to bed and abandoned all idea of driving to London that night.

'You're kissing Jo!' said an accusing little voice.

Joanna pushed Marc away, heart pounding as she smiled shakily at the small, pyjama-clad figure at the head of the stairs. 'He was saying goodbye, darling.'

'Not *he*,' said Polly impatiently. 'Marco!'

Marc bounded up the stairs to scoop his niece up into his arms. 'What are you doing out of bed, *tesoro*? When I came to see you just now you were fast asleep.'

'Want a drink,' said Polly, rubbing her eyes.

'Right,' said Joanna. She went ahead to the room which had once been hers, pulling herself together, giving herself a silent, stinging reproof for such abysmal behaviour. She handed Polly a drink, then watched as Marc tucked his niece up tenderly.

'See you when I get back, *cara*,' he said, kissing Polly's cheek. 'Be a good girl for Joanna.'

'Yes, Marco,' murmured Polly drowsily.

'Ciao, cara.'

Joanna bent to kiss the little girl, then followed Marc downstairs.

'Goodbye, then. Safe trip,' she said brightly, doing her level best to behave like any normal hostess seeing off a guest.

He smiled indulgently, then leaned down to kiss the tip of her nose. 'I hate goodbyes, Joanna Swan.' He strode to the door and opened it, then turned, lifting a hand in salute.

'My friends call me Jo,' she said on impulse.

Marc Anstey shook his black, curly head. 'Doesn't suit you—too masculine. You're all woman, whether you admit it or not. Besides, I'm not one of these *friends* of yours—my feelings for you have nothing to do with Plato! *Arrivederci*, Joanna.'

CHAPTER FIVE

THE period following Marc Anstey's departure for America proved one of the most harrowing, exhausting periods of Joanna's entire experience. Polly, coming to terms with a life from which the last familiar face had departed, relapsed into grief when she realised it would be some time before she saw her beloved Marco again. She threw tantrums, refused to eat, lost weight and generally worried Joanna to death.

'School started last week. Get them to take her this term instead of after Christmas,' advised Mary Lavenham one morning, while Polly was upstairs with Doris. 'I know she's a bit young, but it could be the answer, Jo.'

'She needs something,' said Joanna, sighing. 'She cries most nights for her mother, and in the day she pines for her uncle. As a mother substitute I'm a washout. I'm beginning to think I'm entirely the wrong person to have care of her.'

Mary pooh-poohed the idea. 'Nonsense. The poor little mite doesn't know how lucky she is, Jo.' She waved a hand about her expansively. 'A house like this, with that garden out there—think of the times we had here when we were children.'

Joanna sighed. 'I know. I just hope she settles down soon.'

'Get her to school,' repeated Mary, with the conviction of experience. 'I can't tell you what bliss it's been since Jack and Charlie started there last week.'

Joanna grinned. The Lavenham twins' recent brief visit to Swan House to play with Polly had been lively in the extreme. She could well believe Mary was delighted to have her sons safely occupied in school for a few hours each day. 'How a saint like George ever fathered a pair of devils like your twins I can't imagine!'

'He's not a saint *all* the time,' Mary said demurely. 'Must go. But take my advice, Jo. Send Polly to school right away. Has this uncle of hers been in touch?'

'Yes, of course. He talks to Polly each time, then she's back to square one again afterwards, worse than ever.'

'Then don't let him talk to her.' Mary pulled on an ancient quilted jerkin, eyeing Joanna closely. 'How are *you* coping, Jo? About Paul, I mean.'

Joanna shrugged. 'To be perfectly honest I don't have much time for brooding over Paul, owing to Polly.'

'Good,' said Mary, briskly, and patted Jo's cheek. 'Bring Polly to lunch on Saturday. George will be out marrying someone—and I'll bully the twins into submission, promise.'

Joanna took herself in hand when Mary was gone. Her friend's bracing comments had brought it home to her that she was too anxious to please where Polly was concerned. The child needed sympathy, it was true, but she also needed discipline and common sense if she was to make a complete recovery from the trauma of losing her mother.

While the child was still occupied Joanna rang the village school, had a chat with the deputy head teacher and arranged to take Polly there that very afternoon for a look round. It might, thought Joanna, have been better to consult Marc first. But Marc Anstey was caught up in the hectic whirl of life in Washington, not here on the spot, coping with Polly's tantrums, so she wouldn't bother.

Joanna was secretly very disappointed by his phone calls. To demonstrate how little their parting had affected her she'd been so crisp and cold when he'd first rung that he'd taken swift, easily discernible offence. Since then he'd kept rigidly to a single enquiry about Joanna's health before asking to speak to Polly, his hostile formality leaving Joanna thoroughly depressed. She'd been a fool to expect anything different, she assured herself. It was no big deal. She'd let Marc Anstey kiss her purely because she was in a particularly vulnerable state at the time. When he came to see Polly at Christmas she would make a point of clearing the air, letting him know that the incident was a one-off, never to be repeated.

Polly, to Joanna's relief, was not unwilling to visit the school. When she was ushered into a classroom full of busy, lively children painting in groups at small tables, she drank in the scene wide-eyed. The jolly, vivacious girl in charge seemed on excellent terms with her pupils, the Lavenham twins among them. Polly acknowledged their cheeky grins with a gracious nod, then walked home with Joanna afterwards, lost in thought.

'Would I paint too?'

'Of course, darling.'

'When can I go there?' demanded Polly.

'You can start on Monday, if you like.'

'When's Monday?'

'In four days' time.'

'Want to go tomorrow.'

'No, Polly. Mrs Phillips, the head teacher, said Monday.' Joanna waited, expecting a storm of protest, but Polly accepted it meekly enough. 'Let's go to the village shop and buy a drawing book and crayons, shall we?'

Marc rang that evening, not long after Polly was in bed, but this time Joanna went into the kitchen with the mobile phone and shut the door in case the child might hear.

'Would you mind if you didn't speak to Polly this time?' she asked, when the polite preliminaries were over.

'Why?' he demanded swiftly. 'Something wrong?'

'No. That's the point. There's nothing wrong at the moment, but if you talk to Polly there will be.' Joanna explained about the storms of weeping after his previous telephone conversations, and Marc swore softly, obviously very much taken aback.

'Hell, I'm sorry, Joanna. I didn't mean to complicate things. I thought it would reassure her to hear my voice.'

'So did I. Instead it makes her miss you all the more.' Joanna hesitated. 'Frankly, she seems to miss you even more than her mother—probably because she's accepted the fact that her mother's gone to heaven, whereas you're still available to her.'

'Does that mean you don't want me to visit her when I get back?' he demanded sharply.

'No. Of course not. But I don't think the telephone's a good idea. It unsettles her too much.' Joanna took a deep breath, then explained about the school, and how eager Polly was to start there.

'If she's been so difficult I imagine you're eager for her to start there too,' he said drily. 'She must be holding up your work.'

'I don't care about that!' said Joanna, stung. 'It's just that she's been grieving so much I thought she needed something to divert her, to occupy her mind. I've been frantic with worry about her.'

'I can see that.' He paused for a moment. 'May I make a suggestion?'

'Of course.'

'How about getting her a puppy? Didn't your ideal world include dogs before Paul Clifford put a stop to it?'

'I don't know why I haven't thought about that before,' she said, struck by the idea. 'Is Polly used to dogs?'

'No. But I'm sure she'll quickly *get* used to one if you feel up to coping with yet another call on your time.'

'Are you being sarcastic, Mr Anstey?'

'As it happens, no, *Mrs* Clifford. I'm not insensitive. I realise all this can't be easy for you. As far as I'm concerned you've got the go-ahead to do anything you want to make life easier, for both Polly and yourself.' He paused. 'Joanna?'

'Yes?'

'Since we seem to be communicating again, please don't hang up if I say I probably did myself a whole lot of no good where you're concerned before I left.'

Joanna stood very still, her knuckles white on the receiver. 'It was my fault for crying all over you.'

'I'm glad you did. Otherwise I'd have had no excuse for taking you in my arms. Which,' he added huskily, 'was where I wanted you from the moment I first set eyes on you, Paul Clifford's widow or not.'

Joanna almost dropped the telephone. She cleared her throat. 'I don't think you should be saying things like that to me.'

'I tried my best not to. Surely you've noticed how formal and correct I've been?' He chuckled, then the sound was drowned suddenly by a sudden high-pitched whine on the line, and after a few fruitless 'hellos' into the receiver Joanna replaced it on the handset. She sat down on a kitchen chair, staring into space for a long time before she went up to check on Polly, who, to her infinite relief, was asleep. Afterwards Joanna made herself some strong black coffee and focused her attention sternly on Marc Anstey's suggestion about a puppy for Polly, not sure if this was entirely a good idea. Puppies were small and lovable, but grew into big, unmanageable dogs if they weren't trained properly. Trying to get a little girl to see that she couldn't take a puppy to bed with her might be difficult. The answer was a fully grown dog in need of a home. Joanna rang Mary, her never-failing source on local information, who told her to get in touch with the local Labrador Rescue Group. Soon afterwards Joanna was able to explain her requirements to a sympathetic but brisk lady who asked to call round the following day to inspect the premises.

'You see, Mrs Clifford,' she explained, 'I must make it clear that we are looking for a home for a dog rather than finding a pet for you.'

Mrs Blake duly arrived the following day, took down particulars of Joanna's situation, noted Polly's age, and promised to match the splendidly suitable environs of Swan House with a dog in need of a home.

'Would you like a dog, Polly?' asked Joanna, when Mrs Blake had gone.

Polly was drawing on the kitchen table, as she usually was of late. She looked up, surprised. 'A dog?'

'Yes. We could take him for walks and play ball with him. He'd be great company.'

'That's a good idea, Polly,' said Doris. 'You'll like that.'

Doris's approval was more than enough to convince Polly a dog was a good idea on the whole. 'A big dog?' she asked doubtfully.

Joanna put out her hand at Labrador level. 'About so high. I used to have a dog,' she added casually.

'When you were a little girl like me?'

'Yes.'

'What was his name?'

'I had more than one, darling. When I was small we had one called Bunter, and then there was Pandora, and after that Mabel.'

Polly giggled. 'Funny names.' She went back to her drawing while Joanna made herself some coffee.

After a while she looked up. 'Jo, did you have a horse too, like Snowbird?'

'Yes,' said Joanna sadly. 'I did.' She brightened, astonished, as Polly pushed her sketch-book across the table. The child had made a very creditable attempt at a drawing of Snowbird, copied from one of Joanna's illustrations.

'But that's very good, Polly,' she said in wonder. 'What a clever girl you are. By the way, we're invited to the Rectory tomorrow, for lunch with Jack and Charlie.'

The child beamed. 'I'll wear my new trousers—and wellies.'

'Good choice, knowing the twins.'

That night, for the first time, Polly slept through without waking to cry for her mother. Joanna leapt out of bed early next morning in alarm, sure something was wrong, but she found Polly still fast asleep. Joanna stood very still in the doorway, just gazing at the child, realising just how deeply she'd been worried now those worries were allayed. Polly, she suddenly felt sure, was over the worst.

Lunch at the Rectory was a great success. So much so that George Lavenham returned from officiating at a wedding to find Joanna still chatting comfortably with his wife at the kitchen table, and Polly out in the garden with the twins, running about and shrieking happily at the top of her voice as they played some complicated form of tag.

George Lavenham was that paragon of the male species, a powerfully attractive man who was naturally virtuous, unshakeable in his faith, and, to Joanna's everlasting wonder, the possessor of a sense of humour.

He swept into the kitchen, looking like Joanna's idea of the Angel Gabriel with his fair hair gleaming like a beacon above his vestments. 'Joanna! You look better.'

'I feel better.' Joanna waved a hand towards the garden, where Polly was playing happily with George's sons. 'I think Polly's beginning to settle down at last.'

'She starts school on Monday,' said Mary, looking smug. 'I told Jo it was what she needed. I was right.'

'You're never wrong,' said her husband, kissing her. 'And even if you were it would take a braver man than me to point it out.'

Joanna watched them together, stabbed by a pang of envy. The Lavenhams gave out an aura of oneness her own marriage had never even approached. She got up quickly. 'I must go.'

'Must you, Joanna?' asked George, in tune, as always, with someone else's pain. 'Why not stay for supper? I'm sure Mary can peel another potato or whatever. I can run you home afterwards.'

'Super idea,' said Mary warmly. 'Do stay, Jo.'

Dangerously tempted, Joanna nevertheless found the strength from somewhere to refuse. 'Thanks a lot. But we must go home.' She smiled. 'Best to leave while Polly's enjoying herself. She gets fractious when she's tired.'

'Don't we all?' sighed George, accepting a cup of coffee. He gave Joanna an affectionate smile. 'Next time, then.'

Marc rang again that night. Before he had time to say a word Joanna embarked on a bright, impersonal account of the pleasant day at the Rectory, told him about Polly's drawing and gave him her views on the advisability of a fully grown dog instead of a puppy.

Marc listened patiently until she finished, then chuckled. 'All right, Joanna. I get the message. I'll leave more personal exchanges until we meet again. Face to face,' he added significantly. 'But where Polly's concerned do whatever you like to make life easier. I know you'll do what's best for her. If I hadn't believed that I'd never have left her with you, no matter what Rosa said.'

'Perhaps a fully trained nanny might have done better with her than I have,' said Joanna, sighing.

'Rot! She needs love, not efficiency.' He paused. 'I believe you possess a great deal of love to give, Joanna.'

Something in the way his voice roughened on the last words took Joanna's breath away.

'Polly's easy to love,' she said unevenly.

'So am I!'

'It's not you we're discussing!' Joanna hesitated. 'By the way, Polly keeps asking when you're coming home again.'

'I'm working on it. Just tell her soon, will you? As soon as I possibly can. I miss you. Both of you.'

Joanna caught sight of her face in the hall mirror as she replaced the phone; eyes like stars and a flush which deepened as she realised that Polly wasn't alone in wanting to know when Marc was coming home. It was useless to tell herself that Paul had been dead only a short time, that a respectable widow shouldn't be thinking of another man at all at this stage. The truth of the matter was simple. It was such a long, long time since she'd felt like a wife that it was impossible to think of herself as a widow. Nor, she told herself firmly, was it a crime to find herself strongly drawn to Marc Anstey. He was an attractive, intelligent man who made it clear he found her desirable, an attitude which poured balm on the wounds made by Paul's infidelity.

She sighed. On the other hand, it was a bad idea to throw herself into Marc's arms at the drop of a hat however much she wanted to. Because of Polly the only relationship possible between them was friendship. A love affair, deeply tempting prospect though it might be, was out of the question.

Polly took to school like a duck to water, even happy to have her lunch there once she found Jack and Charlie Lavenham ate theirs in school too.

'You won't know you're born, Mrs Clifford,' said Doris the first day.

Joanna, who felt illogically restless now she had several hours all to herself, smiled ruefully. 'I felt terrible when I handed her over this morning, Doris. I don't know why! Polly went skipping off with the Lavenham twins without a qualm.'

For a while that first day Joanna pottered about, finding things to do instead of shutting herself in the study. But at last, mindful of recent hints from her editor, she sat down at her desk and began, very slowly at first, but eventually with her usual concentration, to work on the Snowbird adventure abandoned when Polly arrived to disrupt her life.

Once the new routine was established, the days began to fly by. Polly, stimulated and diverted by her lessons and the company of other children, was a very different little person. There were times when she still lapsed into grief for her mother, or anxiety over seeing Marc again, but with the resilience of childhood she gradually began to accept her new way of life, an acceptance which speeded up enormously once Sunny arrived on the scene.

Sunny was a golden Labrador, two years old, whose owners had been posted to a job abroad and couldn't take him along.

'His neutered and well-trained,' said Mrs Blake on the telephone. 'A very attractive dog, and used to children, Mrs Clifford. His owners are heartbroken at having to part with him. Would you care to come and see him?'

Two hours later, Joanna, who fell madly in love with Sunny at first sight, had the dog on a lead as she waited outside the school. When Polly ran out with the Lavenham twins, she stopped dead as she saw Joanna with a dog.

'Is that ours?' she demanded, scarlet-faced with excitement.

Rejoicing at the word 'ours', Joanna nodded casually. 'Do you like him?'

'Go on, pat him,' exhorted Jack Lavenham, and Polly, gingerly at first, then more boldly, stroked Sunny's handsome head. The dog, panting gently, looking as though he were grinning from ear to ear, submitted to the caress with such obvious pleasure that Joanna soon had to restrain all three children from giving the dog concussion with their attentions.

'Good move, that dog,' approved Mary. 'Now let me get my little darlings off the poor beast before the RSPCA come down on us.'

Sunny was a very well-trained, beautifully behaved dog, and no trouble at all from the first. It was Polly who posed the problems encountered in the first few days of dog-ownership. She yearned to feed him titbits from the table, and protested stormily because Joanna said Sunny couldn't go upstairs.

'He's a dog, Polly,' said Joanna firmly. 'He'll be much happier if we keep to the rules. And healthier,' she added, 'if you don't keep giving him bits and pieces to eat. He'll grow fat. And if he's fat he'll be ill.'

Polly, quick to learn, thought this over and decided she hated the idea of Sunny being ill, and kept meticulously to Joanna's instructions from then on.

'She adores him,' reported Joanna when Marc rang towards the end of the week. 'She hasn't cried for Rosa at all since Sunny arrived.'

'My idea was a good one, then,' said Marc smugly.

Joanna chuckled. 'An absolute brainwave!'

'If Polly's still asking when I'm coming home, by the way,' he went on casually, 'I am.'

'You're what?'

'Home. I'm in London. I arrived today, jet-lagged, death warmed up, but home.'

Joanna sat down abruptly. 'Oh. I didn't realise——'

'I bade a fond farewell to Washington yesterday, I caught a flight today—or is it tomorrow?' He waited for a while. 'Are you still there, Joanna?'

'Yes. I'm here.' Joanna gathered her dazed wits together hurriedly. 'Shall I tell Polly you'll see her soon?'

'I'll be tied up at the paper until Saturday. If I drive down to Swancote on Sunday morning, could I take you both out to lunch?'

'I'll cook lunch,' said Joanna quickly. 'If you like, that is.'

'I like very much. See you Sunday.'

When Polly heard her uncle was coming to lunch at the weekend her eyes were like stars.

'He can come when we take Sunny for a walk. He'll like Sunny, won't he? Can I get down, please?' Barely waiting for Joanna's permission she left the breakfast table to crouch down by the dog, telling him how much he'd like Marco, and what fun it would be to go for walks together.

Joanna watched indulgently, wondering how Marc would react to the change in his niece. Polly was a different child from the woebegone little creature he'd left behind.

Instead of racing by, time dragged interminably until the weekend. In vain Joanna ordered herself to stop behaving like a schoolgirl with her first crush. She had to force herself to concentrate on her work, to banish the clever, olive-skinned face which kept coming between her eyes and the page. She was glad when Friday afternoon came round at last, and she could officially abandon work for the weekend.

'What's up?' demanded Mary, as they waited outside the school for their charges. 'You're like a cat on hot bricks. Work going badly?'

'Concentration's bad,' said Joanna with truth.

'Hardly surprising, is it!' Mary eyed her, frowning. 'Something wrong, Jo?'

Joanna smiled sheepishly. 'Nothing more than usual. Life's a bit hectic these days, that's all. Not that I'm complaining,' she added hastily.

'You're not brooding over Paul?'

'Paul?' Joanna turned wide blue eyes on her friend.

'Yes, Paul,' said Mary drily. 'Your husband.'

Joanna blushed to the roots of her hair. 'No. Oh, Mary, I should be. But I'm not.'

'Glad to hear it,' said Mary succinctly, then waved. 'Brace yourselves. Here they come.'

Happily Saturday was a fine, sunny day which meant Joanna could channel both her own and Polly's energies by taking Sunny on walks as long as Polly's small legs would allow. Jack and Charlie came to tea, which put the finishing touch to both her own and Polly's exhaustion, and once George had collected the twins and Polly was in bed Joanna retreated to put her feet up on the sofa with a new novel. Sunny, apparently as glad as Joanna for a rest, lay stretched out on the floor beside her, snoring gently, while Joanna planned her menu for the next day. She smiled dreamily, abandoning any attempt to disguise the fact that she was as excited as Polly over seeing Marc Anstey again.

After the large doses of fresh air Joanna felt drowsy in the warmth of the drawing-room. Her eyes grew heavy and the book slid, unnoticed, to the floor as she dozed. Suddenly she woke with a start, to see Marc's face, disembodied at the window. For a moment she thought she was dreaming, that his face was some kind of wish fulfilment, then she realised he was smiling and disturbingly real, and she felt a great rush of joy at the sight of him. Stealthily, in an effort to leave the dog sleeping undisturbed, she tiptoed on bare feet from the drawing-room and closed the door behind her before racing across the hall to fling open the door.

'I'm a little early for Sunday lunch,' said Marc without preamble and seized her in his arms, kissing her fiercely, in a famished, unstoppable way which left Joanna unsteady on her feet when he released her.

'I've been dreaming of that,' he said huskily.

'I wasn't expecting you until tomorrow,' said Joanna breathlessly. She brushed past him to close the door with hands which shook so much that she could hardly shoot the bolt.

'I managed to finish up earlier than I thought, so instead of going back to my lonely flat I rang the Lamb and Flag in Swancote, bespoke me a room for the night, then drove down here like a bat out of hell.' He reached out a hand to touch her cheek. 'Are you glad to see me?'

'Would there be any point in denying it?' she asked mockingly.

His eyes danced. 'No. Not after that kiss.' He looked about him. 'Where's this guard-dog of yours, by the way?'

'Asleep in the drawing-room.' Joanna opened the door. 'Here, Sunny. Here, boy. Come and say hello.'

Sunny was shameless in his predilection for the new arrival. Joanna chuckled as the dog fawned over Marc. 'He obviously fancies you like mad.'

'Never mind the dog—does his owner feel the same? If not madly, at least a little.'

He turned to look at her so suddenly that Joanna had to think fast. 'Even if I do, I'm not going to let myself,' she blurted.

His eyes narrowed. 'Am I allowed to ask why?'

'Because I'm too vulnerable at the moment. You must be, too, in a different kind of way.' Joanna's chin went up. 'If ever—I mean if we were to become involved in that way I'd want it to be for normal, healthy reasons, not because our link with Rosa pushed us together.'

'Shall I go out and come in again then?' he asked with sarcasm. 'I find it a little difficult to revert to formality now, after that kiss.'

She grinned. 'I don't require formality, Mr Anstey. Let's just be friends. Good friends, of course.'

'With the accent on the "good".' His eyes lingered deliberately on her mouth. 'It seems a pity. Would you believe that while I was in the States I resisted quite a few blandishments just because of your beautiful blue eyes?'

'I'll try,' said Joanna tartly, leading the way into the kitchen. 'Shall I make you something to eat now?'

'No. I had a large celebratory lunch. I'd like some coffee, though, and while you make it will Sunny here let me go up to see Polly?'

'Try him.'

Sunny was quite happy to let Marc upstairs. He made it plain he would have liked to go too, but in response to Marc's command the dog lay obediently at the foot of the stairs, waiting with his handsome head raised in longing for this new, fascinating human to return.

'Polly looks well!' said Marc, coming into the kitchen. He closed the door behind him. 'She's sleeping like a log.'

'Now we have Sunny we walk a lot. The fresh air knocks her out.' Joanna poured coffee for them both, then sat down at the kitchen table. 'So how was Washington?'

'Hectic.' Marc sat down opposite her, looking to Joanna's eyes even more attractive than before now some of the lines of grief were smoothed from his lean, dark face. He smiled into her eyes, reaching a hand across the table to touch hers. 'How have you been, Joanna?'

'At first it was hard going,' she admitted, withdrawing her hand gently. 'After you'd gone Polly relapsed badly, as I told you. But since she started school she's been a different child.' Joanna explained about the help the Lavenhams had given, and how Polly liked playing with the twins. 'Then Sunny came on the scene.' Joanna grinned. 'She's been telling him how much he's going to like you, and she was right!'

'Children and dogs always like me,' said Marc smugly, eyes gleaming. 'It's a good indication of a chap's character. Paul hated dogs, which proves my point.'

There was a sudden, charged silence, then Marc shook his head. 'Sorry, Joanna.'

She shrugged. 'You can't help how you feel, I suppose. And we can't pretend Paul never existed. He did. And until recently, too. I keep feeling that a widow with any pretensions to sensitivity wouldn't even be here with you like this. We hardly know each other, really, Marc.'

'Owning to pressures beyond our control we've got to know each other faster and more intimately than we'd ever have done if we'd met in the usual way.' He captured her hand again, caressing it gently. 'Nothing on earth will alter the fact that Rosa and Paul are gone. But you and I are here and alive, Joanna. Is it so terrible to be attracted to each other? Neither of us is hurting someone else, as Paul and Rosa did. Paul was no husband to you, not for years, anyway. Why should you feel guilty about wanting to live and——?' He stopped short, his eyes completing the sentence for him as they held hers.

'I see your point,' she admitted. 'But I doubt if the world at large would feel the same.'

'I don't give a damn about the world at large. The opinion I care about is yours.'

'Is it? Then in my considered opinion we should go into reverse a little. Get to know each other better before——' She paused, flushing.

'You stopped at the interesting bit.'

'You know perfectly well what I mean.'

Marc smiled. 'Yes, Joanna. I know exactly what you mean. And I won't tease you any more. I'll do my utmost to behave. But it won't be easy,' he added, his caressing eyes bringing heat to her cheeks.

They spent the rest of the evening in the drawing-room, Sunny on the floor beside Marc's chair while they caught up with each other's news.

'You must be pretty tired,' she commented, after yawns began to punctuate Marc's conversation rather regularly.

'I haven't caught up on myself yet. I've been working flat out to get back home to finalise a little matter I embarked on some time ago.' He stretched luxuriously, looking very pleased with himself.

'Am I allowed to ask what it is?' asked Joanna, curiously.

'A new job. It was confirmed today. As from the first of next month I shall no longer go a-roving to foreign parts. I shall be foreign editor of the *Citadel*, and based in London. Are you going to congratulate me?'

Joanna looked at him uncertainly. 'I don't know yet. How will the new arrangement affect Polly—and me?'

Marc stared at her, astonished. 'You don't honestly think I'd take her away from you now that she's settling down in Swancote?' He paused. 'Unless that's what you want, of course.'

'Of course it isn't,' she snapped. 'How can you even suggest such a thing?'

He passed a hand over his face, then leaned forward in his chair. 'Shall I tell you why I put in for the new job, Joanna Swan? Because it meant being based permanently in the UK. And why did I want that? So I could see more of you—and Polly too, of course. It beats me how you could think I'd take her away from you!'

Joanna quailed before the fierce light in his eyes. 'I'm sorry, I'm sorry.' She pushed a glossy wing of hair back from her face. 'It's just that I've grown so attached to her already—I couldn't bear the thought of losing her.'

His eyes softened. 'I realise that. So, now you've had time to calm down, am I allowed to ask if you welcome the idea of having me around more often? In my function as Polly's legal guardian, of course.'

'I think I can handle that,' said Joanna matter-of-factly, hoping he had no inkling of how much the idea thrilled her. 'Were there many people after the job?'

'Hundreds! But with me in the running, of course, no one else stood a chance.'

'So modest!'

He gazed at her, sighing. 'This is going to be very difficult for me, Joanna.'

'What is?'

'Trying to keep my distance. You must know I'm straining every muscle to stay where I am instead of coming over there and taking you in my arms.'

'Take Sunny for a walk in the garden instead,' she said briskly. 'I'll make some sandwiches while you're out.'

Marc laughed ruefully and jumped to his feet, clicking his fingers to the willing dog. 'You're a cruel lady. Come on, hound. Let's go cool off in the night air.'

Joanna felt absurdly happy as she put a snack together in the kitchen. It was useless to tell herself that a woman who was thirty next birthday shouldn't be feeling like a starry-eyed teenager, that one look from Marc Anstey's black eyes shouldn't be enough to melt all her resistance. Not that she was going to let him know that it did. Nor, she thought bleakly, was she going to let him make love to her, no matter how much she wanted him to. It was all too sudden, too new. They had known each other far too short a time to rush into something which would inevitably end in tears. Polly's, as well as her own.

CHAPTER SIX

JOANNA woke next morning to a feeling of anticipation she knew at once was due to Marc's unexpected reappearance. She sang off-key as she showered and dressed, deciding to stop worrying about relationships and just enjoy the day with a fascinating, charismatic man who made it flatteringly clear he found her desirable. She put on a new strawberry-pink wool shirt and grey flannel trousers then went in to Polly, who was sitting up in bed, tongue between her teeth in intense concentration as she sketched the row of battered teddies on the shelf. Polly held up her face to be kissed, then went on with her masterpiece while Joanna marvelled at the way the child had contrived, with a minimum of basic lines, to portray the characteristics of each separate bear.

'Goodness, darling,' said Joanna. 'That *is* good.'

'I like drawing.'

'I know you do. But could you go back to it later? Sunny needs a walk.'

Polly agreed.

'Guess who came to see us last night?' said Joanna, smiling, when they were out in the garden.

Polly's bright black eyes looked puzzled. 'I don't know. Who, Jo?'

'Your uncle! He came home a day early.'

Polly stared, her lower lip quivering. 'Marco! Didn't he come to see me?'

'Of course he did, the moment he arrived. But you were fast asleep. Don't look like that,' added Joanna hastily, bending to hug the child. 'He's staying in the village. He'll be here soon.'

In wild excitement the child went careering round in circles with the barking dog, too pent-up at the thought of seeing her beloved Marco again to eat much breakfast when they went in. Joanna hadn't the heart to scold her. She couldn't eat much herself. And *she* was old enough to know better, she reminded herself as she began preparations for the celebration lunch.

The reunion between Marc Anstey and Polly was touching to see, the presence of an excited, barking Sunny a welcome touch of lightness as the child wept with joy to see her uncle again.

'Hey,' said Marc huskily, 'you mustn't cry, *tesoro*! Look, you're upsetting Sunny!'

Quick to comfort the dog, Polly forgot her tears as she pulled Marc into the house and began to talk nineteen to the dozen about the Lavenham twins, and all the new friends she'd made, and the lessons she did at school.

'I like drawing the best,' she told Marc happily.

'I know. A little bird told me.' Marc smiled at Joanna, who was standing a little way apart to allow the other two their moment of reunion. 'And how are you this morning, Joanna?'

'I'm just fine, thank you,' she said with composure. 'Let's go into the kitchen so I can keep an eye on lunch.'

Marc winked at Polly. 'You two go ahead. I've got one or two things to get out of the car.'

'What things?' demanded Polly.

'Wait and see—off you go with Joanna, please.'

By the time Marc finally joined them in the kitchen, weighed down by a large parcel, Polly was jumping up and down with excitement, chattering like a magpie as she hazarded guesses about the contents.

Joanna helped her with the string and brown paper while Marc sat back in a kitchen chair, watching the two intent faces, the one rosy beneath a mop of curls, the other creamy pale under a shining wing of dark gold hair. Joanna's eyes narrowed as she glanced up to intercept the dark, intent look trained on her face.

'A lot of paper!' she commented.

'Just tear it off,' he advised, 'before Polly goes off with a loud report!'

Soon the last of the wrappings were off, discarded on the floor for Sunny to investigate, while Polly gazed, saucer-eyed, at a drawing-board and easel, each a miniature of Joanna's. With them came a package of white cartridge paper, drawing books, a box of paints, one full of coloured pencils, another with felt-tip pens, everything a child could possibly need to paint and draw and colour to her heart's content.

'Well?' demanded Marc. 'Do you like your surprise?'

For answer Polly hurled herself into his arms and covered his face with smacking kisses to express her delight.

'Did you bring a present for Jo?' she demanded at last.

'Of course I did. I left it out in the hall. Fetch the parcel on the hall table, *cara*—and carry it very, very carefully, please.'

Joanna eyed him disapprovingly as she gathered up discarded wrappings. 'You needn't have brought me anything.'

'Why not?' His eyes locked with hers. 'It seemed the natural thing to do. I thought of you a lot while I was away. Did you ever spare a thought for me?'

'You promised——' She broke off, jumping up as Polly came back into the room with Sunny at her heels. She handed a package to Joanna in great excitement.

'Go on, Jo,' she urged. 'Open it.'

Wishing she could have done so away from two pairs of identical black eyes, Joanna unwrapped her gift with unusual clumsiness, lifting the lid of a cardboard box at last to find a mass of polystyrene chips, and at the heart of them a tissue-swathed object which she unwrapped with care then stood still, her teeth caught in her bottom lip. The pearl-white porcelain horse in her hands was depicted in full gallop, mane and tail flying, the workmanship so exquisite that she blenched at the thought of what it must have cost.

'It's Snowbird!' cried Polly in wonder.

Joanna stood the horse gently on the kitchen table. 'No, darling. Snowbird's a pony. This is a horse, like my Saladin. The very image of him, in fact.' She looked at Marc. 'How did you know? That he looked just like this?'

'I didn't. But I hoped. I came across it by chance in Kensington only a couple of days ago.' He smiled. 'The moment I saw it I thought of you.'

'Aren't you going to kiss Marc to say thank you?' asked Polly severely.

Joanna, eyes averted, planted a very swift kiss on Marc's lean dark cheek. 'Now,' she said briskly. 'Where shall we put him?'

Marc consulted Polly earnestly. 'I think he should sit on the desk in the study, don't you? Perhaps he'll give Joanna inspiration.'

Joanna nodded. 'Yes. You're right. I shall want him where I can see him all the time.' And where no one else was likely to see the horse at all, or ask embarrassing questions about where she'd acquired it.

To Joanna the day was a bittersweet blend of pleasure and misgiving, the latter increasing with every minute as the three of them spent the day in much the same way that countless other families were spending a fine autumn Sunday all over the country. They ate a traditional roast lunch together, then went for a walk through the woods with Sunny until it was time for tea, and to the casual eye they appeared like any mother, father and child. But, Joanna took care to remind herself, they were not. Polly was in her care, but the child was not her daughter, nor was Marc Anstey anything other than Polly's uncle. And days together like this could be misleading for Polly, if she got into the habit of regarding the three of them as a family unit.

'Penny for your thoughts,' said Marc lazily, as he stroked the dog's head.

Joanna took refuge in gathering up plates and cups. 'Not for sale,' she said lightly.

'Perhaps I knew what you were thinking,' he said so softly that Polly, absorbed in drawing Sunny, couldn't hear.

'I doubt it.' Joanna hefted the tray, refusing his help. 'What time do you have to leave?'

'Once Polly's in bed I'd better make tracks. Busy day tomorrow.'

Joanna nodded, deeply relieved, yet illogically disappointed at the same time. 'While I see to this lot perhaps you'd like to chivvy Polly into the bath.'

'Right.' Marc got to his feet, yawning. 'Come on, *cara*. Bathtime.'

All too soon, it seemed to Joanna, Polly was in bed and asleep, and Marc was ready to go.

'I don't have to go,' he said, eyeing her narrowly as she walked with him to the door. 'Given the least encouragement I'd stay. For a while at least. But you're on edge, Joanna. And I wish I knew why. Last night I surprised you into giving me a totally spontaneous welcome. But today you're back in your shell and regretting your lapse last night, yet too polite to tell me to get lost. What's troubling you, Joanna? Tell me.'

Joanna faced him. 'All right,' she said flatly. 'If you must know, I'm worried because the type of day we spent together is certain to be bad for Polly.'

His eyes narrowed incredulously. 'How the hell do you work that out?

'Surely you can see! Polly will take it for granted it's the way things are always going to be.' Joanna eyed him unhappily. 'And you and I know perfectly well we can't guarantee that.' She put out a hand in appeal. 'Please don't be angry. It's been a lovely day. I've enjoyed it as much as Polly. But circumstances rule out any kind of—of attachment between you and me, Marc. You've got to make it clear to Polly that one day you'll probably produce some perfectly acceptable aunt for her. Just as I may find another husband.'

'Is this an oblique way of telling me you already have?' he said harshly.

She shook her head, hugging her arms across her chest. 'No. I'm not. If I had I wouldn't——'

'Wouldn't have let me kiss you senseless last night!' Black eyes met incensed blue ones challengingly. 'Well?' he went on. 'Isn't that what happened?

'No,' she said hotly. 'I was too taken by surprise to—to resist, that's all. It didn't mean anything other than that.'

'My mistake. I thought it meant a hell of a lot more than that.' He took her by the shoulders, his fingers digging into her skin through her sweater. 'I could have sworn that I got through to the real you, that you were so glad to see me you forgot that you were Paul Clifford's widow, and I was Rosa's brother. For a moment there we were just two people who'd missed each other and were so bloody delighted to be together again that what happened was the most natural thing in the world.'

'But that's what I'm worried about,' she cried, trying to free herself. 'Can't you see, Marc? I acknowledge the chemistry between us. It's—it's undeniable. But that kind of thing can vanish and leave nothing behind in a relationship. And today we looked like a family, we behaved like a family; a permanent arrangement, which we're not. We're two strangers thrown together by chance, with Polly as the sole point of reference between us other than the chemistry.'

'Is that really what you think?' he said in disbelief. He stood back, his arms falling to his sides. 'You think that without Polly I wouldn't have driven down here like a love-sick schoolboy last night. That I wouldn't have bought you the horse——'

'Which you shouldn't have done—it must have cost a fortune.'

He gave her a look like a thrown spear. 'Bloody fool, wasn't I? But when I found it, all I could see was the look in those big blue eyes when you talked about your beloved Saladin.'

Joanna's head went up angrily. 'I'd rather you hadn't given it to me, whatever your reason. Look, Marc, it's better to put the brakes on now, not when it's too late. The very nature of our link with Polly is bound to have a greenhouse effect on our relationship if we're not careful, forcing it into something intimate whether we want it or not.'

He stood with folded arms, his face grim. 'And you don't, obviously. All right, Joanna. What do you suggest? That I don't come down here any more?'

'Of course not,' she said impatiently. 'Polly needs to see you. I know that.' Her eyes fell before the ice in his. 'But I suggest that next time you take Polly out on your own. I'll make sure she knows well in advance that I'm not available that day. She'll probably be delighted to have you all to herself.'

'Am I allowed to pick her up at the house?' asked Marc bitingly.

'Of course. Please! Don't make this more difficult than it is.' She looked at him in entreaty. 'I've had time to think—last night after you'd gone, today while we were out walking. I know I'm right. Polly must get used to the fact that, while you and I are both constants in her life, we are totally separate from each other.'

Marc gave a short, mirthless laugh. 'I'm sorry for you, Joanna. I don't know what—or who—made you so wary of human relationships, though I can make a bloody good guess. We could be good together. I'm as certain of that as night follows day. Tell me. How long is a guy required to know you before——?'

'Before what?' she broke in hotly. 'Before I let him into my bed?'

'I was going to say before you considered him worthy of trust, Joanna.' He turned away, suddenly, repudiation in every line of his lean, graceful body. 'Oh, what the hell! I don't know why I'm beating my head against a stone wall like this. All right. You win. We'll play the game to your rules if that's the way you want it. I just hope Polly understands.'

Joanna, aware that she should be satisfied now she had her way, felt instead as though all the warmth had just drained out of her life.

'Will you come again next week?' she forced herself to ask.

'Yes. I'll come,' he said morosely. 'I'll be round about eleven next Sunday to take Polly out to lunch. I leave it to you to explain why you're not honouring us with your presence. Goodnight, Mrs Clifford.' Marc opened the door without a backward glance, as though he couldn't bear to look at her, closing the heavy oak door behind him so quietly that the effect was worse than if he'd slammed it in her face.

When the following weekend arrived there was no need to fabricate an excuse for reneging on Polly's outing with Marc. Joanna had the messiest, most objectionable head cold she'd ever had in her life, and felt, looked and sounded so wretched that Mary Lavenham insisted Polly spend Saturday at the Rectory, and remain there overnight, away from Joanna's germs.

'You're a saint,' said Joanna hoarsely from the top of the stairs, as the small cortège prepared to depart, dog included.

'Wrong Lavenham. Sanctity is George's department.' Mary shooed Polly out of the door then looked up at Joanna, lips pursed. 'You're a mess. Get back in bed, so you're fit to have Polly back in the morning. Sorry I can't keep her tomorrow, too, but you know what Sundays are like *chez* Lavenham.'

'I do. In any case, tomorrow she's off on a jaunt with her uncle.'

'Hmm. I'd like to meet this uncle of Polly's some time. He can't possibly be as amazing as she says.'

Joanna made non-committal noises, thanked Mary gratefully, then went to wave to Polly from the window before going back to bed in utter misery, coughing, barely able to breathe, sneezing at such regular intervals that the tip of her nose soon shone red like a traffic light from contact with too many paper tissues.

When the telephone rang late in the afternoon Joanna felt almost too wretched to answer it. Only the thought that it might be Mary with an emergency gave her the necessary energy to lift the receiver.

'Hello?' she said thickly, then gave way to a bout of coughing.

'Joanna?' demanded Marc. 'What the hell's the matter?'

'Got a cold.'

'Only a cold? You sound at death's door. Where's Polly?'

'At the Rectory.' Joanna sneezed three times in rapid succession. 'They're keeping her overnight,' she gasped when she could speak. 'I should be better tomorrow.'

'You can hardly be much worse by the sound of you! Did Polly mind?' he added.

'Mind?'

'Sleeping somewhere else.'

'No. She seemed quite keed—keen. She took Sunny with her. She'll be ready when you come tomorrow. You *are* coming, I suppose?' she asked anxiously, shuddering at the thought of Polly's disappointment if he wasn't.

'Yes. See you in the morning, then.'

Joanna sagged against the pillows in relief. 'Right. Goodbye.'

'For Pete's sake take something for that cold,' he ordered. '*Ciao.*'

Joanna spent a miserable night feeling sorry for herself, her misery somewhat alleviated when she staggered downstairs the following morning to find

Doris on the doorstep with Polly, Sunny and various bags and baggage.

'Good morning,' Doris said calmly, smiling at Joanna's astonishment. 'You do look poorly, and that's a fact. No, Polly, you mustn't hug Mrs Clifford, you'll get her cold.'

'All right,' said Polly reluctantly, her eyes anxious on Joanna's ashen face and red, puffy eyes. 'Are you very ill, Jo?'

'No, not really, darling,' said Joanna, pulling herself together as she stood back for them to come in. 'I feel horrible, and a bit shivery, but only the way you do with a cold. And don't think I'm not grateful for your presence, Doris,' she added, 'but how——?'

'Mrs Lavenham rang me last night. She was worried about you,' said Doris, removing her best coat with care. 'I know what Sundays are like at the Rectory, so I said I'd see to you. I've packed my two off for the day to get spoiled by their Gran.'

Within minutes of Doris's arrival Joanna was back in a bed newly made up with clean linen, a tray of steaming coffee and crisp toast beside her and a hot water bottle at her feet. Polly, allowed to stand in the open doorway for a chat, gazed at her with round, apprehensive eyes.

'Jo...do colds ever make people die?'

Joanna's heart contracted. She summoned up a reassuring smile as she said firmly, 'No, Polly. Never, ever. I'll be up and about again by this afternoon. I'm only staying here now so I don't give you my germs. Now while I eat the delicious breakfast tell me what you did yesterday at the Lavenhams'.'

Her eyes bright with relief, Polly lingered a while to give an account of her stay with the twins, displayed a bruise she'd gained by sliding down the Rectory banisters, then decided she'd better play ball with Sunny in the garden for a while before getting ready to go out with Marco. She lingered for a moment to discuss her choice of outfit for the outing, then went off downstairs to Doris, plainly no longer a prey to fears about Joanna's mortality.

Marc Anstey arrived a little after eleven. When Doris let him in the sound of his deep voice carried to Joanna's room, but not loudly enough to let her know what he was saying. Shortly afterwards Polly peered cautiously round the door. She displayed herself to Joanna in all the glory of a new scarlet sweater and navy trousers, announced she was ready to go, then blew a kiss and ran off to join Marc.

'I told Mr Anstey you weren't well enough for a visit,' said Doris firmly when all was quiet. She plumped up Joanna's pillows then handed her some freshly squeezed orange juice and a couple of cold-cure tablets.

'Thank you, Doris,' said Joanna meekly. 'But don't hang about here too long, or you'll catch my cold.'

'I never get colds. Malcolm and Sheila won't be back until the eight o'clock bus, so I'll stay until Polly's bedtime, Mrs Clifford.'

'I feel guilty lying here,' sighed Joanna. 'It's only a cold, Doris.'

'But a very nasty one.' Doris hesitated at the door, looking a little awkward. 'Your resistance is low, I expect.'

Lower than Doris imagined, thought Joanna, once she was alone. And to more dangerous things than the common cold. In a day or two her coughs and sneezes would be better, but where Marc Anstey was concerned she had a sinking feeling that recovery would take longer. Like the rest of her life, perhaps.

Joanna sighed. It was useless to pretend that she was indifferent to Marc. His slightest touch set off fireworks of response inside her that she'd never felt for Paul. But she just couldn't conquer her deep distrust of the sudden longing to give herself up to a man, body and soul. It would be bliss with Marc while it lasted, she knew, a shiver running through her at the mere thought. But when it ended, as experience had taught her it could, Polly would be heartbroken. And the mere thought of causing the child more grief again was unendurable.

When Marc returned with Polly later in the afternoon Doris was still firmly in charge. She offered Marc a cup of tea, which he refused, gave him the latest bulletin on Joanna's health, took charge of the flowers he'd brought for the invalid, then saw him calmly to the door with Polly, who waved him off, blowing kisses, then scampered up to Joanna.

'Marco didn't stay,' she told Joanna from the doorway. 'Are you better, Jo?'

'Yes, darling. Have you had a lovely time?'

Polly was surprisingly non-committal. Marco had taken her to lunch and then for a drive, during which they'd stopped to go for a walk, but they'd had to run back to the car because it rained. 'You come next time,' said Polly firmly. 'We missed you, Jo.'

'I thought you'd prefer being on your own together,' said Joanna surprised.

Polly shook her head. 'No. I like it best when you come, too.'

'I think Doris has made some kind of little cakes for you,' said Joanna, guiltily pleased that she'd been missed.

'Yum,' said Polly eagerly, about to dash off when she turned back for a moment. 'Marco bought you flowers. Doris put them in a pot.'

'How lovely,' said Joanna, sneezing. 'Oh, drat this cold. Off you go, darling, well away from me and my sneezes.'

'OK.' Polly eyed her anxiously. 'Get better soon, Jo.'

'I will!' Joanna mopped herself up vigorously. 'I'll be fighting fit in a day or two, I promise.'

Marc rang later that night, long after Polly was in bed. 'I wasn't allowed to visit you on your bed of pain,' he said drily. 'Doris appeared to think that one look at you with your red nose and swollen eyes would send me raving mad with lust.'

Joanna giggled. 'I'm sure the thought of lust never crossed Doris's mind——'

'Lucky old Doris.'

There was an awkward pause. 'Thank you for the flowers, by the way,' Joanna said hastily, coughing a little.

'I had hoped to present them in person.'

'Just as well you didn't. I look revolting—and you'd probably have caught my cold.'

'I swore I wouldn't say this, after the way you sent me packing last week, but I missed you today,' he said gruffly. 'Polly did too. She said so in no uncertain terms.'

Joanna gave a shaky sigh. 'It's better this way, Marc.'

'Better for whom, Joanna? It certainly wasn't better for Polly. Nor for me. We were like lost souls without you. So it must have been yourself you were thinking of when you decided to back out of future outings. Own up, Joanna. You're a coward—in a cold funk at the thought of getting involved.'

'I'm not,' she denied, so fiercely it brought on an attack of coughing which rendered her speechless for a while. 'It was Polly I was thinking of,' she went on hoarsely at last.

He laughed scornfully. 'What a load of rubbish, Joanna Swan. You backed out of the arrangement because you're afraid of committing yourself to a normal, healthy relationship where a man's concerned. Polly's just your excuse for running away from me. You're worried I might crack that shell you've been living in, make you feel like a flesh and blood woman in a way Paul Clifford never did.'

'How dare you?' she croaked, incensed.

'I dare because——' He stopped dead. 'Oh, what's the use?' he said fiercely. 'Forget it. I've no right to interfere in your life. Have it your way. Polly's adaptable. She'll just have to accept the failure of her plan.'

'What plan?'

'She thinks it would be nice if the three of us lived together, just like the Lavenhams.' He laughed shortly. 'Don't worry. I explained, in as simple terms as possible, that this wasn't remotely possible. One way and another.'

CHAPTER SEVEN

TO HER intense irritation, Joanna, who normally shook off minor complaints with ease, found it hard to get rid of her cold. One of the contributing factors to her slow convalescence, she knew perfectly well, was Marc Anstey's apparent lack of concern. He rang, it was true, but beyond a perfunctory enquiry about her health said nothing personal other than his regret at not being able to take Polly out the following weekend. He was bidden to lunch by the owner of the *Citadel*, an offer he couldn't refuse.

'If I could talk to Polly for a moment I'd like to explain to her personally,' he said with chill courtesy.

Rebuffed, as he very plainly intended, Joanna took the phone along to Polly's bedroom and left the child alone to talk to her uncle.

When Polly came back with the phone Joanna eyed her closely.

'Are you disappointed, darling? Because you won't see your uncle this weekend?'

Polly nodded, mouth drooping. She heaved a big sigh. 'But Marco said I must be a big girl and understand. He'll come next week. Without *fail*,' she added, in touching reproduction of Marc's forceful manner.

That night Joanna woke with a start. She turned on her bedside lamp to find a tearful little figure standing beside the bed.

'Can I come in your bed?' sobbed Polly.

'Oh, darling, of course you can.' Joanna turned back the covers in welcome, scooping the child into the warm bed. Joanna held Polly tightly, rubbing her cheek over the damp, tangled curls.

'What is it?' she asked gently. 'Are you missing your Mamma?'

Polly nodded, sniffing hard. 'But Marco said she's happy in heaven 'cos I'm safe with you.'

Joanna's throat tightened. 'Did he, darling?'

Polly gave a huge, shaky sigh. 'I just wish Marco could live here too with you 'n' me 'n' Sunny.'

'He can't do that, Polly, because he works in London. You know he's got an important new job?'

Polly smiled proudly. 'Yes. Marco's clever.' She eyed Joanna sternly. 'Why don't you like him, Jo?'

Joanna tried to smile. 'But I do.'

Polly frowned. 'Then why——?' She bit her lip, suddenly the picture of guilt.

Joanna eyed her narrowly. 'Why what, Paola Anstey?'

'Marco said not to.'

'Out with it!'

Polly buried her head against Joanna's shoulder. 'Why won't you let Marco live here? Then we'd be like the twins and their mummy and daddy.'

Joanna lay very still, staring at the ceiling, sending up a silent prayer for guidance before doing her best to explain to Polly that the way things were would just have to do. That not everyone had a family like the Lavenhams.

'Just remember, Polly,' she added, 'that your Marco loves you very much and so do I. But your uncle and I hardly know each other. Grown-ups don't live together until they know each other very well.'

'I live with you, and you haven't known me long,' said Polly unanswerably.

'That's different,' said Joanna firmly, and put the light out. 'Now go to sleep, my cherub, or you won't keep awake in school tomorrow.'

The locations for Snowbird's adventures varied with the seasons. In summer his escapades took place at the beach, but now Joanna painted him against a background of autumn leaves and bonfires, Hallowe'en and Guy Fawkes night. Ignoring her cold, she worked hard while Polly was in school, and at the weekend let the child set up her new easel and drawing-board in the study so they could work together. And as the time went by Joanna convinced herself that her life was full. That it lacked nothing that Marc Anstey could provide.

Marc rang fairly regularly, it was true, but these days it was all too obvious that he'd taken the hint, that he now considered Joanna's role in his life minimal. As far as he was concerned, he made it clear, her sole function was a means of communication with Polly. To Joanna's shame she had to curb a strong urge to eavesdrop on their talks, even to question the child about them afterwards. Then one night, before asking to speak to Polly, he made a suggestion which filled Joanna with sharp dismay.

'As you know,' he said impersonally, 'I start at the *Citadel* soon. Since I'm likely to be tied up rather a lot from then on, while I get to grips with the new job, I thought that instead of just lunching with Polly next Sunday as originally planned I'd take her away for a holiday next week.'

'Away?' said Joanna, dismayed. 'Where?'

'To a Greek island called Chyros. A friend of mine owns a house there. I thought a few days in the sun would do Polly good. And you could have a good rest while she's off your hands,' he added. 'You still sound a bit hoarse. Cold still hanging on?'

'No,' snapped Joanna. 'I'm fine.'

'Good. Would you pack a few things for Polly, then, please? I'll come for her on Friday night.'

'Certainly. Would you like to speak to Polly now—describe the delights in store?'

'Do I detect a hint of sarcasm?'

'I'll just take the phone in to her,' said Joanna distantly. 'She's reading in bed. Goodbye.'

Polly was so excited at the prospect of the holiday that she was hard to handle for the next few days. Joanna would have been hard put to cope with the child if Jack and Charlie Lavenham hadn't come round after school to play with her most days. The twins were deeply envious of Polly's forthcoming trip to the sun.

'As well they might be,' said Mary cheerfully. 'My darling husband's stipend doesn't run to exotic holidays, I'm afraid. And George's principles won't allow him to use any of my money for things like that.'

Mary, the cherished only daughter of comfortably off parents, had been left a considerable private income, which was, in her words, as much use as a sick headache due to her husband's scruples.

'George refuses to use it for anything other than eventual school fees.' Mary sighed. 'He even vetoes raids on my piggy-bank for fripperies like a reliable car, or a few miles of new curtain for the Rectory windows.'

Joanna chuckled. 'He let you buy a new cooker.'

'Ah, yes, but George, saint though he be, loves his food. I said, "No cooker, George, no meals." End of problem.'

Joanna got to her feet as the noise volume increased upstairs, but Mary waved her back. 'Relax. You only charge off when there's a deadly hush, love.' She eyed Joanna searchingly. 'I say, Jo. You look a bit washed out. Cold still bothering you?'

'No.' Joanna topped up their coffee-cups. 'I suppose if I'm honest I hate the thought of Polly going off to Greece next week. I'll miss her.'

Mary, who with her George was the only one in Joanna's confidence regarding Polly, eyed her friend thoughtfully. 'You really adore that child, don't you? I don't know that I could have been so noble under the circumstances.'

'Of course you could,' scoffed Joanna. 'Besides, I don't have much else to fill my life, other than Snowbird, do I? Polly's a handful sometimes, but she's a loving little soul. The house will seem empty while she's away. Thank heavens for the dog.'

'The twins tell me Polly would like her uncle to move into Swan House with you—provide her with a ready-made family,' announced Mary, then stared as Joanna flushed to the roots of her hair. 'Oh, dear. I've struck a nerve.'

Joanna pulled a face. 'Actually it's all your fault. Polly yearns for a family just like yours. She had to be enlightened, as gently as possible, that it just isn't on.'

'How did Marc Anstey feel about it?'

'I'm afraid I'm more concerned with my own feelings—and Polly's of course—than his.' Joanna sighed gloomily. 'We can't play happy families just because she wants us to. Besides,' she added bitterly. 'My experience of happy families isn't exactly extensive, is it, what with my defecting mother—and Paul.'

'Paul's dead now,' said Mary sharply. 'And you're much too young, Joanna, to turn your back on all possibility of a family of your own.' She leaned forward to pat Joanna's hand. 'I know your accident put paid to any more babies, but surely if you marry again you could adopt a child? Polly's a darling, but you can't devote your entire life to her. To be blunt, you could do with a man in your life. Some women function perfectly happily without the blighters, I know, but don't kid me you're one of them.'

Joanna smiled, filled with a sudden urge to confide. 'I'm not. I fancy Polly's arrangement like mad, if you must know, Mary.' She smiled wryly as Mary's brown eyes rounded in astonishment. 'If I followed my baser instincts I'd let Marc Anstey into my life, my bed, anywhere he cares to be. But with Polly to consider it's out of the question. Love affairs end. And if I had an affair with Marc who would be the one to suffer most when it was over? Polly! So I'm not going to let it start.'

When Marc arrived to collect Polly late on Friday afternoon Joanna was so determined to conceal her pleasure at seeing him that her greeting was glacial.

'Everything's packed and ready,' she said, while Polly hugged her tall uncle. 'Not having much idea of the climate on this island of yours, I've put in a selection of clothes. Plus a first-aid kit with various medications Polly might need.'

'It's a Greek island, Joanna, not the wilds of Borneo!'

'It's best to make sure. Can I give you tea, or coffee?'

'Thank you. Tea sounds good.' Marc, looking drawn and sombre as he sat down at the kitchen table, watched Polly playing with the dog while Joanna filled a kettle and clattered teacups on a tray. He looked up. 'You're very pale,' he commented.

'I've been burning the midnight oil to meet a deadline.'

Polly chimed in eagerly to tell Marc about the Snowbird stories. 'Jo tells them to me first,' she added importantly.

'I'd like to see one of them,' said Marc.

'Can I get some from the study, Jo?' demanded Polly, jumping to her feet in excitement.

'Of course.' Joanna poured tea with a steady hand then passed a dish of home-made strawberry jam for Marc to spread on scones still warm from the oven.

He ate and drank in silence for a moment, watching her abstractedly. 'You know, Joanna, the life I lead tends to make me forget that there are places like this, with people like you, who cook proper food and stop for tea, where life is a calm, pleasant affair instead of the rat-race I lead.'

'Before Polly came to live with me I never had tea,' she said, smiling a little. 'But now it's a ritual when we get back from school in the afternoon. Children get used to rituals *very* quickly,' she added with emphasis.

Marc stared at her moodily. 'Possibly. But I still don't see why the three of us couldn't go out together occasionally. Dammit, Joanna, Polly's old enough to understand that it doesn't have to mean a permanent arrangement——' He stopped dead. 'Sorry. Didn't mean to bore you with all that again. And don't worry. I'll take very good care of her. I can't promise afternoon tea on a Greek island, but I'll do my best otherwise——' He broke off as Polly returned, staggering under a pile of large, hardback picture books containing as many of the adventures of Snowbird as she could carry. 'Careful, *cara*, you'll do yourself a mischief—give them to me.'

With Polly hovering at his elbow Marc went through the pile of books, Joanna watching on tenterhooks as he skimmed through one after another without comment.

'I've seen these displayed in bookshops,' he said at last, looking up. 'I didn't know then, of course, that you were Joanna Swan. They're magical. I congratulate you. It's not often that something as artistic as these is so commercially viable.'

Joanna relaxed, concealing her intense pleasure at his praise.

'They're great fun to do, but after this batch Snowbird's going out to grass, I'm afraid. He's had quite a run, but it's over now.'

'Have you anything in mind to take his place?'

She nodded. 'I quite fancy trying my hand at an adult novel. I created Snowbird to get Saladin out of my system. As a kind of catharsis, I suppose. Now I feel ready to tackle something different.'

Marc glanced at Polly, who was gazing at Joanna, drinking in every word. 'Are you ready, *tesoro*? Nearly time to go.'

When Polly had skipped upstairs Marc turned back to Joanna. 'If your Snowbird books were a way of getting your horse out of your system, what's the motivation for your novel? Will that be based on experience, or complete fiction?'

'A combination of both, I imagine. Isn't that how most writers function? You're the journalist. You must know how it works.'

'I'm mainly a hard news man. I don't go much for fiction.' Marc got up, holding out his hand. 'Goodbye, then, Joanna.'

She looked at the outstretched hand, afraid to touch it in case the contact breached the wall of reserve she'd constructed so carefully against him.

Marc eyed her derisively as his hand fell to his side. 'I forgot. Touching's against the rules, of course.'

'Marc——' she began impulsively, moving towards him, then stopped as Polly came running into the kitchen.

'Ready!' she cried happily. She dropped on her knees to cuddle Sunny, planting kisses on his smooth gold head. 'Be a good boy for Jo, Sunny.' She jumped up and threw herself in Joanna's arms, hugging her tightly. 'I wish you were coming too.'

So did Joanna, the urge so sudden and overwhelming that she buried her face in Polly's curls, afraid Marc might tune in to it. 'I'll be here when you come back. Have fun, darling.' She smiled brightly at Marc. 'Enjoy your holiday.'

'I'll try.' He picked up Polly's luggage, his black eyes narrowed as they met Joanna's. 'Take it easy while we're away. You look very pale.'

She shrugged, smiling brightly. 'I'm fine, honestly.'

There were more hugs and kisses from Polly before Marc could get her in his car. Joanna waved them off, her face lint-white under the porch light as the car moved off down the drive, then went back into a house which suddenly felt very empty and still.

Joanna was grateful for Sunny's company when Polly had gone. The Lavenhams had taken advantage of half-term to spend most of the week with George's parents, leaving Joanna with Doris as her only contact with the outside world.

Joanna missed Polly more than she would have believed possible. In a few short weeks the child had invaded Swan House and Joanna's heart to such an extent that she felt like a lost soul with only herself for company. After two days of solitude Joanna was utterly delighted to receive a phone call from Chyros, but Marc managed only a word or two before Polly's excited voice was chattering in Joanna's ear about the flight and the boat to the island and the little white house right by the sea.

When Joanna put the phone down the house seemed lonelier than ever, deciding her to take Sunny for a walk into Swancote to buy stamps. In the post office stores Mrs Birkin the post-mistress

introduced Joanna to the doctor who'd rece
gone into partnership with Dr Penfold, the ma
who'd brought Joanna into the world. Roger Morley was very pleasant, large and fair with a reassuring air about him which appealed to Joanna very much.

'I hope you enjoy living in Swancote,' she said as he opened the door for her.

'I'm sure I shall,' he said, bending to pat Sunny's head as Joanna unfastened the leash from the railing outside. 'I'm glad of the chance to meet you, Mrs Clifford. I've just moved in to old Mr Reynolds' house just down the road from you. I'm your new neighbour.'

Joanna smiled warmly. 'So you're the mystery purchaser! The village jungle drums must be on the blink. I didn't know who bought it. Let me know if there's anything your wife needs. I'll call round when you're settled and introduce myself.'

Roger Morley looked a trifle embarrassed. 'Afraid I'm divorced. I live alone these days.' He smiled ruefully. 'Nevertheless I hope you and your husband will drop in for a drink one evening.'

'Actually, Dr Morley, I'm a widow. A fairly recent one,' Joanna added, to offset any hint of invitation he might have read into her statement. 'There's just me and my little ward, Polly, at Swan House. And Sunny, of course.' With a friendly smile she said goodbye and walked home briskly, pleased that her new neighbour was so pleasant.

Joanna renewed her onslaught on her work with determination, set on despatching the final Snowbird adventures to her editor as soon as possible. When Marc brought Polly back she intended to concentrate on the child. The new project could wait for a while. There was no financial problem now to provide a spur. She could afford to take it easy for a while, get herself thoroughly fit.

Joanna worked like a maniac for three days, breaking off only to let Sunny out into the garden now and then, and to take him for a longish walk each afternoon. She met Roger Morley more than once during these excursions, and stopped to chat for a minute or two, aware that he'd have lingered longer each time if given the least encouragement. He was lonely, Joanna knew. Moving into a new house alone had to be a rather depressing experience, with no one to see if he was hanging the pictures straight or how the furniture should be arranged. He was a very attractive man, she thought ruefully, wondering why her reaction to him was so negative compared with her response to Marc, who had only to come through the door for her hormones to start dancing a highland fling.

Two days before the holidaymakers were due to return Joanna packed up the finished manuscripts in triumph, walked with Sunny to the village to post them off, then did nothing much at all for the rest of the day. And that night she slept more soundly than she had for months, secure in the knowledge that her deadline had been met with time to spare, and that now all her attention could be focused on getting herself and the house in welcoming mood, ready for Marc's and Polly's return.

Joanna was ready hours before Marc was due to arrive with Polly. She'd baked Polly's favourite cake, helped Doris with the house, taken Sunny for a walk, until at last there was nothing left to do but wait. She knew she looked better than she had done in a long time. Deadline or not, the break on her own had done her good as Marc had forecast it would. Now her cold was finally a thing of the past her hair shone with a healthy gloss, and her skin glowed very satisfactorily against the apricot wool of her sweater. Joanna found it hard to fill the time until the appointed hour arrived. When the hour passed with no sign of Marc and Polly she switched on the television to check the teletext section which listed flight arrivals, horrified to find that their plane, far from crashing, had landed on time. Marc should have arrived with Polly long since. Joanna began pacing up and down like a caged tigress, frantic with worry, almost jumping out of her skin when the long-awaited ring of the telephone finally interrupted her.

She leapt across the room to seize the receiver. 'Marc?'

'Is this Mrs Joanna Clifford?' asked a crisp female voice.

Joanna sagged with disappointment. 'Yes.'

'Swanford General here, Casualty Department.'

Joanna went cold. 'Yes?' she said hoarsely.

'We have a Mr Marcantonio Anstey here.'

Marcantonio? thought Joanna, dazed.

'There was an accident on the bypass. Mr Anstey is only slightly hurt, but——'

'Polly?' said Joanna urgently. 'He had a little girl with him, Paola, his niece.'

'Don't worry, she's fine. Shaken, and very bewildered, of course, and crying for you, Mrs Clifford, but she was in the back of the car, asleep.

Mr Anstey suffered slight cuts and bruises, and possibly a mild concussion. He's not fit to drive. Can you come to fetch them? I gather they were due to arrive at your house some time ago.'

'I'll come at once,' said Joanna tersely. 'Thank you.'

Joanna shut Sunny in the kitchen, pulled on a jacket and ran outside to the garage. Blessing the fact that Swanford General was only ten miles away, she drove as fast as she dared, thankful the bypass was relatively quiet by this time. At the hospital she parked the car as near the Casualty entrance as possible, and raced inside, blind to the curious glances of people waiting for treatment. The woman at the reception desk looked up with a reassuring smile as Joanna gave her name.

'Ah, yes, Mrs Clifford. Mr Anstey's just having his wound stitched. Staff Nurse is with Polly in one of the offices.'

Joanna hurried after the receptionist to a small room where a pretty nurse was cuddling Polly on her lap. The child turned as the door opened, her tearful face lighting up like a lamp as she leapt from the nurse's knee into Joanna's outstretched arms, clinging to her like a limpet, burrowing her face into Joanna's neck. 'Marco's hurt,' she sobbed brokenly. 'Will he die, Jo?'

'Goodness me, no,' said the staff nurse calmly. 'Why would he do that? You're uncle's got a wee cut on his forehead and the doctor's making it better right this minute. He can go home with you soon.'

Joanna gave warm thanks to the nurse, who excused herself to go back to work. Joanna sat down with Polly on her lap, smiling down into the woebegone little face. 'Goodness, you're brown. Did you have a good time?'

Polly nodded, sniffing. 'But I wish you'd been there, Jo.'

Joanna hugged her, then put Polly away a little to cough suddenly. 'Sorry, poppet,' she gasped, surprised. 'I haven't coughed in ages.'

The staff nurse popped her head back round the door. 'Mr Anstey's ready, Mrs Clifford. One of the porters will come with you to the car.'

Joanna took Polly by the hand to follow the staff nurse along to one of the curtained cubicles where Marc sat waiting, the dressing on his forehead standing out starkly against a tanned face embellished with several minor cuts and a shiner of a black eye.

'Hello, Marc,' said Joanna, restraining Polly's desire to hurl herself at her uncle. 'Ready to go home?'

'Sorry about this, Joanna.' He smiled ruefully as he took Polly's hand. 'We were unlucky. Some maniac ran into the back of us while we were waiting to get off the bypass on to the Swanford roundabout. Polly woke up with a fright, and I shot against the windscreen. The belt prevented any serious damage, but my car's in a mess.'

'Never mind the car. You're both safe, which is all that matters.' She smiled at him. 'Let's go home.'

Joanna drove very slowly on the way back to Swancote, afraid Polly might be nervous after the recent trauma, but to her surprise Polly chattered like a magpie all the way, recounting the glories of the Greek holiday, and bewailing, several times, the fact that Jo hadn't been there. Marc made no effort to join in the conversation. His explanation at the hospital appeared to have exhausted his powers of speech.

'The nurse said you might feel drowsy,' warned Joanna when they arrived at Swan House. She steadied Marc as he got out of the car, unable to stifle a cough as the cold night air hit her chest.

Marc stood straight with an effort. 'Still coughing, I see.'

'I haven't been lately,' she said briskly. 'Probably a combination of this cold wind and the nasty shock you two gave me.' She grabbed at him. 'Steady! You're wavering all over the place. For heaven's sake forget your manly pride and lean on me, Marc. We'll go the back way, it's nearer. Here's the key, Polly. Can you unlock the door?'

Polly nodded eagerly, eventually managing to open the door at the third attempt. She gave a cry of joy as Sunny hurled himself towards her in tumultuous welcome, and Joanna left them to their ecstatic reunion to support Marc though the hall and into the drawing-room, where he collapsed in relief on the sofa, breathing hard.

'Hell, I'm sorry about this Joanna,' he panted. 'I knew you'd be off your head with worry, but there was no way I could get a message to you sooner.'

'Never mind. You're here now, not exactly in one piece, but it could have been a lot worse.' Joanna piled cushions behind him, then swung his feet up so that he was lying more comfortably. 'You stay quiet for a bit while I give Polly some supper.'

'She had a few bits and pieces on the plane.' He managed a smile. 'She's been so good, Joanna.'

'I'm sure she has. Have a nap. I'll feed Polly in the kitchen.'

Now Polly knew her beloved Marco wasn't about to join Mamma in heaven she ate quite a hearty supper. Grateful for the amazing resilience of the young, Joanna gave Polly a glass of milk, told her to say goodnight to Sunny, then took her to see Marc before going to bed.

His eyes opened as Polly approached on tiptoe, his smile tender as he held out his arms. Polly embraced him with exquisite care, asking anxiously if he was hurting.

'Only a little bit, *tesoro*. Off you go to bed. It's late. I'll see you in the morning.' Marc kissed her on both cheeks then patted her bottom. 'Be a good girl for Joanna.'

Polly looked indignant as she took Joanna's hand. 'O'course I will. 'Night, Marco.'

Joanna let Polly get away without a bath for once. Tonight it seemed more important to get the child tucked up in her bed and asleep than to fuss over whether she was clean or not. Afterwards, in her bedroom for some necessary repairs to her face, Joanna began coughing again. Crossly she decided it must be psychosomatic, and drank some water, then a spoonful of the linctus Doris had brought while the cold was in full force. But cough or not, a look in the mirror confirmed that her earlier glow was surprisingly undimmed by the trauma of the evening. Just to have Marc here in the house with her again seemed to have ignited a visible light inside her.

Joanna returned quietly to the drawing-room to find Marc deeply asleep, his face exhausted above the blood-stained white sweater. The dressing stood out, stark against his tan, the bruise around his eye darker already, giving him a raffish look Joanna found dangerously irresistible. Snatching back the hand which yearned to stroke his cheek, she tiptoed from the room to join Sunny in the kitchen. Not sure what sort of eating mood Marc would be in when he woke up, Joanna cut slices of ham, laid a tray, then collected the book she was reading and went back to the drawing-room to curl up in a chair until Marc woke.

In the warmth and peace of the familiar room reaction suddenly hit Joanna like a body blow. Limp as a rag doll, she leaned her head against the cushion, gazing at Marc's sleeping face as it dawned on her that he'd have to stay the night. Whatever his original intention had been, to drive back to London, or even spend the night at the Lamb and Flag, there was no question of his doing either now. Joanna closed her eyes, a shiver running through her as she thought of how much worse it could all have been. She sat erect, limp no longer, as it struck her that if Marc had been killed she would probably have spent the rest of her life regretting the way she'd kept him at arm's length. She closed her eyes and wriggled back down in the chair, giving way to fatigue which engulfed her so completely that she was soon as deeply asleep as her companion.

Joanna woke to a rough tongue licking her cheek, and shot upright in the chair, blinking up at Marc owlishly as she pushed Sunny away. She jumped to her feet guiltily.

'I must have dropped off. Is it late? I'm sorry——'

'Relax.' Marc grinned, looking a different man after his rest. 'I'd have let you sleep, but this chap was making a fuss in the kitchen, so I took him for a stroll outside. He got back in here to you before I could stop him.'

'A good thing he did!' Joanna pushed at her hair, self-conscious under his amused gaze. 'I'll get you something to eat.'

'Good,' he said cheerfully. 'I could eat a horse.'

Joanna eyed the clock in consternation. 'Heavens, it's past eleven! You must be starving. How do you feel?'

'My head's a bit sore, but I don't feel sick any more.' He smiled as he strolled after her to the kitchen. 'My skull's too thick to succumb to a little bump like that.'

Joanna grinned as she made sandwiches. 'You said that, not me! Sorry, by the way. These are ham, not horse.'

They sat together at the kitchen table, Marc making short work of the food as he gave Joanna a graphic account of the holiday, and how Polly had loved the little sugar-cube house on Chyros. But once Sunny was settled down for the night, and they were back in the drawing-room, the atmosphere altered abruptly.

Marc shot a sombre glance at Joanna as she handed him a cup of coffee. 'I'm sorry about tonight—giving you a shock like that. You took it very well, and I'm grateful.'

'The accident wasn't your fault. Thank heaven it was no worse.' She looked worried. 'But I hope it won't have a delayed-action effect on Polly. It's a wonder she set foot in the car again tonight, on top of what happened to Rosa.'

'Polly doesn't know about the car crash. Rosa died in hospital, so Polly believes her mother was just taken ill, and went to heaven. That's why she gets so uptight about illness in any form.' He shrugged wearily. 'Maybe I was wrong, but at the time it seemed best to keep the truth from her.'

'You were very definitely right,' said Joanna emphatically. 'Otherwise she wouldn't have been so good about coming home in the car tonight straight after the bump.'

'That's because you were driving. She doesn't associate danger or harm with you, Joanna.' His eyes moved over her face broodingly. 'I can't say I feel the same way.'

There was a sudden, fraught silence.

'What do you mean?' asked Joanna at last.

'Don't pretend, Joanna. You know you've been a danger to my peace of mind from the moment I first set eyes on you.' He went on looking at her, until Joanna kept from fidgeting only by sheer strength of will.

'The spare bed is made up,' she said in a strained voice.

One of Marc's slim black eyebrows rose mockingly. 'You mean you're actually allowing me to sleep beneath your roof?'

'What do you expect me to do?' she demanded angrily. 'Turn you out in the snow?'

Marc smiled sardonically. 'You'd probably like to.'

'I wouldn't turn anyone out in your particular state of health,' she said sharply, and got to her feet. 'I'm sure you're tired. If you can manage to carry your bag up I'll show you where you're to sleep.'

'If necessary,' said Marc silkily as he hefted his hold-all, 'I could carry you upstairs as well as the bag, concussion or no concussion, but don't be nervous. I shan't make the attempt.'

Joanna gave him a kindling look, then stalked out of the room ahead of him, slowing down as she mounted the stairs for fear of waking Polly. Marc followed close behind, pausing beside her as they looked in on Polly who lay, arms outflung in total abandon, so deeply asleep that a regiment of soldiers could have marched along the landing without waking her.

'She's worn out,' Joanna whispered as she showed Marc to the spare room.

Marc put down his bag at the end of the bed, then turned to face her. 'Thank you, Joanna, for everything. I truly appreciate your coming to rescue us tonight. I'm sorry I needled you just now. Lord knows you've had a lot to contend with from me and mine lately. You were a wonder tonight.'

Joanna shrugged as she went to the door. 'I just did what anyone else would have done. I hope you sleep well. Goodnight.'

'Goodnight.' He smiled, looking dark and alien, his villainous black eye incongruous against the faded chintz of the Swan House guest-room.

Sure she'd lie awake all night, Joanna fell asleep almost at once, even though Marc lay only a few feet away on the other side of her bedroom wall. But as the temperature dropped in the night her room grew cold and her cough returned to plague her. She woke herself violently at last and shot up in bed, gasping for breath. She switched on her lamp, then stared, her eyes dilating, as Marc slid silently into the room and closed the door behind him.

'Medicine?' he whispered.

Joanna, hand clapped to her mouth, pointed speechlessly to the bottle on the bedside table. Marc measured a dose into the plastic cup beside it then stood over her while she swallowed the linctus down. She tried to smile her thanks, flustered suddenly because his short robe revealed so much long brown leg.

He looked at her questioningly. 'All right, Joanna?'

She nodded wordlessly.

'I've looked in on Polly. She's still out for the count.'

'Thank you.' Joanna swallowed, her eyes on a level with Marc's bronzed chest, her pulse racing as she saw he was breathing unevenly. Slowly, like someone hypnotised, she raised her blank blue eyes to his, and they stared at each other, spellbound, Joanna motionless against the pillows, Marc rooted to the spot. Then Marc let out a great unsteady sigh. As though some giant fist had pushed him from behind he dropped on his knees beside the bed and pulled her into his arms, kissing her like a man at the end of his tether.

Joanna yielded to him without reservation, rejoicing. To feel Marc's lips against hers, the warmth of his lean body, was sheer heaven after the agony, however brief, of believing he'd been killed. She would have told him so if her mouth hadn't been so ravishingly otherwise employed. It seemed so much more important to pull him closer, to welcome him into her bed, than talk. Then Joanna forgot Polly, forgot everything, as a tidal wave of sheer need submerged them both the instant their bodies came into contact. Every nerve in her system leapt in response to Marc's urgency, gloriously in tune with his consuming urge to celebrate life after his brush with danger. He raised his head, his eyes glittering with a question Joanna answered without words, her smile radiant with shared delight.

'I always knew,' he whispered victoriously, as his hands slid in a lazy, lingering caress down her hips. 'Right from the first, I *knew*.'

'Knew what?' She shivered, her eyelids suddenly heavy.

'How it would be for us.' His kisses grew ravenous, his hands moving over her in triumphant possession as his fingertips blazed a trail of fire over her breasts and hips and thighs. But even as his caresses grew wilder Joanna knew, beyond all doubt, that he was deliberately withholding the moment of union until her desire was as great as his.

Nothing in Joanna's experience had prepared her for such bliss. Having been married to a man too concerned with his own pleasure to care much about hers, she now responded in astonished delight to Marc's slightest touch, returning his kisses with an ardour which tested his control to the limit. Her body moved restlessly beneath his, her fingers knotting in the damp curls on his chest, digging into the skin sheathing his shoulder muscles until at last, tantalised beyond bearing, she resorted to a caress so intimate that he was vanquished.

'Diletta mia,' he groaned. The breath left Joanna's body as they came together in a long, sustained assault on the senses, and Marc let out a great, shuddering sigh, burying his face against her throat as their bodies united in a fierce, rhythmic quest for fulfilment.

Joanna came back to earth to the touch of Marc's mouth on her damp eyelids, of his hands stroking her back as he held her against him, whispering gratifying things in her ear instead of flopping over on his back and falling asleep, as Paul had always done.

'How do you feel?' she murmured drowsily.

He laughed, rippling a fingertip down her spine. 'How do you think I feel, woman? Amazed, ecstatic——'

'I *meant*,' said Joanna, pulling away slightly, 'how's your head?'

Marc put up a hand to his forehead in surprise. 'Now you come to mention it, it's throbbing a bit. One way and another I forgot about it before.' He grinned. 'How's your cough?'

She buried her face against his shoulder to stifle her laughter. 'Conspicuous by its absence.'

Marc stuck an ungentle finger under her chin. 'Have you missed me?' he demanded.

'Not in the least,' she lied, giving him a feline little smile. 'In fact I've been seeing quite a lot of Roger.'

His eyes narrowed. 'Who the hell's Roger?'

'The new doctor here, Roger Morley. He's charming.'

'Has he taken you out?'

'No,' she admitted. 'I just meet him now and then when I'm walking Sunny.'

Marc shook her slightly. 'Enjoy making me fry, don't you?'

'Were you frying?'

'You know I was.' He kissed her savagely, his hands sliding round to cup her breasts, 'I'm jealous of any man allowed in your vicinity, if you want the naked truth, Joanna Swan. I may be a civilised Brit on the surface, but scratch it and you soon get down to my Sicilian ancestry.' He bent his head to take a sharply pointing nipple between his lips, the ensuing sensation so exquisite that Joanna forgot her tart rejoinder, bowled over by the astonishing discovery that, far from being a one-off, her experience of love at Marc Anstey's clever hands was not only about to be repeated, but surpassed.

'Well, that's that, I suppose,' she sighed eventually, when they lay at rest at last in each other's arms.

'That's what?'

'Well, if you'd made love to me once I could have passed it off to myself as an accident. Circumstances beyond my control and all that. But twice in a row...' She shook her head, smiling at him.

He propped himself up on an elbow to look down at her. 'Will you believe that much as I wanted you I'd have stopped if you'd called a halt at any stage?'

'Oh, I know that. I suppose, in a way, that's why it happened. I never felt threatened.' She smiled demurely. 'I could tell you wanted me, of course——'

'Full marks for observation!'

Joanna grinned. 'But at the same time I knew you'd never use force to get your wicked way.'

Marc smoothed her hair back from her flushed face. 'Forcing a woman is not my style, *carissima*.' He smiled crookedly. 'Not, I feel obliged to point out, that it's ever been necessary.'

She gave him a dig in the ribs. 'Bighead!'

'Why *did* you let me make love to you, Joanna?' he asked, suddenly very serious. 'What changed your mind?'

Joanna's eyes burned darkly blue with candour. 'When the hospital phoned I thought you'd been killed.'

'The police would have come to tell you that.'

'I know that—who better? But don't forget I'd been worried sick for ages before I heard from the hospital. In the second before I knew what happened——' She shuddered, and he pulled her close.

'I was a coward before, you see,' she went on huskily after a while. 'That's why I sent you away. I was attracted to you so quickly, so—so violently, that the rapport between us scared me to death. I'd never felt like that in my life. I thought it was too sudden, too soon. If only you and I'd been involved it would have been different, but I was afraid of it, sure that if we became lovers it would burn itself out and then Polly would be hurt. So I pushed you away, and you stayed away and I tried to tell myself it was for the best.'

Marc let out a long, unsteady breath. 'Joanna, I want to know exactly how you felt when you thought I was dead.'

'It was only then,' she began, taking her courage in both hands, 'that I learned how I should have felt when Paul was killed. And didn't.'

His arms tightened convulsively. 'Then why were you so hellish distant tonight? You were fine during supper, but afterwards down came the shutters again, closing me out. Oh, no, you don't,' Marc added, holding her fast when she tried to free herself.

'It suddenly occurred to me that you might not be interested any more,' she murmured awkwardly. 'I got cold feet.'

'Are they cold now?'

'No.'

'I should hope not.' Marc held her face cupped in his hands, forcing her to meet his eyes. 'Listen, Joanna Swan. What happened between us just now was just one part—a very wonderful part—of a great many things I feel for you. Of course I *want* you, but I care for you, too. I want to make you happy, make sure you're never hurt again.' He smiled, the light in his eyes melting her utterly. 'Now tell me how you feel about me.'

'Isn't it obvious?' she said crossly. 'Otherwise, Marc Anstey, I would have sent you packing the minute I'd swallowed my medicine.'

Marc's eyes glittered in triumph. 'Does this mean you've changed your mind? About the three of us living together and making Polly's dream come true?'

'Yes.' She smiled, stretching luxuriously. 'Only it'll have to be a weekend arrangement, as far as you're concerned.'

'I'll settle for that,' he said, smoothing back her hair. 'Most people in my sort of job sweat it out alone in London during the week and go home to the country for weekends with the family.' He grinned. 'You realise your main attraction is this house, of course! Saves me a lot of expense. I'm only sorry I shan't have as much time to spend here as I'd like until I get to grips with the new job.' He kissed her lingeringly, then swung his long legs out of bed and sat up, pulling on his robe. 'Besides, you'd prefer a reasonable time to elapse, I suppose.'

Joanna sat up, pulling the covers up to her chin. 'Reasonable time?' she said blankly.

Marc pushed back his dishevelled hair, wincing as he made contact with his wound. 'You've never pretended to feel like a widow where Paul Clifford's concerned, I know. Nevertheless you can't get away from the fact that he's only been dead for a short time. You're so well known in Swancote that it's only natural you'll want to wait for a while before we actually get married.'

Joanna stared at him in utter dismay. 'Married?'

He frowned at her as he tied the belt around his spare waist. 'Yes. Married.'

'But—but, Marc, we don't have to get *married*!'

His face darkened, one eyebrow lifting ominously. 'Why the hell not?'

'I don't know that I can go through all that a second time. I've done it before, remember, including the "death us do part" bit.' Joanna clasped her hand round her knees above the quilt, gazing at his set face in entreaty. 'Look, Marc, I didn't like being married the first time. Don't let's spoil everything with red tape and legality. Can't we just live together, as Polly wants? No strings, no rules, just being together as much as we can, whenever we can. And because we want to be, not just because a piece of paper entitles us to the privilege!'

Marc's black brows flew together, his eyes cold with disbelief. 'Let me get this straight. Are you telling me you can't face marriage with me?'

Joanna shook her head violently. 'No, of course I'm not. But these days it isn't necessary. In fact,' she pointed out, 'you were the one who referred to it as something to evade!'

'True.' His lips twisted in the parody of a smile. 'Like your late, unlamented husband, I'm a Catholic. For me it must be for life. Until now I'd never found someone I *wanted* for life. I'm paying you the highest compliment a man can give a woman, Joanna.'

Joanna gazed at him beseechingly. 'I know, and I'm deeply honoured, believe me. But I can't, Marc. It wouldn't be fair.'

He sat down on the side of the bed, taking her by the shoulders. 'Fair! What the hell do you mean? I don't think it happens to be *fair* for you to profess some kind of feeling for me one minute, then turn me down the next.' He shook her slightly, his eyes spearing hers. 'Joanna. Are you telling me, in a roundabout way, that you don't want me on a permanent basis?'

She shook her head violently. 'Of course I'm not! When I thought you'd been killed I wanted to die too.'

His eyes glittered in triumph, then dulled. 'If you feel like that, why the hell *won't* you marry me?' he demanded violently.

Joanna gazed at him in entreaty. 'Surely you can see why.'

'No. I can't.' He pulled her into his arms and began to kiss her savagely, but when she forced herself to stay limp in his arms he let them fall and stood up. 'Tell me, then,' he said in a voice so dead Joanna shut her eyes tightly in anguish for a moment.

When she opened them the baffled pain on Marc's face almost tempted her to throw herself into his arms and tell him she'd do anything in the world he wanted, just so they could revert to the happiness they'd shared such a short time before. She resisted the impulse, her eyes bright with unshed tears.

'There's something you've forgotten, Marc. I can't give you children—no, hear me out,' she said firmly as he made a move towards her. 'I know we've got Polly, but you'd never be able to have a child of your own.'

Marc hesitated a split second then said roughly, 'That's nonsense. If I can have you—and Polly—that's all I ask.'

Joanna gazed at him in misery. 'You think that now, but one day you could change your mind, find someone able to give you the children I can't, just as Paul did. But he had to remain tied to me—and I to him. I just couldn't bear that a second time.'

Marc seemed to withdraw into himself, turning into a grim, forbidding stranger right before her eyes. 'I suppose there's no point in trying to convince you that it wouldn't happen a second time?' He gave a short, mirthless laugh. 'Obviously not. I realise now why I've never proposed to anyone before. Rejection's bloody hard to take.'

'Oh, Marc, don't! I'm not rejecting *you*. Why can't we just——?'

'Share bed and board on weekends?' he put in bitingly. 'No way. I'm not some tame stud, Joanna. If you don't fancy marriage, fair enough, that's your choice. But as far as I'm concerned it's the only thing on offer. My aim was to share the rest of my life with you, not just a bed now and then.' Marc glanced at his watch. 'I'd better get back to your spare room. Under the circumstances it would never do for Polly to discover me in yours. She'd assume her plan was in full working order, poor little scrap. Goodnight, Joanna—or good morning, I suppose. It's nearly dawn.'

Tears streamed down Joanna's face as he crossed the room. She saw his slim brown hand clench on the white porcelain of the doorknob as he waited to give her time to call him back. When she said nothing he went from the room as quietly as he'd arrived, leaving her alone with her tears, but drearily certain she was right. A man had a right to a family of his own. She could never give Marc a child. And she loved him too much to tie him down to a relationship which might turn into a prison once the first flush of physical attraction died away. As inevitably it would. Paul had taught her that particular lesson all too well.

CHAPTER EIGHT

AFTER A whole week with her beloved Marco in the Greek sunshine Polly was philosophical about his subsequent absence from Swan House. He'd told her, she explained to Joanna, that his new job would keep him very busy for a while. Not even his departure early on the morning after their dramatic return troubled Polly too much. She accepted his explanation at breakfast that he had to return to London by train because his car was being mended, and in her pleasure at playing with Sunny failed to register the constraint between Joanna and Marc over a breakfast neither ate. The arrival of a taxi soon afterwards came as a profound relief Marc only too plainly shared with Joanna. Looking strained, his bruised face colourless beneath its tan, he reiterated formal thanks for her help as he said goodbye.

Joanna forced herself to smile as she repudiated the least need for thanks. 'It was nothing.'

'I'm glad you think so. It was a great deal more than that to me.' He smiled mockingly as colour rose in her face. 'Goodbye, Joanna. Take care of that cough.'

'Goodbye.' Joanna stood at the door, watching as Polly skipped alongside Marc towards the car, held up her arms to be hugged, then blew kisses to her uncle as the taxi bore him away.

* * *

Not for the first time Joanna was obliged to pick up the pieces of a life which had fallen apart. She should, she thought with irony, be expert at it by now.

Years before, when her father was terminally ill, the discovery that very little money went with the legacy of Swan House had been a blow. But Joanna had promised her dying father faithfully that somehow she would find a way to keep the house in the family, and if possible hand it down to her children. She'd been working as a secretary to a merchant banker at the time. After graduating she'd failed to find a post which made use of her art history degree, and in desperation had enrolled on a secretarial course which had landed her a job in the City. The work was never more to her than a means to earn money until she found something more to her taste, but she had enjoyed sharing a flat with two other girls, and had led a fairly hectic social life, met a lot of men, and eventually taken to seeing one of them on a regular basis. When her father had died she'd been shattered, not only by grief, but by the burden of the promise she'd made. Edward, her escort, had defected when Joanna proved poor company in her grief, and in despair at breaking her promise she had been on the point of putting Swan House up for sale when she'd met Paul Clifford.

A self-assured, handsome man in his middle forties, or the prime of life in his own phrase, Paul had taken an immediate fancy to the attractive secretary of the man he'd come to consult. Joanna, smarting from Edward's treatment, had warmed to the mature, self-assured businessman, and accepted his invitations to dinner, and, as she got to know him better, confided her problems about Swan House. Once Paul Clifford learned she was on the point of selling a country house which had been in her family for two hundred years he had acted swiftly, using steamroller tactics to get his own way. He'd bought Swan House and made it over to Joanna on condition that she married him, gave up her job, and set about providing him with a family in the type of home the ambitious boy from the East End had wanted all his life.

During the afternoon walk with Polly and the dog later, Joanna marvelled at the naïveté of the girl who'd mistaken her gratitude to Paul Clifford for love. Now she'd met Marc Anstey she knew, at last, exactly what a lasting adult love should be, what her life still could be, if she could only bring Marc round to her point of view.

'Are you sad, Jo?' asked Polly anxiously.

'No, darling, of course not! How could I be sad when you've come home to me?' Joanna smiled brightly, blowing her nose. 'This wind is making my eyes run, that's all.'

'Marco said to look after you,' Polly said importantly. 'Let's go home. Here, Sunny. *Good* boy!'

Mary Lavenham, a lady of discernment where Joanna was concerned, raised her eyebrows when she heard Joanna had embarked on a novel. 'I thought you might have had a rest once you finished off the Snowbird books.'

'I need occupation,' said Joanna firmly.

It was Mary's opinion that Joanna should go out more and meet people. There was Roger Morley for a start, charming, unattached——

'And very, very nice, but that's all, so stop matchmaking,' said Joanna, chuckling.

'That's better. You don't smile much lately.' Mary hesitated. 'This Marc Anstey—has he upset you, love?'

'The boot, dear heart, is on the other foot. I upset him.'

'Irrevocably?'

'Utterly.'

'No resumption of diplomatic relations? Ever, I mean?'

'"Nevermore," quoth the raven."' Joanna accepted another cup of Mary's tea. 'So let's not talk about it.'

Mary dropped the subject obediently, suggesting instead that it would be excellent therapy if Joanna both wrote the script and used her artistic talent to paint the scenery for the school nativity play, ideas which appealed to Joanna very much. When Marc made his weekly telephone call to speak to Polly Joanna requested the formality of his approval regarding his niece's inclusion in the cast as a shepherd.

'Not the starring role? I'm surprised,' said Marc drily, sounding less formal than he normally did of late.

'Ah, but playing a shepherd involves a crook and toy lambs borrowed from the local craft shop!' Joanna informed him. 'It was something of a departure to cast a girl as a shepherd, of course, but because the Lavenham twins form the rest of the trio a point was stretched.'

Marc laughed. 'If Polly's tales about those lads are true I pity the producer of the play.'

'She's a jolly, competent sort of girl. Besides, Mary Lavenham's warned the twins that Father Christmas will cross them off his list if they misbehave.' Joanna hesitated. 'While we're on the subject, Marc,' she said diffidently, 'what shall I tell Polly you're doing at Christmas? You're very welcome to spend it here, of course.' She waited, tense, as Marc took his time to answer.

'That's very good of you,' he said at last. 'But even for Polly I don't think I could endure a jolly family Christmas the way things are. It would only emphasise all too bloody painfully what we're both missing because you refuse to marry me, Joanna.'

'It's not my fault!' she snapped. 'I can't help it if you're bristling with high-flown scruples.'

'Hell and damnation, Joanna——' He stopped, breathing in sharply. 'It was like a kick in the teeth to have you turn me down after—after what happened between us.'

Joanna fought for calm, shattered by his unexpected descent into the personal. 'I'm sorry. But you know exactly why I refused.'

'I take it you haven't changed your mind,' he said grimly.

'Have you?'

'No, I have not.'

'Then it's checkmate.' She sighed. 'Forget it, Marc. What do I tell Polly about Christmas?'

'Nothing. I'll tell her myself next Sunday when I take her out for the day.'

At first Joanna had looked forward to seeing Marc when he collected Polly for the weekly outing, but he very quickly disabused her of any pipe dream about talking him round to her way of thinking. He quite simply gave her no opportunity to talk to him at all. Joanna's sole contact with him was a moment or two when he collected Polly, and another brief encounter when he brought her back.

At first Joanna was devastated. She'd been convinced that meeting Marc face to face would be sure to weaken his resolve. When she found she was very much mistaken she took her cue from Marc and answered his greetings with polite enquiries about his progress in the new job, then retreated into the house with Sunny to avoid looking wistful as the car took her loved ones away.

Once the script was written and the scenery finished for the nativity play, Joanna felt eager to get to grips with the novel she'd had simmering in her brain for months. Polly's arrival in her life had meant consigning the novel to a back burner in her mind for a while, but now Polly was settled Joanna decided nothing was going to stop her getting down to work again. Work which might, if she were lucky, help her to get used to the fact that Marc was never going to change his mind about their relationship.

It was mid-December when Joanna first became aware of a marked lack of enthusiasm for sitting down at her typewriter each day.

'I'm getting lazy, Doris,' she sighed, making a pot of tea instead of starting work as soon as she returned from the morning walk to school with Polly and the dog.

'I wouldn't say that, Mrs Clifford,' said Doris, setting out cups. 'Mrs Lavenham thinks you're working much too hard over your new book.'

'I know!' Joanna shook her head, amused. 'Quite funny coming from a busy clergyman's wife who never has a minute to herself. As we speak she's probably running up the costumes for the play with one hand and making cakes for the Mother's Union tea with the other. I don't know where she gets the energy.'

Joanna's Christmas dilemma had eventually been solved by an invitation from the Lavenhams to join them for the festive meal at the Rectory, along with George's parents and a couple of Mary's elderly relatives.

Marc, when Joanna informed him of the arrangement, asked if he might visit Polly on Christmas Eve to deliver her presents.

'I can hardly absent myself altogether, nor do I want to. On the other hand maybe it's just as well I'm not around for her first Christmas Day without Rosa,' he said sombrely. 'That way she won't have anything to remind her of previous years.'

Joanna's previous years had entailed a skiing trip for the festivities. Surrounded by other people in a smart, impersonal hotel, she and Paul had managed to rub through it without too much friction, while at the same time neatly relieving Paul Clifford of a family Christmas with either wife or mistress.

'Whatever you think best,' she said serenely. 'By all means come down on Christmas Eve.' She hesitated, then before she could think better of it suggested he come to lunch. 'Unless you prefer to take Polly out, of course.'

There was a pause. 'Thank you. I eat so many restaurant meals I'd appreciate some home cooking. But please don't go to any trouble,' he added distantly.

'Oh, I won't,' Joanna assured him. 'Polly and I have to eat lunch, anyway.'

Joanna, obliged to sandwich Christmas shopping in between her writing while Polly was in school, did her best to throw off a growing feeling of malaise, but with no success. She felt irritable with herself. For years she'd suffered nothing worse than an odd cold, yet since Paul's death she'd been nothing like her usual healthy self. Worried she might be sickening for something dangerous to Polly, Joanna was driven at last to seek professional help. After two consecutive visits to Roger Morley, who was taking over more and more of Dr Penfold's patients, she returned home, dazed, feeling worse than ever. She clipped on Sunny's lead and took him for a walk to the Rectory, where Mary took one startled look and led Joanna to a chair at the kitchen table before reaching for the coffee.

'No coffee, thanks,' said Joanna. 'These days I can only manage tea!'

Mary's bright eyes widened as she changed course for the tea caddy. 'Tummy upset?'

Joanna gave a hollow laugh. 'You could say that. I've just been talking to Roger Morley.'

'Good! I told you to encourage him a bit.'

'The visit wasn't social, Mary. I haven't been feeling too good for quite a while. I thought I'd better see about it in case I had something Polly might catch.'

Mary stiffened. She slammed the lid of the teapot and went over to Joanna, putting an arm round her shoulders. 'What's the verdict?'

'If I tell you will you keep it to yourself? Even from George?'

Mary looked terrified. 'Oh, good heavens, love, what's wrong with you?'

'I'm pregnant,' said Joanna, and burst into tears.

'Is that all?' Mary held her close, laughing with relief.

'Aren't you listening?' wailed Joanna. 'I'm going to have a baby.'

'Well, yes, Jo. I know what pregnant means...' Mary's eyes widened suddenly. 'Oh, glory. But I thought you couldn't——'

'So did I,' said Joanna bitterly. 'But it seems I can, after all.'

Mary handed her a sheet of kitchen paper. 'Mop yourself up while I pour. Or shall I raid George's sherry decanter?'

Joanna shuddered. 'No! Tea, please.'

Mary filled two mugs with a brew strong enough to melt the spoon, then looked Joanna over assessingly. 'You don't look very pregnant. Poor Paul. He'd have been so pleased——'

'I doubt it. It doesn't show yet because the baby's not his.'

Mary choked on her tea. 'Oops!' She eyed Joanna warily. 'Who?'

'Marc Anstey.' Joanna beat an impotent fist on the kitchen table, badly startling the dog. 'It was the night of the accident. Neither of us meant it to happen. It—it just did. But even if I'd deliberately set out to seduce him I wouldn't have given a thought to any consequences. Oh, Mary, what on earth am I going to do?'

'I don't see your problem. Just tell the man.'

'If I do he'll insist on marrying me.'

'I should jolly well hope so!'

'It's not as simple as that, Mary. He did ask me, and I turned him down flat because I thought I *couldn't* give him a child.' Joanna heaved a despondent sigh. 'I suggested we just, well, cohabited, but he wouldn't hear of it. Anyway, I can't just do a complete U-turn now and say, "Hi, Marc, guess what? Problem solved. I'm pregnant." He might have changed his mind.'

Joanna went home soon afterwards, turning off to walk in the woods with the dog before returning to Swan House. It was such a silly situation to be in, she thought angrily. She'd sent Marc packing because she couldn't have his child, yet the words would stick in her throat if she tried to tell him that Dr Penfold had been wrong all those years ago. The diagnosis had never been put to the test for the simple reason that once Paul had been told there was no possibility of further children he couldn't bring himself to touch her. Besides, it was more than possible that Marc no longer cared for her in that way any more. Men changed. She knew that better than anyone. On the other hand if she told him she was pregnant Marc's principles might force him to offer marriage whether he still wanted it or not. And that would be worse than anything.

Joanna ground her teeth impotently. If she'd known there was the remotest possibility of getting pregnant she'd never have let Marc near her that night. She whistled to the dog, then smiled bitterly.

Who was she trying to kid? That night she'd given no thought to anything other than the joy of being in Marc's arms.

Joanna strode back to the house in a mood so black that she found it impossible to work on her novel when she got home. The problems of her mythical characters paled into such insignificance beside her own that she flung away from the typewriter in the end and went off to the kitchen to make a cake for Polly's tea. One thing was certain, she thought, as she whipped eggs viciously. Marc would know, sooner or later, whether she told him or not. So would Polly, not to mention the entire population of Swancote. There was no hope of disguising the fact that Joanna Swan's child would appear in the world a sight too long after her husband's death to be his.

That night Joanna lay on a sofa in the drawing-room once Polly was in bed, too listless to do anything other than stare at the television. Very little of the evening's programme registered, and, once she realised the credits were rolling on a play she'd been pretending to watch, Joanna got up to let Sunny out before bedtime. She stopped dead halfway to the door as the announcer on *Newsnight* informed her that later there would be an interview with the new foreign editor of the *Citadel*. Marc Anstey, Washington-based until recently, would give his opinion on the latest governmental crisis brewing in the White House.

Joanna rushed the dog out to the kitchen and let him out in the garden, then switched on the small portable on the kitchen counter, her eyes glued to the screen. When the camera finally focused on

Marc's face she slumped down on a kitchen stool, elbows on the counter, her face propped in her hands as she looked on the face of the man she loved. She listened to the familiar gravelly tones of his voice, deeply impressed by the assurance and quiet authority he brought to the discussion on current US affairs. As time went on Joanna grew more and more depressed. Seeing Marc on screen like this, self-contained and elegant, his views listened to with obvious respect by the presenter, was a bittersweet experience. She was totally unprepared for her reaction to this informed, lucid stranger. Until now Marc Anstey had merely been Polly's uncle, Rosa's brother, even, briefly, her own lover. Now, watching him on the screen, it was impossible to see him as anything other than foreign editor of a national newspaper, a formidable, rather glamorous stranger far remote from Joanna Swan and her embarrassing little problem.

The rest of the time until Christmas flew by at much too swift a rate for Joanna. Polly, excited by school Yuletide preparations, was harder to handle than usual, and loud in her lamentations when she learned her darling Marco was not only unable to witness her performance in the school play, but too busy to see her at all until Christmas Eve.

'Try to make her understand, Joanna,' said Marc, when he made a second phone call later that evening to explain why he'd upset Polly so badly earlier. 'I can't make it again this Sunday because I've finally set up a meeting with a certain foreign diplomat the *Citadel*'s been after for months. The man refuses to talk to anyone but me. I can't pass up the chance of an exclusive for the paper.'

'Of course not,' agreed Joanna. 'When she's calmed down a bit I'll have a chat with her, tell her I'll take photographs at the play so you can see her with her crook.'

'Thank you, Joanna. I'm very grateful.'

'Not at all,' she returned politely. 'Congratulations, by the way. I saw you on *Newsnight*. Very impressive.'

'Thank you. One of the aspects of the job I like least.' He yawned suddenly. 'Sorry. I've only just got home. No working dinner with anyone tonight, praise be. I yearn for an early night.'

Joanna's eyebrows rose. 'It's gone nine. You work a long day.'

'Honesty forces me to admit I don't actually get to my office until mid-morning these days, ready for the morning conference at eleven.'

'Perks of the new job?'

'In a way. But don't get me wrong. I still get up at the crack of dawn to listen to Radio Four, and get through all the morning papers before I drive to work.'

'Sounds gruelling. Are you settling in well in the new flat?'

'It's chaos at the moment; the painters are still in. But I like being nearer to the job.' There was a pause. 'How's your novel coming along, Joanna?'

'Fairly well,' she lied, reluctant to tell him that she was suffering from severe writer's block due to circumstances beyond her control. 'Right. I'll do my best to put Polly in the picture. See you on Christmas Eve, then—unless some story breaks to keep you away, of course,' she added.

'I'll be there,' he said curtly. 'Goodbye, Joanna.'

End of term arrived, and with it the performance of the nativity play, which Joanna watched, smiling widely despite the lump in her throat, as Polly entered stage-left with the twins, beaming. Joanna dodged about, in company with several proud parents, taking photographs during the performance, then presided over a celebration tea-party afterwards at Swan House, with Mary on hand to help with the tearing spirits of the three shepherds.

Once school term was over Joanna occupied Polly with preparations for Christmas, taking her to the local forestry commission centre to buy a newly felled tree, and letting her help with the decorations when the tall tree was installed in a corner of the drawing-room. Joanna kept Polly busy by enlisting her help with every Christmas task possible for the child, who was in a high state of excitement as she wrapped presents for the Lavenhams and Doris and her beloved uncle.

Joanna had taken her to Oxford to shop the previous Saturday, and the result, a dark red cashmere scarf with a famous designer's signature on it, was being wrapped lavishly in shiny gilt paper printed with scarlet robins. 'Will Marco like it?' asked Polly anxiously, as she stuck a large red ribbon bow to the finished parcel.

'He'll love it,' Joanna assured her.

By noon of Christmas Eve Joanna's state of tension was only slightly less than Polly's. The tree was ablaze with lights, the table in the dining room festive with scarlet napkins and glittering Christmas crackers, a holly arrangement in the centre of the snowy white cloth. Wonderful smells filled the air in the kitchen, where a fillet of [illegible] [illegible] [illegible]earing perfection in the oven, surrounded by roasting potatoes. A pan of fragrant tomato and basil soup sat on the stove, ready to decant into dishes for the first course, and in the refrigerator Polly's favourite lemon soufflé waited to round off a menu Joanna had chosen with care to appeal to a palate used to the sophisticated offerings of London restaurants.

When Marc arrived, at twelve-fifteen to the minute, as promised, Joanna hung back while he fended off the dog as he scooped up an excited Polly, swinging her round a couple of times as he always did. He set her on her feet then came towards Joanna, his smile guarded.

'Hello, Joanna.'

'Hello, Marc.' She took his proffered hand briefly, then led the way into the house. 'Is it too soon to say Merry Christmas?'

'Of course not. Merry Christmas to you both.' He stood in the centre of the hall, smiling, looking so attractive to Joanna that she felt shy.

Which was ridiculous, she told herself, all things considered. Polly danced round him in a fever of excitement, encapsulating all the news of the past few weeks into one incoherent monologue which ended only when he hugged the breath out of her, then swung her up in his arms under the mistletoe hanging from the hall light and kissed her on each scarlet cheek.

Polly slid to the ground, pushing Joanna forward. 'Now Jo, Marco.'

For a moment Joanna was sorely tempted to turn tail and run, but the mockery in Marc's gleaming black eyes put her on her mettle. She moved under the mistletoe and held up her cheek, closing eyes which flew open again in astonishment when Marc took her in his arms and kissed her hard on the mouth.'

'Merry Christmas once more,' he said softly, releasing her.

'I—I must see to the lunch,' said Joanna, backing away, her cheeks rivalling Polly's.

'Let's take Sunny for a run in the garden, Polly. You can help me get some things out of the car,' said Marc, a look of victory about him which sent Joanna off to the kitchen, routed.

The meal was a great success. Joanna's initial awkwardness soon wore off in the face of Marc's obvious effort to make the occasion a happy one for Polly. He was complimentary about the food, and the wine Joanna had chosen, wore his paper pirate's hat with panache and looked so much at home at the head of the table that Joanna began to wonder what on earth had possessed her to refuse his proposal. If she hadn't been so stubborn, her present problem would be no problem at all.

'That's a very pensive look,' said Marc quietly, when Polly was in the kitchen giving Sunny leftovers from the meal.

'Was it?' Joanna smiled brightly. 'I didn't mean to put a damper on things.'

'You couldn't.' Marc smiled, making her heart turn over. 'I wanted you to know I'm grateful for the way you've made Polly so happy, Joanna. I was worried about Christmas—afraid it might revive memories she'd find painful.'

'There've been one or two bad patches,' she admitted in an undertone. 'She asked me if her mother would have Christmas in heaven.'

'Bloody hell!'

'Quite. I said it was definite, because it's the birthday of Jesus.' Joanna smiled ruefully. 'I had to think on my feet, believe me.'

'You do very well,' he said gruffly. 'In fact, you make a wonderful mother. I must be honest—I didn't think so at first, but Rosa knew exactly what she was doing by handing Polly over to you.'

Joanna gazed into his intent eyes, taking her courage in both hands. 'Marc——' She broke off at the sight of Polly advancing slowly into the room, bearing the large crystal bowl of soufflé, with Sunny in hazardous attention. 'Goodness, darling, that must be heavy for you. Thank you very much.'

Joanna's sudden urge to confess was lost as Marc took the bowl from Polly and shooed Sunny from the forbidden territory of the dining-room. It was the wrong time, anyway, Joanna assured herself, as she served the pudding.

'None for you?' Marc tasted his with pleasure. 'Not dieting, are you?' His eyes rested on the fuller curves outlined by her crimson sweater. 'I fancy you've put on a little weight since I saw you last, but it suits you.'

Joanna's stomach gave a sickening lurch as Polly, to her infinite relief, interrupted with a plea for a present-giving session later when lunch was over. 'Marco won't be here tomorrow,' she entreated, her face rivalling the Christmas tree once permission was given.

'But only once we've helped Joanna clear everything away,' warned Marc as they rose from the table.

Once the kitchen was in order, Joanna sent the other two out for a quick session in the garden with Sunny and a ball while she went upstairs and made repairs to a face which felt shiny and hot after the rigours of the morning. In her full-length mirror she scrutinised herself in profile anxiously, but decided that other than a slight new fullness of curve here and there her secret was safe. For the time being.

'Jo!' called Polly from downstairs. 'Come *on*.'

When Joanna joined the others in the drawing-room she felt a sharp pang of yearning. The elegantly shabby room, lit only by the logs crackling in the hearth and the lights on the tree, was a wonderfully welcoming place. The scene before her was the epitome of everything she held dear, not least because Marc held centre stage as he leaned an elbow on the chimney-piece, his chiselled features softened with amusement over the antics of Polly and her dog on the hearthrug.

He looked up, smiling. 'Polly's going to do the honours, Joanna. We've decided that you shall recline gracefully while Polly dishes out the presents.'

Joanna obediently settled herself on the worn brocade of the sofa, while Polly, beaming from ear to ear, presented her uncle with her offering, hanging over him anxiously as he exclaimed with unfeigned pleasure over the scarf.

Polly danced to the tree to get another parcel. 'Look, Marco, this is for you from Jo.'

Joanna's gift, which had taken some time to create, was a framed water-colour of Polly's head and shoulders. Marc gazed at it for so long in silence that Joanna wanted to fidget as Polly was doing, while they waited for his verdict.

'Do you like it, Marco?' Polly demanded at last. 'Isn't Jo clever? I sat *very* still. *And* I kept it a secret! Look, there's my dimple——'

'It's exquisite, *cara*. I'm overwhelmed.' Marc walked over to Joanna and raised her hand to his lips, an oddly bleak look in his eyes. 'My grateful thanks. You're very talented.' He turned to Polly, smiling again. 'These are the best presents I've ever had. I shall wear the scarf always, and hang the drawing on the wall in my new flat. You shall choose where, if you like, Polly. Now the painters are finished you can come to stay with me during the holidays.'

But Polly was more interested in the presents Marc produced from behind the tree. She crowed with delight over a small pair of Levis and some track shoes, too taken up with trying them on to notice Marc's departure from the room until he came back with a small bicycle, complete with balancing wheels. She fairly screeched with excitement, throwing herself at her tall uncle like a missile as she kissed him all over his face.

'You guessed!' she said, almost tearful with delight as she slid down to perch herself on the bicycle. 'Please come outside. I want to ride it.'

'Not so fast,' he said firmly, taking a small package from his pocket. 'Don't you think Jo should have her present first?'

Joanna felt nervous, remembering the porcelain horse, but she smiled with genuine pleasure to find Marc's gift was a relatively inexpensive but pretty antique brooch in the shape of a swan.

'Oh, look!' said Polly happily. 'Just like in *The Ugly Duckling*!'

'It's quite lovely,' said Joanna fervently, and jumped to her feet to thank Marc, only to sit down again with an inelegant thump as the room swam round sickeningly for a moment.

'What's the matter?' demanded Marc sharply.

'Just dizzy,' gasped Joanna. 'I'll be fine in a minute. Must be the heat of the fire.'

'You'd better sit quietly for a bit while I take Polly out on her bike,' he ordered. 'Do you do this often?'

'No.' She smiled brightly. 'I'm fine, honestly. Do take Polly out for a ride. And thank you so much for the brooch.'

Joanna was glad of the breathing-space while the other two were outside, gloomily convinced Marc must think her a total hypochondriac. After a while she pinned the brooch to her sweater and got up to put the kettle on for tea that had lately become an addiction.

When the fading light sent Marc and Polly in at last the latter was sent up to wash while Marc carried a tea-tray into the drawing-room for Joanna.

'What time do you have to leave?' she asked.

'I'll wait until Polly's in bed. I'm not going far.' His smile was sardonic. 'You haven't asked where I'm spending Christmas, but just in case you need to get in contact for some emergency of Polly's, I'm indulging in one of those impersonal, everything-laid-on type of Christmas breaks in a Cotswold hotel.' He handed her a card. 'Here's the number.'

Polly's return ruled out further conversation. From then on until Polly's bathtime and subsequent settling down to sleep, there was no further exchange between them until Marc came downstairs after reading to Polly, his face so hostile that Joanna eyed him in trepidation.

'What's the matter?' she asked.

Marc's brows rose slightly over eyes as hard and cold as jet. 'Polly's just let me in on a very interesting little secret. Only she was guilt-stricken afterwards, because she wasn't supposed to tell.'

'Tell what?' said Joanna, her heart sinking.

'Apparently Jack and Charlie Lavenham heard their mummy telling their daddy,' he said with deadly mimicry, 'that you are expecting a baby.'

CHAPTER NINE

JOANNA whitened as she faced the sudden blaze of anger in Marc's eyes. 'I—I asked Mary not to tell George.' She hugged her arms across her chest. 'I had no idea Polly knew.'

'Nevertheless she does know. As do the Lavenhams. Possibly Swancote *en masse* as well. Everyone, in fact, except me.' Marc pounced, seizing her by the elbows. 'When, Joanna?'

'July,' she said hoarsely.

Marc released her, standing back, his face expressionless. 'Then it's mine, not Paul's. Unless there's someone else in the running, of course.'

His tone lashed Joanna into sudden fury. 'If you have any doubts on that score,' she spat, 'get out. Now.'

'Not on your sweet life. I want a few things cleared up.' Marc stood with long legs apart, his arms folded. 'If the date is July, I must be the father. Is that right?'

'Yes,' she said flatly.

'Quite a bombshell! I thought you couldn't have more children.'

Joanna's chin lifted proudly. 'So did I. But it seems my doctor was mistaken. Utterly ludicrous, isn't it? If Paul had been the kind of husband prepared to take me for better or worse as he was supposed to, he might have achieved his family in the end after all. Not that I could have guaranteed him a son, of course. The child I lost was a girl. So is Polly.'

'For the moment,' said Marc menacingly, advancing on her, 'and just for once, I'm not interested in Polly, and certainly not in Paul bloody Clifford. I'm interested in you, and me, and our baby. When were you going to tell me——?' He stopped dead, suddenly white as his shirt. 'Or were you planning to arrange things so you didn't have to?'

Joanna stared at him in horror. 'You think I'd have——?' She swallowed, gulped hard, then brushed him aside and tore from the room to the small cloakroom off the hall.

When she returned to the drawing-room, ashen-faced but relatively composed Marc was standing in front of the dying fire, his face so masklike that Joanna had no clue as to his feelings.

'Perhaps you'd go now,' she said distantly. 'But first, purely for the record, you may care to know that I was a coward. I lacked the courage to tell you because it sounded like such out-and-out blackmail. Think about it. I wouldn't marry you before for the sole reason that I couldn't give you a child of your own. I just couldn't bring myself to come to you, cap in hand, just because by some practical joke of fate it seems I can, after all.'

'Why the hell not? I had a right to know!' he said bitterly.

'You couldn't have failed to know soon.' She tried a casual smile. 'If my present rate of expansion continues I'm likely to be what is known as "great with child" far sooner than I'd like.'

They stared at each other in hostile silence for a long, tense interval then Marc picked up his coat. 'I need some time to think,' he said wearily. 'Under the circumstances I find it damned impossible to understand your opposition to marriage. I, unlike Paul Clifford, want *my* child to know exactly who its father is. *Capisce*? If you won't marry me that's too bad. But don't imagine for a minute you'll bring up a child of mine in ignorance of the fact that Marc Anstey is its father.' He glared at her. 'I suppose you hate the thought of having my baby.'

'Do you expect me to be thrilled to bits?' she demanded.

'No. I suppose not. On which note I'll bid you goodnight, Joanna. Thanks for lunch.' To her dismay he strode past her, grim-faced, then turned in the doorway. 'I forgot,' said Marc, in a tone which flayed. 'Merry Christmas.'

Afterwards Joanna had very little recollection of how she got through the following day at the Lavenhams'. Looking back on it, she knew that she'd opened gifts, drunk sherry and pulled crackers, eaten turkey and joined in all the merriment and festivities, gone for the ritual walk afterwards, and returned to play silly games and drink tea and hand round mince pies.

'Are you all right, Jo?' asked Mary in private when Joanna said goodbye.

Joanna hesitated, then shrugged wearily. 'You told George; the twins heard; they told Polly; she told Marc.' Joanna kissed Mary's guilt-flushed cheek. 'Don't worry, love. He had to know some time.'

Once Polly was in bed it was a strange experience to sit alone on the evening of Christmas Day. When her father was alive Joanna had brought friends home for Christmas, the more the merrier as far as Richard Swan was concerned. Then she'd married Paul and Christmas had become a commercial, glossy affair. But at least it was never quiet like this, she thought, feeling so lonely and depressed that at long last she gave up the struggle with her pride and rang Marc's expensive Cotswold hotel, surprised that instead of paging Mr Anstey the receptionist put her through to his room immediately.

'Joanna,' she said tentatively when he answered.

'Joanna?' His voice sharpened. 'What's the matter? Is it Polly? Or are you ill——?'

'No, no, nothing like that. I just wanted a word with you.'

There was a long, unbearable pause.

'So talk, then,' he said at last.

'I wondered,' she said coolly, 'if you'd have time to call back here before returning to London.'

'Why?'

'There appears to be something wrong with Polly's bike.'

'I see. Stupid of me. For a moment I hoped you wanted to discuss our little mutual problem.'

Joanna scowled. Marc was right. She did. There was nothing at all wrong with Polly's bicycle. 'We could,' she said colourlessly. 'If you wish.'

'Since when were you so magnanimous about *my* wishes?'

'I agree there are things to discuss——' she began stiffly.

'You bet your sweet life there are!' There was a pause. 'All right, Joanna. I'll come tomorrow afternoon. I'm committed to lunch with someone here first.'

'Thank you,' said Joanna formally.

'I can't stay long. I've got an appointment later in London.'

'I'm only too grateful you can fit a visit to Swan House into your busy schedule at all,' she said sweetly. 'Goodnight.'

'Wait,' said Marc peremptorily. 'Don't hang up. How was Polly's day?'

'On the whole very good. She cried a bit first thing, when we opened her Christmas stocking together in bed.

'Because she always did that with Rosa.' Marc's voice grew huskier. 'All day I've been thinking I should have been there too.'

In my bed? thought Joanna. 'It was your choice to stay away,' she pointed out. 'But don't worry, she was fine the rest of the day. The noise and commotion at the Rectory were just what she needed.'

'It was pretty lively here, too,' he said heavily. 'But it was no substitute for a family Christmas with Rosa and Polly.'

'No,' said Joanna, sighing. 'I don't suppose it was.'

'I'll see you tomorrow, then.'

'Thank you for sparing the time. Goodnight.' Joanna put the phone down very carefully, then, unable to face televised Christmas jollity alone, she went out for a brief, chilly stroll in the garden with Sunny before retiring to bed with the latest bestseller, her gift from Mary.

The morning of Boxing Day passed very pleasantly. Several neighbours called in from time to time for a drink and a chat, kind in their efforts to cheer Joanna up in her first Christmas alone at Swan House, and later, glad to repay Mary's hospitality for the day before, Joanna invited Jack and Charlie to lunch. After a boisterous, noisy meal in the kitchen, she played a fast and furious game of Snap on the drawing-room carpet with the children, took them for a short walk afterwards with the dog, then suggested they draw for a while on the kitchen table. When George Lavenham arrived to collect his sons he was astonished to find peace and quiet reigning at Swan House, as the three children vied with each other to create the best likeness of Sunny.

Agreeing to his sons' demands of a few extra minutes to finish their masterpieces, George admired the artists' work, then accepted Joanna's offer of a glass of sherry in the drawing-room.

'I'm rather glad of a chance for a quiet chat, Jo,' said George, leaning an arm on the chimney piece, just as Marc had done.

Joanna eyed him, resigned, thinking how handsome he looked with his windblown fair hair above the heavy white sweater knitted by his mother, the silk scarf Mary had given him knotted at his open collar. George Lavenham in mufti looked more like a movie actor than a man of the cloth.

'About the baby, you mean.'

George nodded. 'I just wanted you to know that if you don't want to marry the chap, it won't make any difference to Mary and me. We'll give you any help and support you want, Jo.'

Joanna, fully expecting a homily on why she should persuade Marc to do the decent thing, burst into tears.

George put down his glass hurriedly and pulled her up into his arms. He held her close, smoothing her hair, undismayed by the torrent of scalding tears soaking his new sweater. 'There, there,' he said soothingly. 'You've had a rotten time of it lately.'

These kind words, far from drying Joanna's tears, made her cry all the harder, and George fished in his pocket for the large clean handkerchief Mary always provided for use in emotive situations among his parishioners. He scrubbed at her face energetically, winning a wobbly smile as reward. He smiled back encouragingly, then hugged Joanna hard, giving her a smacking kiss, whereupon an ungentle hand hauled him off and hit the Reverend Mr Lavenham square on the jaw with a blow which felled him to the floor.

Joanna dropped to her knees beside George, blazingly angry as she turned to glare up at Marc Anstey, who bent to haul her back up again while George leapt lightly to his feet, his face alight with amusement.

'What in heaven's name do you think you're doing?' demanded Joanna in a rage.

'Dr Morley, I presume,' snarled Marc, advancing on George, who made things rather worse by trying hard not to laugh.

'Don't be stupid, Marc!' said Joanna, incensed. 'This is George Lavenham.'

'Hell—you're not the vicar?' asked Marc in dismay.

George grinned, fingering his jaw. 'That's me. But if you think I'm going to turn the other cheek you're mistaken!'

Colour surged in Marc's dark, arrested face. He spread both hands in apology, stifling a curse. 'Lord, I don't know what to say. Seeing the lights in the kitchen, I came in that way, and Polly sent me straight in here. I thought Joanna was resting. When I found you together I just saw red.' He eyed George ruefully. 'I've had a few scuffles in my time, but I've never hit a clergyman before.'

'You only managed it this time because you took George by surprise,' observed Joanna nastily. 'He boxed for his college.'

'Comes in handy at the youth club,' said George cheerfully. 'Any time you fancy lending a hand we could use you. That's a punishing left.'

Marc smiled remorsefully. 'You're taking this very well.'

'George may be, but I'm not!' snapped Joanna. 'I don't see what business it is of yours who you find in my drawing-room.'

'It is when the man's kissing you!'

They confronted each other like gladiators, oblivious of George, who looked on with deep enjoyment as he finished his sherry.

'I happen to think that what I do, and who I do it with, is entirely my own affair,' said Joanna bitingly.

'Oh, do you! In my opinion the fact that you're expecting my baby makes it very much *my* affair,' returned Marc.

'Rubbish! Besides, George was kissing me purely by way of comfort. Being pregnant seems to have affected my tear ducts. I started crying when he assured me of combined Lavenham support whatever I decide to do.'

'You know bloody well what you're going to do. You're going to marry me, you maddening woman.' Marc turned to George in appeal. 'Surely you agree?'

'Have you asked her?' queried George casually.

'Of course I've asked her!' Marc raked a hand through his hair violently.

'No, you haven't!' contradicted Joanna.

Marc gave her a look which brought the blood to her cheeks. 'I don't want to embarrass Lavenham here, but if necessary I can recall the exact time and place of my proposal!'

She sniffed. 'You haven't asked me since you heard about the baby.'

There was silence for a moment or two.

'I thought,' said Marc with care, 'that you would realise, without my having to repeat it, that the proposal still stood. I've never withdrawn it. You were the one against marriage. Not me.'

Joanna's eyes blazed with scorn. 'How like a man! Can't you see that finding I was pregnant changed everything? Of course I needed to be asked again! Besides,' she added truculently, 'I thought you might have changed your mind. I don't want you tied to me against your will—I've had enough of that.'

'When will you get it through your head that I am nothing like Paul Clifford?' He ground his teeth impotently. 'The bastard wrecked your confidence and gave you such a jaundiced view of men in general you can't trust anyone, most of all me, as far as I can see.'

'But in a roundabout way,' put in George peaceably, 'he was actually instrumental in bringing you two together.'

Marc's eyes narrowed thoughtfully. 'You're right. He was. For that, at least, I suppose I should be grateful.'

'By which I gather you love Joanna.' George smiled. 'It's all that matters, really, you know.'

Marc turned slowly to meet Joanna's startled eyes. 'He's right, of course. It is all that matters. I love you. These past few weeks have taught me that as long as you let me play a part in your life—preferably the lead,' he added with a wry grin, 'I'll accept your terms.'

Joanna stared at him dumbly, wondering how to find a way to let him know she preferred his original idea.

'Um—look,' said George apologetically, 'tell me to push off and mind my own business if you like, but my experience as Mary's husband emboldens me to suggest that Joanna may have changed her mind. About marriage, I mean.'

'Is that right?' demanded Marc, seizing Joanna's hands.

'Yes,' she said faintly.

'Louder, please.'

'Yes, yes, *yes*!'

Marc caught Joanna in his arms and kissed her soundly, then shook her very gently. 'Why?'

She shrugged. 'Because I need a father for this baby of ours, why else? And because I love you,' she added casually, her smile suddenly radiant as he crushed her close, oblivious of George.

Suddenly the door burst open and in came three small people waving pieces of paper.

'Which one is the best, Marco?' Polly demanded. She turned to the twins in triumph. 'He's *my* uncle—he'll say mine is best!'

Six months later, on a hot afternoon in July, a familiar black BMW roared through the village of Swancote and took the turn into the drive of Swan House at reckless speed, spurting gravel in all directions. Marc Anstey took a flying leap from the car and burst into the house, taking the stairs two at a time to reach the bedroom. A nurse rose from beside the bed, startled, as the tall, dishevelled man gathered her patient into his arms and kissed her with a passion the nurse obviously felt out of place in a room where only a short time before the lady in question had been delivered of a child. Nurse Roberts was only slightly mollified when the harassed father turned to her urgently afterwards, demanding assurances on the health of his wife.

'This is my husband,' said Joanna unnecessarily.

'How do you do, Mr Anstey?' said the nurse, turning away to the cradle. 'You need have no fears about your wife. She did beautifully. Would you like to hold the baby?'

Marc received the small bundle into his arms with delight. He settled himself on the bed beside Joanna, one arm around her shoulders, the other holding the baby with an expertise which deeply impressed his wife.

'What a clever girl your mother is,' he said to the small, sleeping face.

'Not so clever,' said Joanna as the nurse left them alone together. 'I was up at dawn this morning, so determined to finish a chapter of the new book I ignored certain early warnings from young Anstey here. By the time I contacted Roger Morley he wouldn't let me risk the journey to Swanford General. He managed to get hold of Nurse Roberts, and we managed the whole thing here between us.'

'How about Polly?' asked Marc eventually, when he could bring himself to stop kissing Joanna by way of fervent appreciation.

'I got her off with Mary without letting on what was happening. Mary came straight back here after taking the children to school, needless to say.' Joanna grinned. 'She said someone had to keep boiling kettles, the way they do in films. Heaven knows what she did with all the hot water—made tea, probably. She's giving Polly supper with the twins before bringing her home, but promised to keep the secret. Polly will be thrilled to bits. She thought she had to wait another week before this little bundle arrived.'

'So did I!' Marc's arm tightened as he bent to kiss her again. 'I nearly went into orbit when Mary rang the office. It was a piece of hard news I wasn't prepared for, believe me.' He removed his arm from Joanna's shoulder to settle the baby more comfortably. 'By the way, how do I address this little personage? When I spoke to you last you were still dithering about a name.'

Joanna smiled at him smugly. 'I thought Richard. My father would be pleased.'

Marc stared at her blankly. 'But that's a boy's name.'

'Well done, Mr Hotshot Journalist! Of course it's a boy's name. We've got a son, darling.' Joanna began to laugh as Marc began unwrapping the little bundle to see for himself.

'So we have!' he said in wonder, then handed the baby to Joanna to put back together again, a process young Richard Anstey objected to in a way which brought the nurse running.

'Try him on the breast, Mrs Anstey,' she instructed, giving Marc a look intended to send him packing.

Marc Anstey, used to confronting far more difficult personalities than Nurse Roberts, settled himself firmly alongside Joanna on the bed again, shocking the poor woman to the core by helping his son find the source of nourishment he was yelling for, whereupon Nurse Roberts retired from the room, routed.

'You've upset her,' observed Joanna, gazing down at the small face at her breast.

'Too bad,' said Marc, unrepentant as he gazed at his wife and son. 'She may as well get used to having me around——' He frowned. 'How long is she staying?'

'Only for a day or two. She can sleep in the spare room.'

But Marc was no longer interested in the nurse. 'You know it's a funny thing, darling, I was completely convinced we'd have another daughter.'

Joanna smiled tenderly at his slip. 'Since we're already blessed with Polly I think a son is a nice idea. We can have another girl next time.'

Marc gazed at her in awe. 'What a woman! I thought new mothers always said "never again" at this particular juncture.'

'I can understand that, I suppose,' she conceded, thinking about it. 'It's dashed hard work, producing a baby——'

'Not for me, it isn't!'

They laughed together, disturbing their son. Joanna transferred him carefully to her other side, pulling a face. 'I'm a bit clumsy about all this, Marc. I hope I get better as I go along.'

'For me you're perfection as you are,' he said matter-of-factly, bringing a glow to her eyes as he bent to lean his cheek against her hair.

Later, when the nurse had wheeled the baby away, Marc smoothed the hair back from Joanna's forehead with a caressing hand. 'Are you tired, my angel?'

'A bit, but so happy.' She smiled. 'I think I'll have a little snooze before Polly comes.'

'While I shall take a bath and have a long, celebratory glass of something.' Marc stretched as he stood up, shaking his head. 'A son! Can you believe, darling, that I had no idea until now that I quite fancied one? Not that a daughter wouldn't have been just as welcome——'

'But having Polly had already taken care of that.' Joanna stretched, wincing a little. 'It's perfectly natural. We're lucky, we've got one of each—who knows? One day we might have two of each.'

He laughed. 'I applaud your enthusiasm!' He paused, looking down at her. 'I'm a lucky man. You were so right, Joanna. Giving Polly to you really was the perfect solution.'

She smiled. 'Not quite. What we have now is perfect in Polly's eyes; she's got her wish about a family just like the Lavenhams.'

'Ah, but she's one up on the twins now. She's got a baby brother as well—cousin really,' he added, chuckling.

Joanna shook her head. 'No fear. Polly's as much our child as the scrap who arrived today, Marc. Rosa gave her to us.'

'And gave you into my hands in the process,' he said, kissing her. 'Once I accidentally hit on the one sure way to get you to marry me, that is.'

'Clever devil!' Joanna smiled drowsily. 'Not, I hasten to add, that I'm sorry you did. After six months of connubial bliss, husband dear, I realise that marriage—for you and me, anyway—was the most perfect solution of all.'

DOUBLY DELICIOUS

Dedicated to
Taylor Rosalie
and Tyler Erin-Marie Crowninshield
With whom our story begins

CHAPTER ONE

MRS DAUGHERTY was one of those difficult women who took to her bed the day after her husband died, leaving her a forty-year-old widow. The illness lasted forty years, spun out with detailed descriptions of every ache and pain, until there were no more neighbours to listen, no more friends to call. So she lived on her husband's government pension, spent all her days calling radio talk-shows, and her nights writing nasty letters to editors.

And then she up and died.

Town gossip in Dartmouth allowed that nobody could have been more surprised than Mrs Daugherty herself. Maggi Brennan went to the funeral, of course. Being the only in-sight neighbour on Tucker Road, she felt *some* responsibility.

The funeral was well attended. Curiosity, more than respect, Maggi thought. And after the preacher was done, she heard one of a passing couple say, 'I'm sure they ought to inscribe on the tombstone, "Well, I told you I didn't feel well!"' All of which sent Maggi up Allen Street in her old Jeep Cherokee in a somewhat bemused mood. There was a tangle at the traffic-lights at Slocum Road. There were two high schools on Slocum, both letting out at about the same time, but Maggi was patient. Her house was empty, except for dear old Aunt Eduarda. There hadn't been a bed-and-breakfast customer in over three weeks, and the spring floods had practically washed her corn crop off the side of the hill.

When the intersection was finally cleared she chuckled at the mass of students and their smoky gas-buggies. For there, but for the grace of God and twelve years, would Maggi Brennan have gone herself. Well, Maggi Paiva in those days. And, still chuckling, she zoomed down the other side of the hill to where Allen Street smashed head-on into Tucker Road, at which point she turned south.

The Paiva farm was set back from the road, with only her forlorn advertising sign on the road itself. 'Brennan's Bed and Breakfast.' Handpainted, with a considerable lack of talent. But she and Robert had laughed when they hung it, five years ago. They had spent the month of July hoping no one would come, and then Robert had gone off as mate on the fishing trawler *Katherine Mary*, out of New Bedford.

And had never come back.

His name had been added to the plaque in the Seamen's Bethel. There seemed to be something so desperate about that. He held no place in the burial grounds where she might cry. He was just—lost at sea. Five years ago.

It might have been the date that brought tears to Maggi's eyes. The date, or Mrs Daugherty's funeral, or the deadly dull mist that was falling, or the fact that her parents were in Florida and her two brothers were working in Chicago. So for just a moment Maggi let the motor idle while she felt sorry for herself, and then, mustering up her practical mind, dried her eyes and drove up the narrow unpaved drive and pulled up beside the old farmhouse. There was another day to live, in the endless succession of days, and she would live it as best she could.

She climbed out of the car, brushed her burnished auburn curls off her face, dabbed at her wet green eyes, and started for the house. Moments later, as if he had been following her, an old motor-home pulled up alongside hers, facing the swamp, and a tall red-haired man climbed out and came over to where she waited, one foot up on the back porch.

'Do I find Miss Brennan?' he asked. 'Maggi Brennan?'

Maggi smiled for the first time that day. He had such a delightful Irish brogue—restrained, but still present. Robert had been a third-generation Irish-American, who could muster a brogue for party purposes only. This man sounded so natural, so—nice.

'Mrs Brennan,' she assured him. 'Margaret. That I am.'

'Heaven be praised,' he replied. 'I wasn't sure. The good Father pointed you out at the funeral. And thank the lord you and your people come from the Old Country.'

'Old Country?'

'Ireland, of course.'

'I—think you've made a mistake,' Maggi said. 'I *married* a Brennan. Before that I was a Paiva. My family comes from Portugal.'

'Oh.' Flatly said, as if he considered Portugal to be the end of the world. 'Well, it can't be helped. Look, I'll bring them in.'

'I wish I might know what the devil you're talking about.' Maggi was tired, and after the initial interest in his brogue, she was willing to send him about his business. Unless—good lord, suppose he wanted bed and breakfast? 'Are you looking for accommodations?' she asked tentatively.

'Me?' He looked disdainfully past her at the house. Built in 1786, it seemed to be tired. Originally it had been constructed on an east-to-west line. Now it leaned gently southward. The weathered shingles were uniformly grey. Fourteen rooms, one bath, and a roof that leaked. The farm itself had long since stopped paying for itself; lost travellers looking for a bed for the night were few and far between—but necessary. But the way he looked at her house gave her the mad inclination to kick his ankle. Never before had she seen such a look of sheer disgust.

'We *do* have running water,' she said stiffly. 'Duke Patterson stayed here, you know.'

His face lit up. 'The Irish duke?'

'No, the heavyweight boxer,' she snapped. 'Why don't you——?' She was about to tell him just what he could, when another car pulled up into the yard. 'An invasion of locusts,' Maggi muttered.

'Ah, Mrs Brennan! I've finally caught you at home!'

Maggi struggled with her face, massaging it at least into neutral. One of the facets of learning. Her mother was always insistent on politeness, even with people you couldn't like. The second man was about five feet eight, somewhat rotund, dressed well, and too well known to her for pleasurable meeting. He and she were of the same height, but her one-inch heels gave her the advantage.

'You again, Mr Swanson?' Her first urge now seemed more appropriate. She should have turned on her heel and walked away, but it was too late. 'This makes the third time in two weeks. Surely you must be aware of my decision by this time?'

'But times change,' he said. She hated that cheerful note in his voice. As well as the absurd little hairpiece he wore. And his persistence.

'Well, they haven't yet,' she told him as she folded her arms over each other and stood four-square, blocking his movement in every direction but out. 'And if you were to ask my honest opinion, I don't think they'll ever change in the direction you want. I have no intention of selling the farm. Not to you!'

'Tax time coming up soon,' he reminded her, cheerier than ever. 'You'll have to have a great deal of ready cash around for that, Mrs Brennan. I'm offering a good price, you know.'

'No, I don't know,' she replied. 'It seems to me when you bought the land at Mallow Farm you didn't exactly give Mrs Turner a fair shot, did you? Wasn't there some talk about an investigation? The District Attorney? Things like that?'

'All gossip.' He took a backward step, bounced off the Irishman, and nearly fell over. 'All gossip, Mrs Brennan. Why, you never saw a happier customer than Mrs Turner.'

'Damn you!' Maggi took a step in his direction, her jade eyes glaring at him. 'I visit Mrs Turner in the nursing home every Saturday. Don't you tell *me* what a happy customer she was. Get off my land!'

Old Mike came around the corner of the house at just that moment. One hundred and ten pounds of white Dalmatian with black spots, a grey muzzle that bespoke his age, and a stiff pair of arthritic hind legs, the dog could, on his best days, look fierce indeed. This was one of those days. He ambled around the end of the porch, came to a stiff-legged halt, and growled.

Mr Swanson suddenly remembered a whole host of other appointments, which he gabbled about as he backed away from the pair of them, and then broke for his car. Mike sat down and began to search out an itch with his back paw. Maggi, cheered by the encounter, grinned and started for the kitchen door before she remembered her other visitor. He was still there, unfortunately, leaning negligently against the side of his van, a broad grin on his face.

'Hounded by salesmen?' he enquired. 'My name is John Dailey, Mrs Brennan.' Maggi nodded and folded her arms over her chest, glaring at him. Anyone who doesn't like my house doesn't like me, she told herself, and her eyes dared him to say something more.

'State your business, Mr Dailey. I have a million things to do.'

'Even better, let me show you.' He walked back to the side door of the motor-home and lifted out a little bundle, handling it as if it was fragile. With the package at his shoulder he walked up on to the porch, brushed by her and went in through the open door. Faithful watchdog Mike got up, sniffed at the man's heels, and followed him in, tail wagging.

'Hey, I—just a minute here,' Maggi started to object, but was completely ignored. She stood at the door, her eyes following the broad back of him. Maggi Brennan had had an ordinary upbringing, mixed with a reasonable number of men, and a brief marriage, but somehow was still a little naïve for twenty-nine. But she possessed the most cynical conscience in south-eastern Massachusetts. And just at that moment she took a good look at John Dailey and realised just how—ugly he really was!

'You could close the door.' All of six feet or more, Maggi thought. He wore a brown cardigan sweater, jeans, and work-boots. A craggy sort of face. Those little semicircle lines that most people sported from nose to mouth in his case were deep crevasses. His face might profit by a good ironing, Maggi thought. His dark eyes were wide-set, his nose boasted a tiny bump in its middle. Dark, deep eyes, and, lord love us, red hair, almost as red as my own, she thought.

'There's a draught,' he prompted. A deep voice that seemed to rumble after itself, like the fading noises of a thunderstorm.

'Thunderstorm,' Maggi said, not yet back on an even keel.

He looked at her quizzically, with his head cocked slightly to one side. 'The door,' he repeated, as if addressing some imbecile child. Maggi shook herself out of her trance, and managed to close the door. It was a heavy oak old-fashioned affair. When it closed it shut off the outside world completely, and left the kitchen saturated with silence. From the living-room she could hear the sounds of Daffy Duck. Aunt Eduarda was at her usual morning entertainment. Formerly an avid participant in life, Aunt Eduarda was a retired bilingual schoolteacher, but the loss of her husband some years before had divorced her from life, left her gradually withdrawing into herself.

The man was standing with his back towards her. The bundle at his shoulder stirred and the soft pink blanket fell back. A tiny face poked out into the light, a toothless mouth yawned at Maggi, one large blue eye opened, followed immediately by the other, and the baby giggled at her. And with that one micro-second of contact Maggi Brennan fell in love. With the child, of course.

Good lord, she thought quickly—a homely man, and a lovely baby. Watch out, Maggi Brennan. You always were a sucker for a cute little baby! It was a sore subject. She and Robert had spent a riotous honeymoon month in this very house, and there had been no baby. Somehow she felt as if God had cheated her. One little baby would have made a world of difference. Just one little baby. And here it was. God was being good to her, finally. But the man upset her, tilted her off her sound, sensible base.

'What?' The man took a step in Maggi's direction. Self-consciously she backed away from him. 'Are you acquainted with children?' he asked. He was gently patting the baby's backside.

'I live here,' Maggi snapped at him. Anger was always a good palliative. 'This is my home. I don't know a darn thing about babies, and just what in the living hell do you think you are doing, Mr Dailey?'

Aunt Eduarda was partially deaf. Selectively deaf. She seemed to hear nothing that didn't suit her, but babies were a favourite subject. She came puffing in from the living-room, strong and white-haired and seventy, and lively as the day was long. 'What a lovely child, Margaret.'

Maggi smiled. Aunt Eduarda was a second-generation settler in the land, spoke English like a schoolteacher, and Portuguese like a lover, and never *ever* called her Maggi.

'She is, Auntie, a beautiful child. She belongs to this gentleman. His name is Dailey.'

'Dailey?' Aunt Eduarda's mind was turning over—slowly but inexorably turning over. 'No, I don't know any Daileys. I know a d'Avide. Perhaps a relative?'

John Dailey seemed to change from monster to gentleman in the flick of an eyelash. Aunt Eduarda put out a wrinkled hand. He took it and cherished it in one massive paw, and the smile that lit his face was gentleness indeed. 'Probably a relative,' he said softly, and his deep bass voice seemed to caress the room. 'A great many Irish families have Iberian forebears.'

'Men have no way with babies,' Maggi heard her aunt say. 'Give me the child.' The exchange was made. Dailey stepped back a pace and smiled at them both. The baby cooed and snuggled up against the old lady's shoulder. But if there's anything I don't need, Maggi thought, it's an attachment to this—man. And his child. Something had to be done to break up the mutual admiration society.

'Why don't you ask your wife to come in, Mr Dailey?'

'I don't happen to have a wife,' he returned.

'Everyone who has a baby has a wife,' Maggi snapped. 'That's the way it is!'

'Is it so? Why?'

Despite her age and her experience in life, Maggi still retained a habit that she hated. She blushed easily. As now. Her cheeks turned red, she stuttered, and her mind totally deserted her. 'Because!' she muttered.

And the baby began to cry. With great enthusiasm, her face as red as a beet, she wailed for all the world to know. Maggi, who had never dealt with a child under six, backed off a step or two.

'I don't have a wife,' Dailey repeated. 'Here—you hold her. She thrashes around a great deal. Her name is Priscilla.' Aunt Eduarda was unwilling to give up her prize. She held the baby out with the sort of expression on her face that dared Maggi to take it. But Maggi hadn't even considered such an act.

'Me?' Maggi squeaked. Her anxious hands managed to cling to the kicking infant as its soft body pressed against her unfamiliar shoulder. The soft sweetness of the child was like a hypnotic charm. And don't let the *child* sway you, Maggi insisted to herself, but her caution was already too late. 'Er—where's the child's mother?'

'I said that she doesn't have a mother,' he repeated. 'Here, hold her up against your shoulder, like so. Now pat her back, gently.'

'You weren't patting her *back*,' Maggi grumbled. 'What a father you are!'

'I'm not her father, and I wasn't whacking her.'

'I'm afraid she'll slip off my shoulder,' Maggi said anxiously. She shifted the baby into the cradle of her arms, and the infant began to nuzzle at her breast. 'She's hungry——'

'She's not *hungry*; I just fed her ten minutes ago. I know what she wants. Stretch her out on the table there and tickle her stomach.'

Before she could object he walked out, leaving the door open behind him. Mike went along, as friendly as a frisky pup. 'Watchdog,' Maggi muttered as she paced up and down the room, rocking the baby. 'Know-it-all,' she grumbled as she watched his back, bent over something else in the car. 'Nothing I hate worse than an arrogant male know-it-all!'

But if there was one saving grace within Maggi Brennan it was honesty. You can try to fool yourself, she sighed inwardly, but it hardly ever works. The man is undoubtedly ugly, but he's all man. The size of him, the swift, decisive movement, the certainty of everything he does. He might not please Maggi Brennan, but I'll wager you could find fifty women within a ten-mile radius whom he *would* please! Even if some of them might have to put a plain brown paper bag over his head in the beginning!

'Oh, stop that foolishness!' Maggi snapped at herself. The baby, who had stopped to catch its breath, started to roar again. 'I wasn't talking to you,' Maggi apologised desperately as she laid the child down in the middle of the table and began to unwrap the blanket from her. The tiny legs, free of entanglement, kicked. One hand went to her chubby baby-face, and her thumb went into her mouth. It seemed impossible, but with her mouth full of thumb the child was still complaining. Maggi shook her head, disgusted at herself, as her mind wandered. Babies. She could hear herself say it. 'I'd want four, Robert.' Those had been halcyon summer days, so long ago, when their days were full of laughter, and their nights with wonder. But when summer died, so did Robert and all her hopes.

Maggi shuddered. The baby squealed, and managed to work up a real tear. Maggi dashed the one out of her own eye and tried a few soothing noises. Aunt Eduarda was doing a sort of dance behind her, trying to take over the baby's care. Behind her back she could hear John Dailey come back into the house. For all his size and weight he moved like some soft-footed panther, bypassing her and laying another identical package down beside the first.

'And this is Prudence,' he said softly as he unwrapped the blanket. Priscilla, the crying baby, turned her head slightly to look at Prudence, still asleep. Her wandering hands flayed around, then managed to touch those of the other child. Her wail dropped off into a cough, and was replaced by a sigh and eventually a smile. Prudence opened both her eyes and the two stared happily at each other.

'Like two pins,' Maggi whispered.

'Identical twins,' John said from behind her. 'They miss each other.'

'You mean all that crying was because she——'

'Because Prissy woke up and found that Pru wasn't with her. That's it, Mrs Brennan. You don't know a great deal about babies, do you?'

'I confess, but I could learn,' Maggi admitted as she bent over the gurgling pair. 'How do you know which one is which?'

'I don't,' he said, laughing. 'But I hope by the time they get old enough to be concerned someone will have learned how to tell them apart.'

Maggi looked up at him, full of the feeling of sharing. He had bent over with her, and now his face was only inches away from her own. She stared at it, mesmerised. He had a Roman nose, and that hump in the middle looked as if someone might have stepped there—hard. His dark eyes, almost black, were as big as limpid pools. He hadn't shaved recently. His beard was as red as his hair—and hers. For some reason she had to fight the urge to reach up and touch his cheek, but she managed to avoid the impulse. Fine thing, she thought. He doesn't have a wife; the children have no mother? What sort of biological miracle is this? And—*someone* will have to learn? Not him, someone? What's going on here?

Prissy—or Pru—hiccupped. Dailey picked up one of them and rearranged her on the table, so that the two were side by side, touching, head to foot. The babies gurgled for another moment, then, as if on a signal, both pairs of blue eyes closed. 'Now, let's get down to business.'

'Business?'

'Business,' he repeated. 'It's a little personal. Perhaps we could get your——'

'Aunt. Aunt Eduarda.'

'Perhaps we could get Aunt Eduarda to watch the children for just a moment while we step next door. There are several things that must be explained to you.'

Her aunt promptly sat down in the rocking-chair and gestured. He gathered up both babies and laid them in her arms, across from each other. And then, before Maggi could say, 'What the——?' he had her by the arm and ushered her into the living-room.

Feeling besieged, Maggi sat herself down on the sofa. The springs were rather old. He took a quick look around the room. It needed no great brain to see he was less than impressed, which made her more angry than before. She folded her arms and glared up at him as he paced back and forth.

'Well?'

'Not well at all,' he said, sighing. 'It's been a difficult week.'

If he wanted sympathy, he had come to the wrong confessional. Maggi leaned back against the sofa, planted her two feet flat on the floor, and waited.

'The babes,' he said, and then hesitated. 'These two little ones are the great-grandchildren of Mrs Daugherty,' he said slowly. 'Their mother died at their birth. Their father was lost in the Troubles. Arrangements had been made for the girls to come to live in America with their great-grandmother. They have no other living relatives.'

'You—you're not a relative?'

'No. Just a courier. The town fathers at Turoshish knew I was coming over on business—you know Turoshish?'

'Not a bit,' grated Maggi.

'In County Roscommon,' he went on. 'A very poor place. Sending the babes to America was beyond their means, but, of course, children under five fly for free, and I volunteered——'

'You? A man? Why couldn't they have sent a nurse?'

That did finally bring a smile. 'They did—two of them. Most of our Irish nurses are already over here,' he said, chuckling. 'Working in the American hospitals, they are. The ladies had to go on to their new jobs when the babes and I were held up by Immigration.' He stopped in front of her and looked down. 'And there's nothing special about two little babes. Any woman could care for them, and what any woman can do, a man can do better.'

Which only added more fuel to Maggi's anger. 'A lot you know,' she mumbled. 'But why did you bring them to me?'

'It was the only thing I could think to do,' he went on. 'We landed in Boston and the two tykes were that sick, so we were held up, and, by the time we came south to New Bedford, Mrs Daugherty had already passed on.'

'Which still doesn't answer my question,' Maggi insisted. 'Watch my lips. Why did you bring them here?'

'Ah, and well now, that is the difficult part,' he said grimly. 'I contacted Mrs Daugherty's lawyer. The lady left everything to the babes, as you might expect. And—er—she appointed you, Mrs Brennan, to be the executor of her will—because of your kind heart and disposition, so the will said. So that's it. I was commissioned to bring the babes over the water. I've done that. You are their legal guardian, and so I'll leave them to you and be on my way.'

'Hey!' Maggi came up out of her chair, shaking. 'Me? Executor? Why, that old house of hers is about to fall down any minute—and I don't know a thing about babies!'

'Ah, but you always have your aunt,' he said, as if it all meant nothing more to him.

'Seventy years old and—no, just a minute! Just a *darn* minute!' She sank back in her chair, totally confused. 'How—how do I know you aren't making this all up? How do I know that you're not just a—childnapper?'

'Kidnapper,' he corrected her. 'Yes—*bona fides*. To be truthful, I'm a solicitor. My card.' He fumbled around in the pocket of his jacket. 'Ah—here.' He handed her a calling card and an envelope that crinkled as she touched it. 'From the mayor of Turoshish.'

Maggi managed to focus her eyes. It was an ornate letter, on high-quality paper, and sealed at the bottom with a red wax seal. And she couldn't make head nor tail of it. Dear lord, I've been driven mad, she told herself, and now I'm going blind!

'I—can't seem to read this,' she muttered. He leaned over and took it back for just a moment. But his eye was caught by her wedding-ring. 'Maybe your husband can read it?'

Maggi swallowed hard. The reminder was too painful, on this particular day. 'I'm a widow,' she responded hoarsely.

'Why, of course,' he said, and that cat-and-mouse smile was back. He leaned over her shoulder again. 'They've written this letter all in Gaelic. It's the way of things in the western counties.' He patted his coat again and found another document. 'But here's a copy of Mrs Daugherty's will and all.'

Maggi knew for a fact that she wouldn't be able to read that either, no matter *what* language it was in, but she was saved from admitting it. One of the babies in the kitchen began to whimper.

'I can't—settle this in my mind,' she told him faintly. 'I—why—why don't you stay overnight, and then maybe I'll get it all straight, and—it's late, and you really can't get anywhere from here, and——' And I wouldn't have the faintest idea what to do with two little babies, she told herself. Not a darn idea!

'I suppose I could do that,' he said. 'I've become attached to the little ones.' For the first time since he had come into the house Maggi Brennan wasn't quite sure that she really hated his guts at all. Not *quite* sure. But it didn't really matter. She had fallen head over heels in love—with two little babies.

CHAPTER TWO

MAGGI rolled out of bed at quarter to six, her normal time, an hour after her rooster began his sunrise complaint. It was a long-ingrained habit, seven days a week. After all, the egg harvest was presently the only paying concern on the farm, and she was a woman who liked to expend her efforts on first priorities. But it hurt. Her biorhythms never hit a peak much before eleven o'clock. So she fumbled with bare feet on the cold floor, scuffed into her slippers, and was actually at her bedroom door before she remembered she had guests.

The upstairs part of the house was quiet; there were noises from downstairs. Faint, but noises anyway. Maggi managed to stagger along the upstairs hall to the babies' room, guiding her half-blind walk by dragging one hand against the wall; the big crib in the nursery was empty. So was John Dailey's bed, she noted as she hurried back in the other direction. It was a long corridor, and Aunt Eduarda had two rooms at the very end. The nursery was midway. And without giving it a thought she had assigned John to the bedroom just opposite her own.

Freudian? she asked herself as she peeped around his half-open door. Of course she knew better, and grinned at her own stupidities. It was purely accidental, this room assignment. For the life of her, she could barely stand Mr Superiority, despite his interesting brogue.

One of the difficulties of living in a female household for years was the habit of neglecting clothing. Had she not stubbed her toe on the hall table, she might well have waltzed down to the kitchen in her filmy knee-length silk and lace nightgown. More lace than silk, to be honest about it. A detour back into her own room secured some cover—an ancient green robe that had fitted her well when she was sixteen.

John had found a use for her old playpen. It was set up in front of the hearth in the kitchen, and both the children were lying in it foot to foot, cooing at each other, stripped to their nappies. A mobile toy was stretched across the playpen, half a dozen plastic butterflies revolving in the heated air. A blaze was crackling in the fireplace, and the chimney was drawing well. The tiny dancing flames seemed to hypnotise the children. They spared Maggi a grin as she walked over to them.

Mike, the huge Dalmatian, was baby-sitting, stretched out flat on the stone flags of the hearth between the flame and the children, and only coincidentally in the warmest part of the house. Two empty nursing bottles stood in the centre of the table. 'Well, at least you've eaten,' Maggi offered. The two children gurgled. 'Where's your dad? I mean—your uncle? I mean your—whatever.' It seemed impossible to refer to him as the courier. The children made no translatable response.

Maggi shivered, not from the cold, but rather because, as they said in New England, something had just walked over her grave. She pulled her shabby old robe tighter and debated momentarily whether to clean up the kitchen or get herself a mug of coffee. Which is to laugh, she told herself. Clean-up-the-kitchen comes in dead last any day, and twice that far back today! She grumbled as she made for the kettle and burned her finger. Someone had left it on the stove, on 'simmer'. Some kind soul. And not Aunt Eduarda. She hardly ever got up before noon.

Whatever else he was, John Dailey was a thoughtful man! It was an idea to gnaw on as she made herself a cup of instant decaff. There was a noise from outside. With her warm mug cupped between both hands she wandered over to the back door and peered out between the ruffles of the curtains. Who else? Her Irish courier, of course.

He was stripped to the waist, glaring down at her dull axe, an ocean of split logs surrounding him. Working like a Trojan, she told herself in admiration. Cursing like a Trojan too, and wearing only a pair of ragged blue denim shorts to cover the essentials. There's more to him than just the average bear, she told herself, her mind filled with a strange excitement.

Robert had stripped well too. But Robert had been tall and thin, built like a whippet. This man was solid muscle from shoulder to thighs, like a solidly planted fire hydrant. And wasn't it a surprise that she had thought of Robert? During the last two years she had seldom recalled Robert's physical proportions to mind. Not that she had forgotten him—the memory was too precious for that. Rather, he had retreated from the foreground of her mind, and occupied a tiny little corner, almost as if he were enshrined in a side chapel in the church of her life. In a sense, the thought hurt. Enshrined in an out-of-the-way corner! It didn't seem right, but the thought was too painful to pursue. She put the idea aside; there would be more time later to examine it.

The crash from outside was Dailey's exclamation point. He threw the axe down against the chopping block, where it penetrated half the width of the steel head, and the handle vibrated visibly in the early sun—weak sun, filtering through mist, like weak tea. And now he stretched as if he meant to tear the branches off the apple tree in front of the house. Then he picked up an armload of wood and sauntered up the path.

Maggi felt a strange feeling start at the pit of her stomach and run up her back. She suppressed the spasm quickly. Not since Robert died had she experienced such a startling feeling. It was not the sort of thing a good Catholic widow could consider. That he might drop all that wood just where he stood, and——! 'I'm not that kind of girl,' she muttered, in her most superior manner—and heartily wished it might be true!

Don't get caught at the door, she told herself. He'll think the most awful things about you! So she backed away in the direction of the gas stove, and was smitten by a housekeeping idea. When he banged into the kitchen, gleaming with sweat, she handed him the coffee mug she had just filled. He took it with a welcoming grin. When she threw one of the kitchen towels over his shoulders and began drying him off he nodded again.

'Nice. A man could get used to this kind of living.'

'Good morning,' she managed to squeeze out of a partially paralysed throat. Somehow, in the doing, she eventually lost the towel. It was minutes before her tactile fingers told her she was working on bare flesh.

'Hey, no need to stop on my account.' A bit of whimsy as he slowly turned to face her.

'Yes, but you'll want a shower,' she stammered. 'Have you had breakfast?'

'Not since I acquired those two little rascals,' he said, chuckling. 'They take up so much time of a morning that I hardly have the chance. Why are you staring at me like that?'

'Because you're—unusual,' she told him honestly. 'You're the only man I know who could do for babies the way you do. And you unmarried yourself, with no home examples.' She blushed and stepped away from him. Distance was a great protector. 'At least, I——'

'Even Irish girls ask.' He laughed. 'Yes, I'm a bachelor. We tend to marry later over there, you know. And besides——'

Maggi shivered again and hugged herself, sure protection against dragons. He walked over to his duffle bag, which lay in the corner, among the variety of bags and packages and boxes that a pair of babies required.

'And besides?'

'And besides, I had this.' His big hand pulled a tattered old book out of his bag and waved it in front of her. '*The Care And Feeding of Babies*, by Dr Leonard Appleby, Dublin, 1927.'

'By the book?' she gasped as he advanced on her and thrust it into her arms. 'You can't raise children by a book! An *old* book!'

'Nonsense, Mrs Brennan. Women raise children every day. It's not knowledge they get as a prize in their breakfast cereal, you know. And anything a woman can do, a man can do better.' He reached over and patted the cover of the book. 'Read it. The best instruction you'll ever get.'

'Some day you're going to have a massive headache,' Maggi told him glumly, shaking her head from side to side.

'How so?'

'When your skull splits under that swelled head!'

'Why, you little imp!' At first she thought he might be angry, but the corner of his mouth twitched a couple of times, just before he leaned over and kissed her.

Maggi *Brennan* hadn't been kissed by very many men; Robert had been a very possessive husband. But Maggi *Paiva* had played the game since her fourteenth birthday, and knew a thing or two about kissing. Or thought she did.

She had expected a barrage, an assault, from such a big strong man. Instead his lips were warm and moist and gentle, teasing at her own. He tasted—nice. Her sensitive tongue moved to savour the rest of him; the strongly masculine odour filled her nostrils, and awakened some sleeping animal deep in her being. It was as if she had awakened from a dream, to find herself riding the roller-coaster over at Lincoln Park.

He was holding her loosely, just enough so she could feel pressure at her back, but not close enough to soothe her desire. Maggi could feel a sense of loss closing in on her. There was too much space between them. The book in her hands tumbled to the floor as she arched up on the tips of her toes and flung her hands around his neck. His arms tightened, lifting her slightly off her feet, plastering her against the entire length of his body. Her tongue penetrated his half-opened mouth as firestorms raged up and down her spine. Whimpering, she pressed closer.

One of his big hands slid down her back, cupping her buttock, lifting her higher. Her awakened breasts pressed into his bare chest, separated by only the thickness of her old robe. She wriggled herself from side to side against him. He groaned—and Prissy began to yell for attention. Or was it Pru?

The adult pair froze, pinned against each other by the sound, like a pair of butterflies on a display board. He broke away from her mouth, still holding her. Maggi panted, desperately seeking air, as the fever cooled; he appeared calm and collected, in fact a little cold and distant, but there was a gleam in his eyes that hadn't been there before. The babies joined together in a duet, and a tiny smile formed at the corners of his mouth. Maggi, too tired, too bewildered for anything else, hung in his arms, her hungry eyes telling him everything—but he wasn't looking. Over her shoulder he was already assessing the twins' needs.

When her feet touched the floor she staggered for a second. The movement brought his attention back. And that grin.

'Well, Maggi,' he said, and she could hear the chuckle behind every word. 'Lie down here. I want to talk to you.'

He could not have chosen his words better. They fell on her head like a pan of ice-water. Anger replaced want; anger and perhaps a touch of embarrassment. 'I'll bet you do!' she snapped as she backed away from him and fumbled at the belt of her robe, which had come undone. 'But—but just because I'm a widow you needn't think I'm in need of stud service, Mr Dailey!' The sentence had started at a whisper and ended up as a full gale as her temper escaped control. The babies interrupted her. Their little complaints had grown massively, fed by the anger they could hear in the adult voice. Maggi clapped one hand across her mouth and stared at him through enlarged eyes.

'No, of course you don't,' he agreed, as he stepped back. A shutter seemed to have closed over his face, and the smile disappeared. 'Look, Mrs Brennan,' he said as he picked up one of the twins and comforted the child, 'we need to be outspoken with each other.'

Maggi, who had duplicated his move with the other baby, looked at him over the child's head cautiously. 'Outspoken?'

'Outspoken,' he repeated. 'I don't mind staying around for a few days—to help you get your feet on the ground, so to speak. Just because I come from Ireland doesn't meant that I'm one of those peep-o'-day boys. So please to understand this—I'm not eager to rush to the altar myself, nor am I interested in operating a stud service for some American widow. So do you not be in such a hurry to deny me the things I've never asked for. Right?'

Maggi was so startled that she almost dropped the baby. 'Thank you very much,' she muttered. Squeezing her eyes dry, she summoned up Robert, dear laughing, loving Robert. To her total surprise, no picture surfaced. She could not, no matter how hard she tried, remember what her dead husband looked like.

It was that shock more than anything else that stiffened her backbone and allowed her to move away from him; another moment of sniffling brought her tears to an end. He hardly seemed to notice or care how cold she had become.

She put the baby she was holding back down in the playpen. Pru—or was it Prissy?—immediately sent up a howl of rage. Ignoring them all, Maggi walked over to the back door and slipped on the boots that waited in that dark corner, then shrugged herself into the cape that hung behind the door.

'And what are you up to now?' he asked. The frown had spread from his lips across his whole rugged face. 'The children——'

'This is a farm,' she snapped at him. 'If the hens don't lay, we don't eat. And they won't lay if they're not fed.' With which she slammed the door behind her and marched off up the hill to the chicken coops. There were four of them, two hundred hens, and four roosters. She hated every inch of the coops, and every feather of the birds, but they were her last resort.

'Nobody can made a living from farming around here,' her father had told her two years before. 'Look around you, child. All you're doing is working yourself to death. Houses, that's the growing thing these days. Sell off the land and live on the proceeds.'

'Sell off Grandpa's farm?'

'He wouldn't turn over in his grave, dear,' her mother had coaxed. 'Your grandfather was a very practical man. He knew the jig was up when his own son refused to farm and became a computer analyst.'

But Maggi had grown up close to her grandpa, and treasured what *he* treasured, and although she recognised that designing computer programs was a highly profitable trade, her stubborn mind refused to give in. So while she filled the feeders with mash and gathered the eggs and cursed the smell, she thought about Grandpa, and resolved two things. First, if she was *bound* to handle the twins she would learn how, and second, just as soon as possible she would get rid of this imperious Irish lawyer. 'After all,' she told herself, 'lawyering isn't a very respectable trade. As Uncle Jaoa always said, lawyering rates just below used-car salesmen these days!' Since Uncle Jaoa was himself a lawyer, he should know!

An hour later she had no further time for tears. The twelve dozen fresh brown eggs were packaged and waiting for the supermarket pick-up, the hens were all fed, the coops swept out, the barn cat fed, and her back hurt.

She stretched mightily, then stopped just long enough to look up the hill, at the broad spread of eighteen acres of cornfield. Sweetcorn, the kind called 'bread-and-butter' corn. Eighteen acres, all harrowed and planted and prayed over. And all the seed swept out of it and down the hill in the massive flooding rains of two weeks ago. A total loss, including the price of the seed. Shaking her head disgustedly, her mind burrowing at other solutions to her innumerable problems, she dragged her feet down to the kitchen door, kicked off her boots, and walked in.

John Dailey looked up as if she had merely stepped out to powder her nose. 'Breakfast,' he said, as if it were some major operation. 'Oatmeal.' And now each of the adults had a twin in one hand, a plastic spoon in the other, and were shovelling cereal mixed in warm milk as if feeding the furnace of an old-fashioned steam locomotive.

'How the devil do you know when she's full?' Maggi asked plaintively.

'She'll tell you,' John replied. 'Only allow a little more time between spoonfuls. She'll end up with wind pains.'

'Yeah, sure. When I slow down she gives me that dirty look, as if I were stealing the stuff off her plate!' Curiously, Maggi had forgotten for the moment all her anger and fears and disgust. Feeding babies was a simple thing. Why should it be so interesting?

'Be firm. She's only a baby. And stop to let her take a deep breath now and again, like I'm doing.'

'She's—you know she just spat up all over your shoulder?'

'That's why the nappy between my shoulder and her mouth. Lord, don't you know *anything*?'

'I was an only child,' Maggi announced huffily. It wasn't true, but she had to say *something* to this impossible man.

'Well, don't feed her any more. Once she starts to spit it up she's obviously full.'

'They ought to put a gauge on the outside,' Maggi muttered as she watched him out of the corner of her eyes. There was no doubt about it, the man had the knack. And you have to love a man who loves kids like that, don't you? she thought, and then quickly answered herself. Hell, no, you don't have to!

By nine o'clock the babies were both fed, exercised, loved. 'And now it's time for their bath,' he announced.

'Bath? In the morning? In the tub?'

'Yes, yes, and no,' he replied. 'They need a bath because they're dirty, I like to do it in the morning because that suits me, and no, not in the tub. You have a big kitchen sink there, and I thought we could use that. It's wide enough for the two of them.'

'Did you know that you're an infuriating man?' she asked, tight-lipped.

He gave her a grin, an infuriating grin, as he tested the water in the sink with his elbow, and then picked up Pru—or Prissy. 'Watch carefully. Here's how you do it.'

By eleven o'clock Maggi was exhausted. The twins were cooing at each other on the rug in the living-room. Which had required a complete and sanitary house-cleaning—the sort of thing Maggi applied often. Sometimes as often as twice a year. The little music box inside the teddy bear played 'Take Me Out to the Ball Game'. Mike had taken up his watchdog role between the children and the fireplace. The old grates and fenders and fireguards had been resurrected from the attic, polished, set up. The kitchen had been cleared and washed and pummelled until John Dailey was satisfied. And Maggi, reduced to being the scrubwoman in her own house, went over to the big captain's chair and flopped into it like a puppet whose strings had been cut. And by this time John was beginning to look, in her imagination, like the Hunchback of Notre Dame, with none of the Hunchback's redeeming features.

He stalked around the kitchen one more time. 'We have to be absolutely antiseptic about things,' he murmured, as he checked the container in which half a dozen bottles were being sterilised; weighed the kettle that was boiling more water for tomorrow's formulas; pulled out a dozen or more little bottles of baby food and stacked them on the shelf. 'We've got to go shopping pretty soon.'

'Yeah, sure,' said Maggi as she finger-combed her hair and settled back against the chair rest. Eleven o'clock, and you're not even dressed, her conscience nagged. And you're falling out of that nightgown. You need to get into a conditioning programme! And since Dailey had just sauntered out the door and left 'going to take a shower' hanging on the air behind him, she felt justified in mumbling, 'For heaven's sake, what a slave-driver the man is!'

That was the cue for the telephone to ring. It was a wall telephone, across on the other side of the room. The two children squirmed around at the sound, and for a second it looked as if Prissy was going to cry. It *had* to be Prissy, Maggi had decided. Prissy had more hair than Prudence; three or perhaps four long strands more. Of course, you had to look closely. Neither one had a lot going in the hair department; what they had was blonde, and hard to see in any case. And while she was considering this the telephone rang again. And this time it was Pru who formed a tight little mouth and swelled up prepared to yell.

Maggi pulled herself to her feet, all the while making soothing noises, and managed to snatch the instrument up before it rang again. 'Hello,' she said angrily. 'You're disturbing my babies!'

'Well, really, Mrs Brennan.' The man at the other end sounded as if he might have been shocked. Maggi was convinced that she didn't care a bean for him or his shock.

'And just who are you?' she demanded with all the disdain of a New England matriarch.

'Er—Mr Small,' he said. 'Of the firm of Small, Small, and Ditmore, Mrs Brennan. We were, until her death, Mrs Daugherty's lawyers.'

'Were you really?' Maggi was almost shouting. 'You're the mob that steered all this trouble in my direction? What in the world did you mean by appointing me executor?'

'You mustn't yell with babies in the house,' said Aunt Eduarda as she hurried down the stairs and cuddled the child who was yelling. Maggi waved an impatient hand.

'Do I—er—take it that the babies have arrived?' the voice on the telephone asked.

'You can take it any darn way you want,' Maggi snapped. 'What in the world did you think you were doing?'

'It was Mrs Daugherty's idea entirely,' the lawyer defended. 'Your name was on her lips immediately. The only Christian woman left in Dartmouth, Mrs Daugherty insisted. She used to tell us how you brought her dinner one day when she was sick.'

'Lovely babies.' Aunt Eduarda chortled. 'This one reminds me of you when you were—but, oh, dear, you always had such a temper!'

'Spare me,' Maggi muttered to her aunt. 'Yes, they're adorable.' And then into the impatient telephone she said, 'Once in ten years, would you believe? The ambulance brought her home from the hospital. How could I help but do *something*? I made her up a tray of left-overs and——'

'And left your name forever in her mind,' the lawyer said. He made a peculiar noise. It *might* have been laughter.

'Not funny,' Maggi grumbled. 'Not funny at all. What the devil do I know about raising kids? And two of them at the same time! There ought to be a law!'

'Ah—well,' the lawyer said, 'there is nothing in the will that requires you to be a baby-sitter, Mrs Brennan. All *you* are required to do is administer the estate. You might, for example, turn the children over to the State division of Child Services.'

'I couldn't do that,' Maggi snapped. 'Turn these two little darlings over to some State orphanage or something? Never!'

'A commendable attitude.' Mr Small cleared his throat. 'Perhaps you could hire someone to help out? Someone who might have—temporarily, of course—a reason to stay in the area?'

'I couldn't afford it,' said Maggi, discouraged. 'I can barely——' Feed myself, was the rest of the sentence, but there was no sense in broadcasting *all* her problems to the world.

'But—if you are considering the sale of Mrs Daugherty's house,' the lawyer continued, 'there would be a prospective income. With houses going the way they are this month, I suppose you might get a hundred thousand dollars for it. And we, of course, would be willing to advance on that prospect, Mrs Brennan. Would you like us to put the house on the market?'

'On the market?' Maggi's mind had gone scrambled again. 'It's falling down! It's almost two hundred years old!'

'Ah,' the lawyer said, and that dry chuckle came through the wires again. 'Then let's say a hundred forty thousand. Antiques draw much higher prices these days.'

'And the roof leaks.'

'All the better, Mrs Brennan. It would be a challenging bargain. Shall we?'

'Just like that? I decide?'

'Just like that, Mrs Brennan.'

'And—what do *you* get out of it?' Scattered brains or no, Maggi Brennan's practical streak was still there.

'Oh, we might make a dollar or two,' the lawyer said. 'Six per cent sales commission from the estate, perhaps eight per cent from the buyer, an odd penny or two for filing and fees and little things of that nature. You needn't worry about us, my dear.'

'Dear heaven, no,' mumbled Maggi. 'No—I mean yes. But all that money belongs to the babies. I can't just——'

'No, you can't just,' Mr Small interrupted. 'You are limited to disbursement of funds entirely for the use of the children. As I said, you could hire a baby-sitter. The estate would pay for the children's food and clothing, and for anything required because of having the children in your home. For example, babies require a great deal of clothes washing. A washing-machine might be acceptable.'

'And leaks in my roof?' Maggi asked wistfully.

Another of those dry chuckles which might have been a laugh came down the telephone line. 'No,' Mr Small said. 'Repair a leak in *their* roof, yes; in your roof, no. After all, this is a very small estate, and there are still medical bills to be paid.'

'And you would advance me something to carry me through until the sale is final?'

'The estate would, of course.' Mr Small mentioned a monthly sum that caused Maggi almost to bite her tongue.

'I—er—yes,' she said, sighing. 'Almost at once?'

'Almost at once. We shall send you your first maintenance cheque by the first of the week. Mrs Brennan? Mrs Brennan?'

'Yes,' Maggi said firmly, but with a queer quirk in her voice. Money. Income. Hire somebody. 'I'm still here. Yes, sell—if you please.' A hand reached over her shoulder and covered the telephone mouthpiece. A very large hand.

'Trouble?' John Dailey asked softly.

'Nothing to speak of,' she returned, looking him up and down speculatively. Hire a lawyer? Well, in the United States he *wasn't* a lawyer. He was unemployed, for a fact. Of course, shaved and showered and dressed, he looked to be some high-priced unemployed. I'll ask him, she told herself. But not this minute. Not falling out of my nightgown while he's dressed like some country lord.

She turned her attention back to the telephone. 'Yes, Mr Small,' she said, and sat holding the telephone instrument for some minutes after the other end had been disconnected. The lord *does* provide, she told herself, but with some limitations. Consider the lilies of the field? But in peculiar ways.

'I'd like to talk to you about something important,' she told Dailey in her most prim and prissy voice. 'After I dress, of course.'

'Of course.' He smiled down at her, and she could hardly help but note that it wasn't her emerald eyes he was staring at. It was the soft white corner of her breast, almost slipping its halter. No, he's not interested in such things, she told herself sarcastically as she got out of her chair and went around him, heading for the stairs. Aunt Eduarda sat in the rocking-chair, mindlessly cuddling one of the girls, while John played with the other.

It was cool as she went up. May had come with bright sunny days, but away from the warmth of the fireplace one could raise goosebumps. Or were all those the result of this insane 'John-attack' through which she had just suffered? It was a question that haunted her as she went into the bathroom and stripped. Or perhaps it was John himself that haunted her? There was something more to all this than his indisputable male charisma. Of that there was plenty.

'And you, girl, are just ripe for that,' she told herself as she turned on the hot water and stepped into the shower. 'Over-ripe.' She used her Irish Spring soap with enthusiasm. It left a wonderful odour behind it, and she wanted all the advantages she could get. If you're thinking of this as a war between the sexes, she told herself, forget about it and surrender. You're unarmed. It'll save a lot of time and bother!

'Hah!' Mrs Robert Brennan retorted as she reached for the shampoo. Her wedding-ring glistened in the rain of water, but the hand that wore it moved to her own capacious breast and caressed it and remembered. And forgot what her name was. From force of habit she snatched up a towel and wrapped it around her waist, picked up her handful of nightclothes, and marched smartly out into the hall, heading for her room. Directly in front of her John Dailey stood with his mouth half open, a look of complete surprise on his face. He recovered first.

'I came up to get clothing for the girls,' he said. It was obvious that wasn't what was on his mind, but Maggi was so surprised herself that she wasn't thinking clearly. 'I'm going to take them for a walk.'

She arched her eyebrows, and stood there in front of him, a lovely vision of a great deal of adult female. Evidently he thought so too.

'Lovely view,' he said gruffly, as if there were something caught in his throat. She followed the direction of his eyes, turning her head slowly downward, to where the rounded rise of her firm breasts were definitely his target.

'Oh, help,' she muttered, and fled for her own room. As she slammed the door behind her she could hear that laugh, deep, strong, earth-shaking. It hung in her ears for a long time as she huddled herself up on her bed, totally ashamed of herself, and yet—perhaps a little proud!

When she came back down some considerable time later she was dressed from neck to ankle—a loose-fitting white cotton blouse with a frill of ruffles down the front, a pair of navy blue trousers, which might have been just the slightest bit too tight, and a wide leather belt to mark off a waist that needed no marking. And shoes with two-inch heels, because a girl needed some protective camouflage when dealing with such a tall man—such a big man. Such a troublesome man!

He was sitting in the living-room, having started a second fire. The twins were sprawled out in abandon on the rug. He put down the morning paper when she came in. 'I took them for a walk,' he said, like some judge condemning a prisoner to death. 'All by myself.

And fed them lunch.' And where have *you* been, was the unexpressed thought.

'I—took a little longer than usual,' she explained, and then blushed at the need to. What did *he* have to say about it? He was only a bed-and-breakfast guest in her house, for goodness' sake. He and his two lovely little babies! I could kick him out and keep the babies? she thought.

'No matter.' He waved her half-hearted comment aside. 'We need to talk business.' My house, she emphasised to herself as she walked across the room to the over-stuffed chair furthest from his seat on the sofa. *I'm* in charge in these parts!

'We *do* need to talk business,' she said pertly. She set both feet firmly and flat on the floor, the heels trim and on line, brushed down her blouse, and squared her shoulders. 'I'm not quite sure I understand all this business about visas,' she began. He offered a smile and nodded. 'Just where do you—and the children—stand?'

'Well, the children have no problem,' he said. 'Their father was an American citizen, their mother held a green card, and their grandmother, of course, is a citizen. The INS, the Immigration and Naturalisation Service, had recognised the children as citizens. Oh, there may be a little paperwork here and there, but nothing more.'

'And for yourself?'

'Ah, for myself,' he said, settling back down in his chair and extending his long legs in front of him. 'Somewhat different. I have come over on a ninety-day tourist visa, to conduct some business. At the end of that time I must return. Unless, of course, I were to find myself some recognised employment——'

'Not lawyering?'

'As you say, not lawyering. You Yankees seem to have enough of your own lawyers.'

'What other trades might bring you more security?'

'Hard to say,' he said, chuckling. 'I'm not well trained in other lines. I can farm; the United States doesn't need farmers. What they want are people who are—oh, qualified tradesmen. Plumbers, nurses, repairmen. Or someone willing to work in trades Americans want but won't work at. Things like maids and nannies and service people—you know the sort of thing I mean?'

Maggi very carefully crossed both sets of fingers on both hands. What she was about to propose was as stupid an idea as anyone could wish for. Only a woman with her back to the wall could think of offering. Only a woman who had come to completely love two little infants, and hadn't the training or money to keep them, could consider the idea. Only a woman who was unable to sort out her feelings for a strange Irish con-man could offer.

'Mr Dailey,' she said softly, 'would you consider working for me as a nanny?'

Instead of rising in wrath, he smiled at her and shifted his massive weight in his chair. 'I thought you'd never ask,' he replied.

'Only temporarily,' she added hurriedly.

'As you say, only temporarily,' he agreed, and sighed a tremendous sigh, as if he had been holding his breath for some period of time.

CHAPTER THREE

'I THINK I'm just too tired,' Maggi complained as he urged her out of the door. They were celebrating the end of their first two weeks together, she and John and the babies, and he had threatened mayhem if they didn't get out of the house for a time. 'I never realised how much trouble a pair of babies can be. How in the world does a natural mother survive?'

'By mobilising all her family, her friends, and especially the grandmothers,' he told her. 'You've been cooped up in that house now for too long. So today we go touring.'

'And make more work for me—I mean, for ourselves?'

'It's illegal and unwise to give kids morphine,' he said, chuckling. 'But once this van gets moving you'll see that travel puts them right to sleep. They love the sound of the open road. Now hop in and buckle up, lady.' The battered old van had succumbed to considerable washing and polishing, and now looked quite attractive.

Maggi found it hard not to obey as she climbed up into the high front seat, pushing the lunch basket ahead of her. He just seemed to overwhelm one, and that bothered her. She shifted uneasily in the bucket seat and looked around. The twins were already aboard, each strapped into a complicated child-seat behind the driver's cubicle. They seemed none the worse for wear. Aunt Eduarda had opted out. Much as she loved children, she loved her soap operas more. Riding shotgun, so to speak, was Mike. He was sprawled out flat in the narrow corridor leading back to the van's self-contained bathroom and bedroom facility. Her dog offered her a vague tail-wag before closing his eyes. 'Some protection you are!' she muttered as the van bounced down and up under John's considerable weight. She watched the man warily out of the corner of her eye. He had slammed the midships door behind him, and was coming forward, checking every detail, much as an aeroplane pilot might. It was a reassuring little gesture.

It all seemed so natural as he bent over each child and checked the safety-belts, but when he came all the way forward and did the same for her, Maggi was shattered. Inadvertently or otherwise, his elbow brushed across her breasts as he performed the simple check. She caught her breath as sensation replaced reflection. He must have heard her quick hissing intake, because he stopped for a second and smiled at her. Not until he buckled himself into the driver's seat was Maggi able to draw another breath. And he heard that too.

Maggi knew she had one massive problem. It had appeared at her shoulder every morning for the past two weeks: a bed torn and twisted from the violence of her dreams. A body soaked with perspiration. Muscles aching. All purely physical, she reminded herself firmly. The reason why good little virgins stayed 'good' was that they didn't know what they were missing! And Maggi, with one month of wedded bliss behind her, had found that experience too wonderful to ignore. Only the fact that she really hated this man kept her from—whatever one wanted to call it.

Brazen it out, she decided. Explore his weaknesses—if any. 'You've had a great deal of experience driving wide-based vehicles like this?'

'You bet.' His hand moved among the array of switches and gears, and the motor fired up and settled down. 'I've been driving this monster for——' he leaned forward to read one of the meters '—for one hundred and thirty-two miles!'

It wasn't a tremendous mileage, on the American scale. 'But you've had plenty of experience in other big vans like this one?' she asked hesitantly.

'No. I always liked a small car—sports cars when I could afford them. But you needn't worry, I can handle this little darlin'. It's only thirty-one feet long, anyway. As easy as catching Paddy's pig.'

'Yes, of course,' she mumbled, not knowing a great deal about pigs, and nothing at all about Paddy. She pulled her seatbelt up another notch, wiped off the clammy palms of her hands and then locked them securely around the edges of her seat.

'I wouldn't want you to have a heart attack,' he commented as he went about the business of turning the van around. 'If you don't mind, lean back in your chair. I have to use that mirror outside your window to see what's going on.'

'I'm not the class idiot,' she told him huffily, and gave him the back of her head while she looked out the window.

'Ah, a girl of spirit,' he drawled. Maggi shrugged her shoulders at him. He was, after all, only an employee. But after he had made his sixth attempt to turn around in the narrow yard outside the house, she could not suppress the giggle.

'Why don't you drive up to the barn?' she suggested. 'There's a lot more space up there.'

'I was just going to do that,' he grumbled. 'I've been practising down here in case we run into a problem on narrow streets. And there's nothing I hate worse than a female know-it-all.'

'How nice for you,' she murmured, and turned back to contemplate the surrounding property. She could hear him chuckle behind her back as the van moved smoothly up the hill and turned easily in the great circle in front of the barn. He pulled to a stop, however, just as he had the nose of the vehicle pointed in the right direction. One of the babies behind them stirred and fretted.

'Just as good as opium?' she asked sarcastically.

'Well, when we hit the open road,' he returned. She had forced herself to turn in his direction. One could hardly carry on a conversation with one's back turned. That was one of the many things she knew about etiquette. Her mother, descended from a long line of Yankees—down-east Yankees, that was, not the general term used all over the world—had brought to her marriage a single copy of *Mrs Godey's Ladies' Book*, printed in 1886. It contained everything there was to know about manners. And then she had spent endless hours teaching her daughter the difference between absolute right and all those half-truths.

'So how do we get there?' John added.

'How do we get where?'

'You mean I didn't tell you?'

'Mr Dailey,' she snapped, 'despite the fact that I'm the employer in these parts, you've been issuing orders all morning. I don't take to receiving orders. Not once have you said anything about where you want to go!'

'Take that,' he said under his breath, and grinned. 'Would you feel better if you could slap my face?'

And that, curiously, answered her other question. The one she had been hiding in the back of her mind. He isn't really ugly at all, she told herself. Those crevasses—if they were a little shorter they could be dimples! He's never going to be handsome, not ever. But he certainly looks to be—dependable? Trustworthy? What was it that Mother always said? A girl must be neat and good-looking; a boy only needs to be employed!

'Well?' he asked.

'N-no,' she stammered. 'Why would I want to——? No, it wouldn't make me feel better. Where do you want to go?'

'I want to see the fishing fleet,' he said. 'I've heard about the New Bedford fleet for years. Biggest in the country, I hear?'

'Maybe not the way you mean it,' she replied. 'It may not have the largest number of boats, but its catches bring in the most money of any port in the country. You don't—you don't want to go down to the wharfs and crawl around among the boats and things like that? I haven't done that in years.' A deep sigh accompanied the statement. There were too many remembrances down among the wharfs.

He gave her a quizzical look. 'I'd be satisfied just to look. It's just curiosity, I don't intend to go into the business. I suppose you know all about it?'

'I did once. But after—well, I just couldn't bring myself to——'

He slowed the van and came to a stop so he could look over at her. There was more sympathy in his voice than she might have expected. 'I'm sorry, Maggi, I made a bad choice of subjects. I keep forgetting about your husband. Please forgive me.'

And so do I, Maggi thought glumly. Keep forgetting Robert, I mean. And John sounds so—concerned. He's much like Robert, really. Big and strong and not exactly handsome. Kind. 'I wouldn't want to disappoint you,' she said. 'There's a place out on the bridge where we could see the whole harbour. Would that do?'

It would. So she furnished him directions, the van started rolling, the babies were lulled into sleep, and the sun seemed to shine a little brighter. Heading north on Tucker Road, she pointed out all the sights to be seen in the small, widely scattered country town of Dartmouth. Housing was springing up everywhere on the right-hand side of the road, while the land to the left swooped down to the Paskamansett River. A brook, it would probably have been called elsewhere; river was somewhat overdoing it. John nodded politely as she pointed out the post office, stared at the fire station when they came to busy Route Six, and made appropriately respectful noises when they turned east and headed for the city.

'You didn't mention that hellacious traffic jam behind us,' he said, chuckling, as they climbed the hill beside the Country Club.

'No,' she said glumly. 'That's the Dartmouth Mall. Some of us would rather forget its existence. That whole area was once a delightful little country corner, with the river, a watermill, and—they've cemented everything over. Of course, it adds considerably to our tax base.'

'All in the name of progress?'

'All in the name of progress. That building over there is where I spent my high school years.'

'A year or two ago,' he teased as they went down the hill. The idea startled her. She knew he was teasing, and yet—how very nicely it was done!

'To be honest——'

'No,' he interrupted. 'Let's not be honest today. Let's just enjoy. This is the city limit?'

'Just right there.' She pointed to the marker, and the little pond that marked Buttonwood Park, the city's biggest recreation area.

'We seem to be going up and down, and not very forward,' he questioned as they started downhill again at Kempton Street.

'A series of ridges,' she explained. 'They run parallel to New Bedford harbour. I forget the exact dimensions, but the city is about twelve miles long and two miles wide—something like that. Founded in the 1770s, and became the world's biggest whaling centre. That's where we get the name, the Whaling City. All gone. There now, dead ahead, that's the harbour.'

They were poised at the top of the hill at County Street, where urban renewal and change had opened a view to part of the tidal harbour.

He had nothing more to say as he manoeuvred them down the final hill and on to the bridge that connected New Bedford with the town of Fairhaven, on the other side of the harbour. When, at her direction, he pulled off the road into tiny Marine Park, he brought the van to a stop, breathed a sigh of relief, and patted the steering-wheel.

'Well, we fooled 'em again,' he told the van.

'What?'

'When I leased this van they bet me I'd pile it up in three months,' he said, chuckling. 'And we fooled 'em again. Come on, let's walk around.'

'I—wish you had told me that an hour ago. I'm sure I could have found something that I just had to be doing—elsewhere!' The quaver in her voice was artificially manufactured. She had ridden with a hundred worse drivers than he. He always seemed to be on the alert, checking his mirrors, gauging the traffic beside and in front of him.

He flipped the switch that turned on the air-conditioner and leaned in her direction. 'You know, you have the finest hair I've ever seen on a girl!'

Maggi shifted uneasily in her seat. He had lulled her into a false sense of security, and the conversation upset her. Automatically her hand went to her hair and struggled to bring some order among the curls. All to no avail, as usual.

'You didn't get it,' he commented as her hand moved aimlessly. 'Bend over here.' Maggi had no idea what he was talking about, but was so firmly in his thrall that she leaned over in his direction and trembled as his hand ran through the curls, seeking.

'What is it?'

'Nothing.' He laughed, a full-throated sound that filled the van with its pleasure. 'I just had the mad notion to run my hand through your hair.'

'Well—really!' She snapped her head back so quickly that her neck hurt. She rubbed at it and glared at him. Neither seemed to faze him in the least. He unstrapped himself from the driver's immense seat and moved out into the corridor. Even for a man of his height he could move around comfortably, albeit with head slightly bowed.

She watched warily as he rearranged the blankets and checked the air-conditioner vents. 'The noise of the machinery will keep them down for quite a while,' he explained. 'Tell your dog to guard them. Come on.'

'Tell my dog?' Maggi gasped at the thought. The dog would do as he pleased; he always did. At this moment he didn't seem too displeased to move aside and let them both pass to the midship doors. And when they were by Mike raised his head to look around, sniffed at the babies' feet, and went back to sleep again.

'But we just can't walk off and let the dog take care of them,' she protested.

'Modern science answers everything,' he said, chuckling. 'Our citizens' band radio is also an amplifier. I push this switch and—presto, every deep breath they take is funnelled up into the loudspeaker on the roof. Come on, girl.'

John offered his hand as she scrambled down the three steps to the ground. She hesitated fractionally, and decided it wasn't worth the trouble to fuss about a hand. People held hands all the time, she told herself. Little people and big people and—besides, she thought, if you're holding his hand that's one thing he can't use to get you into more trouble. She stuck her head out of the door. True to his word, she could hear the sound of the babies breathing.

John looked back at her as if he might have heard her thought. His big hand was still stretched in her direction. She dropped her own small paw into it, and it promptly disappeared.

'Trouble?' he asked.

'Nothing. Just clearing my throat.' And a quick change of subject. 'Isn't it wonderful, smelling the sea?'

'And the harbour and the fish and the seaweed,' he added, grinning. 'All wonderful.'

'Well, it's a working harbour,' she snapped. Marine Park was really a small island that served as a mid-harbour support for the long bridge. They were facing south, looking at the massive wall of the hurricane dyke that shut off the inner harbour from the outer, and from Buzzards Bay. The dyke was a huge wall of stone, with a massive steel gate in the middle, put up to protect the low-lying land inside from the ravages of another hurricane. It had been a big success, Maggi told him. 'Since the dyke was completed not a single hurricane has come by in this direction! And over there are——' She was waving towards the New Bedford side of the harbour, and the array of docks in the South Terminal. Where not a single fishing boat was tied up. 'Damn!' she muttered. 'I wanted to show you the fleet—and there's not a single boat in port. They must all be out on the fishing grounds!'

'Not to worry.' He was standing slightly behind her. The wind, which had been a mild breeze out in the country, was blowing in good force, streaming her hair behind her, and pushing her back against him. Two warm arms steadied her gently. And then moved further forward and tightened around her. His voice was close to her ear. She shivered again, and not from the cold.

'You're very proud of your part of the world, aren't you.' It was a statement, not a question. She pondered it, unwilling to admit to herself that it was his nearness, not his statement, that affected her. Cut it out, she told herself firmly. He's only a man. You've been held by a good many men, my girl. And practically all of them better-looking than this one. Maggi exerted a little strength, trying to move away from him, but either he was too strong, or she wasn't really trying—And I don't want to know which, she thought.

'I don't see any boats.' That voice at her ear again, close enough so she could feel the warmth of the words. 'But there are plenty of factories. Tell me more.'

She leaned her head back against his chest and tried to catch a glimpse of his face, with no success. 'That's part of the New Bedford renaissance,' she told him in her best tour-guide voice. 'The whaling industry died out after the Civil War. Petroleum oil was too much competition. So the city went downhill. Then in the 1880s cotton became king. Spinning of cotton thread in those days required humidity. What better place to build a factory than here on the banks of the river? The city became rich again on cotton—until the 1920s, when the mill-owners abandoned their buildings and workers and moved south—cheap labour. And then, after the Depression, all those buildings were standing empty, and hundreds of small industries moved into them—mainly the rag trade. And that's all.'

'That's enough,' he said still at her ear.

You've got to stop that, she told herself. My lord, girl, you're a sucker for this smooth line, the sympathetic voice. Get your show on the road before he overwhelms you. Before you learn to enjoy it, Maggi girl!

'If you would kindly turn me loose,' she snapped. 'I'm not that kind of girl.' His arms immediately opened and freed her. She moved away a step or two, and felt immediately lonely.

'I never supposed you were, so why do you keep saying that?' he commented, watching her like a hawk.

'I—I didn't mean to imply——' And the sentence just could not be completed. It was almost impossible to keep her face from flushing. But the wind had done its work. Her cheeks were already rosy.

'I see,' he said. Obviously, he didn't, but Maggi had no intention of explaining. Why give this man a single bit of information to use against her? Why tell him that she wasn't afraid of John Dailey, the hunter, as much as she was afraid of Maggi Brennan, the widow?

'I'm sorry I've spoiled your day,' she told him.

'You haven't spoiled anything,' he replied. 'It's a grand view, I love the sight of a working city, and you're just about the best tour-guide in the area.'

'That's not saying much.' She was rebuilding her weakened defences, restoring her own confidence. 'Since I'm the only tour-guide in sight. I feel I ought to do something more——' And the idea struck her. 'Look, I brought some lunch stuff with me. Why don't we go over to Fairhaven and picnic at Fort Phoenix?' She pointed out to him the promontory stretching to their south where the old fort sat. The fort itself, just outside the hurricane barrier, was out of sight, but he didn't seem to mind. They walked slowly back to the van, struggling against the wind. It wasn't really all that much wind, but it was the best excuse she could offer herself for taking his arm.

When he parked the van in the area just outside the state park at Fort Phoenix the place was almost empty. 'Too cold for swimming,' she told him as she stepped out of the van. 'That's the Atlantic Ocean out there. It doesn't get warm enough for bathing until some time in July.'

He came around to join her. 'The kids are still asleep,' he reported. 'And the amplifier is on again. Whatever happened to the nice warm Gulf Stream?'

'Oh, it's out there somewhere. Out beyond Nantucket Island. It's *still* too cold to swim.' The sun was brilliant on their heads. Maggi pulled the scarf out of her limitless handbag and tied it over her head. The offshore wind was chilled. They stood for a moment, looking out towards Ireland, some three thousand miles away. 'That's taking the long view, of course,' she teased.

He came up behind her again and put an arm around her waist. 'We're going to stand here until the wind blows us away?'

'Coward,' she said, laughing. 'And I thought you were very brave, driving the van up Fort Street.'

'Well, I was,' he admitted modestly. 'How narrow can the streets get?'

'Narrow? They used to drive the streetcars right up the middle of that street. Of course, there weren't many drivers around who were willing to contest the passage with a thirty-ton streetcar.'

He squeezed her just the tiniest bit, and she was immediately caught up in her panic. Do I shake because he's there, or because I don't want to be there? It was a question she still could not answer.

'Do you know they have a large number of crazy drivers in this town?' he enquired.

'Not really,' she replied. 'All those crazies you saw are from out of town. Come on, let's take a look at the fort.' Before he could answer she grabbed his hand and began towing him up the massive natural rock on which the old revolutionary war fort was established. He looked for only a minute at the battery of ancient muzzle-loading cannons, emplaced to command the entrance to the harbour, and then let her pull him further, up to the top of the stone parapet.

'Now that's a view,' he agreed. And it was. The fort was located on the elbow of a hook-like peninsula, with the shank extending further out to sea.

'Sconticut Neck!' she yelled at him, pointing to the land mass to their left. 'New Bedford.' She pointed across the harbour to where a similar point stretched out to sea. 'There must be a dozen promontories in the area, all creating little bays and harbours. New Bedford and Newport are the biggest anchorages.'

'And Fort Phoenix? Arisen out of the ashes?'

'Well, how did you know that?' She looked back at him in surprise, and at that very moment a massive gust of wind pushed her into his arms. To keep from falling off the back of the parapet he dropped to the ground, taking her with him. They ended up nose to nose, laughing. Watching closely, she saw the laugh disappear as his face became solemn, intent. Oh, dear lord, she told herself, he's going to kiss me.

And he did. It was not a challenging kiss. Not as wild and strong as the ocean wind. Instead it was warm and comforting and—highly desirable. She found it almost impossible to draw away from him. And he mumbled some words that the wind swept away. If only he didn't look as if he were carved in granite!

'Let's get over to the leeward side of the fort,' she said. 'When we get out of the wind it'll be warm, I promise!'

A little smile twitched at his lips, as if he knew just what was going on in her mind, but he was up gracefully and followed her around the perimeter to the far side, where the wall was barely four feet high, and jumped down outside. What she had promised was true. The minute the ancient stone wall cut off the wind they began to appreciate the heat of the sun. She gestured to a protruding rock and used it as a seat. He sprawled out in the grass beside her.

'Now,' she said, unwilling to let him set the agenda, 'you said you were a hurler. Tell me about hurling and the professional football.' He chuckled. He knows what you're up to! she thought immediately.

'Hurling,' he mused. 'Well, it's a lot like your game of field hockey, only much more ferocious. Nobody wears pads, there aren't so many rules and formalities, and—well, altogether it's a game of weaponless terrorism. One can accumulate a few scars here and there, but can't make any money at it. As for the Irish professional football, it's what you people call soccer—only we really know how to play it. I was on the All-Ireland team for four years. The money wasn't bad at all. It paid for my law degree. End of story.'

'You mean—that's all?'

'That's all,' he agreed. 'Our sort of soccer is relatively sedate, as long as you can keep the fans in the stands. If things get out of control then you have trench warfare. Kill or be killed. Great sport.'

'But——' She searched his strife-marked face with concern.

'Now you see why I became a lawyer,' he interrupted, laughing. 'I was such a bad player that I was lucky to get out of the league with my life!'

'And *then* you went to law school.'

'As you say,' he replied. 'Now tell me about yourself. Or Fort Phoenix?'

Luckily he gave her a choice, and the old fort won. Babbling at high speed, she jumped into the story. 'New Bedford was a famous port back in those days—the revolution and all that. So they built this fort to keep the British fleet from invading.' She looked down at him to see if he was listening. Those big dark eyes followed her every move. Self-consciously she tugged at her windbreaker.

'But they did,' she continued. 'There were a lot of boats here in the harbour—little fishing boats. And the British claimed that they were privateers, just because each one of them had a cannon to protect themselves with.'

'What a stupid conclusion!' he interjected.

'Yes, well, so they brought a whole fleet up into Clark's Cove, and landed forty thousand troops. Or maybe it was only four thousand. Or maybe four hundred.'

'There's some discrepancy in the figures?'

'Well, you don't have to be sarcastic! So they landed the marines over there in New Bedford, and they marched all the way through town and burned everything down. And at the same time they landed a force down there on Sconticut Neck, which is up behind the fort.'

'And of course the cannon were all facing out to sea and couldn't fire behind them——'

'You've heard this story before,' she accused him.

'Not at all. Just my normal analytical mind at work. You tell a story beautifully, Maggi. Your eyes light up, and you have the world's best gestures, and——'

'Stop that! If you don't want to listen, then you——'

'I want to listen,' he assured her hurriedly. 'Where does the Phoenix arise from the ashes?'

'Later,' she snapped. 'Where was I?'

'They were coming up behind us——'

'Yes. They came up behind the fort and——' It was getting harder and harder to tell the story. Somehow or another one of his hands had come around her waist and was resting just below the curve of her breast. She talked faster. 'They came up behind and there was a terrible massacre, and they burned the fort to the ground. And then their battleships—well, at least one frigate. That must have been a pretty big ship. It came into the harbour and burned all the little fishing boats.'

'Terrible,' he said solemnly. 'Terrible.'

'Yes,' she hurried on. 'And then the militia from Wareham arrived, and the New Bedford militia, which had been over in Newport waiting for an attack there, came back.'

'A lot of men?'

'Oh, maybe two or three hundred.'

'Against forty thousand!' He whistled in astonishment. She decided to keep her face pointed towards the harbour.

'Yes. And the militia drove the British out and sent them scurrying back to their boats, and the town of Fairhaven voted to rebuild the fort——'

'Up out of the ashes.' He chuckled.

'Yes, out of the ashes. Because they knew that the British would never come back if they knew the fort was there to defend the harbour. And it was successful!'

'Great!' He sat up and smiled at her. Or grinned, if that was a better classification.

'It's all true!' she told him very firmly.

'Of course it is. How many more times did the cowardly British attack?'

'They never came back. The French fleet appeared off Chesapeake Bay, and the British admiral called all the ships south to Yorktown.'

'Lucky for him,' he said solemnly. 'How many died in that terrible massacre?'

'You mean right here at Fort Phoenix? I don't know. But in the whole battle—it lasted for twenty-four hours, you know—I think four men were killed, a dozen wounded, and the British fleet lost six men by desertion. So there!'

'So there indeed.' And now he was definitely laughing. Laughing and squeezing her gently.

She jumped up and glared at him. 'I'm going to report you,' she announced fiercely. 'There must be somebody I can report you to. Unpatriotic laughter in the face of the enemy!'

'I can't allow that to happen,' he told her as he climbed to his feet. 'I'll lose my green card and have to give up being a nanny. The American green card, by the way, is actually blue.' He laughed again as he gathered her up. 'I can't take that chance. I'll just have to shut your mouth, *acushla*.'

'Oh, no, you don't,' she stammered as she backed up a couple of steps, her hand covering her mouth. 'Listen—one of the babies is crying!' They weren't, of course, but it was the first excuse she could come to. She turned and ran, almost tumbling down the face of the rock in her hurry, thankful she had worn her trainers for the trip. The hurrying was not required. John sauntered after her as if he had all the time in the world.

As a result, by the time he arrived she had warmed the still-sleeping babies' bottles, set out their lunch, and deployed the large container of fried chicken she had brought with her. Fried chicken, mashed potatoes, coleslaw. And she sat herself down on the opposite side of the feast, leaving him to sit on the stair of the van, safely separated from her by six Southern-fried chicken legs.

'I know when I'm licked,' he said, laughing. 'Did you cook this yourself?'

'Of course I did. Those little red bits are *linguiça*. Portuguese sausages. They're a little peppery. And there's some beer in the refrigerator, and——'

'And everything's fine,' he assured her. 'Slow down. Calm down. Like any sensible lad, if I can't bite the lady, I'll settle for fried chicken.'

'How gracious of you,' she muttered, and dug into the food as if her life depended on it.

The babies were awake a few minutes later. It was hard to tend to their needs in the narrow van, but they managed. When the children were back in their seats Maggi managed to squeeze by John, out into the open air, just in time to see another car pull up beside them.

'Maggi? Maggi Brennan?'

Maggi walked over to the car and looked in. 'Stella! It's been a long time.'

'And we're neighbours, love. I live down Tucker Road now, about a mile from you. How are things going?'

'Well,' Maggi reported. 'And you?'

'Working downtown,' Stella replied. 'In a law office. What's this I hear about you living with some foreigner? The whole town's gossiping!'

'There's nothing to it,' Maggi protested. 'Nothing at all.'

'Where there's smoke...' Stella offered archly. 'Some gorgeous hunk? Oh, lord, is that him?'

Maggi flashed a look over her shoulder. John Dailey had just come around the front of the van and was standing there looking at them. And for some reason Maggi just did not want to introduce John to her old schoolfriend. 'No, I'm not living with him, I'm employing him,' she said firmly. 'And we have to go right away. Maybe I'll see you again one day.'

'Maybe I'll come over some night,' Stella suggested, chuckling. 'I'm sure I can find some work for him myself!' All of which convinced Maggi that the neighbours were already talking too much, and it was long past time to go, before any more female sharks came ashore. She wheeled and made for the van, tugging John's arm as she passed him.

'You're not going to introduce me to your friend?' he asked as he followed along.

'No, I'm not. Are the babies ready to go?'

'Suddenly maternal,' he said as he checked the seat straps and slipped into the driver's seat. 'Now I wonder why?'

'Well, you can wonder until hell freezes over,' she snapped at him.

He was laughing as he eased them out of the car park. The two babies behind him gurgled, sharing the joke. Maggi tightened her seatbelt and glared out of the window as they headed down the tree-shrouded avenue that was Fort Street, heading home. It started to rain before they reached the bridge. She was glad for it. It matched her spirits.

CHAPTER FOUR

'WOMAN'S work is never done,' grumbled Maggi several days later. 'Well, hardly ever. We might as well be married, the way we're going on!' The statement was casually made, off the top of her head; the moment she heard what she had said her face turned a violent red and she clamped a hand over her idiotic mouth.

She could see John's face, too, all the way across the kitchen, as the steel shutter fell again. He shook his head and said gently, 'I thought we'd settled that idea. I'd rather not discuss it again. The word "married" frightens me. At least the way things are now you have all your nights off.'

'How nice for me,' she muttered as she stuffed another load of baby clothes into the brand-new washing-machine. 'It's hard to believe that just two little babies require a daily laundry service. But I want you to know that I'm not going to let you buy everything in the world for my house. I can't imagine what you're using for money! When you decide to go back to Ireland you'll have to take it all with you!'

And that's another problem, she told herself. For a man who didn't have two pennies to rub together when he arrived, this man seemed to have more money than he knew what to do with. Although she was paying him well, it hardly added up to all the things he had purchased. 'You seem to be made out of money,' she accused him. 'Like Finian's Rainbow? Found a pot of gold outside your village?'

She was not too far away to see the startled look that swept over his face and was gone. 'Not exactly,' he answered abruptly. 'Of course, we poor Irish have the saving habit. I talked with your lawyer. You have to have a clothes-washer, so I just ordered one on your account.'

'You—you just charged it to my account?' Anger boiled over and gibberish ran out of her brick-red mouth. 'You just——'

'To the executor's account,' he soothed, but Maggi was beyond soothing. 'You wouldn't want to lose all this equipment,' he challenged. 'If the babes are to stay here, this stuff will be in use for a long time. And the estate can afford it. Anything else for the drier?'

'No.' Deep breathing. Fifty breaths, steady and slow. Somehow she managed to stem the tide of anger. In a sense he was right. She needed the equipment, she knew, but to just charge it off to her—it boggled the mind! Ten more deep breaths. 'I think that's all the laundry, but I need to sterilise the bottles, and get another quart of boiled water.' She nibbled her lip for a moment. This was the time to make the announcement. 'And the babies are going to stay here,' she said quietly.

From out in the living-room, television and all, she could hear Aunt Eduarda give a muffled cheer.

'Good,' he said. 'Although I'm not one to know much about the subject, I think you might make a good mother. How do you propose to do all that?'

'Why——' Maggi had given it some thought, but the answers she had found so far were not too agreeable. 'I intend to adopt them, of course.' Only when I went to the Division of Child Services they made a great many noises about "stable home and family life" and "We seldom allow adoptions into one-parent families," and "If you were married, and your husband had a sufficient income, Mrs Brennan," and "You have to fill out these ten thousand forms." Well, perhaps not that many, but hell!

When she lifted her head he was studying her face, as if trying to read behind the cover. 'Well, now,' he said, 'I think everything is under control, and I have to get up to Boston to see the Immigration people.'

'About your green card?'

'Blue, actually,' he corrected her.

'Both of the babies are napping?'

'Of course they are. When did you ever see one of them doing something that the other wasn't? I'll be back by dinnertime. What are we having? Steak and potatoes?'

'Last night we had potatoes and steak,' she reminded him. 'How about a tuna salad and soup?'

'Ah,' he said, shaking his head dolefully. 'You must know that the Irish culture begins and ends with potatoes. I'm a growing boy. Why don't we stick to what we know?' He was gone out of the door before she had a chance to rethink the problem. Steak was just too darn expensive, Aunt Eduarda didn't like it, and the moment the door closed behind him she had other ideas to worry her.

Marriage, for example. In barely three weeks she had fallen desperately in love with two little girls. Desperately. If she were married she could adopt them without any trouble. As for income—well, she might just give up the struggle and sell the farm. Forty-six acres, nudging against the limited land of the housing estate under construction up the hill, would bring a sizeable income. It would last long enough for the children to grow up, graduate from college, and have their *own* families. The thought tickled her funny-bone. 'Here I am barely making ends meet,' she muttered, 'and already I have grandchildren! Where in the world could I find a nice man who's interested in marrying me? Not John, certainly. He's said that, and I'm coming to believe him. Besides, who could stand a dictator like him around the house, twenty-four hours a day?'

'I'd rather have kale soup,' Aunt Eduarda called from the living-room. 'With sausages!'

'Yeah, growing,' growled Maggi as she moved to the door to watch John, starting up the van out in the front yard. The vehicle started at the touch of his finger. Everything he owned seemed to work—including her! She smiled at her own temerity.

He doesn't own me, she reminded herself, I'm renting *him* by the day. Maggi Brennan, bottle-washer-in-chief. Assistant baby-minder. His van works because he tinkers with it; is he tinkering with me? A little shudder ran up and down her spine, having nothing to do with the temperature or the wind. Smiling a secret smile, Maggi started the bottles in the steriliser, and filled the kettle for the boiled water needed in the babies' formula.

Quarter past one, she noted as she left the kitchen. For the first time this week I've actually had breakfast and lunch! Will wonders never cease? I wish I understood what I'm up to. That man has moved into my home and taken over everything! He's not the sort of man I really like to have around, and he makes me mad more often than he makes me happy—so why don't I up and send him about his business?

She knew the reason. Despite her anger there was no denying the shivers that he sent up and down her spine. Shivers of—anticipation? All physical, of course. There was certainly no romance involved. 'And I'm not the sort of girl to jump into bed with him at a minute's notice,' she muttered as she wandered out to the living-room.

The twins were fast asleep and smiling, under Aunt Eduarda's cheerful eye. Because the day was a little more chilly than previously, they were dressed in their wool pyjamas—the pyjamas with the feet cut out of them, so they could touch each other. Mike managed a single tail-wag as Maggi came in.

'Boy, have *you* got it made,' she grumbled at her dog. 'Sleep all day in comfort, never miss a meal, no more living out in the barn—and I don't think I've heard you bark in a month of Sundays!' The old dog opened his mouth in a massive yawn and put his head down again. Maggi sat down in the rocking-chair. Just for a minute, of course. She was no longer affected by the sheer physical effort of being a substitute mother. So no one was more surprised than she to find she had fallen asleep.

She slept until someone tugged at the tip of her shoe. Maggi opened one eye; Mike was playing watchdog, mouthing the toe of her shoe and shaking it, rather than barking. Even the dog knows you don't disturb two sleeping princesses, she thought. And then she managed to work the other eye open.

She had been napping for an hour. The babies were still asleep, although both had rolled over on their stomachs, Prissy to the left, Pru to the right, so that their feet were still entangled. Aunt Eduarda was trying her best to figure out the use of the two spring-loaded baby chairs that she and John had bought the previous day. And someone was walking up the path leading to the kitchen door.

He's back again! For some foolish reason the idea excited her. But Mike wasn't behaving as if the lord of the manor were returning. In fact the dog's teeth were showing as he padded out to the kitchen door. Maggi followed. One of the first things John had done was to disconnect the noisy doorbell; somebody pushed the button a couple of times, muttered disgustedly, and knocked. She whipped the door open.

'You again, Mr Swanson? Don't you have somewhere important to go?' Mike was unable to restrain the soft but threatening growl. But Swanson had worked up his courage, and stuck a shoe in the half-opened doorway.

'Come to make you a better offer, Mrs Brennan,' the little man said jovially. 'Been authorised to increase our offer by ten dollars the acre. How about that?'

'If you don't get your shoe out of my door you won't be able to walk for a month,' she said. He started to say something more, but Mike growled again. The agent quickly retrieved his toe.

'But think what you can do with the money,' he said. His face still wore that jovial smile, but his words belied the idea that he was having a good time. 'You don't seem to realise the problem,' he insisted. 'You must know that my firm is building those luxury condos behind your farm. The project won't be economical if we can't expand on to your land. You wouldn't want to see it all brought to a stop, would you? The town would suffer severely, you know. A lower tax-base, more unemployment, fewer homes.'

'And all my fault?' Maggi straightened out her suede skirt, and finger-combed her hair while she waited.

'Well—er—probably,' he announced.

'And you would be one of the unemployed, Mr Swanson?'

'Why—yes, to tell the truth.'

'Good,' she snapped. 'The answer is no. Goodbye.'

He stood there on the stoop, rocking back and forth on his heels, a hangdog look coming over his face. 'I can't take no for an answer,' he said in anguish. 'It would ruin me!'

'Then I suggest you start looking around for other employment,' she snapped. 'There's only one thing more I want to tell you, Mr Swanson, and that is goodbye!'

Swanson, caught in the weight of her disapproval, took another look at Mike's bared teeth and decided that nothing was worth further effort. He turned and left. And almost knocked over the elderly grey-haired woman dressed in an almost masculine navy blue business suit, who was just climbing out of her State car.

State car, Maggi nudged herself. Blue licence plate with white numbers, on an otherwise inoffensive red Ford Escort. Danger signals? From the Bureau of Revenue—the State income tax people? Maybe I should have filed last year, even though I didn't make any money to speak of?

Or the Health Board? There had been a lot of complaints about the swamp on her land—something to do with odours? And in the meantime the woman was walking slowly up the path, and smiling as she saw Maggi standing in the door. And that's the worst kind, Maggi thought. Civil servants who smile as they escort you to the guillotine! Maggi Brennan swallowed hard, and prepared to defend the pass at Thermopylae to the last man—or woman, as the case might be.

'I'm not accustomed to the walk,' the woman said as she climbed up on to the stoop and put out a hand. 'Mildred Fagan, from the State Bureau of Child Services. This *is* the place where the Daugherty twins live? And that lovely Mr Dailey?'

Child Services? Dailey? For the life of her Maggi couldn't remember the name Dailey at all, and then her mind cleared. 'Yes, Mr Dailey works here. Forgive me, but it's all been so sudden that I forget names, and——'

'Yes, we were contacted by the Immigration people. But I came because of your application for adoption. Evidently our clerk was given to understand that you might remarry soon, and so I've been sent along to check the other aspects of the case,' Ms Fagan said. 'But not to worry.' She gave a professional glance down at the gold ring on Maggi's left hand. 'You *did* get married?'

'I—why, of course, I did, but——' Truth is a precious commodity, Maggi told herself. As priceless as pearls. So it shouldn't be spread around too much, right? If the woman wants to think I've gotten married again, why should I spoil her day?

'No need to explain. That's a lovely ring. Now if I may see the house, and the children?'

'I——' Before Maggi could work up another word Ms Mildred Fagan was walking by her into the kitchen, her clip-board at the ready, her little bifocal glasses perched perkily on the end of her stubby nose. Mike gave her a friendly little wag of encouragement, and wandered off to stand guard over the children.

'Nice,' Ms Fagan commented. 'It's a good idea to have a dog or some pet available when raising children. Especially a short-haired dog. Dalmatian, is he?'

'More or less,' Maggi agreed. 'His mother was registered with the American Kennel Club.'

'Mixed blood.' The State inspector nodded sagely. 'Always the best, as far as temperament and intelligence are concerned.' Maggi shot her a quick glance. Behind those ridiculous little glasses sparked a pair of blue eyes as full of intelligence as anyone could ask. And a little smile, as if the pair of them shared some secret.

'Neat kitchen,' Ms Fagan went on, checking off half a dozen spaces on her clip-board. 'Well scrubbed.'

'John and I do that every day,' Maggi offered. Two more checks on the other end of the clip-board. 'The babies are in the living-room.'

'Mr Dailey isn't here at the moment?'

'Well, no.' Maggi stopped for a second, trying to decide how much truth she should spoon out. 'We have a good working arrangement, you know. I'm home with the children today, and he's gone up to Boston to the INS—the Immigration people.'

'Old-fashioned,' Ms Fagan mused as she slashed at three more blocks on her pad. 'The Commonwealth loves that. And my boss does too. Now, the children are——'

'Through that door.' Maggi held the door back for her guest. Mike, who had gone back to guard duty, came to the open door of the living-room, then retreated. Aunt Eduarda had figured out what to do with the little dangling chairs. Each of the two babies was ensconced in a canvas seat, with their legs projecting from holes in the bottom. The entire affair was suspended from the top frame of the door by a huge spring, so that the child could bounce her feet off the floor, and the spring would provide a momentary free ride. At the moment they were bouncing themselves up and down like Yo-yos, squealing their delight and at the same time exercising their little legs.

'Darlings!' Ms Fagan gushed. 'A guard dog. And a lovely fire.' A brief pause as her head came up from her inspection. 'You *do* have central heating?'

'Of course. But the babies love to see the fire—the sparkle and all that, you know. And the fireguard is doubly safe. John has welded it in place, with a small door up here through which we can feed the wood.' She indicated the place. 'But since it's too warm for both fireplace and——'

'Of course.' The smile was back again. 'Aren't they both darlings? Can you tell them apart?'

'That's Prissy.' Maggi pointed. 'So the other must be——'

'Prudence. Of course. How clever you are, and in such a short time.'

Yes, Maggi told herself, I'm clever. And good-looking. And righteous. And old-fashioned. And I'll probably not get to finish a sentence until this lovely lady leaves, after which the lord will undoubtedly strike me dead for all the lies I'm telling! 'Yes, it's been difficult,' she murmured. 'And this is my Aunt Eduarda, who lives with us and helps out with the children.'

Ms Fagan smiled and made a few more positive slashes on her report form. Aunt Eduarda, who hated officialdom with a passion, withdrew into n comprehension, and said a few words in Portugue

Maggi blushed and refused to translate. 'Is there something more you want to see here?'

There wasn't time for an answer. Promptly on cue Prudence noticed their presence and gurgled up at the pair of them. Priscilla instantly followed suit. The two of them contemplated the adults peering over them, turned their heads at precisely the same time to check on the fire and on Mike, then returned to the adults. At exactly the same moment, the little pair of mouths opened and they began to complain.

'Oh, dear,' Ms Fagan said and stepped back.

Proving she's only a textbook baby-minder, Maggi's conscience noted. Show her how it's done, shall I? Me with all my experience?

'It's normal,' Maggi assured her visitor. 'This is about the time they both turn up with wet diapers. Would you like to carry one of them out to the kitchen while I take the other?'

She bent over the swing to unloosen the straps, lifted Prissy up and passed her over. Ms Fagan made a gingerly reception, somewhat on the order of a maiden aunt at her first exposure to a wet niece. With Pru in her own hands, Maggi led the way. With practised skill she balanced the baby on one shoulder while spreading a thick cotton blanket over the kitchen table. And demonstrated that she was a fast learner indeed. At least the inspector was impressed.

'A little diaper rash there,' Maggi pointed out, just as if she knew what she was talking about. 'Probably from the change of water—in her formula, you know.'

'Of course.' Ms Fagan was becoming just the slightest bit glassy-eyed, as if she were learning too much too soon. But she gamely reset her bifocals on the end of her nose and watched while Maggi spread ointment and powder and kisses.

'We're still using throw-away diapers,' she commented. 'We might go to the all-cotton ones if that rash persists. How's that?'

'Commendable.' Ms Fagan was over by the door, looking up high on the wall. 'Your wedding certificate?'

Maggi looked over her shoulder, keeping one hand on each twin's stomach. They were starting to roll. In another week or two they would be squirming on their stomachs. Or so her book said. She could only spare a corner of her mind for Ms Fagan. 'Yes,' she answered. It was true. A week after Robert died she had, in a rage of loneliness, snatched the parchment up, framed it, and hung it there. And hadn't looked at it in over three years. 'Did you want to read it?'

'No need,' Ms Fagan replied gently. 'You know, wearing bifocals it's impossible to look *up* and read without breaking my neck. Bifocals were made for looking *down*. No, don't bother. It's enough to know it's there.' One more slashing check on her pad, and she folded it up and came back to the table.

'All wonderful,' she chirped cheerfully. 'Everything in perfect order. Loving concern, capacity to care, marriage—all wonderful. These children can look forward to years of concerned parenting.' A brief pause while she moved her glasses and stubbed at her curiously wet eyes. 'And the Commonwealth will save a potful of money. I'm happy to give official assent to this temporary guardianship, and, I hope, to the adoption. Now, if you would sign here?'

From under the lip of the pad on her clip-board she extracted a long official form that had already been signed in innumerable places by half a dozen strangers. Ms Fagan indicated the proper line. With bold strokes, Maggi signed, 'Margaret Brennan'.

'Ah, you don't use his name?'

'His name? No, I never——'

'Many women don't,' Ms Fagan agreed. The smile was still there.

'Is that wrong? Did I——?'

'No, everything is fine. I won't wait for Mr Dailey. We don't need his signature. We women can take care of these things, don't you think? Goodbye—Margaret.'

'Maggi—everyone calls me Maggi.'

'Then goodbye, Maggi. And may God bless this little family.' A lovely benediction which left Maggi stuck with two babies who needed to be moved, her mouth half open and her eyes glued to the door as Ms Mildred Fagan made herself scarce. A funny thought bothered Maggi. Somehow she had put her foot into a very deep hole indeed. One with a large trap at its bottom.

The might and power of the Commonwealth of Massachusetts was walking down the path on the shoulders of Ms Mildred Fagan, having been lied to, either by commission or omission, on practically everything that was important. Just who is doing what to whom? Maggi asked herself as she managed to get both babies up on her shoulders, and back out to the safety of the living-room rug. And just what is the Commonwealth going to do when it finds out about all these lies? Oh, I'm so glad you've married, Maggi

Brennan. Do they still execute people for false swearing?

John walked into the house just after five o'clock; a quietly dangerous house. He could feel the atmosphere the moment he opened the kitchen door. 'I'm back!' he called—not too loudly. For some reason he felt caution might be required.

Dinner was simmering on the stove. He detoured by and lifted the lid. Soup. And next to it an asparagus salad—just what a big growing boy didn't care for. It heightened his caution. Mike came strolling in out of the living-room. The dog cocked his head to one side as if censuring.

'Look, whatever it is, I didn't do it,' muttered John as he scratched behind Mike's left ear. 'Of if I did I didn't mean to. Or I've forgotten about it. Where is she?' The dog was too intelligent not to understand. He licked at the hand that was being so nice, and turned and led the way back into the living-room. Maggi was sitting in the rocking-chair, a baby in each arm, playing with them both at the same time.

'I'm back,' he said after it was plain that she intended to ignore him.

'Do you say so?' She looked up at him for just a moment and then went back to the children.

'Look,' he sighed, 'even Pontius Pilate held a hearing!'

'Thank you for edifying me.'

It was the coldest thank you he had ever heard. Only his indignation warmed him. She thinks she can twist me around her little finger, he told himself bitterly. As typical a female as ever there was. And maybe she can! Good lord, how did I ever get in this mess?

All I thought to do was gain a week or two, to figure things out, and——

'Your dinner's ready,' she told him without looking up again. 'It's on the stove. I'll have mine later.'

'Soup——'

'Is there something wrong with soup?' she flared up at him, her cheeks turning blush-red. The sudden noise disturbed both babies. One of them whimpered. Maggi jiggled them both up and down for a moment, restoring comparative calm.

'No,' he offered tentatively. 'There's nothing wrong with soup. I love soup!'

'How nice.' Her voice had become deceptively soft, but the strained look still formed around her eyes and mouth. 'I had a visitor while you were away. A lady by the name of Fagan—Ms Mildred Fagan.'

'I don't know anyone by that name,' he replied, trying to fathom what went on behind her busy forehead. 'At least, I don't *remember* anyone by that name.'

'Ms Fagan was from the Department of Child Services,' she said, again with that deceptively cool voice. 'She inspected the place, checked on the children, filled out a form, and went away. You'll be happy to know that *we* passed inspection, *Mr* Dailey.'

He let out his breath in a big whistling sigh. 'For a minute there you had me fooled,' he said. 'We? We passed inspection. I thought you were going to say she was repossessing the kids.'

'Very funny, Mr Dailey. No, she gave me to believe the adoption would be successful. I put the papers she left up on the refrigerator.'

'All right, Maggi,' he said firmly, 'I can see you're out to stick the needle into me. Get to the point. If this specious argument has some point!'

And that, thought Maggi, *is* the point. This specious argument hasn't any point at all. I'm suffering from a guilt complex, and he hasn't a thing to do with it. Well, I've talked myself *into* the problem, and now it's up to me to work my way out. To begin with, I need either to give up the children, or find a husband. Lord, how do you go about that these days? With Robert and me it was so simple. We dated from grammar school days, and married. All the good ones went early in the marriage game. What's left on the husband market these days but old maggotty stock? And here I am taking my frustrations out on poor John!

She was so angry with herself that tears were flowing, and she just could not bring herself to stanch them. So she put the babies down in the crib, stood straight as a die, hands at her sides, and let the rivulet roll down her cheeks.

'Hey—Maggi!'

She moved back a half-step. 'Don't touch me,' she muttered.

'I won't.' Instead he held out his arms, and like some sort of zombie she walked into them. He cushioned her head on his chest. And the strangest thing of all was that neither of the children cried. A minute passed, Maggi raised her head.

'What a fool I am,' she sobbed. 'I'm getting your shirt all wet, and I only ironed it this morning! I've done a terrible thing, John.'

'It can't be all that much of a problem,' he said, his lips just at her ear. 'Tell me about it.'

'I—that's the problem,' she stuttered. The tears were drying up and her courage was coming back. 'I can't tell you. I just can't.'

'It's a terrible problem but you can't tell me about it? I thought we were friends, Maggi Brennan.' He tugged her with him back to the rocking-chair and sat her down. She promptly stiffened her back, dashed the last remnant of tears away, and mustered up all the sternness she could find. He paced up and down in front of her while he marshalled his thoughts.

'Do we play "what is it"?' he asked. 'Is it bigger than a breadbox?'

'Yes, they are,' she said quietly.

'Ah, then it's about the babies. And the Child Services person?' Maggi nodded. 'They wouldn't let you adopt the kids because you would be a single parent?' Maggi nodded again. 'But that isn't an immediate problem,' he mused. 'As long as you are the executor of the estate the children are yours, no matter what the Child Services people have to say. Unless, of course, they can prove that the children are being abused by being in your care. Which, Maggi, would never happen. You *said* you passed the examination; nothing else matters.'

'I—had to tell the inspector a lie, John. A very tiny little lie.' Her lovely green eyes stared at him. He moved not a muscle.

'I would rather think a word or two not highly important,' he said. 'You know that everyone in the world tells a lie now and again. Some are inadvertent, some not. It could hardly be important, lass. Now, can we get the little people fed and ready for bed? That's the important thing?'

Maggi stared at him without saying another word. She lacked a great deal of education, did Maggi Brennan, but she was not one of the world's stupid people. It wasn't even a word-lie. It was a 'lack-of-word' lie. As she studied his face, strong-marked in the evening light, she wondered what he would say if she blurted it out? I let Ms Fagan believe I was married to you, John! What would he do? Turn and run? It wasn't something she wanted to tell him, not today. But some day Maggi Brennan's famous loose tongue would slip, and the whole game would fall apart. Poor Maggi Brennan, wishing for the stars.

'Very well,' she told him coolly, 'I'll say nothing more. You'd better get your supper before we get to work with the children.'

'Soup?' he said and sighed.

'Your steak is in the oven. The girls have been fed, I'm having the soup and salad, and you'd better hurry up, because the kids need their playtime with their nanny.'

He came over to her and leaned down. 'Don't keep putting me down, Maggi. I might——'

She squirmed back an inch or two. 'You'd better watch your Ps and Qs,' she warned him. 'I've got two big brothers.'

'Two of them?' he queried softly. 'OK, I'll be careful.' Which proved to be an instant lie as he leaned closer and kissed her gently. 'And which one was that?' he asked as he looked down into her dazed face. 'A P or a Q?'

It rained again that night, a cold, driving rain. But not cold enough to quench the fire within her.

CHAPTER FIVE

DISASTER struck at four o'clock the next morning. The great pouring rains had come to a stop. Both babies woke up long before their normal time, wailing. Maggi had barely closed her eyes, and now she had to force them open again. She snatched at the robe at the foot of her bed and staggered down the hall. Aunt Eduarda was coming from the opposite direction, and they met at the nursery door. The night-light, plugged into a wall socket, was brilliant enough for them to see the trouble: the plaster ceiling in the centre of the room was bulging ominously downward, and a steady drip of water fell into the crib, directly below.

'Meu Deus!' Aunt Eduarda muttered as she made the sign of the cross, and then snatched one of the babies up in her arms protectively and backed away into a dry corner.

'Good lord!' Maggi echoed as she picked up the other. Prudence—or perhaps Prissy—struggled in her arms, glared at her out of those big blue eyes, and then blew a bubble and laughed. And John Dailey appeared in the door.

'What in the name of the seven saints is going on?' he asked, at a level just below hurricane force. Both children flinched, and one of them whimpered.

'You needn't roar and curse,' Maggi responded in her most Puritan manner. 'I think it's pretty obvious. We have a leak in the roof!'

'Leak? It's more like a river. Right over the babies' bed? How convenient!'

She glared at him. Lack of sleep, bad dreams, sudden disturbances, his towering temper, all added up to a firestorm in Maggi's mind. 'Yes,' she told him, her voice loaded with venom. 'I arranged it just that way on purpose!' If she had been a little taller they would have been nose to nose, with little Pru squeezed in between. The baby seemed fascinated by the argument. Maggi's empty hand was clutched tightly into a fist. Luckily Aunt Eduarda stepped in.

'Bastante!' the little lady roared at them. 'Enough! You, Margaret, you take the babies to your room, no? Change the clothes. Entertain.' And then, turning her back on Maggi and glaring fiercely at John, 'And you, eh? With the big noisy mouth, and all the muscles. You take the crib down to Maggi's room, while I am to get new sheets. And dry it off, the crib, quietly. *Comprehend?*'

The pair of them, suitably reprimanded, set about their assignments. Maggi felt better about it all as she heard John cursing under his breath as he struggled with the massive crib. And so, by six o'clock, the two children were dreaming again, their bed inches away from Maggi's, and all the adults had fallen asleep as well.

But the woodpeckers woke Maggi up again about eight o'clock. They were drilling a hole in the world, almost directly over her head! Woodpeckers or hammers. Disgustedly, she swung her feet out on to the floor again. The twins seemed able to sleep through it all. Muttering a few choice Portuguese phrases under her breath, Maggi searched out her robe again and staggered downstairs. Off the side of the porch a fragile old ladder leaned against the wall of the house. It seemed too ancient to be climbed, but curiosity ruled. She carefully sidled upward, skipping the two slats that looked too far gone to bear her weight, and when her head reached the level of the gutter she dared to look up.

'You!' she snapped. 'I might have known!' John, dressed only in a pair of ragged denim shorts, was squatting on the incline of the roof, a hammer in his hand, and half a dozen roofing nails in his mouth.

'Me,' he managed to say. 'Who were you expecting? James Bond?'

'I was expecting peace and quiet!' she raged.

'Well, you'll never find that—not with people like you around,' he returned. 'Now get off the ladder before you break your neck!'

'You'd like that, wouldn't you?' she snarled, and almost fell off the ladder as he started in her direction, anger flashing from every rugged corner of his face. One of his hands cupped her chin.

'No,' he said, very distinctly, 'I wouldn't like that at all. And I don't like girls——'

'Women,' she interjected.

'Women.' He savoured the correction as if he might wish to dispute it, and then changed his mind. 'I don't like women who insist on putting words in my mouth. Now—get—back—down—that—ladder!' Maggi closed her eyes. Heights and violent men both upset her very easily. With her eyes still closed, she crabbed her way back down and fumbled for a chair on the porch. Catching her breath fortified her strength, and when John scrambled down moments later she was—almost—ready for his attack. Which didn't come.

Instead he pulled up a porch chair beside her and looked out on the farm for a moment. 'It could be a lovely place,' he said softly. Maggi looked up in surprise. He was staring uphill to where the cornfields lay. 'I suppose you'd be reluctant to leave it?'

'I—really don't know,' she replied. 'It's my home, and I've never been anyplace else.' A moment's pause. 'Well, I went to Washington DC with my high school class. Once. It was a four-day trip.'

'Home is where the heart is,' he said, sighing. 'Look, Maggi, you and I have to talk. Somewhere where we aren't trapped by an aunt and two babies and an ancient dog. Do you suppose your aunt could watch the babies tonight and we two go out to supper?'

'I—I'm sure Aunt Eduarda could look after them—when they're asleep,' she stammered. 'As long as the——'

'I *fixed* the roof,' he interjected. 'Replacement shingles, hot tar—enough to hold things for a few weeks. The inside ceiling is pretty bad; I'll get to that this afternoon. But you need a whole new roof, you know.'

'I know.' She stabbed at her eyes. Some sort of water seemed to be trying to sneak out. 'I—just can't afford it.'

'We'll talk about it tonight,' he said gently. 'Kids still asleep?'

'Like a pair of logs,' Maggi answered. 'Prudence snores. Did you know that?'

'No, I never knew that.' He sprawled out, relaxed, and his eyes half closed.

'You seem to be able to do almost anything in the world,' Maggi said softly, wistfully. But he was already asleep. And how about that? she told herself. You snore too!

It was eight o'clock that night before they were able to get the children settled, Aunt Eduarda soothed, and the arrangements made. Not that Maggi's aunt was a terrible problem. Flaky she might be, but her knowledge of baby care was voluminous, and her desire to take care of the girls was immense. So by nine o'clock John and Maggi were seated at a small table in the very front of Davy's Locker, a fine seafood restaurant facing the harbour, out on the pier on East Rodney French Boulevard.

Night had already fallen, and through the big glass windows they could see the sparkle of lights on the water. Ships came up the channel, their red and green running lights twinkling as they made for the entrance to the inner harbour. The Butler's Flat lighthouse beacon still flashed, even though no longer used for navigation. There were dim lights, like a tiny string of pearls, down the length of Sconticut Neck in the distance. And an occasional spotlight lit up Fort Phoenix, all the way across the harbour.

'I'm tired.' Maggi sighed as she rested both elbows on the table and cupped her chin in the palms of her hands. 'I don't know why, but I'm tired.'

'The babes will become mobile,' he said. 'That increases the work. And you have the chickens, and you're still trying to do something about the corn?'

'I must,' she replied. 'I can't just let it all—well, you wouldn't understand. Lawyers don't——'

'I was raised on a farm,' he interjected. 'A big farm for Ireland—fifteen hectares.' When she looked at him, bewildered, he translated, 'Say roughly two and a half acres per hectare.'

'That *is* a lot,' she agreed. 'And I suppose you grow potatoes?'

'Not likely.' That big smile played around his lips, and teased her out of her doldrums. 'The Daileys came up short. We have more rock than turf. We raise sheep, and cut peat. Now, what about mobile babies?'

'*Will* be mobile?' she repeated, exasperated. 'Both of them can roll now. Prissy can go either way; Pru seems only to roll in one direction. And they get on their stomachs, struggle up on hands and knees, and rock back and forth. Any day now they'll be crawling.'

He lowered his menu, and Maggi was warmed by that special smile that had come to mean so much to her. 'There's too much work here just for you,' he commented, running his eye up and down her frame. 'You've lost ten pounds in three weeks.'

'Fourteen,' she corrected. 'But who's counting? Are you still having trouble getting your green card?'

'That's part of what we have to talk about,' he assured her. 'Things aren't exactly the way you think them, Maggi.'

'I'm not blind, John. I can see. I was hoping you might tell me, instead of making me dig it out.'

'Yes, well.' The waiter interrupted them. John looked considerably relieved at the appearance. 'What's good to eat in New Bedford?'

Maggi straightened up and shook her head in disgust. Every time she approached the door to his character something slammed it shut again! 'We're a fishing port,' she answered. 'Try the New England clam chowder for starters. And the boiled lobster. The asparagus is nice—maybe a tossed salad?'

He was easily pleased. He collected her menu and his own and returned them to the waiter. 'For two,' he ordered. 'And a whiskey sour for me—Maggi?'

'Hmm?' It was hard to concentrate her attention on the conversation when, augmented by candled shadows, he looked so attractive. And wasn't *that* a surprise! It hardly seemed a breath ago that she had thought of him as ugly!

'Drink?'

'Yes, please. A—Martini.'

The chowder and the drinks arrived at the same time. Thick, succulent chowder, heavy with milk and cream and clam juice and a few slices of potato.

'It actually has *clams* in it,' John commented as he spooned up the last of the cup.

'Why, of course.' She set her spoon aside and searched out the corners of his face. He was not to be allowed to escape completely. 'Now, tell me about it. You're not really interested in a green card, are you?'

'I shouldn't say that. I *am* interested, but I don't stand much chance of getting one.' One of his strong brown hands came across the narrow table and took hers. 'No, Maggi. No green card, no permanent emigration for me. And that's what we have to talk about.'

Maggi's throat was blocked. *No emigration for me?* Nothing to keep him in Dartmouth? Only the babies were the tenuous line that held him close? She shivered.

'Air-conditioning?' he asked anxiously.

'No—nothing. Nerves. Tell me about your—family—in Ireland?'

'All right. There's myself and three sisters. My father owned the farm in Roscommon, outside the town of Tulsk. We live in a tiny village, to be sure. And we own a considerable amount of land in the mountains, over the border in Mayo.' A bigger grin. 'I've got to go down to Connecticut tomorrow—an overnight trip. Think you can handle things?'

And how's that for caring? her conscience nudged at her. You're working too hard, Maggi. You're losing weight. You look like a skeleton. So he's going to help out by running off to Connecticut. Whoever heard of a more ridiculous state? Only the people who live there can spell it! Probably he has some woman down in Hartford, just waiting for him! Maggi, who hadn't talked to herself for at least a year, was struck speechless—for a time. 'Try spelling Massachusetts,' she muttered bitterly.

'What?' John looked at her, his head cocked to one side.

'Nothing. I was just clearing my throat. Of course I can handle things. We girls are getting along fine!'

'I don't doubt that part. Now, where were we?'

'You have a family in Ireland,' she prompted.

'So I do. A fine farm, and a county-wide law practice.'

'You can make a living at law?'

He chuckled. 'America may have the most lawyers in the world, Maggi, but Ireland has the most lawsuits. Per capita, that is. Yes, I make a living at it. Not a *great* living, but a living. So you see, my home is there. I have sisters to support—until I can marry them off, of course.'

'Of course,' muttered Maggi, unable to define why there should be such a pain in her heart.

'And my mother still lives in Ballydooley. Loves the big cities, she does.' He waited for her to laugh, but she didn't understand the joke. Ballydooley was a nice town, but hardly a metropolis. 'So that's part of the problem,' he said moodily.

'I—still don't understand.'

He reached over the table again and took her hand. 'You're a fine broth of a lass,' he said softly, 'but our worlds are far apart. I have obligations in Ireland, and you have obligations here in Dartmouth.'

'And that means?'

'And that means that one day soon I must go. I came to transact some business, Maggi. The bringing of the babes was incidental. My business here in the States would be more profitable and more quickly realised if I were an American citizen—but that seems to be out of the question. So I need to work at something until the deal I've started comes of age, and then I have to go home. A farm and a law practice just can't prosper when the man of the house is on the other side of the water. Nor could I abandon my hopes in Ireland, not with my mother and sisters so dependent on them. You do understand?'

No! No, I don't understand! she wanted to shout at him, but her pride stifled the words. 'So this is some sort of declaration,' she challenged him. 'You've been blowing hot and cold for weeks now, but you don't really want me?'

He groaned. 'I'm saying that there's no permanent relationship possible between us. I didn't say I don't want you. A man would be a fool to live in the same house with a woman like you and not *want* her.'

'Then I think you'd better explain in more detail,' she snapped.

'Explain?' His voice rose high enough to attract attention from the neighbouring tables. His hand locked on her wrist like a handcuff as he swallowed and tried again, softly. 'It's very simple,' he half whispered. 'I want you well enough, Maggi Brennan, but I can't have you. I'm doing my best not to reach out and take you, girl. There's still a little bit of honour left in the Dailey clan. But some days you're harder to refuse than others. And I'm not sure how long I can hold out. Now, how does one attack this red little monster on my plate?'

So she explained, carefully, about New England lobsters, about the bib provided, the claw-breakers, the meat picks, and while he ate with gusto she moved her hands mechanically, and her mind played tricks on her. John is going home to Ireland—soon. And I'm going to stay in Dartmouth with the children, and cry a lot! And Child Services is going to take the kids away because I'm not married, and I'll grow into a bent little widow—and heaven help me, I've fallen in love with this crazy Irishman! But he's going home to Ireland soon, and in the meantime maybe he will or won't seduce me, and I don't think I have the strength to resist if he does. That last bit sprang up out of nowhere, and left her trembling at the strength of its passion!

She managed a great deal of meaningless conversation to boot, told him about her Yankee mother and her Portuguese father, and about the decline of New England farming, and the dangers in being a fisherman, and—just to get even with the hurt he had inadvertently done her—how much she had loved Robert, and how happy her marriage had been.

After the meal he led her out on to the pier and they stood for a time, looking out over the bay, he with his arm around her shoulders, she holding herself in, fighting against the pain. And so when he took her home again they were both disgruntled, and lied to each other about how happy a night it had been.

'I've checked the twins,' she told him a few minutes later. 'Aunt Eduarda is fast asleep in my bed, and now I think I'll take Mike for a walk.'

The dog, who understood a few words like 'Mike' and 'walk' and didn't enthuse about the latter, sidled out of the door and went to hide in the kitchen. Maggi watched enviously, and then turned to study John's face as he picked up the paper—and found those dark eyes of his studying her over the top of his page. He's going to Connecticut tomorrow, she thought. A woman waiting for him down in Hartford, perhaps? Nonsense. *My* man wouldn't do a thing like that! *Hah!* But he isn't *my* man!

Mike was doing his best to blend in with the kitchen rug when Maggi came out looking for her jacket. 'Are you coming?'

The massive old dog closed his eyes. I'm sleeping, the message came. 'You old fake,' Maggi muttered, but she left him where he lay, and went out into the cool of the night.

The walk was probably the best thing that could have happened to her. She wandered up the hill by the barn, circled the chicken coops, and climbed further to the boundary of her land to look over the fence at the construction site, where buildings were in confusing stages of completion. 'And that's what I ought to do,' she told herself disgustedly. 'Sell off the land. Why end up as the last farmer in Dartmouth?

It's like catching a space-available ticket on the *Titanic*!' And so she walked the perimeter of her land, kicked at the lumps of earth, and came in again just after midnight, strangely refreshed. The babies were upstairs in their crib, fast asleep. Maggi peeped in, then looked in across the hall. John Dailey was hunched over the little desk in his room, half shadowed by the light of the lamp, resting his chin in the cup of one hand. There was a harried, brooding look on his face.

Fearing that he might hear, Maggi slipped out of her shoes and stole back to the spare room. A shower, a brief read, and before the clock struck one she was fast asleep, a tossing, restless sleep. A dream bothered her—her grandmother's face, young and hauntingly beautiful. 'Love the man, not his land,' the face repeated. '*I* never hesitated when my man wanted to leave the Old Country.'

When the babies woke her up in the morning at five-thirty, John was gone. The sun immediately lost its sparkle, the house reverted to gloom, and suddenly Maggi felt an intense loneliness settle in on her.

The babies noticed the new atmosphere immediately, and became fretful. Pru refused any of her cereal; Prissy could not be satisfied with her bottle. Maggi tried walking them one at a time, with no good result. In the end she yelled for help, and Aunt Eduarda hurried to the rescue. They each put one of the babies to their shoulder, camped out in the rocking-chairs, and managed to subdue, if not satisfy them. The whole affair taught her a lesson. It was easier to be a mother to two *cheerful* kids than almost anything.

The hens were not all that co-operative either. The season was fast approaching where calcium was in short supply, and so all the eggs were thin-shelled, easily cracked, and markets did *not* buy eggs that were already cracked. They might *sell* them, but they didn't buy them. That afternoon Maggi called and made an appointment with Dr Jonas, one of the paediatricians in the nearby Dartmouth Medical Plaza.

The following day was worse. It rained. There was nothing more dismal than a dank drizzle in New England. The whole world turned dark. Things that had the tendency, ached. The world withdrew inside itself, except for the milkman, the paper-boy, and the postperson. And if one lived in a house with a leaky roof, well——!

So the babies were fed and cuddled and left to play, and the adults ate kale soup and home-baked bread, and Aunt Eduarda was pleased by it all. 'It's about time we had some decent Portuguese food on the table,' the old lady grumbled.

'Yes,' Maggi returned absentmindedly. 'I wonder where I could get an Irish cookbook.'

'You must be *doente*,' her aunt muttered as she spooned another plate of soup. 'Sick over that man!'

'Not me,' Maggi defended stoutly. 'I wonder if it's hard to learn Gaelic?' Her aunt gave her a withering look. And the next morning Maggi called the bank.

'Mortgage?' Mr Oliviera was a dry stick of a man who examined each word, turned it over and upside-down, before letting it slip out of his mouth. He was also the senior loan officer at her bank, and an old friend of her father's in the local Shriners' lodge.

'Why, yes, Margaret, the bank could certainly grant you a mortgage. On the house or the land?'

'I—hadn't considered,' she said and sighed.

'But you have to remember, *caro*,' he rumbled on, as if she hadn't said a word, 'that when you mortgage you have to pay. What sort of income do you have to make payments from?'

'I—hadn't thought that far.' Glumly said. Maggi Brennan, idiot first class, she told herself. Pull up your socks and get down to the nitty-gritty!

'Then I recommend that you think some more. Now would be a good time to sell the land. Not all of it, perhaps—say twenty acres?'

'I—I hate to sell the land,' she repeated, 'but my taxes are due, the roof leaks, and if I can't fix it the babies will——'

'Babies? Yes, I did hear something about babies. What does your father say, Margaret?'

She noticed the switch to formality. Not Maggi any more, but Margaret. It set her back up. 'It's *my* farm,' she snapped. 'My father is a nice man, and he's in Florida, and needless long-distance calls are a waste of money, and—how do I go about selling the land? I don't want that man Swanson to get his hands on——'

'I understand. Let me ask around, spread the word in the right places, and——'

'And then who can I get to come right away to fix the roof? I can't wait.'

'Ah, that I know,' Mr Oliviera answered, chuckling. 'I have two hungry sons in the construction business. I should send them?'

'You should send them,' Maggi agreed. '*Muito obrigado*, Uncle Manny.' She stood for a moment with the instrument in her hand as he chuckled and hung up. And that's what friends are for, she told herself. Or relatives, no matter how distant. But I don't have any relatives in Ireland!

Before the day was out the two Oliviera boys came by, as hungry for business as their father had indicated, and willing to perform on credit, having been assured by Uncle Manny that Maggi was a sound customer. So when John came back late the next day the yard was already strewn with equipment and supplies, and half the bedrooms were unusable.

'So the babies and I will be using your room,' she summed up for him. 'It's only for a few days, of course.' And I'm the owner, and I'm the boss, and he's only a nanny, for goodness' sake, she told herself firmly. So why am I shaking all over? 'And you'll have to use the couch until they get through!' And there, she told herself, that was firm enough—wasn't it?

'But the couch is too small for me,' he grumbled.

'I have an old sleeping-bag,' she offered as an alternative. 'You could sleep in the living-room in front of the fireplace.'

'Somehow I knew I'd be in trouble,' he said. But though his voice was complaining, his eyes were sparkling at her. 'Do I have to fight the dog for position in the pecking order? He likes to sleep by the fire.'

'That's entirely up to you male types,' she told him primly. 'A mere female like me wouldn't dare intervene.'

'Would you excuse us for a moment, Aunt Eduarda?' He was out of his chair before the old lady could respond. Around the table, behind Maggi, he pulled her chair back from the table and swung her up out of her seat, with her feet dangling four or five inches off the floor.

'I'm glad to see you too, mere female,' he murmured in her ear, and then he kissed her.

'That's not fair,' she complained as he set her down, still holding her against his muscled chest.

'If there's anything I've learned,' he told her, grinning at her aunt over Maggi's shoulder, 'it's that it doesn't pay to be fair when you're arguing with Maggi Brennan.'

'Show-off,' she muttered, but was not entirely displeased.

'I'll get the dishes,' Aunt Eduarda said complacently. Notice she's not startled to see me kiss the help, Maggi's conscience nagged. Probably he does it all the time.

'I'll go and move the furniture. Are you going to help, Maggi?'

'Lord, no. It's my time to play with the girls, and after the dishes are done I'll give them a bath. No, furniture moving is for big strong men. Isn't that so, Auntie?'

'I hate that title,' that worthy said, rolling up her sleeves. 'Call me Tia—a good Portuguese word.'

John chuckled at the evasion.

Maggi stalked over to stand directly in front him, intending to do him a serious damage, but before either of her hands could move he swept her up in a bear-hug. 'Put me down,' she demanded. 'I don't see a single thing to laugh about. I'm going to——'

'I'm sure you are,' he interrupted. And kissed her again.

There was nothing for it after that. Gasping for breath, Maggi leaned against the wall, wondering why the joints in her knees were so fluid. John winked one eye at her and headed up the stairs, in full possession of all his faculties. But if kissing doesn't bother him at all, she thought, why is he perspiring so much?

'Bless you,' Maggi muttered cynically at his retreating back. 'You're really worth having, after all. You think!'

'What was that?' asked Aunt Eduarda.

'I said bless us,' Maggi repeated. 'Lucky the babies are so small!'

'Yes, isn't it?' the aunt returned. 'And thank goodness you have a dishwasher machine now.'

'I do?' Maggi looked vaguely around the room, now crowded with shining white appliances, and stamped her foot as the anger rose. 'When did he sneak *that* in?'

CHAPTER SIX

'LET me say one thing for you,' said Dr Jonas. 'I'm happy to see that you don't insist on dressing the twins in identical clothes. You can't begin too early emphasising that they are two separate and distinct individuals. You make a good mother, Mrs Brennan.'

Maggi shook her head and glanced over at John. They had both tried to explain the situation to the receptionists. Four separate explanations, in fact, in the past half-hour. John shrugged his shoulders, as if to say, 'Let them have it their way.'

Maggi, made uncomfortable by the whole idea, winced and started to explain yet again, only to be interrupted by the doctor.

'Despite all their travelling, and their environmental changes, the babies are in excellent shape,' he rambled on. 'I don't see any major problems in either of them. They are both right at the proper developmental point. You should be giving them more liberties now. They're ready to crawl, and they need some range-of-motion exercises, as I illustrated to you—preferably just after their baths. And one more thing. Raising twins is sometimes harder on the parents than it is on the children. You should hire some help. At least once a week you both need to be away from the babies, off by yourself.'

'But we don't get out much,' Maggi volunteered. John frowned down at her, as if she were revealing the location of the family fortune.

'You don't have to go out,' the doctor added, chuckling. 'Go upstairs together, lock the door behind you, and do what comes naturally. Anything to get away from the kids!'

'Well!' Maggi exclaimed.

'Sounds good to me.' John was laughing at her. She refused to look up, to meet his eyes. And what she was thinking she had no intention of letting him know.

'And that's all I can tell you,' the doctor said. 'Obviously you're doing something right. Just keep at it. Level-headed, and stuff like that.'

'Don't worry, we're raising them by the book,' John said. 'I'm keeping a firm hand on Maggi's wild ideas.' Both he and the doctor laughed.

All men must have their little foibles, Maggi told herself grimly. They shift on a second's notice from arrogant dictators to lovable small boys. And throughout it all they think we women haven't the brains to come in out of the rain! If I ever have a baby I'm going to insist on a female paediatrician. Preferably one with children of her own!

She was still fuming as they made their way down the hall of the practically new medical-office building, and out into the sunshine of Dartmouth Medical Plaza. Prissy rode in a backpack with one tiny fist clutching John's thick hair, gabbling all the way. Pru was lording it over the world quietly in a cuddle-pack resting on Maggi's breast.

'That was very clever of you, dressing them differently,' said John.

Yes, clever, she told herself. I started the day late and never did catch up, so I dressed them in whatever came to hand. What a clever, clever woman am I! But rather than admit it, she offered him a sunny smile and walked on into the stream of pedestrians roaming the Plaza.

'Maggi! Maggi Paiva!' The shout came from halfway across the open Plaza. Maggi stopped and turned. John continued, wrapped up in his own thoughts. A young man was racing in her direction. He was of medium height, blond as a Viking, thin, dressed in a three-piece grey suit, the epitome of good looks and sophistication.

'Henry? Henry Peterson!' Memories, flashbacks. Henry Peterson at her high school prom. He had danced with her once. He hadn't worn gloves at the dance. She could remember his cold hand running up and down her spine, unlimited by her practically backless evening gown. The son of a moderately wealthy family with great aspirations. The best catch in the whole school—until she had met Robert, of course. And not seen since—when? Since their fifth class reunion, years ago! And here he was, with a big grin on his face, sweeping her up and swinging her in a circle.

'Maggi Paiva,' he said with a gusty sigh. 'How long has it been?'

'Several years,' she recounted, and pushed him away. Prudence, crushed between the two of them, wailed. He moved back, embarrassed.

'Oh, dear,' he apologised. 'I didn't realise you had a child, Maggi. I read in the paper that Robert died——'

'Five years ago,' she reminded him. 'But I——'

'She doesn't have one, she has two.' John was back, towering over the pair of them. If looks could kill they would both have been dead, Maggi thought.

'Two of them?' Henry moved a step or two further back, a discouraged look on his face.

Maggi stole a quick look up at John's face. He's playing dog-in-the-manger, her conscience reported. Don't let him get away with it! Henry is a very handsome young man! She muttered as she wheeled on him and glared.

'They're not mine,' she told Henry over her shoulder. 'They belong to—I'm their——' and then stopped, because it was too hard to explain. The two men stared at each, like a pair of pit bulls circling. 'Mr Dailey brought them over from Ireland.'

'So that's the way of it,' Henry said. 'Baby-minder.' He threw another glare at John, who seemed to be gritting his teeth. 'Look, Maggi, we have a million things to talk over. Why don't we get together over a drink?'

'I'd like that,' Maggi agreed softly. She had no idea what Henry might want to talk about, but watching John steam in the background did something for her ego. 'Why don't you come out to the house? I'm living at my grandfather's farm. You know the way?'

'Indeed I do. Remember when we had that hayride just before Christmas?'

Lord, do I remember, Maggi thought. He didn't pay me a minute's worth of attention. I didn't have the build I have now. But when Gramps caught him in the hayloft with those two cheerleaders, boy, did we *all* remember that! 'I remember,' she murmured.

'How about tomorrow night?'

'That would be fine. About eight?'

'About eight,' he agreed as he leaned forward to kiss the tip of her nose. He walked away jauntily, hands in pockets, whistling.

'So what happened on that hayride?' John demanded. His scowl was dark enough to bring monsoon rains.

'Nothing,' Maggi said. 'It's really none of your business.'

'None of my business?' he thundered. 'What the hell do you mean, none of my business?'

'Well, I'm not *married* to you,' she returned heatedly. 'Thank heaven for little favours. You've blown hot and cold for long enough. There's nothing in our relationship except business, Mr Dailey. And if I decide to go out with Henry, it has nothing to do with you. You just do your duties, and keep your hands to yourself, and we'll get along fine! And if that embarrasses you, all you have to do is stop shouting, then nobody in the Plaza will know about it!'

'I wasn't shouting,' he muttered. 'I never shout. I never lose my temper! Come on, Pru isn't going to stop fussing if you don't walk her!'

Which was all true, Maggi reflected. About Pru fussing as long as they stood still, that was. Never loses his temper? Hah! I'll twist his tail again a time or two! Maggi began to move slowly along at his side, close enough so that the twins could see and assure each other. Ideas raced through her brain. Hold it, her conscience insisted. Try anything like that and he'll beat up on you. That's like trying to soothe Stromboli with Alka-Seltzer tablets! But it *had* been a good idea, and she hated to give it up.

'There's nothing to it, John. Henry's just an old acquaintance. We were in school together.'

'An old boyfriend, was he?'

'Not exactly,' Maggi admitted. 'And, to tell the truth, I can't understand why he popped up so suddenly. He never——' You don't have to tell him everything, her conscience interrupted. So Henry never paid you a bit of attention. There's no need to broadcast that to the world!

'He never what?'

'Nothing.' Maggi sighed. Pru had stopped crying, lulled by the movement and the warmth. If only John could be soothed as easily as Prudence, she thought. Maybe he deserves more information. 'Nothing happened at the hayride,' she told him. 'That is, nothing happened between him and me. He remembers the wrong woman.'

'Well, that's *some* consolation,' the man beside her grumbled.

Yes, Maggi thought. Some, but not much. Why is he acting like a sore-headed bear? Obviously we haven't heard the end of this little episode!

What with one thing and another, Maggi was hardly any further ahead at eight o'clock the following evening, dithering as she stood in front of her wardrobe. The children had been moved back into their own room after the roof was repaired, and John was in the nursery now doing his best—or worst—to sing them to sleep.

'So I'll try the blue,' Maggi decided as she consulted her watch. She really had little choice. Four 'nice' dresses, and a wardrobe full of jeans and blouses. So the blue would have to do. It was the newest of the lot, barely five years old. She slipped it on over her white slip. It fitted a little more loosely then she remembered, not clinging so closely to her well-rounded hips, flowing outward in a wide skirt just at her knees, moulding her full breasts. The little white Peter Pan collar provided a demure match for the touch of lace on each sleeve. Although, it was one of those dresses that showed nothing—but revealed everything. She turned back and forth in front of her mirror and smiled. Henry Peterson truly meant nothing to her, but what woman didn't like to try out her weapons from time to time? The dress swished as she—— 'Wriggle my rear,' she muttered. 'I'll do it whenever I wish!' It was an item which had risen more than once, to John's anger.

Downstairs, Aunt Eduarda was giving the kitchen a final turn-out. Since the arrival of the babies the old lady had thrown off her retreat from the world and taken an active interest in everything that went on. She came smiling to the living-room door as she heard Maggi come down the stairs.

'Is this the young man who telephoned? Said he just had to know where you were, so I told him you were at the doctor's.'

So how about that? Maggi thought. Our meeting wasn't all that spontaneous after all. Henry knew exactly where to look when he decided to *accidentally* bump into her. Oh, well, women are schemers too, and as a matter of fact I like men who put a lot of thought into the pursuit.

'Oh, my,' her aunt commented as Maggi pirouetted to show off. 'My, what a lovely thing you are, my dear! That's what we used to call "wickedly demure" in my day.'

Maggi halted in mid-stride. 'Not *too* overdone, is it?'

'Not the slightest.' Aunt Eduarda grinned at her. 'It's fine enough even for churchgoing. You're not responsible for what men think, my dear.' There came a knock on the front door. 'And there he is now. I'll leave coffee on the stove. Now that I have my own television set up in my room I won't have to disturb you for a minute.'

'I don't want to drive you away,' Maggi protested.

'And I don't want to be the fifth wheel on this wagon,' the older woman remarked as she made for the stairs. Maggi watched her go, stood in front of the wall mirror to smooth both dress and hair, and went for the door. The knock sounded again.

She stood at the door, trying to calm down. Not since before her wedding had she dated a man, and she was uncertain and anxious. Things *did* change over the course of the years. Anybody who told you you hadn't changed in years was probably trying to sell you a used car. Or a bridge. She wiped the palm of her hand on the handkerchief balled up in her fist, and reached for the doorknob.

'Good evening,' Henry Peterson said. 'Look at you. You haven't changed a bit, Maggi!'

Maggi gulped as she almost swallowed her tongue. She waved him in and closed the door behind him. In the soft glow of the lamps he appeared not so angular. He was meticulously dressed, and carried a little spray of gardenias which he pressed on her.

She fumbled. Flowers had not been her thing since her brother-in-law Jake had smashed up her old car and tried to make amends. 'Thank you, Henry,' she managed to get out. 'Won't you sit down?'

He scanned the furniture, and chose the couch. Cautiously Maggi backed into the kitchen and found a vase that would do. 'Sit here by me,' Henry invited, patting the cushions beside him. Maggi gave him a timid smile and chose the chair opposite.

'I want to be able to see you,' she explained. He seemed to take that as some sort of compliment. She could see him swell inside his tan suit.

'It's been a long time, Henry.'

'Yes, a long time. But there was Robert, of course, and he and I didn't get along well.'

'I didn't know that.' She squirmed to plant both feet on the floor. The chair had been built with a deep seat, for big men like Robert—and John Dailey, she thought. So with her feet flat on the floor she occupied about three-quarters of the chair and had nothing to lean against. 'What have you been doing with yourself?'

'Oh, this and that. I went off to college, you know.'

She didn't, but hated to admit it, so she nodded and smiled. Curious, her conscience interrupted. Most men would say 'I graduated from college'. Why this 'I went off to college'? 'How nice. And now?'

'I'm in the real estate business,' he continued.

'Oh? I thought you might be at the bank. Your father was something at First Bristol, wasn't he?'

'I thought I might try banking.' Henry was looking very embarrassed indeed. 'The old man wanted me to—a father-and-son team, so to speak. But then I discovered I wasn't—compatible. So I switched.'

'A wise thing to do,' she acknowledged. 'Although I like First Bristol. I do all my banking there.'

'I know.' He grinned across the space that separated them. 'I hear your name mentioned from time to time. Only this week, for a fact, Dad mentioned you at the dinner table. That's why I decided to get in touch with you.'

And what do you say to something like that? Maggi did. 'Oh, really?'

'How about that drink you promised me?'

She was up out of her chair like a shot. 'Bourbon? Scotch?'

'Scotch on the rocks,' he said, and got up to come over behind her. The little cabinet-cum-bar sat in the far corner of the room. As she stretched for the Scotch he leaned over past her and reached it down, his body pressing against her back. 'I remember, Maggi,' he breathed into her ear. 'You were always one hot lady.'

She moved away, disconcerted more by the smell of his after-dinner mints than his words. 'Was I? I don't—quite remember it that way.' His hand reached in her direction. She filled it with his drink glass. At least that kept one of his hands occupied.

'Don't you remember that football rally in our senior year?' he coaxed. 'We went up into the project booth at the gym. Remember? That was a pretty wild hour or so, I sure remember.'

'You almost got expelled,' she returned in a confiding tone.

'I knew you'd remember.' He laughed. 'We ought to take up where we left off.'

'There's only one problem,' she told him, pushing him firmly away. 'That was Mary Anstruther, not me. She married, you know—a great big guy who works down on the dock. You want to be careful what you remember about Mary. He's a very possessive type of fellow.'

'There must be some mistake,' he muttered, taking quick refuge in the glass of Scotch in his hand.

'Probably,' she said, sighing. 'I was always the shy one. Sometimes I wish it could have been me that had all those adventures—but life's like that.

Henry took that as some sort of forgiveness. His grin returned, and he moved back to the sofa to re-group. 'You're not drinking?'

'I never do,' she replied softly. 'Nor smoke.'

'Well,' he said, fumbling to get his cigarette case out of sight, 'tell me about yourself.'

'There's not much to tell. After I graduated I took a secretarial course, but never cared for the work. And then Robert took me away from all that—and then—and then I've done odds and ends of things ever since. You know, I was never the ambitious type. And you? You never married?'

He shifted uneasily in his chair and finished off his drink. 'Yes, I married. But it didn't work out. She was a real nag, Betty was. Do this, do that, jump! And her father—a big faker. He lived like a millionaire, but all on borrowed money. They finally sent him to the slammer for embezzlement, and we were divorced.' He lifted his empty glass up and rolled it around in the light.

Maggi jumped at the hint, refilled the glass, and returned to her original seat. But Henry had acquired a little Dutch courage and wanted none of that. 'Over here,' he demanded, patting the couch cushion beside him.

So why not? Maggi thought. The whole idea was to try for a little adventure, wasn't it? The whole idea, her conscience nagged, was to make John Dailey jealous. Come on, babe! She made a face and came over to Henry's side.

The couch was old, from her grandmother's day. As soon as she sat down the springs sagged, throwing her against Henry's thigh.

'What a good idea,' he muttered, and tossed down his second drink. 'So I hear that you're thinking of selling the farm?' And immediately Maggi understood why her high school hero had come to look her up.

'Perhaps,' she said, sighing. 'I was *thinking* about it. Not very hard, you understand, but thinking.'

'Now isn't that something?' he murmured, shifting his body in her direction so that his shoulder was behind hers. His empty hand fell on her knee. His eyes were so close that she could almost see the dollar signs in them.

And this is where it's supposed to become interesting, Maggi told herself. Just hang on for a moment, and all sorts of things will happen. Just as soon as I get over the disgusted feeling I have! How much is rumour saying? That I plan to sell off the whole place?

'It's not true,' she told him gently.

'What's not true?'

'It's not true that she's a hot kid.' The voice came from the middle of the stairs, where John Dailey was standing, half in the dark. Maggi jumped like some fourteen-year-old whose father had just caught her making out with the boy next door. Luckily Henry's glass was empty, for it clattered to the floor and rolled against the wall. Mike came in from the kitchen to investigate; John came all the way down the stairs and stood in front of the fireplace, gazing moodily into the embers.

'Well, really!' Maggi gave both dog and man as dirty a look as she could summon up. The dog came over to the sofa and lay down in front of her, his muzzle resting on her shoe top. John moved over to the rocking-chair and sat down, picking up the evening paper.

'Don't let me bother you young people,' he said from behind the paper. 'I've been so busy I didn't have a chance to catch up on the news.'

'I think I'd like to have another drink,' Henry said.

'I think I'll join you,' Maggi muttered.

'In that case, I'll have one too,' said John from behind his paper fortress. 'The usual, Maggi. And go easy on the Scotch for yourself. You know how sick it made you the last time.'

She might have said something really nasty, but unfortunately what he said was true. A true believer in non-drinking, John had driven her to it with his tongue, with disastrous results. And now here he was doing it again! Grinding her teeth together to keep from answering, she went over to the bar and made them each a drink. 'I'm having coffee, myself,' she stated flatly.

'Good idea,' John returned. 'Know anything about babies, Peters?'

'Peterson,' Henry returned cautiously. 'No, I don't know anything about babies. Can't say that I'm interested. Do you live here?'

From out in the kitchen Maggi strained to hear the answer, and managed to burn her finger on the coffee-pot. By the time she returned to the living-room John was lecturing, Henry was leaning back on the sofa with a defeated look on his face, and Mike had withdrawn to his favourite place in front of the fireplace. Defiantly Maggi returned to the couch.

'Don't let us tie you up, John,' she interrupted. 'I'm sure Henry isn't interested in babies. Not every man is.'

'You are surely right,' John agreed.

The agreement surprised her; his warm, slippery tone frightened her. John Dailey, wheeler-dealer, was up to something big!

'That's a shame, too,' John continued. 'Knowing how much *you're* interested in children, Maggi, I doubt if any man who didn't like babies would stand a chance with you!'

'Oh, I'm interested.' Henry, startled out of his confusion, made a desperate attempt to get back into Maggi's favour. 'Of course I'm interested. Carrying on the family name, and all that. Who wouldn't be?'

'I'm glad to hear that,' John replied heartily. 'I have a couple of books and magazines here. You should look at them in your spare time. Anybody who's contemplating marriage ought to be up on this stuff.'

He deposited the handful of books in Henry's lap with a thud. Maggi took a close look at her visitor. Henry Peterson looked less and less like a man contemplating marriage as every second ticked away. 'You need another drink,' she offered in comfort.

'Not if he's driving,' John warned. 'Drunk driving is a terrible thing these days.' Before Maggi could think of a suitable response there was a tiny wail from upstairs, followed shortly by another. Both babies were complaining. 'Your turn.' John gestured towards the stairs.

It really wasn't her turn, according to the careful rota they had established. He was responsible for the babies from six at night until two in the morning. But Maggi had become so conditioned that she bounded up the stairs as fast as she could go. The nursery was not quite dark; a tiny seven-watt night-lamp was plugged into the baseboard socket.

Maggi snatched at little Pru. She had known, without knowing how, that Pru was the one who began the crying. More dominating Prissy had joined in for the fun of it. She cuddled Pru and walked the floor a few times, her eyes busy searching. One of the curtain rods had fallen down; the clatter had probably awakened the baby. A few more steps and Pru, tired from a day full of exercise, was fast asleep.

As soon as her sister—her partner-in-crime, Maggi told herself—went silent Prissy gave up and rolled over. Another few minutes to be sure they were settled, and then Maggi carefully sorted out the curtain rod. It was not something once could fix in the dark; its replacement would be added to the long list of tasks already on the list for tomorrow. But at this exact moment Maggi had an immensely important job to do. She crept out of the room on her rubber-soled shoes and almost ran down the stairs. John was behind his newspaper again.

'Where—where's Henry?' she snapped at him.

The top of the paper lowered just far enough for his eyes to show. His innocent, naïve eyes. 'Your boy-friend? Oh, he said something about a previous engagement. And he said he'd call you again soon.' The paper snapped back up again. Maggi bounced off the last two stairs and stalked across the room to confront him. The dog scented the air and scampered for the kitchen.

'Just what the hell do you think you're doing?'

'Who, me?' The paper lowered about halfway. 'Reading the paper. Did you see where Mike Greenwald is going to hold out? That kid wants more than a million dollars to play for the Red Sox. Can you——?' Maggi snatched the paper out of his hands and very slowly began to shred it, page by page. 'Hey!' he objected. 'I haven't finished the——'

'Believe me, you've finished,' she told him grimly. 'Now just what the hell do you think you were doing?'

'Stamp your foot,' he suggested.

'I will,' she threatened. 'Right on your head I'll stamp. Well?'

'This is hardly fair,' he murmured. 'I ought to have time to consult with my lawyer.'

'If you don't get to it,' she spluttered, 'I'll—I'll——' But her anger was too much for her, and the words tumbled around and got trapped in her mouth.

'Interesting,' he said. 'You seem to have a terrible case of distemper.' He was up on his feet, trapping her in those two massive arms, before she could take evasive action. 'Now listen, Maggi.' He gently pulled her head flat against his chest and held it there with one hand, while the other coursed her back. 'The guy is a loser—a real loser. Whatever he's interested in, it's not your delectable little body—well, at least seduction is only his secondary interest. I don't know what's leading the little man on—but even if he's sincere he's not for you.'

'So tell me something I don't know,' she muttered. 'Whatever gave you the right to come down here and poke yourself into my life like that? You had no right!'

'No right? Maggi!' His hand left her cheek and his fingers walked gently through her hair. 'Look, Mrs

Brennan, you can't expect anything else from me. There I was at the head of the stairs, listening while that pea-brained idiot made love to *my* girl. No red-blooded Irishman could put up with that!'

She managed to push herself away from him, as much as an inch or two, far enough away so she could watch his face. 'I'm not your girl,' she said in anger. 'Watch my lips. I—am—not—your—girl!'

'What?' His hands fastened on her shoulders and stood her off at arm's length while he examined her face. 'You're not my girl? That's a lie, isn't it?'

It required a little more concentration, but she managed. 'I am not your girl,' she announced.

He lifted both hands up in the air in a surrender gesture, and moved three or four steps back. 'Can I be wrong?' He sounded amazed. 'I was wrong once before, but that was twenty years ago. You're not my girl?' She nodded her head. His hands dropped to his sides. 'You're not my girl?' he asked mournfully.

'Got it in one,' she said. 'I am not your girl.' And he's playing a game, she told herself. He's having more trouble keeping from laughing than I am. Besides, when he moved away he left me feeling—cold? Lonely? Disappointed?

'Thrown over for a mutt like Henry Peterville,' he muttered.

'Peterson,' she corrected. 'I can't stand him.' His grin spread. So did hers. 'All he wants is my money, and since I don't have any—well . . .'

'You're not my girl? We have to test the theory.' He extended both arms in her direction. She rocked back and forth on her heels for a moment. Every time you give in to him, you make it that much more impossible to ever stand on your own feet, her conscience warned. Maggi struggled with the thought, and then flew across the intervening space and into those warm protective arms.

'See?' he said disingenuously a moment or two later. 'Your body thinks that you're my girl.'

'Maybe it knows more than I do.' She sighed contentedly. 'Convince me.'

He kissed her. Three short words, supposedly all one needed to cover the contact of his warm moist lips, the penetration of his tongue beyond the barrier of her teeth, the fire that shot up and down her spine, the roiling in her stomach, and that maddening scream of *want* from further down. She trembled as her arms went up around his neck, pulling herself upward against the steel of him until one foot was off the ground and the other making contact only by toe. Both his hands were around her; the one pressed in the middle of her back, welding her to him, crushing her firm full breasts against his chest muscles. The other wandered south, made circles in the centre of her tiny waist, dropped to caress the round fullness of her hips and buttocks, and circled back again, and they finally ran out of breath.

'You're not my girl?' he whispered in her ear as his arms still held her in thrall.

'Maybe I am,' she gasped. 'Maybe.'

'Another twenty seconds of this,' he warned, 'and there won't be any maybes.'

A tiny bit of sanity tugged at Maggi's brain centres. She had been raised to strict disciplines, strong morals; caution dictated a stop. Her sigh was massive as she dropped her hands. He let her settle on her own feet again, but she could see the disconcerted look on his face.

'Still only maybe?'

'Still only maybe,' she agreed, stepping away from him. 'Propinquity, that's all it is.'

'I guess so,' he said regretfully. 'Propin who?'

'You know what it means,' she lectured. 'Lawyers know everything about words. It means we're living too close to each other. We've become too involved—because of the babies, of course.'

'Yes, of course.' He definitely sounded mournful about the whole affair, her ears reported. 'Propinquity. I'll think about it.'

'Where are you going?' He had one hand on the stair-rail, and already she regretted that she had stopped him.

'I'm going upstairs,' he told her. That little grin was playing with the corners of his mouth again. 'I'm going to get a cold shower. And if you really want to preserve your—propinquity—you'd damn well better get out of my way!'

Maggi jumped at the fierceness of his statement, clapping her hand over her mouth to shut off any smart remarks that might surface. He was gone in a second; in three she heard the shower rattle. Cold water? Does that really do any good? she asked herself. One of her hands wandered from her flank up over her breast and down again as she struggled with her own internal devils.

There were glasses and cups all over the room. While her mind dreamed her practical hands went to work, picking up. The coffee in her mug was lukewarm; she drank it in one swallow, and wandered out to the kitchen with her hands full. Mike followed after her, wagging his tail in funereal beat.

'Cold showers?' she asked the dog. 'Come on, let's take a walk.' For once in a dozen years the big Dalmatian came without a protest. Even the dog feels sorry for you, she told herself. You had your chance and you blew it. One day that man is going to get you in his bed and you'll be——

'Happy?' she muttered as she closed the door behind her and stepped out into the cool white moonlight.

CHAPTER SEVEN

'HIM again?' John Dailey was standing at the kitchen sink, supporting Prissy in her bath. The baby was all gurgles and smiles, kicking away at the water, while Pru, being held in the other end of the white-tiled sink, was leaning against Maggi's hand, fretting a little. Maggi was using her other hand to hang up the telephone. John did not exactly look best pleased.

'Four nights this past week,' he grumbled. 'Doesn't he realise that you have work to do?'

'True love,' Maggi said with a sigh as she batted her curly eyelashes. 'And flowers again today. Do you know, the last man to send me flowers was Herbe LeGrande, way back there on my fourteenth birthday!' And then, to the baby who was almost successful in sitting up by herself, 'Kick your feet, love. Exercise is good for you.' Prudence didn't agree. She whimpered.

'That's a very long time ago,' John muttered.

'Thanks a lot,' she snapped. 'I heard that. It wasn't as long ago as *your* fourteenth! And besides, Henry sent me that lovely box of chocolates for my birthday!'

'I brought you a birthday present too,' he protested glumly. 'Doesn't that count?'

'Of course it counts,' she said, feeling ready to chop him up into little pieces. It had been a difficult day, and she might well have tried to murder her mother, never mind John Dailey. 'But it's not a contest, you know.' The babies both splashed at the same time, catching him as he leaned over. He spluttered, wiped his eyes, and looked daggers at her.

'If it is a contest, Peterson isn't within miles of the starting line.'

Maggi, who had a considerable amount of water dripping down her face too, glared back at him. 'I was trying to be nice, but that doesn't pay, does it? Once you get into your black bear act there's no pleasing you. He sent me chocolates; you gave me a pair of scrubbing brushes for the bath tub. Now what kind of a gift was that?'

'Why are you screaming at me like a fishwife?'

'Because that's what I am!' she shouted. 'Robert was a fisherman and I was his wife! Why do you treat *me* as if you and I have been married for ten years?'

'Twenty,' he grumbled. 'What does Peterson want?'

'What else?' She picked Pru up and folded her into the warm towel. 'He wants me to go out with him Saturday night.'

'You can't do that!' Prissy was giving him a hard time. Slippery as a little eel, the tiny creature was giggling and twisting and kicking. 'You can't do that,' he repeated as he finally captured the little rascal and bundled her up.

'That's funny,' Maggi replied. 'I thought we'd settled that before now.'

'Settled what?'

'Use more powder,' she instructed. 'She's beginning another rash. I thought we'd settled that you don't tell *me* what to do.'

'Well, somebody has to tell you,' he snapped. 'You know darn well what he wants.'

'I'm not so sure.' She looked up at him as she stretched Pru out on the kitchen table. 'I thought at first he wanted my money, but I don't have any. Maybe it's my pure white body—or the farm? I keep forgetting that he's in real estate. Maybe I *will* go out with him on Saturday.'

'Lord, if he wants the farm give it to him,' grumbled John. 'Don't fool around. But watch that other bit. I want your pure white body for myself!'

'Sure you do,' she said disgustedly. 'You want me at your own time and at your own convenience. You don't fool me a bit with that come-on of yours. You've got a good thing going for you here in my house——'

'I don't know about that convenience business. And you're not exactly paying me a princely sum for looking after the children,' he reminded her.

'Princely? Even at the going rate I'm not sure I'm getting my money's worth, so knock off the come-on!'

'Come-on? Lady, you haven't seen come-on yet. You still can't go out with him on Saturday. That's the night we're taking off.'

'What are you mumbling about now?' She was using only half her mind on the interchange. The other half was busy leading Prudence through her battery of little exercises. Ordinarily the little monkey would be all smiles. Tonight she was bothered by something.

'Saturday night,' he repeated. 'Dr Jonas. Take a night off once a week. Go lock yourselves in your bedroom and see what happens. *That* night off.'

She looked up at him, using one hand on Pru's stomach to hold her in place. There was caution in her eyes. 'I'm not too bright,' she said, 'but I didn't exactly come down in yesterday's rainstorm. Lock myself in a bedroom with you? What is this, feeding time at the zoo?'

John shook his head in disgust. 'You can't really be Portuguese—I've heard that they're kindly people. How many bodies have you left by the roadside, killed with that rapier tongue of yours?'

'I never keep track.' She looked up at him again. He had finished with Prissy, and was supporting the baby against his shoulder with one capable hand. He had never before said anything about her brittle wit. How could he know that she used it to protect herself, to cover up the marshmallow centre at the core of her being? 'John?'

'Yes?'

'I—don't mean to be—it's just the way I am. I'm sorry if—did you have something planned for Saturday night?'

'In a manner of speaking. I've hired an LPN nurse to come in and watch the kids from six o'clock on. The American Ballet company is in town. They're performing *Swan Lake* at the Zeiterion this weekend. I thought we might go along and see the ballet, and then pop over to the Twin Piers for a late supper.'

'Oh, my, that *does* sound attractive.' She was wavering. 'But I did promise Henry.'

'And what was Henry Liverpool offering?'

'Peterson,' she corrected automatically. 'I'm not sure. He mentioned something about lifting a few down at Bunratty's. I get the suspicion that he intended a few rounds of wrestling in his apartment afterwards.'

'Well?'

'I just don't know.' I've got to hold to my principles, she told herself. This business of giving in to him whenever he turns on the charm has got to stop! She flashed him another quick look. 'I'm sorry you've gone to all the trouble of hiring a nurse. I always thought I'd like to be a nurse. I think it had something to do with those cute caps they wear, rather than the work. But then again I heard that Bunratty's is a swinging place, and I haven't been out on the town in a dog's age. Come on, let's get these darlings into bed.'

'That's all this relationship means to you—the children?'

'That's all I can take care of at one time,' she returned. 'I don't think I'm in the market for a quick affair, which is all you've been offering.' He mumbled something under his breath and headed for the stairs.

Maggi went along behind him to help put the children to bed. Her conscience bothered her. After all, these two little mites who had grabbed at her heart deserved her complete attention, and all her squabbling with John Dailey was taking the edge off their need. It took more than a little doing this time, getting them down. Pru fussed and grumbled. Prissy watched her twin with wide blue eyes, not knowing whether to join in or not. In the end Maggi sang to them, something of a relief from John's cracked baritone. When they both came downstairs Aunt Eduarda had just finished in the kitchen. The three adults sat for a while, meditatively, in the silence of the living-room. A sort of truce hung over the former battlefield.

Maggi was not much of a woman for meditation. Silence bothered her, and olive branches were really her thing. 'How's your American business venture going on, John?'

He lowered the paper and shook his head. 'You wouldn't believe. I've had three bids already, and it's only been three weeks since I made the first contact. If things go on the way they appear right now I might be forced to re-examine all my future plans.'

'So it's something you have that you want to sell?'

He ducked his head behind his paper. 'More or less. Lease if I can, sell if I must. It depends on the offer.'

A rattle of pages seemed to put a full stop to that line of conversation. I don't know why I keep trying, she thought bitterly. He doesn't want me to know, and that's the end of that. She snapped on the television and clicked her way through all the channels without finding anything she liked.

'Something wrong, Maggi?'

'No, nothing. Just a little twinge,' she told him. 'I shouldn't have put raw onions in that seafood salad.'

'It wasn't the onions, it was the salad,' he said. 'Poisonous stuff, salad. Anything green is poisonous.'

'And with that sage advice, I think I'll go out on the porch and get a little air. It's a lovely balmy night.' Aunt Eduarda gave them both a twinkling grin, and marched slowly out into the kitchen to get her shawl.

'She's not getting any younger,' Maggi said as the old lady disappeared out into the moonlit darkness. 'Ever since she retired from the school system she's been at a loose end.'

'No, none of us are getting any younger.' John folded his paper and dropped it in his lap. 'I didn't know she was a teacher.' Which was more conversation than she had heard in the past two hours. And then he threw her a curve. 'How does it feel to be thirty?' He ducked just in time. Her pillow landed squarely in the place where his face would have been.

She struggled up out of the sofa. 'I'm going for a walk.'

'I'll come with you.' He laid the carefully folded paper down on the end table.

'No, thank you. I need to think.'

'I'll help. I'm a great thinker-helper.'

'I'm sure you are, but tonight I feel the need to fly solo. Besides you're on baby-watch until two in the morning.'

'Spoilsport!'

'You'll never really know,' she said, sighing, and went out on to the porch. Although it was a warm night for early June, there was still a chill in the air, and she was wearing only a sleeveless dress. She walked over to the rail and looked out, wrapping herself up in her own arms.

'You two seem to be forever bickering.' The chains on the porch swing squeaked as Aunt Eduarda got up and came over to join her. There was no sting in the words; it was not an accusation.

'He's a hard man to understand,' Maggi admitted softly.

'The babies?'

'Wonderful little creatures. I always wanted babies of my own. I'd love to be mother to these two, but——'

'But you can't stand Mr Dailey?'

'I can't even say that.' Maggi laughed at herself. 'Can you imagine that? I'm thirty years old and can't make up my mind!'

'Happens to us all at some age,' her aunt replied. 'Twenty—thirty—forty. Sooner or later. It has something to do with God's design to populate the earth.'

'You don't mean I'm smitten by the maternal yearning? Surely not every woman goes through that?'

'Perhaps not, dear. But most do. You just can't see John as the man for you?'

'I don't know, do I?' Maggi said bitterly. 'He's explained to me very carefully that he's here on a temporary kick. As soon as he finds out about this hush-hush business deal of his he expects to load up and go back to Ireland. And in the meantime here's slow-witted Maggi Brennan to entertain him—locally, that is.'

'It's not exactly a one-night stand,' her aunt admonished. Maggi's head snapped around and she stared. Her Portuguese aunt was so much out of character that it puzzled her.

'No,' Maggi returned, still bitter. 'It's more like a one-month lease. I don't see myself as his mistress, but more like his concubine-in-waiting.'

'Maggi!'

'Yes,' Maggi snapped. 'And even that's a lie. No, he hasn't had me in his bed—yet, but it's a subject close to the top of his list. Goodnight, *Tia*, I'm going to walk up the hill a way and see if I can't puzzle this whole thing out.'

She stamped down off the porch, rattling a loose board on the steps as she went. Just one more thing that needs fixing around here, she told herself as she followed the silver moon-path up towards the fence that separated her farm from the apartments building site.

The Jones boy had re-ploughed her lower ten acres on the same day the men had come to repair the leaky roof, leaving the twenty-acre tract that lay next to the building site for possible sale. But not to Swanson and his gang of pirates, she assured herself. And shortly after the ploughing a pair of schoolboys had come to seed the area. Five acres in sweet corn, the kind called salt-and-pepper, guaranteed a good local market and a money crop. The other five were set in hilled potatoes, for her own family's consumption. She had been lucky to get the school kids. With unemployment in the Greater New Bedford area standing at 3.3 per cent, she had been lucky to find *anybody* to do stoop labour.

With one foot in a furrow she found herself repeating her grandfather's age-old custom: she reached down for a handful of soil and tasted it. But her mind was on John Dailey, and she could hardly remember whether the ploughed land was sweet or sour. John Dailey, itinerant heartbreaker. The wandering lawyer, bon vivant, and all-round womaniser. And I'm the woman, she thought. How now, brown cow?

She puzzled at it from all angles, accepting, rejecting, changing—all to no avail. It was a no-win situation. A good, well-raised Portuguese girl had only one relationship with a man. Marriage was the name of the game. He certainly didn't have *that* subject in mind, but Maggi was wavering, and could actually think of herself as accepting second-best.

If he would offer even that, she reminded herself. So far this week he had acted like a self-centred spoilsport, not wanting her for himself, but unwilling to see her go to any other man! How exasperating could a man be? If he would only proposition her, at least she'd have the reward of a good strong turndown! So now, Maggi Brennan, she thought, how do you entice a man into making a proposition, just so you can turn him down to boost your ego?

It was a subject beyond her ken. So be proud, she told herself. Suffer a little. Eat a little dirt and cry up a storm! Which sounded like good advice, so she did.

The wind was in the right direction to bring her the sound from the bell-tower of St Lawrence's Church, down in the city, striking twelve. Having solved nothing, but feeling much relieved, Maggi snatched up a twist of long grass to chew on, and went back down the hill.

The house was quiet when she came in. Closing the door shut out the vague meandering of the breeze and damped the hoarse song of the frogs in the swamp. Instead she heard the murmuring as her electric kitchen muttered and cycled and hummed to itself in the darkness.

She felt her way to the stairwell, slipping off her hard-heeled shoes to mask her passage. At the top of the stairs she paused from force of habit, and stole down the hall to the nursery. The night-light plugged into the baseboard socket cast an eerie pink glow over everything.

The two babies were fast asleep in their massive crib. But while Prissy had turned over on her stomach with her knees bunched up under her, content, Prudence was lying flat on her back, arms outstretched, stirring restlessly. With infinite care Maggi readjusted the blankets, fingered a kiss on both foreheads, and went back out into the hall.

A slight glow of light from the half-open door of the last room down indicated that Aunt Eduarda had fallen asleep with her TV set on. A few steps up the hall the door of John's bedroom had swung half open, due, Maggi remembered, to a slant in the two-century-old flooring. There was no night-light in his room, but a splinter of moonglow had evaded his curtains. She stopped to watch.

John Dailey was asleep as well, and there was evidence of difficulty in settling down. All his blankets had fallen off the far side of his bed, and the sheets had twisted up under his feet. One of his arms lay at his side; the other was wrapped around his head. He slept without pyjamas, all the male magnificence of him displayed by moonlight.

Startled, Maggi drew a deep breath. It whistled around her windpipe as she tried vainly to suppress the noise. The sleeper moved an inch or two, and then settled again on his side. Maggi held her breath, unable to tear her eyes away from the spectacle. It had been a long time, a very long time, since she had seen such a sight. It awoke yearnings, needs, that pounded at her and shook her, body and mind together. Memories?

No, her conscience dictated cruelly. Not memories. There was a time and a place, but those aren't the reasons why you react now. This man isn't a shadow, a recall of your dead husband. This man is real, distinct, calling you. And you want him, Maggi Brennan! The bitterness of the accusation hurt. She crammed her fist over her mouth to stifle the scream of pain, and ran for her own bed.

Safe behind her own closed door she sank into the chair by her window and wrestled with her ghosts. The clock downstairs chimed twice before she donned her shortie nightgown and climbed into bed. It chimed again before her eyes closed in troubled sleep.

It was probably those troubled dreams that allowed Maggi to hear that first protest from the nursery. It started out as a tiny whimper. By the time it was repeated Maggi's feet were on the cold floor, and she was moving towards the door. She had, from studying the book, expected some floor-walking in the middle of the night, but in all the weeks the twins had been in the house they had slept gloriously through the night. If one presumed, of course, that night ended by five-thirty in the morning.

So when the baby transferred her complaints to a higher register Maggi was already in the nursery, bending over the crib. And by that time both of the twins were bellowing. 'Easy, baby,' Maggi crooned as she lifted Prudence up, blanket and all, and rested the child on her shoulder. A few casual pats on the back, a little pacing up and down, certainly that would be all that was required. If the original complaint came from Prudence.

Left in the bed by herself, Prissy squirmed towards the head of the crib on her stomach, yelling. Handling two at a time was too much. Maggi was about to sound the general alarm when John padded into the room, barefoot, wearing a pair of pyjama bottoms that just seemed to hang on his hips, defying the laws of gravity. He snatched Prissy up, and tried a little of his male magic.

'I don't know what's wrong,' Maggi whispered. She laid Pru down on the bathinette table, one of the late additions to the nursery, and began to strip the baby of her shirt and nappy. The ceiling light came on as John flipped the switch. Prudence was kicking her feet awkwardly, chewing madly on her thumb, and yelling loudly enough to alert the town's volunteer fire department. Priscilla, still in his arms, ran into a coughing fit, choked, and started yelling in earnest.

'I can't find anything wrong,' Maggi whispered.

'Hell, with all this yelling there's no sense whispering. Which one started the trouble?'

'I don't know. I *thought* it was Pru. Maybe it's both of them. One of them doesn't necessarily have to be imitating the other, you know.'

'Then move over,' he grumbled, 'and let me see if it's this one.'

Maggi hurriedly shoved Pru into a Pamper and was brushed aside as he moved up to the table and stripped Prissy. Several minutes of serious study, and he sighed. 'I can't see anything wrong. Try walking them again?'

'Diaper her and give her to me,' Maggi directed. 'I'll walk both of them while you check that book. There *has* to be something. Did you read the whole thing?'

With both babies in her arms, fourteen pounds apiece, she began to pace again, humming what she hoped was a restful song.

'No,' he confessed as he fumbled on the top shelf in the corner. 'I only got to chapter seven. You?'

'Six,' she mumbled. 'Chapter six. It's not a book written for high-speed reading. Hurry up. You don't suppose they're hungry? You did give them a bottle after dinner?'

'Don't nag,' he grumbled. 'Nothing I hate worse than a nagging woman. I gave them a bottle. Here's that damn book.'

'Each?' I don't intend to nag, she told herself, but he's only a man. You have to be sure! It tore at her heart to see the two little ones in pain.

'Yes, each. Dammit, do you want me to run downstairs and get another?' He hardly sounded best pleased about the whole idea, but Maggi was not about to let him shirk his responsibilities.

'Better you than me,' she told him. 'And stop cursing. Who knows what the pair of them might remember as they grow up?'

'All right, all right.' He made a dash for the door, and evidently stubbed his bare toe on the little occasional table that stood in the hall just outside the nursery door, for several short Gaelic words floated in the air behind him as he limped along the hall. Maggi had the insane urge to clamp her hands over the babies' ears, but all her hands were in play. She tried to cover the sounds by singing a little louder. The babies gave her no good reaction as she zoomed through the two lullabies she remembered; when she shifted to 'Yellow Submarine' one of the children stopped crying, almost in disbelief. But it was only a temporary cessation.

From downstairs there came noises. Doors slammed, things crashed on the kitchen floor, various words were almost shouted. 'That'll teach you to be a father,' Maggi whispered. 'Er—whatever.' She thought a great deal more. He would make a fine father, once he learned to control his language! And I'm not sure, she told herself, how many other fathers would be up in the middle of the night, helping out with the children. Probably the whole difficulty would be left to their wives! I'm lucky to—and then her spirit dropped through the floor—to be a prospective parent. Which reminded her that Ms Fagan was coming—a thought she didn't care to entertain!

There was just no time to be sorry for herself. John was back, moving at the speed of a world-class father, with a half-filled bottle in each hand.

'Sorry about that,' he said. 'There was only one full bottle in the refrigerator.'

'You warmed it?'

'Dammit,' he growled, 'why do all women think men are idiots where babies are concerned? Of course I warmed it. Give me this one.' He relieved her of the baby on her right shoulder, and passed her one of the bottles. She tilted the baby down across her breast and tempted the little lips with the bottle. Prudence automatically opened her mouth, took a quick gulp, and rejected it. The other baby, in John's arms, accepted the feast and began sleepily to feed.

'So it's Pru,' he guessed. 'She's been fussing all night.'

'But I don't know what's the matter!' Maggi wailed. 'Check the book again.'

'I'm checking, I'm checking.' He stretched Prissy out on the bathinette, supporting her bottle with one hand while he leafed through the manual with the other. Prudence was wailing like a banshee, and Prissy gave up her quiet feed and joined the chorus. Maggi paced the floor madly, rubbing the child's back, trying to sing. He held Prissy down with one gentle hand on her stomach as he madly searched through the book.

'What in the loving world is going on here?' Aunt Eduarda was at the door. Her grey hair was braided over her shoulder. The lace collar of her nightgown projected up out of her green robe. Her glasses were perched on the end of her nose.

'I don't know what's the matter,' Maggi said wearily. 'It seems that something's bothering Pru, and Prissy is crying in sympathy. I suppose we'd better call the doctor—or head for the emergency-room? John?'

'Maybe you're right. Hold this one, Aunt Eduarda, while I go find some pants.'

'Don't be in such a hurry,' the old lady chided. 'Babes in the woods, the pair of you! You've done fine as long as everything was working well, but at the first sign of trouble you blow your stack. Which is the one that started the problem?'

'This one,' Maggi replied. 'Pru.'

Aunt Eduarda came over in front of them and looked the baby over casually. Then, to Maggi's surprise, she stuck her index finger in the child's mouth. The child yelled all the louder, but the aunt was grinning as she retrieved her finger.

'There's nothing really wrong with this child,' she reported. 'Wait right here, the both of you. I'll be back in a moment.'

'Don't ask me,' John said, catching Maggi's glance over the old lady's head. 'Pace a little faster.'

'I'm beat,' Maggi replied. '*You* pace a time or two.'

'I don't dare to,' he reported solemnly. 'My pyjama bottoms are about to fall off.'

'At this hour of the day who would care?' she snapped. 'Or are you one of those super-equipped models?'

'Hey, don't knock it,' he told her. 'Just pace. Sing a little, and——'

And Aunt Eduarda was back, humming a little Portuguese tune, a tiny bottle in her hand. 'Now then, if you two would stop glaring at each other?' She unscrewed the cap, collected a couple of drops of the liquid on her finger, and stuck the finger into the baby's mouth. One precious minute passed, and almost as if on cue baby Prudence stopped crying, gurgled at them, and fell asleep. Prissy kept up her serenade for an additional moment, grumbled to herself, and fell off to sleep. The quiet that descended on the room was startling.

'Dear heaven,' Maggi whispered.

'Teeth,' Aunt Eduarda said quietly, and gave them both a big smile.

'What is that?' John demanded, pointing to the bottle.

'A form of benzocaine,' the aunt said. 'In my day we used paregoric, but that's a derivative of morphine, and it's gone out of style. The pair of them will be cutting teeth for the next few months, so you might as well get used to it. I'll leave this bottle on the shelf here, shall I?'

'Why not?' Maggi moaned. 'Teeth! Why couldn't I think of that?'

'Because you're not their mother, and he's not their father,' Eduarda commented. 'Now do you suppose we could get back to bed? It's well past the shank of the night.'

'Now how stupid can I get?' Maggi asked the empty night as they watched the aunt disappear down the hall.

'No more stupid than me.' John stood close to her, one arm around her waist. The babies were sleeping soundly. Maggi moved away from him nervously and straightened out the crib and the blankets. He recaptured her again as she completed the task and gathered up the two baby bottles.

'Come on,' he added as he snapped off the nursery lights and ushered her out into the dark corridor. It was in that second, as they stepped across the threshold, that Maggi became alarmingly aware of him. With the crisis passed she was almost overwhelmed by the knowledge of him, pressing hard against her flank, his bare upper torso touching her, warming her through the thin cotton nightgown she was wearing. A strange excitement ran up and down her spine, originating in that little swell of her hip where his hand rested.

The night was filled with a huge electrical charge. He was as much aware of her as she was of him. She could actually breathe in the excitement that crowded down on her. She shivered. He held her closer.

'Cold?'

'N-no,' she stuttered. 'Not really. I forgot my robe.'

'Yes, I noticed.' His hand drifted further, until it rested on her flat, trembling stomach. Alarms were ringing in her mind; she purposefully ignored them. At her door they stopped. 'We've hardly two hours before the twins will be up and about for the day,' he said. 'We have a lot to talk about. Shall we?'

'I—don't mind,' she stammered. Without being able to search his face in the dim light she was momentarily doubtful. But of course, she thought, he's a typical virile male. It isn't words he wants. Not with his hand inching upward, reaching across the soft wisp of cotton that was her gown. It isn't words he wants, and—dear heaven—it isn't words I want, either! Still, I can't just—surrender. That isn't the way I was raised. Perhaps a rearguard action will show some alternative? 'But—the bottles—they have to go back to the refrigerator or they'll spoil.'

'Damn! I should have ordered another refrigerator for upstairs!'

'No,' she spat at him. 'That would be a terrible waste of money, and besides—take the bottles downstairs and then——'

'Come back?' he interrupted.

Maggi took a deep breath to steady her nerves. When push came to shove there had to be some sort of commitment. He had finally thrown down the gauntlet, and she was faced with the demon choice. And I love him, she told herself in the hush that followed.

'And come back,' she agreed, suppressing the note of desperation in her voice.

CHAPTER EIGHT

INSIDE her room, Maggi paced. There was a lock on her door. There was still time to change her mind. She could easily get dressed and run away. It wasn't too late to join a nunnery. Her mother would never approve of this. Neither would her father. Her dog wouldn't approve. Heavens, what am I doing? she thought.

It was a question that had no answer. She was already committed. Now all she needed was to get back her nerve and go through with it. It's just like swimming, she lectured herself. You never really forgot. And once you get in, the water will feel fine. 'Sure it will,' she muttered sarcastically. 'But what about once *he* gets in?' Stop the double entendres, babe. All over the world there are thousands of women, right this minute, who are doing the same thing and enjoying it! 'Planning to do it,' she corrected. 'And some of them are great bloody fools!'

A girl was in desperate straits when even her conscience gave up on her. The alternatives flashed in front of her; she brushed them off. *Vai diminuir*, she told herself in her fast-fading Portuguese. 'Take it easy.' There was a cool wind blowing in through her half-opened window. She shivered as she pulled her nightgown over her head and folded it neatly at the foot of her big comfortable bed. It had been her signal, she remembered, for Robert. In this very room. In this very room. She walked slowly around the room, touching bed and bureau and chair, saying goodbye to her memories before she locked them firmly away. Her hands cupped her breasts for a moment. Her flesh was as cold as the night. It had all been so long ago; she was a mental virgin, with a virgin's fears, and a widow's anticipations. There was a noise on the steps. She flipped off the lights and slid under the covers, pulling the sheets up to her chin.

He did not come.

She shivered, reached out desperately for an extra blanket, and huddled herself up in a ball. Make believe you're asleep, she told herself. Her eyelids slammed down like jail bars, but her mind still ran on and on. A woman can't just *do* something like this, she half sobbed. There has to be a reason! So you like sex, her conscience suggested. But not that much! So tell yourself that you're in love with him! I don't have to *tell* myself. I *am* in love with him, but I dare not let him know that. I suppose I could lie about it if he asks, couldn't I? I didn't have any compunction about lying to the State inspector. And, besides, it's only a little lie. A little lie now and then can't hurt! And maybe—you know damn well it could be a lot of fun and games.

And on the other hand, she assured herself, I'm really doing it for the babies, aren't I? Isn't that a great line? But the inexorable facing of the truth could not be denied. I don't care why I'm doing it, I'm just doing it! Where the hell is he?

Night sounds seemed to have slowed almost to a stop. In the distance she could hear the mournful wail of the siren at the Dartmouth fire station, the call for volunteer firefighters to report in. In the other direction the foghorn on the New Bedford hurricane dyke sounded. And still John Dailey didn't come.

The clock downstairs struck the half-hour. A fire truck rumbled south on Tucker Road, its beeper sounding softly. He's not coming, Maggi thought ruefully. After all that, he's not coming! An owl coughed in the old oak tree outside her window. He's not coming! She shook with spasmatic pain. Something—some strength, some excitement—flew out of her body. She felt bereft. The clock struck the next quarter-hour.

Damn him! Maggi snarled to herself. Damn all men! There's not a one of them to be trusted! And at that moment the latch on her door clicked, and he came in.

You're asleep, Maggi commanded herself. You're asleep. You can't be responsible for anything that happens while you're asleep! Her eyes were glued shut; she struggled to slow her breathing as his footsteps padded across the room. There was a new smell in the air—soap and aftershave. He'd stopped to shave! Maggi swallowed hard.

The other side of her mattress sank, there was a movement of the blankets that now almost covered her head, and a wave of warmth enveloped her. It was almost impossible for her to lie still, but she struggled to do just that. He shifted his weight in her direction, and the entire bed shook. The bed stopped shaking, but Maggi's tense body did not. His warm hand had just landed in that little niche at her waist where her hip blossomed out. A warm, confident hand.

'Maggi?'

She struggled to keep from answering. He moved nearer. She could feel the contact as his hip touched hers. The hand coursed upward, hesitated a moment to draw circles around her navel, and then climbed upward, a finger at a time. When it arrived at the curve of her breast she could no longer stand the suspense. Her nerves were shattered; her body remembered what her mind was trying to forget. She half turned in his direction, only to be pushed back flat on her back as he inched himself closer and brooded over her. Somebody moaned in the darkness. His fingers had conquered the satin mountain, and the bronze sentry at the top had sprung to mindless attention.

'Oh, lord,' somebody muttered.

Lips. Cool, wonderful lips. They kissed the pulse-point on her neck, shifted to the lobe of her ear, and then coasted effortlessly to and over her mouth and were gone.

Fire flashed up and down her spine. The hand on her breast came slowly down the declivity and attacked the other mountain, producing the same result. Despite her determination to remain still, her hips quivered, jerked, and her head spun.

'Fast asleep, Maggi?' His lips were at her ear. She could hear the overtone of laughter as his sharp teeth nipped at the lobe nearest him. Once again his head moved. Those warm lips marched down the side of her face, down her neck, into the valley between her breasts. A moment of withdrawal. She gasped and twitched uncontrollably. Teeth were nipping at the bronze peak of her breast. Nipping, and then sliding deeper as his lips savoured the honey of her.

'Nothing to say, Maggi?' His tongue plagued one nipple, while his hand trapped the other between thumb and forefinger and gently massaged it. The sensations were playing in colour behind her eyelids. Brilliant splashes of red and orange. Vaulting silver rockets against the backdrop of green and blue. Somebody moaned; Maggi reached to the depths of her self-control and found just enough power to freeze her body in position. It was a fruitless victory.

He inched himself a little closer. She could feel the weight of his chest on her. His head was below her chin as his mouth tasted and teased. The hand that once had conquered her breast slid off the pulsing mound of softness, making for the flat plane of her stomach. She gasped involuntarily. He stopped all actions.

Don't stop! she wanted to yell. Don't—what are you doing to me? But her mind still held tentative rule. What am *I* doing? I'm asleep, aren't I? It can hardly be my fault if he——

He did. The hand returned to her stomach, twirled in circles for a moment, then dived lower. Without consulting Maggi, her legs spread, opening to the new invasion. One finger flicked against that most responsive point in her entire body. He chuckled when she jumped.

His mouth caught up to hers in a deep, moist kiss that only added to the fire, and locked her head in position as he gradually shifted his weight on top of her. Her legs granted him room.

Maggi found herself alone in her head, faced with a thousand impulses of pleasure and warning, unable to stifle any one of them, not wanting to. What do I do now? she thought, and the voice of her conscience gave her the answer. When seduction is inevitable, lie back and enjoy!

'Still sleeping, Maggi?' He was up on his knees, hands resting gently on her breasts, laughing. Her body was beyond control. She writhed and twisted, her hips urging him on. Don't stop! she screamed to herself. Her teeth were clenched so tightly that her gums hurt, but the reflex was lost in the merging pleasure signals as he leaned forward and entered her.

It had been a long time between for Maggi Brennan. And he was warm and moist and experienced. She welcomed him as he filled her to overflowing, welcomed him and urged him on with both wild hands.

He plunged deeply, strongly, rhythmically. Her legs came up around him and she fluttered her hips against him, unable to match his rhythm. His hands swept under her buttocks and steadied her to the pace. What seemed like hours of enjoyment were really only seconds. Together they smashed themselves on the peak of the little death, and as with a symphony orchestra where the cymbals had sounded the last note, they collapsed in perspiration-laden silence.

Three or four minutes passed. Minutes while his weight came down on her, his head by hers, his hands gentle in her hair. 'Good lord,' somebody said. Maggi was still having trouble with her breathing. She panted as if she had run a dozen miles. He moved slightly, fumbling for something on her bedside table. After a moment or two he lifted himself up on his elbows, and wiped her forehead with a tissue.

And then, with a little laugh, he rolled himself off, and she heard him say, 'What kind of a stud am I, if the girl doesn't even wake up?'

The passion was gone in an instant, replaced by rage. 'Stud.' The word echoed through the empty corridors of her mind. Just because I'm a widow you needn't think I'm in need of stud service! She remembered saying that to him when he first arrived. And he hadn't believed her. Instead he had waited for his chance, and proved what a stupid fool she was. Her blood boiled. No, I didn't need stud service, but I got it, didn't I? she told herself. And that's all it was to him. Stud service! Any woman would have satisfied him; I was the only one at hand! Rage rode high on the crest of her guilt. The feeling swamped her. This one act was the height of sin. She had been unfaithful to Robert's memory in the worst possible way. And John Dailey was laughing at her.

Don't get mad, get even. Wasn't that the right saying? How? What single thing could she do to stab him in his ego? Out of the maze of all her readings, all the little giggling conversations with her friends, popped the perfect answer.

She rolled over on her side, laid her tiny hand across the hard muscles of his stomach, and giggled drowsily. 'Thank you, Robert.'

There was a moment of silent disbelief. She could feel his muscles stiffen in surprise. And then he vaulted up out of the bed like a just-released jack-in-the-box. There were perhaps half a dozen well-chosen short Anglo-Saxon words said, a couple of which Maggi had never heard before—but which needed no explanation. She could see his dark shadow against the darker background of the room. He picked up what clothes he had worn and turned in her direction to repeat some of the words she didn't want to hear. In self-protection she ducked under the blankets and blocked her ears. He slammed the door behind him.

Maggi's moment of triumph passed quickly. She tossed and turned in her bed, but could find no comfort. What she had done was indefensible, and yet so wonderful. And he hadn't been altogether proper either. She argued with herself for half an hour, and finally convinced herself that it was all *his* fault. After which she got up to remake the bed. She climbed back in, but was still unable to sleep. Eventually, because she was so physically tired and yet so thirsty, she got up again, stole across the hall to the bathroom for a glass of water, and returned to the chair beside her bed. Dawn was stippling the hills with grey light.

One of the twins stirred, and began to fret. Thank the lord for that, Maggi sighed to herself as she fumbled for her nightgown and robe and padded down the hall to the rescue.

The day turned sour just after sunrise. A cool north-east wind heralded the arrival of more rain. The house was dark. Aunt Eduarda came downstairs at seven o'clock, to find Maggi and the two girls already in occupation.

'They've been fed,' Maggi said. Hiding the gloom in her voice was a sometime thing; Maggi Brennan had acquired a full-blow guilt-complex. Her aunt looked more closely at her as she continued, 'By the way, don't make up any more fires in the living-room. I'm going to put the little rascals out on the rug from now on.'

'Then I'd better clean the fireplace out,' Eduarda replied. 'Did you have any more trouble after I went to bed?'

'Not with the children,' Maggi said glumly. She noticed the stare. 'Oh, I meant—I just couldn't get back to sleep again.'

'No, of course not.' Aunt Eduarda had lived a full life. It wasn't hard to deduce what the trouble might be. 'And I'll go look for something to block the living-room door so our two little pigeons can't escape.'

'That can wait until you've had breakfast.'

'No, it really can't,' the old lady said. 'I'll have to eat on the run today. We need a considerable amount of groceries. I planned to take the jeep and go over to Almacs. They're open by eight o'clock in the morning. I take it that the mister is sleeping in?'

'I don't give a darn *what* he's doing!' Fire replaced despondency in a second, flashing out from Maggi's eyes and from her lips.

'No, I can see that.' Her guess confirmed, Aunt Eduarda made herself a quick mug of coffee and went out into the living-room. Deprived of her audience, Maggi mumbled to herself, and then set about bathing the two little girls. By nine o'clock Eduarda had gone and the two children were exploring the confines of their new world.

The entire living-room rug was a wide plain to be explored. Between the two of them a soft rubber ball made a good toy. John had installed a stainless steel mirror on the side of their playpen, and, once spotted, it turned two lovely little girls into Narcissi. With both of them enjoying life, Maggi stole a moment to go up to dress. Nothing special, just her looking-after-babies uniform—a light turtleneck sweater, black trousers, her rather elderly plimsolls, and her hair brushed and caught back in a ponytail. And now she was hunched up in the rocking-chair in the living-room, feeling sorry for herself.

A knock at the front door.

That was the oddity of it all. In typical country style, practically every visitor came to the side door, the kitchen door. To have visitors at the *front* door was strange. Maggi got up slowly and moved in that direction. Both babies rolled over on their stomachs and seemed to be watching her. Maggi's smile brought two in return.

It required two hands to wrestle with the old and seldom-used latch. 'Henry! What in the world are *you* doing here? Come in, come in.'

Henry Peterson came in, grinning. 'Oh, I thought I'd mix business with pleasure,' he said. 'Oops!'

'I forgot to tell you. Watch out for the girls, they're mobile.'

'A couple of entries in the snail race?' He walked around the children in an exaggerated half-circle and took the best chair in the room. 'I don't have much experience with kids. I sort of like to keep them at a distance. I didn't think you had either, Maggi.'

'No, but I'm learning fast,' she replied. 'Double tuition, so to speak, doubly precious. Coffee?'

'Don't mind if I do. I was out a little early today. A big transaction.' He was rubbing the palms of his hands together as if savouring the profit. Maggi managed to hide her smile, and went out into the kitchen to fetch his drink.

'Black, two sugars?' she asked when she came in. Aunt Eduarda had stretched a fire-screen across the doorway, which made the trip hazardous, but the trip was made without spilling a drop.

'You remembered!'

'Well, it was only three nights ago, for goodness' sakes. That's not long to remember.' She dropped on to the sofa beside his chair and coiled her legs up beneath her. For some reason she was feeling very—kindly—towards Henry Peterson. In comparison to some *other* men she knew, Henry was a pet. He was at his best dressed, but looked as if he could use a little ego-boosting. Which she was ready to provide. 'Now, tell me about your great sale?'

'It's the condos up above your house,' he told her. 'My, you make good coffee.'

'Instant,' she said, shrugging.

'And you look a sight for sore eyes,' he continued. 'So early in the morning!'

I know I don't, Maggi told herself, but I deserve to look nice. And to have some man tell me so! 'Thank you, Henry. What about the condominiums?'

'Three of them are finished,' he said cheerily, 'and my firm has been awarded the sale and lease rights. Would you believe, in one hour this morning I've sold four apartments?'

'Well, good for you. I suppose there's a handsome commission.'

'I'll say there is.' His grin expanded. 'Sets me up for a couple of months, Maggi. Too bad there isn't more space up there on the hill—I could clean up a fortune.' He sipped at his coffee, watching her over the rim of the mug with those slate-coloured eyes of his. 'And so could you, Maggi.'

'Me?'

'You. You've got almost twenty acres of land just sitting around doing nothing. Just sitting there going to waste.'

'Lying fallow is what we farmers say,' she told him, and offered a small smile to cheer him on. She had heard his tale before, but then it had been known as Swanson's song. Do you suppose Henry——? No, he wouldn't join up with that pirate!

'I know you don't need money these days,' he rambled on, 'but here's an opportunity you shouldn't bypass, Mag.' She hated that name. Nobody but her brothers used it, and then only when teasing. And only when prepared to run. All her good spirits evaporated, but Henry failed to notice. 'You know,' he continued, 'for just ten acres you could——' and he named a sum of money that caused Maggi's eyes to boggle. She had no idea what land might bring, and might not want to sell, but just as a figure to dream about—well!

'Do you really think so, Henry?' He nodded agreement, his smile so big that it was about to swallow him up.

'Positive. Maybe even more.'

She tendered him a sweet smile. Henry Peterson lit up like a Christmas tree. 'I don't think I can really commit myself to a sale like that. I'd have to talk to my lawyer and his accountants, you know. Uncle Jaoa is out of town at the moment.'

'Ah, of course. He's still representing the family?'

'As you say. More coffee?'

'No.' Henry consulted his ornate wristwatch. 'I really have to be going. There's a great deal of paperwork involved in all this. But—Maggi? You'll keep me in mind if you ever *do* decide to sell?'

'I'll keep you in mind.' You and Mr Swanson, Henry. You two could be blood brothers under the skin. I wonder if you're Siamese twins? The thought was father to the question. Henry looked at her in surprise, and whipped a handkerchief out of his pocket to wipe his forehead.

'Swanson? Yes, I know *of* him, of course. We might have met a time or two in the past, perhaps.' He rose from his chair. Maggi was standing with her back to the staircase, and heard the steps that came halfway down and stopped. *He* had finally condescended to get up! *He* obviously had too much exercise last night. Perhaps *he* wasn't as young as he thought—or she thought! With all those thoughts squirrelling around in her mind, she missed what Henry had just said.

'What? I—was thinking about something else, Henry.'

The agent shifted from one foot to the other. 'I said, I thought we might celebrate tonight, Maggi. I've two tickets to the ballet at the Zeiterion. How about it? You were always a dance fan. We could have a night of it. Dinner, perhaps.'

Maggi heard the soft growl from up on the stairs, and was urged to higher levels of drama. 'Sounds good. Maybe we could eat at the Twin Piers?'

The growl from up on the stairs was repeated, with even more venom behind it. Henry, who was missing all this byplay, produced a crocodile smile. 'The Twin Piers? Why not. I haven't eaten there since Hector was a pup. Of course. I'll pick you up—say around seven o'clock?'

'And dinner afterwards? I'd love that! Can you get a reservation that quickly?'

'No trouble,' Henry assured her as he made for the front door. 'I'll use my father's name.'

'I'll use my father's name,' John jeered as he came down the stairs, but Henry was long gone by then. And then, mournfully, 'How can you do that to me, Maggi? That was *our* plan.'

Maggi folded her arms across her breasts and glared up at him. He looked as if the wrath of the lord had finally caught up to him. He was wearing yellow pyjama bottoms and a tired T-shirt. If possible, the shirt looked stronger than he did. His hair was a mess, he needed a shave, and his eyes had shadows under them. Maggi sneered. Both the babies saw him as he stepped off the bottom stair, and gurgled a welcome. So what do *they* know? she asked herself.

He went to them immediately, kneeling down on the floor to offer a kiss. And then he creaked back up to his feet. 'I need a cup of coffee,' he announced.

'Good for you.' Maggi was doing her best to stab him dead with words.

'Oh, my gawd!' he groaned as he collapsed on to the sofa. 'You're not pleased with me?'

'You could definitely say that. Definitely.'

'And you don't intend to bring me any coffee?'

'I'm thinking,' she returned. 'I can't decide whether I ought to let you die as you are, or get you a mug of coffee and pour it all over you.'

'And you don't plan to go out with me tonight?'

'I wouldn't go around the corner with you,' she swore.

'Nice girls don't talk like that, Maggi.'

'I'm not a *nice* girl!' she shouted at him. 'I'm a thirty-year-old shrew, and I don't like people who creep into my——'

'But you were asleep, Maggi.' She had the grace to blush, to turn wine-red at his soft comment. 'So therefore no matter what bad things I might have done, you wouldn't know, would you, Maggi?'

'Why, you——'

'And let me tell you something else,' he continued in that same soft drawl. 'I've had a lot of experience, and you were magnificent, Maggi Brennan. Absolutely magnificent! The next time——'

'Don't hold your breath, *Mr* Dailey,' she hissed. 'There won't be a *next time*. What kind of a woman do you take me for?'

'You're the kind of woman I would take for any price,' he announced grandly. It was the last straw; Maggi was the camel. She raged, pouring out gibberish as she searched the room for some weapon. Henry's coffee-mug, not quite empty, stood on the occasional table. She ran for it, screaming. The babies heard, and began to scream for themselves. John, being a wiser man than she had thought, made for the stairs at speed.

Which was perhaps unfortunate. Maggi was aiming at him where he stood, just by the bottom step. With her usual skill the mug headed for the fourth step up, just as his foot landed there. The mug bounced off his skull with a satisfying thud, and broke into a dozen pieces.

He stopped for a second, staggering. Both hands went up to the side of his head, just above his ear. He glared down at her and said two very bad words having to do with her parentage, and then staggered up the stairs and out of sight.

Maggi, standing with both hands over her mouth in the middle of the room, was moaning. Prudence and Prissy were screaming. Her frantic mind was completely at sea. She had never really meant to hit him; for twenty years she had been throwing things at her brothers, and had never yet hit either of them. And now this. Go upstairs and comfort him, her conscience nagged. You owe it to him. But her common sense intervened. One does not go into the cage with the bear after sticking a thorn in his foot! And besides, somebody has to stay with the babies. Instead of a little romance you can change a couple of diapers!

Which she did. And then walked them both until she discovered that Prissy was also cutting a tooth, which required a long search for the benzocaine, because Aunt Eduarda didn't get back until eleven, and only she remembered where the bottle of painkiller was located.

Henry arrived promptly. It was still raining outside. He was driving a smart little convertible, with the roof up, and wearing—for some reason Maggi couldn't understand—a white dinner jacket with dark trousers. And a cummerbund. That last was a mistake. Henry was losing his schoolboy athletic shape, and the crimson cummerbund, wrapped too tightly around his waist, protruded just a tiny bit. None of which swayed Maggi from her plans to achieve vengeance.

She dressed up to the limit. Her hair was up, her dress was a beautiful satin calf-length sheath split high on one thigh, and it sparkled by lamplight. Her three-inch heels gave her a definite advantage over Henry, and she carried her nose so far up in the air that even Mike, the dog, was impressed.

'Have a good time!' Aunt Eduarda called. John grunted as Maggi went past him, and buried his nose in his paper. Maggi took Henry's arm with a flourish, and was laughing gaily at his second-hand joke as they went out to the car. Behind her, John crumpled up his newspaper and threw it at the fireplace. Aunt Eduarda covered her mouth to hide the smile. Evidently the man knew very well how much of a good time Maggi meant to have—and didn't appreciate it!

Not all American cities had the advantage that Washington DC obtained. Nationwide contributions and government support built the National Theatre, so that all who lived inside the Beltway could seek culture. Washington residents never did understand that the boundary of their fairy kingdom, the Beltway, was to the rest of the nation, merely Route 95 South. But little America wanted culture too.

The Zeiterion was one of those classic movie theatres built in the 1920s, where baroque design, small stages, magnificent lobbies with huge chandeliers, were all the thing. The theatre had fallen on hard times, and was barely rescued from the wrecker's ball by a subscription drive throughout Greater New Bedford. Rebuilt, reconditioned, self-supporting, it now attracted touring performer groups from the big city. And local residents went to see and be seen.

Which was fine with Maggi. Except that, during the drive into the city, she had discovered that Henry's folding roof leaked right above her seat. But when a girl was hugely determined to have a good time, she could put up with many minor annoyances. The ballet was astoundingly good; the dinner at the Twin Piers was excellent, but the rain blanked out the windows, leaving no view of the working harbour, and leaving her to stumble along with Henry's limited conversation.

It was midnight before they started back. To get out from under the leak she shifted over on the front bench seat, only to discover that Henry considered the move an invitation to—whatever a man could do while driving one-handed. When they came up in front of the house he made a massive attempt, she slapped his face, and was thoroughly soaked as she ran for the house. The light was still on in the living-room. She stopped outside on the porch to rearrange herself as best she could, while Henry drove off with an angry spurt of tyres. And Maggi went in at the front door.

'Well, it's about time you got home.' John was in one of his more friendly moods.

'I don't see what it has to do with you,' she offered over her right shoulder as she made for the kitchen. He followed along behind. The kettle was full and whistling.

'I'll make you some coffee,' he offered. She plumped herself down at the table and nodded, too tired to consider much more fighting. The hot coffee cheered her just a little. Caffeine, she told herself, just what I need.

'Did you have a good time?' He was sitting directly across the table from her, nursing his own cup.

'Wonderful,' she said, but was too tired to put any emphasis on the right syllables.

'You look like a drowned rat!'

'Thank you.' Was that a cold enough tone? 'Your friends speak well of you too.'

'You didn't have any sleep last night,' he added. 'And now you're up late, after dashing around all evening—did you fall into the harbour?'

'If I did I'd be dead,' she muttered. 'There are so many PCBs in that water that——'

'You would have been better off here at home with me.'

'Hey, let's get this straight! This is *my* home, not yours. And you demonstrated very successfully to me last night that I'm not safe in my own home. Not at all. Heavens, what will my mother say!'

'Does she have to know?'

'That woman can squeeze information like she was peeling an artichoke. I couldn't keep a secret from her if I wanted to.'

His index finger was busy tapping the top of the table. It was beginning to get on Maggi's nerves.

'Look,' he said, still using that soft deep voice, 'we have a lot to talk about.'

'I don't see it that way,' she muttered, ducking behind her coffee-mug. 'You said you wanted to *talk* to me last night, and look what happened!'

'That's what we have to talk about.'

'I don't believe this.' Water was still dripping down Maggi's neck. She got up and located a dry kitchen towel as she fished around for the pins in her hair.

'Here, let me help.' He had the right pin immediately. When he pulled it out gently her hair cascaded down like a float of logs after a jam was cleared. And then he took the towel from her and guided her back into her chair.

He was a gentle massager. 'You've had a lot of experience at this?' she asked.

'Moderately. Look, Maggi——' A brief pause as if he was searching for some special words. A lawyer, looking for words? she asked herself.

'Maggi—last night was a terrible mistake on my part.'

'You can say that again!' The towel was half over her face, hiding her expression, for which she thanked heaven.

'Yes, I know that I broke all the rules of hospitality. And I don't suppose you had any protection?'

Good lord, Maggi told herself. It never crossed my mind. I never—good heavens!

'I thought not,' he said. His hands were gently rubbing down to her scalp just over her right ear. 'There could be consequences, Maggi.'

Her heart thumped down into her left shoe. There *could* be. Just because she had never been pregnant before, it didn't mean that—oh, lord.

'I know you get along well with the twins,' he added. 'You love them, and they love you.'

'Yes.' Barely a whisper.

'And now I have an added responsibility.' She stole a quick look at his face. He didn't seem exactly happy about the whole situation, whatever it was. 'Despite all our differences, Maggi, I think that you and I will have to——' He had stopped rubbing, and moved around in front of her. She used both hands to push her hair back and out of her eyes. He looked so determined, so sincere, and yes, almost handsome!

'Have to what?' she asked in a very small voice.

'Have to get married,' he concluded. Maggi could not provide an answer. She was too busy trying not to swallow her tongue.

CHAPTER NINE

Two days later Maggi and John were still walking around each other like a pair of nervous cats. They went through their morning devotions with the twins, he dashed off to the city to 'tend to business', he said, while she did the laundry and a thousand and one other things which babies required. And thought.

Marry him? The thought frightened and teased and charged her. He was a wonderfully handsome man—she had come to acknowledge that. A man of fidelity and hard work and enthusiasm, who had burdens in Ireland—and considered her to be just one more burden. Maggi hated the thought. To marry a man just because one night they had—she had—become another of his responsibilities? No word about 'love' and 'happy ever after'? The idea chilled her.

And so did the idea that Ms Fagan would be appearing soon, specifically to meet her husband. And if Maggi failed to have one the State would undoubtedly foreclose on the children—or whatever lawyers called it—and take them away. And that, Maggi knew, she could not allow. So perhaps it was enough that she loved the babies, and loved John Dailey too. Perhaps it didn't matter if he couldn't return the favour.

She should do it for the babies. That sounded just right to her New England conscience. Marry him for the babies' sake. Discount the fact that you love him, and he's one hellion between the sheets! Put all that aside. Make the sacrifice just for the babies. And soon. Ms Fagan had called again, and would be in Dartmouth, for sure, by Friday next!

'And every time you look at each other,' Aunt Eduarda said as she slid her cake pans into the oven, 'it's as if you expected each other to say something you didn't want to hear. What gives with you two?'

'He—asked me something,' Maggi replied. 'And I—just don't know the answer. The right answer, that is. I'm still thinking.'

'Big secret,' her aunt said sarcastically. 'I can read the question on his face, and the answer on yours. He asked you to marry him, didn't he?'

'Dammit,' Maggi snapped, 'he had no right to tell anybody! I hate a blabbermouth!'

'He didn't tell me a thing, dear. Not a single word. He's not that sort of man.'

'So you just guessed?'

'An educated guess,' Aunt Eduarda returned. 'I have three daughters of my own, Margaret. All married.'

'And you just read minds?'

'Faces.'

'If you know all that much, what's the answer on my face?'

'No, you don't catch me in that trap. Figure it out for yourself. In years to come I don't want you to go around saying that your aunt talked you into marrying him! Or *out* of marrying him. Shoo—buzz out of my kitchen. Go watch the children. I don't want my cake to fall!'

'*My* kitchen,' Maggi grumbled under her breath, but she went anyway. Prissy did much to improve her temper. The little girl had finally achieved a pinnacle. For several days she had been rolling over on her stomach, bunching her knees under her, and rocking back and forth. This morning she pushed and rocked and fell forward—and repeated the exercise half a dozen times. As a result she had managed to move a good three feet, all in one direction. The baby accepted it nonchalantly; Maggi crowed like a demented mother. Prudence, the quieter of the two, merely watched.

When John came back that day Maggi had made up her mind. She cornered him in the living-room after lunch. 'Any luck today?' Maggi, firmly committed now, still needed some casual conversation to edge into the *pièce de résistance*.

'Plenty of luck,' he returned. 'All bad!' But he wasn't able to maintain that poker face of his. A little wisp of a smile teased at the corner of his mouth, and his eyes lit up. 'That's a lie, Maggi. I've stumbled on to something. A contact in New York relayed my offering to a man in Sacramento, and I think I *might* have an answer to all our problems.'

'I'm glad,' she returned simply, and moved over to sit beside him on the sofa. Not closely. He was crowded into one end, she took the other, her nose pointed straight ahead at the fireplace. 'I've been thinking,' she began. He let the words hang in the air.

'About—us. Getting married, you know.'

'I know.'

And you're not about to help me a single bit, are you? she thought. 'It—just doesn't seem to me to be a very romantic thing, this courtship of ours.'

'Ah.' Only one word, but he did move across the sofa until his thigh touched hers, and his arm draped itself casually around her shoulders. It took some of the sting out of her thoughts.

'I've only ever had one other proposal,' she said. The words came out painfully. 'There was—

excitement in the air. Flowers, sweet words—I don't know how to take this idea of yours.'

'There was plenty of fire,' he told her. 'In your bed, Maggi. It can be that way every night—well, almost every night, you know.'

'But you—you think that's enough?'

'Some things can't be changed. That other time was long ago. You were very young then.'

'And that's it? I'm not young any more, so it can't be—sweet?'

'What would you like me to do? Get down on one knee? Bring flowers? Write love poems?'

'Well—no, but you needn't be sarcastic about it! Dammit, it's all so—businesslike.'

'And I'd be doing *you* a favour,' he retorted. 'Two favours. You know you want to stay with the twins, and by marrying me you'd be guaranteed that. And then, admit it, Maggi, I'd be providing you with a considerable service—in bed and out.'

'There you go again,' she spluttered. 'Sex! Is that all you men think about?'

'No, it isn't,' he said. His arm tightened around her shoulders. Her head seemed to fall naturally on his shoulder. 'No, it isn't, Maggi.' His voice was at her ear; the words were but whispers. 'But it'll do to start on. Thousands of couples marry without knowing if they're sexually compatible. We already know we are. Think what might develop from that?'

'Oh, lord,' she muttered, wringing her hands. 'I—wish my mother were here. I wish I——' A tear formed at the corner of one eye. She brushed it angrily aside. 'All right,' Maggi Brennan said through a mist of tears, 'I'll marry you.'

She expected that he might be joyful about the whole affair. Not so. He squeezed her gently. 'I thought it was going to drag on for weeks,' he said, sounding very self-satisfied.

'Well, don't put it down to your great charm!' she yelled back at him. 'You've got about as much charm as a dead mackerel!'

'And a face to match,' he interrupted. Her head snapped around in his direction. He was smiling, and she felt terrible.

'No, that's not true. Not a bit.' She shifted to face him, and one of her hands went up to stroke his craggy face. 'Not a bit true,' she insisted. 'Beauty is in the eyes of the beholder. You are truly a beautiful man.' And of course you're going to let him get away with all this? You've only known him for six weeks. I can see mountains of diapers in your future, Maggi, and rivers of tears and sweat, and—— 'Oh, shut up,' she interrupted, and then settled herself with her back to the sofa and her hands folded primly in her lap.

'But of course I realise that you're only doing this because of the twins.' A quick look out of the corner of her eye, and he was still smiling.

'If it weren't for the girls,' she stumbled on, 'I wouldn't dream of—well, I wouldn't. I don't even know where we would live. Or if you expect—more children—or anything!'

'I understand.' There it was again, that touch of cynicism. 'I expect we would live somewhere other than here, but that's something we could talk over. As for children, of course I would want children. And you needn't worry; I don't think twins are the normal thing.'

'And I'd have to sell the farm?'

'You wouldn't have to do anything you don't want to do,' he assured her. 'We could hang on to the farm. Fix it up, put in some modern equipment—whatever you want. It's *your* farm. But I do insist on one thing. I'm the provider in the family. I may perhaps not be the *best* provider you've ever met, but those are the rules of the game.'

'Well, that's all settled, then,' she said in a very small, very subdued voice. 'All right, I'll marry you.'

She had intended to ask him to kiss her, but the asking wasn't necessary. He pulled her over in front of him, lifted her up, and totally destroyed her fragile equilibrium with a kiss that lifted her up off his lap and glued her to him, vibrating and shaking with the passions that overwhelmed her. She was breathless when he had finished with her. His arms released their hold and she fell from want of muscles of her own.

'Now do I suppose we've reached the end of all the shilly-shallying?' Aunt Eduarda, a broad smile on her face, stood at the door. Maggi snapped up, managed to hit John's chin with the top of her head, and swung her feet to the floor. Somehow the buttons on her blouse had become undone, and she could not for the life of her remember when *that* had happened. After fumbling with the buttons her hand wandered to her hair.

'Yes, I believe we've agreed to a marriage,' John said. Maggi hated that laughter behind his words. Hated it, and ground her teeth. 'Haven't we, Maggi?' A finger pinched at the fold of flesh just below her ribs to encourage an answer.

'Yes,' she responded weakly, 'I believe we have. Is there a contract to be signed, or something?'

'Maggi, what a thing to say!' Her aunt was really upset. Maggi was immediately contrite. But all John did was to lean back on the sofa and laugh until tears came to his eyes.

* * *

That night, however, attitudes changed. John had gone out again in the afternoon, something he rarely did. After supper, after the babies were rocked away into the Land of Nod, he came downstairs and cornered Maggi as she sat in the living-room with her embroidery.

'That's the first time I've seen that,' he said. She looked up from her work. He seemed bigger than ever, a tall square threat that loomed over her forever.

'Something I took up years ago,' she explained. 'When I found out that I couldn't knit worth a darn. It tends to soothe the spirit.'

'The nervous spirit?'

'You could say that.'

'There's something we need to talk about. I know it won't be easy for you, but—well, it's a matter of principle with me.'

She set her work aside and patted the place next to her on the sofa. That troubled expression she had seen on his face several times before was in full spate again. Maggi took a good look, then settled back, her hands folded in her lap.

'I know,' he said slowly, 'that this marriage of ours troubles you.'

She nodded agreement. What troubled her was the complete lack of those little words, like 'love you'. The words a woman loved to hear, especially before a marriage. But those were just the words he never had offered. He was apparently tied up in those big words, like compatibility, propinquity—things like that. Which, she admitted, had a place in life, but not *first* place. So she waited for what he had to say. It almost knocked her off her seat.

'I realise, Maggi, that even after all these years you are still very much in love with Robert. I see it all around me. Robert's marriage lines on the kitchen wall, Robert's furniture, Robert's wife. That's a pretty terrible handicap for a man to work against, and I have no intention of breaking up your chain of memories, but—there's *one* thing that has to change!'

And I never even guessed, Maggi told herself, horrified. Is it really that way? Haven't I gradually put away all those memories? Not forgotten them, no. Robert was too much a part of the springtime of my life for me to forget him. Is it true? Am I comparing John to Robert? Am I holding on to the past too strongly?

'I'm sorry you feel that way,' she sighed. 'What is it that I must change?'

'You're willing to make a change?'

'Of course I am. What is it?'

'This,' he said, reaching over for her left hand. 'I can't feel right about coming up on *our* wedding while you're still wearing Robert's wedding-ring.'

Maggi looked down at her finger in surprise. She had worn that ring for so long that she had forgotten it was there. And now it glittered in the lamplight like a tremendous roadblock to the rest of her life. 'I'm sorry—I don't wear it as a badge or a token. It meant so much to me years ago, and I—I just forgot to take it off. I'll—you have every right to say what you did. I'll—oh, lord, it's stuck!'

'Oh, brother,' he muttered. 'The dead hand out of the past?'

'No. Stop talking like that,' she ordered. 'It's just that—well, my finger is swollen. Soap!'

He trailed her out to the kitchen. Mike was curled up on the throw rug in front of the sink. He moved reluctantly. With great care Maggi laved her hand in soap, poured it on until the bubbles concealed everything. After a little judicious wiggling back and forth the gold ring finally slid over her knuckle and broke free.

'You scraped your knuckle,' he said. There was a suspicious sense of apology in his voice.

'It's nothing important. Nothing at all.' She rinsed her finger and used the small hand towel to dry things off. The gold ring rested in the palm of her hand as she looked it over. And then, with the feeling that she was severing her last connection with Robert, she slipped it into pocket of her apron. 'Satisfied?'

'I'd feel better if you gave it to me,' he said savagely. 'I'd like to throw it off that stone wall over in Fort Phoenix.'

'Not that.' She pulled the ring out and turned it over in the light. 'This is a family heirloom now. We'll put it away for our oldest son. It will mean something more to him, to give his mother's ring to his bride.'

He picked the ring up out of her hand. 'Lord, I can't keep up with you, Maggi. But when you're right you're right. Only—Maggi—if you don't object, *I'd* like to keep it.'

'You have no reason to be jealous of Robert.' She handed him the ring, which he pocketed. To emphasise her point she stretched up as far as she could on the tips of her toes, put her arms around his neck, and kissed him. There was no way she could match the enthusiasm of *his* kisses, but she did her best. After a moment of stunned surprise he joined in the effort, and from that moment on neither of them had a complaint about the quantity or quality.

It was more than a few minutes before he led her back out to the living-room. 'I forgot something,' he told her as he swung her back down on to the sofa. Maggi watched as he fished in his pockets and finally came out with a small square box. 'I was just passing by a jewellery store downtown when I happened to notice this thing they had on sale in the window, and so I thought——'

'John Dailey,' she interrupted, laughing, 'you are the biggest con artist in Dartmouth! Just happened to be passing—on sale in the window—— Did you think I would believe a cockamaimy story like—ooooh!'

He slipped the little platinum band out of the box. A brilliant baguette diamond cast miniature rainbows around the room. The centre diamond was circled by diamond chips. It was not large; it *was* brilliant. It said a great many things. Of all the options available, Maggi chose to belive it said *love*! He deserved another kiss. He accepted what she offered, and then stole a few more on his own. There might have been further developments, but one of the babies upstairs whimpered. They both jumped to their feet, and, holding hands, dashed up the stairs to the rescue.

'We're getting very practised with teething,' he whispered as he escorted her down the hall a few minutes later. 'Now they both have a tooth.'

'All the better to bite you with,' she said, giggling. They stopped by her door, and that excitement seemed to build up in her body again. She shivered. His arm tightened around her.

'Would you want to...?' she suggested, gesturing towards the door.

'I want to like mad,' he murmured, 'but I've been on a guilt trip since the last time, and I don't think I could carry that load until our wedding-day.'

'Which will be?'

'How about the day after tomorrow?' he suggested, grinning down at her.

'You think you can wait that long?'

'You think *you* can?'

'Hey, I asked you first!'

'You don't realise what a highly self-controlled man you're talking to. I *could* spend the whole night in your bed and never lay a finger on you, woman. That might be nice.'

'Spending the night or not laying a finger on me?'

'That does it,' he said, administering a tiny chastisement on her bottom. 'Get to bed, lady. I'll be along in a minute, and you'll see just how self-controlled I can be.'

Which *I* am not, Maggi told herself. If he dares to come, I'm going to jump on him! She watched wistfully as he turned back to his own room, and then she went in, turned on her bedside lamp, slipped into her long flannel nightgown, and climbed into bed. The gown was one of her winter specials, something she would never think to wear in the summer. But it covered her from neck to ankle, with only a pair of tiny buttons at the bodice. If he wants to play platonic love, she thought, I'll give him a run for his money. And I *won't* jump on him!

So she plumped up her pillow and lay back, waiting. There was no long delay. See? the voice of her conscience said as he came in at the door. It's become old hat with him. No shave and shampoo this time, babe. What you see is what you get!

Maggi had no rebuttal. What she saw astonished her. Their last meeting in the buff had also been in the dark. This time her bedlamp was enough to penetrate every corner. He came in wearing a big smile and a robe, walked over to the side of the bed as haughtily as Julius Caesar, and let his robe slip to the floor. Maggi gasped.

Never had she seen a man in such superb shape. His upper torso would have made Conan the Barbarian envious. His legs and thighs were carved in steel. And when her eyes managed to focus on what came in between, she was hard put to keep from giggling. His eyes, following the line of hers, looked down with a very self-satisfied expression.

'It is often said,' he pontificated, 'that when God makes a man with a really ugly face, he provides him with certain utilitarian improvements in other areas.'

'Dear lord, stop boasting and come to bed,' she commanded. The uneasy excitement was building, sending successive waves of anticipation up from her stomach to her mind.

'I didn't say a boastful word!'

'Just standing there like that, you're boasting,' she insisted. She reached for the lamp and snapped it off. He slid into the bed on the opposite side. Maggi was still fighting off the giggles as she stretched out, flat on her back. The bed was fairly large, but with him there beside her, also flat on his back, their thighs touched. A tingle shot up and down her spine. And one of his feet ran down her leg from knee to ankle.

'What in the world are you wearing?' he demanded. 'It feels like a burlap bag!'

'You wouldn't know if you weren't touching me.'

'I said I'd not lay a finger on you. That's my toe.'

'Typical lawyer talk!' Maggi squirmed a bit further away. Not that there was much room for manoeuvre. His toe followed, worrying at the hem of her nightgown. She clamped down hard with her other foot, just as he managed to push the gown up to her knees. Silence, overwhelming silence filled the room for a matter of minutes.

'Oh, hell,' he grumbled as he rolled over on one side. His big left hand seemed to fall naturally across her waist, and then climb up over her engorged breasts to her neck. 'What the devil are these buttons for? So damn small. I can't hardly get my fingers on them.'

'That's what they're for,' she told him, suppressing another giggle. 'To keep marauders out.'

'I'll rip the things off,' he threatened.

'You and whose army?'

She could feel the bed shake as he made a concerted effort, but the seams of her nightgown were precisely doubled and sewn, and without some little nick or break to offer the start of a tear he was going nowhere. 'All right,' he groaned, 'I give up. Have mercy!'

'What happened to the entirely self-controlled man? The one who wasn't going to lay a finger on me?'

'I lied, Maggi. Come on now, give me a break!'

She might have extended his torture, but on this night she was no passive participant in the exercises, and could wait no longer herself. Already panting, she slid out of bed, shed her nightgown, and climbed back in again. Her return was heralded by a grunt of satisfaction. For another moment they lay side by side, his hand on her breast, hers at his waist. And then the lull was broken. Not in some slow, symphonic way, but with a mighty crash as they turned on each other in mad attack, melding themselves each to the other in frantic frenzy.

Like two titans meeting on a barren plain they smashed at each other, she on top, he below. Her hand guided him; he entered her deeply and compellingly. She rode him as if he were a wild mustang, leaning forward to drag her heavy breasts across his chest as his hands at her hips balanced her and urged her on.

So quickly passion flared, and as quickly peaked in rapture. She dropped on to his perspiring body, completely exhausted, completely satisfied. She tried momentarily to roll off, but his huge hands prevented it. His massive heart beat just under her ear. 'Oh, my,' Maggi whispered.

'Oh, my, indeed. Maybe we should get married tomorrow,' he suggested.

'I think it takes several days for the marriage licence,' she told him. 'Besides, why would we want to spoil such a good thing? Let's not talk about tomorrow. Can we do it again?'

'That cheeky tongue of yours is going to get you in trouble one day,' he said with a chuckle. And then he carefully explained what she might do to help him do it again. She was a good student. They both fell asleep just before dawn, and the babies might have cried for hours if Aunt Eduarda hadn't been in the house.

'What is so rare as a day in June,' Maggi carolled as she came down the stairs, dressed in white shorts and a pink short-sleeved blouse. It was ten o'clock in the morning of June the fifteenth.

'Well, I'm glad one of you is happy,' Aunt Eduarda called out from the kitchen. 'The mister got the babies fed and changed, and then he bugged out for the city.'

'He wasn't happy?' The idea gave Maggi a little shock. Everyone should be happy on this fine day. Never before had she seen as fine a day!

'Oh, he was happy all right, but complained about losing his strength. What in the world did you do to him?'

'Me do something to him?' Little Mrs Innocence giggled as she danced around the kitchen table and stopped long enough to give Aunt Eduarda a kiss. The elderly lady grinned back at her.

'You must remember that men like to think that they're in control.'

'Oh, he's in control,' Maggi sang. 'He is, he is, he is. Oops! Where are the kids?'

'Outside on the porch. He moved their playpen out there and set your mangy old hound——'

'My honest and sincere old dog,' Maggi interrupted. 'Let's give every dog his due—or his day? Is that how it goes?'

''Scoot out of here,' her aunt ordered. 'I'll bring you your breakfast outside, and you can commune with nature.'

'I've never had a better offer,' Maggi said solemnly. 'You've been a blessing to me—to us, *Tia*.'

'Go on with you now,' that worthy remarked as Maggi waltzed out of the kitchen door. 'You and the children have given me something to live for! Scoot!'

Maggi did. The babies were glad to see her. Both were kicking and gurgling contentedly. She picked them up one at a time, offering a hug and a squeeze, and a few love-words for each. Mike, stalking over to check up on his charges, received a neck-scratch for reward. Maggi looked out across her farm, smelled the air, hugged herself gently, and sat down in the rocker to savour life.

It had been a wild night, a night such as she had never seen before. Her breasts were still a little tender; her pelvic bones ached. And not for a moment would she make complaint! There was so much more that she knew about John Dailey now. The ugly face had disappeared; he might never be outwardly handsome, but he was good and kind and exciting. Sex was a game he played, and played well, but it was not all of him. He was a man of deep compassion, selfless love, hard work. The twins would grow up in his care and be the better for it. And me, she thought, I'll grow up in his care, and I'll be the better for it too.

Blissfully she leaned back in the rocker and set it going with her toe. Up the hill, where her corn was planted, there was a tiny fringe of green. High in the eaves of the barn swallows played. This loving place might not be her home for life, but home was where John was, and who could ask for more? When he comes home, she promised herself, I must tell him all these things, and then I've got to call Mom and Dad and tell them the news! She held her left hand up to the sun. The diamond trapped rays of light within itself, and sent them back out as scattered rainbows.

Her dog came over to the rocker and stretched himself out on top of the foot that was propelling everything. Maggi offered him a smile. The twins squealed in excitement. One of the sparrows had landed on the rail of their playpen, and was preening himself in the soft shadows of the porch. Priscilla shook her rattle at the bird and laughed again. If there was traffic over on Tucker Road, Maggi could hear not a murmur of it.

Aunt Eduarda came out with a tray, loaded with eggs and toast and bacon, and a mug of coffee. Maggi polished it off with enthusiasm, and set the dishes aside. Everything was quiet again. She leaned back and closed her eyes.

The car woke her up gently. It buzzed up in front of the house. Thinking it was John, she forced her eyes open. The little red sports car looked nothing like the battered van. Maggi shook her head and smiled. Henry Peterson. Someone else shared the front seat, but she couldn't make out who it was. Henry opened the car door, hesitated with both feet on the ground, perhaps talking to his companion, and then shut the door behind him.

Aunt Eduarda came to the door to look, holding her hand up over her eyes to screen away the sun. 'Mr Peterson?' she asked. Maggi nodded. Eduarda picked up the empty tray and took it back into the kitchen.

Henry was taking his time, shuffling along like a condemned felon. When he reached the porch steps he stopped, and looked up hesitantly.

'Maggi? Can we talk?' He looked nothing like the neat, suave man he had formerly been. He wore a jacket and tie, but the tie was askew. The top two buttons of his shirt were unfastened. His camelhair jacket looked as if the camel was still in it with him. His handsome head of hair was betrayed by the light wind blowing up out of the swamp. The neat blond triangle just over his forehead was actually a hair-piece. Maggi, feeling as happy as anyone could get, left a little tingle of compassion for him.

'Come up, Henry. Of course we can talk.'

He stumbled up the stairs, stopped for a moment at the top, then moved up beside her on one of the wicker chairs. 'Maggi, I'm in a tight spot. The worst ever.'

'You know I'll help you if I can,' she said softly. 'For old times' sake, Henry.'

'Thank you, I needed that,' he said, sighing.

Her aunt interrupted, as she came out bringing a tray. 'Iced tea,' she announced. 'Mr Peterson looks as if he could use a drink.'

'I could.' Henry grabbed at one of the glasses. 'Oh. Tea.' But he took the drink anyway, and sipped at its ice-polished rim. Aunt Eduarda stopped for a moment to chatter at the babies, and went back into the kitchen.

'So tell me?'

'I thought——' he stammered. 'I thought I could make a killing with the big boys. He guaranteed I could get my hands on a lot of bread; instead I find that I'm the sheep to be sheared.'

'He who, Henry?'

'Mr Swanson. He's over there in the car.'

'I see. So tell me what happened.' Maggi glared in the general direction of the car, then turned her attention back to the young man.

'He offered me a share in the condos up on the hill. I—er—borrowed a lot of money and bought into the development. A lot of money.'

'Borrowed, Henry?'

He shrugged his shoulders and refused to answer.

'And then?'

'And then I found out the whole thing was like a pack of cards. The original backers had ducked out. Swanson dumped a big part of it on me——'

'But I thought the apartments were selling like crazy, wasn't that what you said?'

'It's complicated, Maggi. What apartments there are sold quickly. But there aren't enough of them to carry the expenses for the whole development.'

Maggi stared at him as she ran her hand through her unruly hair. The picture was becoming more clear than she cared to admit. 'And what you're saying is that if you don't get a large part of my land, you go into bankruptcy?'

Henry got up and paced nervously, wringing his hands together in understated anguish. 'No. What I'm saying is that if we don't get a large part of your land I'm going to jail!'

'So you didn't *borrow* the money. Oh, Henry, what a stupid thing to do.' Over at the car Maggi could see the other door open. Swanson was coming towards them, walking rapidly over the rough ground. 'You what, Henry—embezzled the money?'

'Not exactly, but close enough. Two hundred and fifty thousand dollars,' he admitted abjectly, his head down, unwilling to meet her eyes. 'Out of my father's accounts!'

'Good lord! Does Swanson know?'

'About the money? Yes, he knows.' And by that time Swanson was at the porch. Smiling as always, a bon vivant to the end. He climbed the stairs. Mike growled at him, but the man was driven by something stronger than his fears.

'So, Mrs Brennan.' He pulled a handkerchief from his pocket and wiped his florid brow. '*We* are certainly in a pickle.'

The word jarred on Maggi's ears. '*We* are?' she asked.

'Yes, the three of us. You would hardly want your young man to go to jail, would you?'

'I'm not sure——' she started to say, and just at that moment the old van appeared, chugging away on five cylinders as John brought it up in front of the house. It was hard to believe that such a large man could vault out of the car, but that was exactly what he did. He waved to Maggi. She could see the ear-splitting grin on his face as he waved a paper in his hand and ran for the porch. John was just at the foot of the steps when Swanson made his last pitch.

'But surely, Mrs Brennan, you wouldn't stand idly by and see Henry go to jail?'

'I have a suspicion that it's you that ought to go to jail,' she told him bitterly. 'And I know a good lawyer, *Mr* Swanson.'

John heard the last part of the conversation and pulled to a stop. 'I'm sorry, love,' he said, 'I didn't realise you were holding a conference.' And then, too eager with his news to wait any longer, he waved the paper at all of them, vaulted up the porch, and snatched Maggi out of her rocker and into his arms. 'I've got it!' he roared. 'I've finally found the right man! Our problems are over! Aren't you glad?'

'I'm ecstatic,' she said, and meant it. 'But we seem to have this problem.'

'Mrs Brennan is going to sell us some of her land,' Swanson said.

'Mr Swanson *thinks* I'm going to sell him some of my land,' Maggi snapped. 'I'd sooner dig it all up and make an alligator swamp out of it! Mr Swanson ought to be in jail—but I think he's fixed it up so that Henry is the fall guy!' Her eyes flashed anger at the pair of them.

'Ah, Henry.' A condescending greeting from the winner to the loser. Maggi heard that edge in the words and smiled. John put his arm around her waist and, with his other hand, lifted her left hand again so that the other two men could see her engagement ring.

Henry Peterson ducked his head again. He was on the verge of crying. The high school hero had fallen very far indeed. Mr Swanson, on the other hand, seemed to swell up with anger. 'I thought you said you had the woman sewn up?' he roared. Henry ducked even further. 'And you, lady. You don't even know what your loving man is looking for, do you?' It really wasn't a question.

John went suddenly silent. His hand around Maggi's waist tightened. 'You know what I was looking for?' His voice was silky-soft, dangerously soft.

'Everybody downtown knows what you're looking for,' the little man replied hoarsely. 'Hell, they're taking bets down at the court-house on what's going to happen when she finds out the truth about your little game.'

Maggi felt a sudden chill. John's arm was gone. There seemed to be clouds screening the sun. John moved a step closer to the agent. 'What about my Mrs Brennan?' The ice was still in his voice, but Swanson was too excited, too enraged, to hear more than the words.

'Ask him, Mrs Brennan. Go ahead and ask him!' he shouted, almost dancing with excitement. 'Go ahead, ask sweet-talking Mr Dailey!'

'I—don't know what you're talking about,' Maggi stammered.

'I think, Mr Swanson, you'd better leave,' John said as he took one more step forward. 'I can read the future, you know. I can see you falling down those steps and breaking your arm. Maybe both your arms. It would be a shame——'

'All right, I'm going!' Swanson yelled. 'I'm going. But tell the little bitch all about it, why don't you? Tell her what happens the moment you marry her! Go ahead!' It was his last defiance. He turned and ran as fast as a portly middle-aged man might. Henry, tears in his eyes, was right behind him. Maggi, stunned, fell back into the rocker and took a deep breath.

John stood at the top of the stairs, looking steadily after Henry's car until it disappeared down the drive.

When he turned around his face was a stern mask. 'Well, Mrs Brennan?'

'Well, what?' Maggi shivered and wrapped her arms around herself. There was a foreboding that hung over her head. Even the babies were quiet.

'You don't know what he's talking about?' John asked.

'No—I—what?' His face was rock-like, ugly, stern.

'I told you how difficult it was,' he said in a monotone. 'I needed desperately to become an American citizen. The moment we marry, Mrs Brennan, I no longer need a visa. Married to an American citizen I can become one myself. It's as simple as that.'

'Simple?' Maggi staggered up from her chair, trembling. 'Is that what it's all about?' she muttered. 'The whole thing—the babies, the proposal, the ring—and the bedding just to be sure?' Her voice was rising, cracking, as she fought back the tears. 'That's it? It's true? You want to marry me just to—— Damn you,' she muttered, struggling with the ring on her finger. 'I gave you everything last night. Everything! Can't you——?'

'We shared each other,' he said softly. 'Shared each other. It was a mutual thing. I don't owe you anything for a night in bed. We shared equally in the pleasure.'

'For a night in bed!' she yelled. 'Is that what it was? A one-night stand?'

'Two-night stand,' he interrupted. She could see that his fists were clenched in anger, but he spoke softly. 'Let's not denigrate things. But, Maggi, you knew——'

'I didn't know a thing. Not a thing. You've never ever met a woman as stupid as I am! We can't marry, Mr Dailey. To be married requires the involvement of two hearts, and you haven't one to involve, have you? Take your ring and get out of here!'

'If you really believe all that, it's just probably the smartest thing I could do this year,' he said bitterly. She dropped the ring into the palm of his hand. He flipped it over a couple of times, then wound up like a baseball pitcher and threw it out into the trees.

Maggi watched it fly through the air. There were tears in her eyes, tears she could not stanch. Behind her, John took one step in her direction. She whirled round, hatred flaming at him. 'Not gone yet?' she screamed. She turned away from him and ran off the porch, headed for her refuge in the barn.

CHAPTER TEN

MAGGI sat on the porch swing, one foot caught up beneath her, the other gently rocking her back and forth. The twins, one on either side of her, had finally fallen over into her lap and were fast asleep.

Aunt Eduarda came out of the house, wiping her hands on her apron. 'Asleep?'

'For an hour or more,' Maggi replied softly. 'We had a hard morning playing ball. They play too hard, I think.'

'No,' her aunt said, 'you *work* too hard, *caro*. Look at you—all skin and bones. He's not worth it. Forget him.'

'No, he's not worth it,' Maggi agreed. Of course he's not worth it, she thought. He's been gone six weeks. Forty-two days. One thousand and eight hours. And I've counted them all. How's that for forgetting? Sixty thousand four hundred and eighty minutes, but who's counting?

'Not worth it,' her aunt murmured. Prissy was stirring, and they both hushed. It was easy to tell the two girls apart now. Prissy had four teeth to Pru's three, and was definitely the leader.

'It isn't him,' Maggi continued. 'There's just been lots to do. Maybe we can settle down now. Mr Small called to say that Mrs Daugherty's house has been sold—for a fantastic amount, *Tia*. I put it in a trust fund at the First Bristol. There's enough to keep the girls through to college. And I finally did sell that top twenty acres to the development people.'

'To Mr Swanson? I wouldn't believe that, Margaret.'

'No, not to Mr Swanson. His company went belly-up and——'

'His company did what?'

'Went bankrupt, Aunt Eduarda. A new corporation bought up the assets—and my land.'

'And that poor young man—Henry something?'

'The new outfit kept him on, love. He's at the bottom of the ladder, but if he keeps his nose to the grindstone he'll prosper.'

'Crazy language.' Her aunt sniffed. 'Belly-up—nose to grindstones. Better you should study your Portuguese, Maggi.'

Feeling a little guilty, Maggi managed to slip the book she had been studying under her thigh, out of her aunt's sight. Basic Gaelic. It didn't make a lot of sense to study Gaelic. He would never return. But after all, it had been *her* fault that he had left. She had lied to the State inspectors; what difference did it make if he was shooting for American citizenship by marrying her? Six weeks. It seemed like forever.

They could have been married by now. Happily ever after. Carefully she fingered the gold necklace that she wore under her blouse. For three days after he left she had spent all the daylight hours that God sent, on hands and knees, searching the scrub brush into which he had thrown her ring. And now she cherished it, suspended on the same chain that held her little gold cross. It was all she had to remember him by. All the treasured memories. Not until he had gone did she understand how much alike John and Robert had been. Oh, not physically, but all the other ways—tender, sensitive, compelling. How else could she have loved John had she not loved Robert first? The thought came easier now. Love. The tender trap.

Aunt Eduarda, who had been studying her niece's face as she half dreamed, coughed. Maggi snapped back to the present, and her slight movement wakened the babies. Their blue eyes popped open at almost the same second. Rosebud mouths formed a little gurgling bubble, then they laughed joyously, displaying their dagger-teeth.

'Healthy children,' Aunt Eduarda commented. 'They wake with a smile. Now you, Margaret, always you woke with cries.'

'Don't bet your bottom dollar on smiles,' Maggi returned, and at that moment both the children screwed up their faces and began to complain. Wet nappies—always at this hour. Maggi wriggled her way out from between them. They had grown like weeds. And never, Maggi thought, did I ever conceive that I would have to race my aunt to see which one of us could change those wet diapers!

As it happened the race was a tie, each woman managing one child. And after a change, a wash, came considerable cuddling, until Tia Eduarda's age caught up with her and she stood up, rubbing her back. 'I need my own nap,' she told her niece ruefully.

'You need your soaps,' Maggi teased. 'The girls and I are going up the hill to watch the goings-on across the fence. They're a lot like me—they love to see other people working.'

They made the trip in the two-seater stroller, a recent acquisition. Priscilla insisted on riding in front, queen of all she surveyed. Prudence accepted the back seat gladly, spending half her time leaning backward far enough so she could see Maggi, loaded down with all the accessories needed for travelling with babies.

The oak tree stood on the west side of the new fence. Maggi spread out the two blankets and set the pair down in the middle. They would soon enough be moving. Across the fence two carpenters working on the roof of the nearest apartment called and waved to them. A nearby bulldozer operator tooted his horn. Pru jumped at the sound; Prissy giggled and waved until a pair of black-capped chickadees nesting in a hollow of the tree came out to greet them. Maggi was having difficulty keeping her own eyes open. The heat of New England summer lay heavy on the land, and the light breeze that stirred the oak leaves brought hardly a penny's worth of coolness. But the babies wanted watching. They were both mobile, both crawling, both adventurous, and both cooler than she, wearing only a nappy.

And the more she stared at them, watching, the sleepier she got. So when someone called her name from just down the hill she assessed it as part of her daydream. But the call was repeated, and the babies were responding excitedly. Maggi sprang to her feet, still not quite in control. Looking westward, into the sun, she could see only a blob, a shadow, but her heart told her what her eyes could not see.

She stood, trembling, unable to move or flee.

'Maggi?' called a voice.

And now she was held back by guilt. John had come back. Angry? Vengeful? The other figure stopped. She raised her hand to shade her eyes. John Dailey, dressed casually, standing, waiting for her to make a move, as she waited for him. No further words. For a moment they stared at each other, and then he raised his open arms. After that there was no need for words. Forgetting the babies, the audience over the fence, the chattering birds, she hurled herself down the hill at him, slammed into his precious body, and felt those arms close around her, sealing her off from all her worries and troubles, in safe haven again.

Not until Prissy squealed did they come back to reality. The baby, having crawled off the blanket in their direction and rubbed her soft knee on a rock, meant the world to hear her complaint. Pru, the more cautious one, was still sitting in the middle of the blanket.

'Hi, girls,' John called softly. He gave Maggi an extra squeeze, and led her back up to the blanket, his arm wrapped securely around her. 'All my girls!' Suddenly they were all down on the blanket, a giggling mass of people, all trying their best to be first in his arms—or any other part of him they might grab. A gentle wrestling match ensued, until he pulled Maggi close to him again. 'I've been a fool,' he said.

'Me too,' she echoed.

'I lost my bloody Irish temper.'

'We Portuguese have a temper too,' she admitted. 'John? There's something I have to tell you.'

'Confession time?'

'Yes.'

'Well, I have a few things to tell you too.'

'Me first—ladies are always first. You remember Ms Fagan, the inspector from the Child Services?'

'Ah. The one who was coming to take the children away?'

'I—told her we were married. A long time ago, when she first came. It seemed like such a *little* lie at the time. I loved you very much.'

'Ah.'

'Well, aren't you going to yell and scream?'

'Not me. Did she come as scheduled?'

'No. Somehow or another she caught chickenpox from one of her nephews, and they had to take her off all the children's cases. But she's better now. They called to say she'll be here tomorrow.'

'Doesn't leave us much time, does it?'

'For what?'

'Oh, for this and that,' he said, chuckling. 'Now it's my turn.'

'OK.' She sat up and leaned back against him, nuzzling his chin with her curls, making believe it was the wind that gave her the shivers.

'I finished that little business I told you about. It took me long enough, and I didn't dare write to ask you to wait. I was afraid you'd say no. I'd not be an easy man to live with, Maggi.'

She nodded and kept her mouth shut.

'You're not going to ask me what business it was?'

'I'm—reformed,' she murmured. 'Aunt Eduarda told me that men don't care to divulge all their secrets. That women shouldn't pry.'

'Men don't care to get splinters when they hug their girls either,' he announced. His hand was wandering across the sharp bone of her hip, and up under the curve of her breast, where there was still adequate soft flesh to attract the male.

'So I'll eat a little,' she said. 'Now, about that business——?'

'So much for reform,' he said, chuckling. 'Well, I thought you'd found me out that day you asked if I were playing at Finian's Rainbow, finding a pot of gold and all.'

'I don't understand.'

'Gold,' he said. 'I told you I owned a few hectares of rock up on the mountain in Mayo—on Nephin Beg. What's that American phrase? There's gold in——'

'Them thar hills,' she said, excited. 'Real—real gold?'

'Real gold,' he confirmed. 'The Germans have been taking it out by the sackful. I don't know if there's any gold in my particular plot of land, but the Pacific Mining and Metal Company is willing to pay good money to find out. So I sold them a ninety-year lease—and we have enough money to settle all our problems.'

'That much?'

'Well, it depends on who's saying.' He laughed. 'Enough to buy my mother an annuity, and to provide each of my sisters with a dowry. So I spent the last of it over the boards in Dalgenin's Pub, buying a pint for all the lads in Ballydooley. And here I am, with a strong back and a weak mind, ready to claim my woman, *acushlah*. Is my job still available?'

'I—you're too good a man to be somebody's nanny,' she said hesitantly. 'Why don't you—marry some American girl and get to be a citizen?'

'Not a bad idea,' he agreed. 'Anybody in mind?'

'Well, except for the babies, I'm not doing anything this afternoon.'

'What a lucky afternoon this is,' he said solemnly. 'There's visitors down at the house.'

'Then I want to stay here,' she said, nestling up against him.

'Maggi, there's a question.'

She sat up in spritely fashion and paid strict attention. A woman needs to concentrate at important times like this, she told herself. But it wasn't the question she expected.

'Would you come and live with me?' he asked. 'Even if it means going back to Ireland?'

Come, live with me and be my love. The old poem rolled through her empty head and sent echoes flying in all directions.

'I know how you feel about your home,' he added apologetically.

'Don't be silly, John.' She tried to pull his head down to her level, and did manage to kiss his chin. 'I love you,' she told him. 'My home is in your heart. Nothing else matters.' While he stared she pulled her gold chain out and displayed it.

'You—found it?'

'It took me forever,' she told him. 'May I wear it again?'

'I'd like that,' he assured her, and helped to slide it on her finger after she unclipped it. And then he grinned down at her and pulled her to her feet. Both the babies immediately complained. He chuckled as he picked them up, and handed one to her. 'We have the cart before the horse, lady. And there are people at the house you have to meet.'

'No, I don't,' she insisted. 'If we wait long enough they'll go away. They always do.'

'Not this crowd,' he told her. 'One of them claims to be your mother. She looks like you.'

'Oh, gawd!'

'The other one says he's your father. He's making threatening noises. And the other——'

'There's another one?'

'A Mr Small, he says his name is. A lawyer. He also informs me that he's a justice of the peace, licenced to perform marriages.'

'Oh, my!'

'That's what I said. Going to back out now?'

'We need a licence.'

'I've got one in my pocket.'

'You're sure this is right, John?'

'Of course it is,' he insisted. 'How else can I get to stay in the country with my family?'

'Yes, I can see that.' There were tears in her eyes. Tears of happiness.

'Of course it's silly, us getting married when we already have two children!'

'Oh, lord,' she exclaimed. 'Ms Fagan will be here tomorrow.'

'Late, I hope,' he commented. 'We're going to get married, shoo all these people out of the house, get Aunt Eduarda to watch the girls, and you and I...'

'Yes? You and I?'

'Are going upstairs and get a good night's sleep!'

'I'll bet we are,' she said, laughing. 'And you'll never lay a finger on me?' Her laughter set the babies off, and finally he joined in as the four of them hugged and kissed and burbled, and finally made their way down the hill in the direction of *happily ever after*.

MILLS & BOON

Mills & Boon are proud to present three new romantic stories in one passionate volume by bestselling authors Elise Title, Pamela Bauer and Tiffany White.

We know you'll love our **Valentine Bachelors**...

Nicholas, Tristan, and Alec—three very sexy and very single men who find that the only date they have on New Year's Eve is consoling one another! Determined to find the woman of their fantasies by Valentine's Day, they each run a very special personal ad...

Available: January 1996 *Price:* £4.99

Available from WH Smith, John Menzies, Volume One, Forbuoys, Martins, Woolworths, Tesco, Asda, Safeway and other paperback stockists.